About the Author

Laura Roybal has a Bachelor's in English and history from New Mexico Highlands University and a Master's in Theology from the Franciscan University of Steubenville, Ohio. Her three previous novels, *Billy*, *Dear Bobby*, and *Blood Brothers*, are young adult novels. She has three children, sixteen grandchildren, and two "honorary" grandchildren. She lives with her husband, Richard, on a small ranch in the Sangre de Cristo Mountains north of Santa Fe, New Mexico.

The Patriarch: Delvin Matthew Lachlan

Laura Roybal

The Patriarch: Delvin Matthew Lachlan

Vanguard Press

A CIP catalogue record for this title is available from the British Library.

ISBN 978-1-83794-258-9

Vanguard Press is an imprint of
Pegasus Elliot Mackenzie Publishers Ltd.
www.pegasuspublishers.com

First Published in 2025

Vanguard Press
Sheraton House Castle Park
Cambridge England

Printed & Bound in Great Britain

Dedication

For Richard: Thanks for your patience and support. And with love to Tim, Sean, Eve, Bianca, Grace, Benjamin, Ian, Maria, Kyra, Joshua, Sebastian, Zachariah, Ignatius, Daniel, Andrew, David and Philomena.

Charleston, South Carolina: October, 1839

Although whaling may have been a lucrative business for owners and investors, it was not so much for the men below decks. But, when he stepped off the gang plank and onto the dock, Devlin Matthew Lachlan had a small stake in his pocket, and a goal for the rest of his life. He did not know how exactly he would achieve his goal, but he did know that his aim in life was to become one of the well-to-do – "quality folk," he called them – those people who always had enough coal for heating, enough food to eat, clothing that did not itch and burn like the raw, rough-spun wool he had worn as a child, and medical care when they grew ill. And he wanted, eventually, a family. That was a hazy picture: an unknown number of kids wallowing around on the rug as an unseen female figure sat doing fancy embroidery and he rocked by her side, all of them well-fed, content, healthy, educated, maybe reading books and newspapers to each other, as he had read to the other men in the down time on the whaling ship, being one of the few literates on board. Yes, he could read, and he knew his arithmetic. He even had a bit of philosophy, science, French and Latin. He had had a very good early education, and he had kept it up all these years at sea, reading anything he could get his hands on, from political tracts and newspapers to philosophical treatises, and he had managed to learn a bit about business as well. Not a bad start at learning, he thought, for a man of his estimated years. Estimated, because he had no idea how old he actually was. He was pretty sure he was younger by two or three years than the fourteen years of age he had declared himself to be when he was first able to obtain a job on a ship almost eight years ago. He was tall for his age then, he was still tall now, tall and broad-shouldered, but when he paused to look at his reflection in a store window, he was not impressed with what he saw. He looked like what he was: a hulking young sailor. To manage his dream for the future, he would have to find more gentlemanly employment and for that, he would have to look more like a gentleman. The small stake he had in his pockets went mostly towards that end. Step one was a clean set of clothes. Nothing fancy to start with, just something clean. Because Step Two involved a bathhouse, and lots of soap and hot water to scrub off eight years of salt and sweat and the stink of dead whales. He dressed in his new clothes after several rounds with a scrub brush and walked away leaving his old clothes piled in a corner to be taken out with the trash. Then he went looking for a barber. Not some hair cutter down by the docks. If all he wanted was to hack it off, he could have done that by himself. No, he needed a good establishment, and he walked until he found just the right one.

"I'm going to be working as an accountant," he told the barber, and the man not only started to work on his hair, but had a boy scrub and massage his hands, dig the grime from under his fingernails and cut them short and neat.

Bookkeeper actually was a possibility. He had worked as such for the whaling captain. The man's math ability was poor, and he was certain he was being cheated when he went into port. He was. On top of his other duties (not excused from them) Devlin began keeping the books for the ship, figuring the weights and volumes of what they brought to port, market price, tariffs, what they should receive in return, deducting wages and expenses from the totals. When the other men went ashore for beer and women, Devlin accompanied the captain to the sales offices, bargaining, figuring. But, when he decided it was time to leave the whaler and head permanently for shore, he did not receive a penny extra in pay for his long hours of extra work, not even a "Thank you." Well, the man was low-class. What could one expect?

Devlin examined himself in the mirror the barber held for him. Though his beard was still youthfully thin, the man had been able to sculpt a decent set of mutton chops on his cheeks, and his hair was short, with a slight wave, styled elegantly. The sun had bleached most of the color out of it over the years, but the barber had trimmed away all the ragged ends, leaving behind the sunshine gold of his natural hair color. His skin was still sun darkened, but his eyes were as blue as a summer sky. All in all, not bad. Devlin nodded in approval and purchased from the man a boar-bristle hairbrush, shaving razor, soap, mug and brush, and a bottle of the stinging (but pleasant smelling) lotion they had slapped on him when his shave was done.

The barber recommended a tailor, and he went to get measured. He paid in advance for a coat and vest, two pairs of trousers, two shirts and a collar.

"Must it be whalebone?" he asked.

"It's the best, sir. And it is all we carry. Is there a problem?"

He never wanted to even think about whales again, but a collar was necessary, and a cravat, and the tailor then directed him to a cobbler. He was measured again, drawings made of his feet, and he was assured a good pair of boots in a week. He found himself a boarding house where the rates were reasonable and included two meals a day with his bed, and then he started to walk. He still wasn't sure exactly what he wanted to do, but it would be in an office, not as a laborer. So, he explored the city, and he looked at options. Work in a store? In the offices of the buyers and sellers of commercial goods coming in from the docks or the plantations? He hadn't realized quite how big the world really was off the deck of a ship. Importers and exporters, government offices and military officers, sellers and buyers, growers and tradesmen, lenders and borrowers, writers and printers. The dream had seemed so simple, the reality was going to be harder than he thought. He felt like a child who has found tuppence in the street right outside of a sweet shop: so many choices it was difficult to even decide to go inside the door.

Then he found it. He did not have training for things like law, but he knew numbers, and numbers were what they worked with in a bank. He waited until his suit and boots were finished, dressed himself carefully, brushed his hair, and walked into the big marble and gilt edifice of the Merchants' Bank.

It was more impressive even than the manor house had been. Sweeping marble staircases, polished stone floors, desks made of heavy, dark wood, gilt framed mirrors and huge paintings not just hanging on the wall but painted right into the ceiling. He realized he was gawking when someone stepped up and asked him,

"May I help you, sir?"

"I would like to speak to the personnel manager, please."

"Do you have an appointment?"

Stumped. On the other hand… "Yes," he said confidently, and the man bowed and escorted him up the big staircase to a large office. More gilt and marble, heavy wood and oriental carpets.

"Name?" the man behind the desk demanded when his escort had closed the door behind him. The man was looking at some sort of book, an appointment book.

"I do not have an appointment," Devlin said. "But, I am an experienced bookkeeper, and I am looking for a job."

Besides reading and math, his earliest education had included elocution. The words rolled off his tongue not with the Scottish burr of the sailors he had worked with, but with the rich, rolling tones of British aristocracy. As he had hoped, the accent got the attention of the man behind the desk. The man looked up. He took in the styled hair, the tailored suit, and the hand-made boots. Still, he didn't hire him on the spot. He tested him first.

Add this column of numbers. He did it frontward and backward to double check himself. See why these two ledgers don't match. That was almost too easy. The ledgers were off by nine dollars. Anything off by nines, he had learned long ago, meant a transposed number. He found the discrepancy in seconds and figured which of the two numbers was the correct one by reading across the lines to see what they were multiplied from, presented the proofs to the man behind the desk.

He was hired. Not only was he hired, but he was given a desk on the second floor where the bank's main officers worked, rather than being one of dozens of clerks and bookkeepers lined in rows in the great, echoing third floor where the big windows let in the most natural light. Light likely made the work much easier for them, but he heard the room was drafty and unheated in the winter, and unbearably hot in the summer so that windows had to be left open, letting in swarms of biting flies. No, his desk was down here. Not in an office, though. That, he was sure, would come later. Just now his desk was located in a cool, dim, marble hallway, right outside the door of Vice-president Perkins Frost.

"What are you, some sort of receptionist?"

Devlin looked up to find a woman standing by his desk with a handful of documents. He could not help but notice that she was a very pretty young lady. She was small and dark haired, and her eyes were a shade of golden brown that was accented by her dress. On first glance, it seemed to be plain brown, but it was actually a deep shade of copper muslin with a fine brown print of leaves. The cut was stylish, yet modified enough to make it more practical for work. Like most gowns of the era, the neck was cut wide across the shoulders with a deep V in the center front, matched by the V at the waistline. But the V at the neck was not so deep, and the neck opening less wide than was fashionable, leaving much of her shoulders covered. Although hemlines were getting longer and most skirts dragged on the floor, hers was slightly above that, and the hem was trimmed with a stiff gold silk braid that helped hold the skirt wide without so many petticoats. Also, there were no silly puffs on the sleeves. Rather they were gathered enough to give free movement at the shoulder and were long and straight and covered from wrist to above the elbow with the same green sleeve garters the men in the accounting rooms wore.

"Do you work here?" he asked in surprise. He had never seen a woman wearing sleeve garters before.

"No, I just thought I'd wander in and steal some important papers," she said. "Of course, I work here. Who are you and why are you guarding Frost's office door?"

"Guarding…" he repeated. And suddenly, he felt like a fool. Deeply chagrined he realized then that he had not been hired for his math skills or polished accent, but for his size. Again. Why else was he sitting here with so little to do right outside the door of the man who handled the most cash in the bank? In the weeks since he had been hired, Devlin had accompanied Frost on several visits to warehouses and docks and other locations where he had delivered cash payrolls, with Devlin standing next to him, innocently thinking he was doing something important.

He gave a snort of amusement now, as close as he could come to laughing at himself here in these elegant halls, where he had so wanted to work.

"Yes. I think you got it right the second time. Guarding," he said. "Why else would he have hired me?"

"Why else indeed if that is the opinion you have of yourself? Buck up, man! Have some confidence. Is he in, by the way?"

"Yes, he's in. And I've never announced anyone, so I assume you can just go inside also. Unless you want me to announce you, Mrs…?"

"Rogers. Miss Emma Rogers," she said.

So, he stood and walked around his desk, tapped on the big oak doors and stepped inside in his best imitation of the old manor house butler to announce, "Miss Rogers to see you, sir."

And Frost accepted the behavior as perfectly natural and expected.

"Thank you, Devlin, show her in."

Not, "Mr. Lachlan." Not even plain "Lachlan." His first name, as one would address a child, an underling, or a servant. Sitting at his desk again, Devlin considered this, and wondered how he could have been so ignorant. Pride, he knew, was the first of the Seven Deadly Sins, and now he understood that lesson a little better. He would admit to pride. It was what had convinced him that someone with no formal education at all would be hired to some important position in a bank.

"Don't pout," Miss Rogers said, coming out of the office, now empty handed. "It makes you look too young."

"I'm not pouting," he said. "I'm trying to decide, if I can ever be taken seriously for my abilities, or only seen as brawn to their brain."

"That's pouting: harping on that comment I made about you guarding the door. Look… What's your name?"

"Devlin Lachlan."

"No, seriously," she said. "What is your name?"

"That is the name I was given, when I was quite young, and it is the only name I have ever known."

"Really? Interesting way of phrasing it. Anyway, Mr. Lachlan, what I started to say was that you should never let someone else's opinion of you rule how you see yourself. Not that that was my opinion of you, I was just trying to be witty."

"If your wit fell short, that is my fault, not yours. I'm afraid I was taking myself too seriously. I should thank you for knocking me down a few pegs."

"I'll be glad to do it again, anytime you like. You'll find me in the basement: Documents and Printing." With that she hurried away, the small heels of her slippers tapping rapidly on the smooth stone floor.

Charleston Harbor was still a main port of entry for ships coming to the United States from ports of call all over the world, and Devlin knew that, especially early in the morning, goods could be purchased at stalls near the docks. He went early the next morning and found what he was looking for in plenty of time to return downtown to the bank before opening. When noon came, and Frost dismissed him for his thirty-minute meal break, he took his prize down to the basement in search of documents and printing. The office, if so it could be called, was a walled off section of the basement in a back corner. One had to thread between bales of stored paper and other goods to get to it. He knocked on the door and was greeted with a summons to enter. Inside, the room was quite large. A long, high table ran the entire length of the wall that had grime-covered windows that looked into the rest of the basement. Small windows high on the opposite wall brought in some light to augment the lanterns hanging from the ceiling. There was a large piece of machinery towards the back, and the room smelled of ink and machine oil. Miss Rogers was sitting on a high stool at the long table, working.

"Oh. It's you," she said when he entered.

"Is that a bad thing?"

"No, it's good, since I doubt you have come to interrupt my lunch break with work. That is, you've never been sent on that particular errand before. Or perhaps you did come to bring some document that Frost needed yesterday and forgot to send with the others, in which case, no, seeing you would not be a good thing."

"I came to bring a gift," Devlin said, and he held out to her the orange he had purchased that morning.

She studied him and the fruit carefully before commenting: "Interesting. Suitors tend to offer flowers. Bank presidents come down with loads of work they want done in record time. You bring fruit. Any particular reason?"

"I just thought that you were a person worth getting to know better, and it seemed like a good peace offering."

"I accept," she said, holding out her hand. He placed the orange in it with a small bow. "Only if you will share," she added, "And because you are so wonderfully naive and such a fascinating enigma."

She peeled the orange. Its strong fruity scent even overpowered the tang of machine oil. She split the peeled orange and offered him one half, nodding towards a chair that had been brought in for people who had to wait for their documents. It was a leather-covered chair, once probably very expensive, though now the leather was cracked and the seat was slightly sunk in.

"What makes me so naive and enigmatic?" he asked, peeling off a section of orange and biting it in half. He managed to catch the juice that dripped off his chin on the palm of his hand and lick it off while she was

15

looking down at her own section of orange.

"You are naive because you believe what people tell you, and you think that nice clothes and a fine accent will open doors for you. And because you seriously believe I did not see that."

"Sorry!"

"Why apologize? It shows me you have brought me a very nice present, not some ancient, dried-up old bit of fruit. Oh, by the way, thank you for that."

"You are welcome. You still haven't answered the second half of my question."

"Yes. Enigmatic. First of all, you are probably one of the few people in this entire building who knows that word and can conjugate it correctly."

"I doubt that."

"I know that. You are enigmatic because you are so contradictory. That accent again, for one thing. Pure King's English. Yet your name is as Scottish as a tartan kilt. You were actually doing some of Frost's bookkeeping for him, when I peeked over your shoulder, doing it better than he does it himself. You know the systems, the numbers, you write with a very careful, elegant and easily legible hand. Yet, your hands themselves, despite the care you have obviously taken to make them look as though you have never done hard labor in your life belie that idea. You have worked with your hands, worked hard. Who are you, Mr. Devlin Lachlan?"

"Nobody," he said. "Which, I was hoping, is a condition I could begin to remedy by working here at the bank instead of shifting bales of cotton on the docks or chopping blubber off a whale."

"See. Naive," she said, giving him a grin.

"You're a bit of a contradiction yourself," he said. "Speaking of accents, yours labels you as what would be called a 'lady.'"

"Where you come from, maybe. Around here, I think the preferred term is 'southern aristocracy.'" As she said it, she bit into a slice of orange. Juice squirted and ran down her chin to drip on her skirt. She grabbed a napkin from the worktable to clean it with, but only succeeded in spreading the mess. "And wasn't that a fine demonstration of aristocratic behavior?" she laughed.

Devlin grinned himself. "Not at all. It was a demonstration of the behavior of a woman who is sure of herself and in herself and doesn't need to put on airs or pretend oranges aren't sticky to feel secure in her role in life. Which is what, exactly? Why do you work in a bank?"

"Because I, like yourself, would rather slave at minuscule wages where I can make a pretense of high society rather than drudge in a kitchen or boarding house."

"If you truly are 'southern aristocracy,' why do you need wages?"

She ate in silence a moment, then said more seriously, "my father was a gambler."

"Was?" Devlin noticed.

"In the tradition of a true southern gentleman, he shot himself in the head after he lost everything. Mama went to live with some relatives in Savannah, who rather lorded it over us anyway since their plantation was so much bigger and better than ours."

"But *you* didn't go?"

"I went. But I refused to stay and play the role of the poor relation. They were willing to stand me a couple dresses, nothing too fancy, for a coming out ball or two, hoping, of course, that I'd get invited to other balls, and snag one of the less desirable bachelors to get both myself and him off the market and save them any further expense."

"I don't understand," Devlin said.

"Balls?" she said. "Debutantes? Coming out? None of this rings a bell?"

"I've heard the words, and I've seen a ball…"

"From the outside?"

"Uh… yes, actually. What were you coming out of?"

"A young lady," Miss Rogers explained, "of high society, when she reaches marriageable age, 'comes out' into society. The balls and parties and teas and gowns are announcements to all the young men sniffing around that another female is ready to be taken to wife. Eligible young bachelors are invited to the parties. Men who might be nothing yet, but who show promise of making something of themselves are the low rung. After all, they might not make it, right? Sons of important planters or politicians are the highest. Girls aim high, but so do the young men. They want someone who is pretty – to show how powerful they are, I suppose. If politics is their goal, they are searching for alliances with older, more powerful politicians – the girls' fathers, of course. And most of them are looking at the size of the dowry offered to take the girl off her parents' hands, or, even better, the only child of a rich man."

"I thought women could not inherit money or property."

"They can't. Their husbands can."

"I begin to see," Devlin said.

"Have you been down to the market?" Miss Rogers asked.

"Obviously..." Devlin said, raising what was left of his half of the orange.

"The slave market," she corrected.

He had seen it, when he was first walking around, exploring the town. When he realized what it was, he left quickly and avoided the area ever since.

"Charleston was once the greatest importer of African slaves in the thirteen colonies, or the United States."

"That is illegal now, though," he said. "Not just here, either, it is international law."

"That is correct. That is why the slaves still coming into this country are brought in through less well-known ports now. But you can still openly buy and sell human beings on an auction block or through a dealer. Personally, I never saw any significant difference between an auction block and a coming out ball. They are stripped to the waist and paraded in front of potential buyers. We were dressed in gowns and jewels and paraded in front of potential husbands. I have seen that for some there is little difference in the life of a household slave or a housewife. They do the same labor and are expected in many cases to perform the same services for their master, whether he owns them because he bought them or because he married them."

"That is a bit cynical, don't you think? I mean, it is possible for people to be 'happily married,' to actually care for each other."

"Oh, I'm sure it is possible. But my mother's cousins were not looking for a life-partner for me. They were looking for a male human being of any age or position in life, but lowly enough himself to agree to accept only a token dowry to take me off their hands. So, I took myself off and came back to Charleston, and convinced the man who caused my father's demise to put in a good word for me at the bank. And here I am."

"What exactly do you do?"

"Rewrite documents so they are legible and therefore legal. And I print up some things that can be used for a multiplicity of purposes, just with blank lines instead of names and dates. Like this."

She handed him a piece of paper that had the bank's name, and the words "Pay to order of" and a long blank. Another blank, followed by the word "dollars." There was a blank at the top for a date, two at the bottom for signatures. "Bank draft," she said. "And there are other things, receipts that are half printed and whoever is making it out just fills in the rest. Things of that nature."

"Can't you just buy that sort of paper?"

"Yes, but there happened to be a printing press in the basement of this bank – God only know why. And there happened to be a young lady of substance who needed employment. So, I print the paper for the bank, and I hand-write documents, and I stay down here most of the time, out of everyone's way where no one can see me and wonder why this bank has started employing lowly women."

"And you call me an enigma."

"And so you are, still. But figuring you out will have to wait. If you leave now and take the stairs two at a time you might be able to get back to your desk before the clock strikes twelve-thirty."

Devlin glanced at the clock above the door and, grimacing, stood up.

"I hope you'll let me visit again," he said.

"Wednesday," she said. "It's day-old bread day at the bakery near my boarding house. I'll bring enough for two."

II

"Ground rules," Emma said as she split the loaf of crusty French bread with him. If the crust was a little crispier that it would have been fresh, it was still soft inside and delicious.

"We take turns?" Devlin guessed.

"Well, yes. But I was thinking we can't meet for lunch every day. Let's say just…"

"Wednesday and Friday?" he suggested.

She considered, pulling off a piece of her bread.

"I was going to say once a week, but I think I can live with twice. I normally don't even eat lunch. I have breakfast and dinner at my boarding house, but I skip lunch to save money."

"So do I," Devlin said.

"Seriously?" she asked him.

"Very seriously."

"And what are you saving those pennies for?" Emma asked him.

"Partly habit, I suppose," he said. "It took me eight years to get a big enough stake just to make myself look presentable enough to inquire about a job at a bank. If I save more, I might someday have enough to… I don't know, exactly. Move higher up the social ladder somehow."

"Still so naive!" she teased.

"I'm learning," he grinned. "It occurred to me that you're probably right: one doesn't climb the social ladder through promotions from being a lowly a bank clerk. But…"

"Oh, this sounds exciting!"

"I don't know about exciting. But… working in the bank is giving me an opportunity to learn about business and society and someday I'll find what I'm looking for."

"What are you looking for?"

"I don't know. But I'll know when I find it. Opportunity of some kind."

"May I make a suggestion?"

"Yes, please."

"Cultivate some friendships among the people who work with loans, even if it's just the clerks who help with the documentation. Opportunities are more expensive than you can save up for with your lunch money."

"All right. Good plan. Now, you tell me what you are saving money for."

"Art supplies," she said.

"Art supplies," he repeated. "Like… paint?"

"Mostly watercolors. Oils are pretty expensive. And chalks and pencils. And the proper paper, of course."

"Of course," he said. "Because young ladies are taught piano and voice, embroidery and drawing, yes?"

She gave him a cold look, and after a moment she set down her bread and picked up the heavy drawing paper that had been in front of her on the desk when he came in. He took it from her, not expecting much, and was surprised enough that his eyebrows crept up into his hair.

"I apologize for my tone," he said. "This is... this... are you a professional artist?"

"No, but only because galleries aren't interested in works by females, and without some display of my pictures, I can't get commissions even to do portraits."

Devlin examined the work. It was a street scene of downtown Charleston. But, while he saw the city as mostly grey buildings on grey cobblestone streets, she saw it brilliant with color. The sky above the buildings was deep blue. Bright yellow, pink and orange flowers bloomed in boxes below most of the windows, and some of the windows were shaded with brilliant red striped awnings. Green grass peeked between sidewalk cracks. Ladies in brilliant-colored gowns and parasols walked next to men wearing blue and tan suits, not just black, as he mostly saw in the bank. Even the carriage horse in the corner had on a flower-trimmed yellow straw hat.

"That is beautiful," he said sincerely. "That's why you complain about being bothered with work on your lunch hour, but always seem to be working on something, isn't it?"

"Yes, it is."

"You know, maybe if you signed the paintings 'E. Rogers' instead of 'Emma R.' the art galleries wouldn't notice..."

"They'd still notice a female person bringing them in."

"What if I took them?"

"And pretended to be E. Rogers?"

"No, I'd be his... her friend, just helping out."

"Well, you can try," she said. "But I think I live in the wrong time. People seem to like dark, somber paintings right now. Don't ask me why. The world is dark enough."

"I don't know about that," Devlin said. "I only know I'll never see this city the same after looking at your picture. Painting. Whatever the proper term is."

"Hobby, I think is what most people would call it," she said, accepting the paper back and studying it. With a small sigh, she set it down. "I've been thinking about you, you know."

"Really?"

"Don't look excited. I've been thinking of using you, rather like Frost does."

"You need a bodyguard?"

"Sort of. The woman who runs my boarding house is very strict. Young ladies do not often live away from family, and I am not allowed to do anything that she considers 'unseemly', or I could get thrown out. Not many places will let a single woman stay at all, so I can't really risk that. But she's a Methodist, and I have always been High Church Anglican, and I would very much like to start going to my own services again."

"What does that mean?"

"Excuse me? What does what mean?"

"Methodist… Anglican… services…"

"Church, love. I'm talking about attending church. Surely you go to church every Sunday. Don't shake your head at me!"

"I don't think I have ever been inside a church in my life," Devlin said.

"There you go getting all enigmatic again. With that accent, you're not Anglican? Or at least Episcopalian?"

"I don't really know what those are," he said.

"Christian Protestant denominations. British ones, in fact. And you're showing your naiveté again. *Nobody* climbs the social ladder in the south if they are not a regular church-goer! Northerners can be philosophers or even atheists. Southerners are Christian."

"Oh. And you want me to go to church with you, is that what you meant?"

"Now you've got it!"

"Kind of a chaperone, like she normally chaperones you to her church? But do you really think your dragon-lady will permit a strange man to accompany you instead of herself? Isn't strange men what she is protecting you against?"

"Yes, but I think she will pull in her claws if I tell her you are my father's cousin, come over from the Old Country, and here with Mother's approval. You look plausible enough. You do have a tall hat and a walking stick, don't you?"

"I don't need a cane to walk with."

"You are hopeless, you know? I have a lot of work to do on you. Tall hat, walking stick, and pick me up at my boarding house at seven-thirty

Sunday morning. I'll write down the address for you. It's not far from the bank, and the church isn't far from where I live, so we won't need to waste our pennies on a carriage or anything."

"Yes, ma'am, he grinned, reaching for the paper she had written on. "Anything else, ma'am?"

"Alas, we have once again reached our time limit. But I gave you my life story, very soon I expect you to reciprocate."

"I'll think about it, he said.

III

Not sure, where else to go, he returned to the tailor who had originally outfitted him. It turned out to be the right choice, as there was a good selection of walking sticks available. He had the hat, of course. No well-dressed man ever went out in public without a hat. But as he had told Emma, he didn't need help to walk, so he had not thought about a stick.

"I had wondered, sir, why you didn't ask for one before. I assumed it was something you already owned, or because my stock is a bit meager."

"Apparently," Devlin said, "I didn't ask because I am so naive."

"Er. Yes, sir," the tailor said, not sure how to take that comment. Instead, they began looking through the available walking sticks. Most of them were too short.

"I'm afraid this may be the only one I have for a man of your height," the tailor said apologetically, holding up a rather plain stick with a simple brass top.

Devlin looked it over, tapped it on the floor. Examined the price. He had suffered momentary panic as the tailor showed him canes with gold and ivory tops, hidden daggers and swords and all kinds of other expensive additions.

"This one is fine," he said.

And Sunday, right on time, he was knocking on the front door of a two-story stone house about two blocks from the bank, arrayed like all the other gentlemen walking on the street in a formal suit with a tall hat and a shiny-topped stick. A black woman answered the door but did not escort him inside. He was left waiting on the step until the dragon-lady herself came to inspect him. She was suited to the nickname he had given her even before he met her. She was broad-built, arrayed in green finery that made him think of scales. Her grey hair was barely allowed to peak around the corners of her bonnet, and her eyes… He'd met cut-purses and bar fighters with friendlier eyes.

He didn't just tip his hat, he removed it. He introduced himself and announced his intention of escorting Miss Rogers to church. Forewarned, she acquiesced after giving him a hard look, and finally, Emma came downstairs. Her Sunday clothes were a bit more stylish than her work-day dresses, with puffs at the elbows of the sleeves and more petticoats. Like the dragon lady, she wore green today. But hers was a rich shade of green, not too dark, but somehow deep in color, and trimmed in copper ribbon and ecru lace so her eyes came alive. He bowed. He replaced his hat and offered her his arm, and they went down the steps and turned up the street.

"I feel ridiculous," she said.

"You look marvelous," he replied.

"I meant that I am short, even for a woman I am short, and you are probably the tallest man in the city. I feel like Daddy is taking me for an outing."

He laughed, and then she did also.

The church was tall and ornate, and she would have elbowed him for staring if the ladies were not seated on the opposite side of the isle from the men. He listened. He followed the men around him in standing and sitting and giving responses. He was not unaware of Christian beliefs. No one who read as much as he did could have gone without reading the Bible, cover to cover and in Latin as well as English.

When services let out and they met again in the vestibule of the church, he escorted her on a stroll through some of the parks and waterfronts of the city. They had tea and cakes at an outdoor café overlooking the harbor and the fort on an island near its mouth.

"That was delightful," she said when they finally returned to her boarding house. "Much better than the usual dreary Sunday with the Dragon. Same time, next week?"

"Of course."

"You don't need to buy lunch, though."

"Maybe a picnic?"

"Maybe. I think our weather is starting to turn on us, though. We'll discuss it Wednesday. I look forward to hearing your life's story."

Charleston, South Carolina, November 1839

He still wasn't sure he wanted to discuss it. Oh, there was nothing awful, really, about his past. It was just... odd. He didn't really know if he remembered playing in the dirt with nothing but sticks and rocks for toys and being picked up by a girl he thought of always as "The Young Lady," or if he had heard it had happened, and so wove it into his actual memories. He must have been younger than four years old then. He didn't even know if he had been in the stable yard of the manor house, or somewhere else entirely. He didn't know if he had been snatched away from his parents or if he really was an orphan. He just knew that he had been, possibly just for a single moment, alone, and The Young Lady had stopped the carriage to pluck him out of the dirt and take him home with her. Later he estimated that she must have been about eight or nine years old herself at the time, young enough to still play with toys, old enough to be bored with even her very fancy dolls. So, she had picked up and carried home with her a live doll to play with, and her father had let her keep him, as if he were a stray kitten. She had washed him up and combed out his uncut yellow curls, very pleased with her new acquisition.

He did not remember a word of Gaelic, but he must have spoken it in his limited, childish vocabulary, since at first he and the Young Lady didn't understand each other. Rapidly, probably because he was young enough to be learning to talk anyway, he picked up English. She kept him with her through all of the day, except for dinner with her father in the dining room. Pets were not brought to the dining table, nor toys, which is more what he was to her. He sat with her through her lessons with the governess, careful to be seen and not heard, since any noise from him at all would get him sent outside – not just out of the room, but out of the house, very often into the cold northern winter, with nothing to wear but the silk finery she liked to dress him in. So, he played the part of a doll and was silent, but he could listen, and watch, and learn. And, as it turned out, the Young Lady decided playing governess was a good game. When she was dismissed from her own studies, she made him act the part of a pupil and she got to be the teacher. And she was a strict one. His hands were slapped with a stick if he did not write his letters properly or if he spilled the ink. He was refused playtime in the few warm, sunny days available if she thought he was too slow at his book. But, even young as he was, he somehow knew that learning was important. He studied hard at the lessons she gave him, and at the ones her governess gave her. He learned to read, learned geography and history. He was quick with numbers, and in a few years had outpaced her in arithmetic. He privately mimicked the governess's lessons in elocution until his pronunciation was perfect, and he picked up more of the Latin and French than the Young Lady did. And, when she was got bored with playing with him, he had quietly read on his own: books from the school room first, then anything he could reach from her father's big library.

Then one day they moved.

"They moved where?" Emma asked.

"I have no idea. I must have seen packing going on for some time, but I don't think it really meant anything to me. Then, one day I was sent out to the woods to get some berries, and when I came back, the house was locked up and they were gone."

"She just abandoned you?"

"Me, and a pile of old toys: the rocking horse she had outgrown years ago, a broken doll. Her blocks. And, yes, me."

"So, when you said your name was 'given' to you, that's what you meant, isn't it? You were a toy for that girl, and she named you, like she would name a stuffed rabbit or a doll."

"Yes. I have often wondered if it meant anything. 'Lachlan' could have been the name of the manor house, or of the county. Or just something she made up."

"It means 'land of many lakes,' you know."

"Yes that I do know." He paused. "They took the cat," he said. And left him, he didn't bother to add.

"What happened after that?" Emma asked.

He shrugged.

"I waited around for a while, thinking they would come back. They had left before: on afternoon drives, once for a week or more in the city. Of course, those times the house was open and there were servants, and even if it wasn't anybody's job to feed me, I knew where the kitchen was. I ate all the berries. I drank water from the well by the stable. It was probably about three days later one of the tenant farmers driving by the front gate saw me sitting there waiting and asked me what I was doing. I told him I was waiting for the family to come back and he said they weren't coming back. They'd lost the estate. Most of the tenants were being evicted. He gave me a ride as far as the coast with his family. I spent the winter doing odd jobs for public houses and inns by the waterfront - hauling water, cleaning, stacking wood – for food and a corner to sleep in."

"How old were you?

Another shrug.

"I don't know, but I do know I was starting to grow. Maybe that's why they abandoned me: I wasn't small enough to be a toy any more. I was easily the same size she was when they left, and I added inches over the winter."

"So, you have no idea how old you actually are, or when your birthday is?" Emma asked.

"No. Does it matter?"

"Everyone needs a birthday. I think… yours will be January first. That's a good day for a birthday: the start of the New Year."

"And how old will I be come January first?" he asked, smiling.

"I'm not sure. Tell me, how did you get a job on a ship? Surely you had to be twelve or older even to be a cabin boy."

"I was big as most of the men when I started, so I told them I was fourteen, but I probably wasn't. I was more likely eleven, twelve at the outside, considering how much I still grew after."

"And then you spent eight years on a whaling ship?"

"Yes."

"Then… Twenty."

"Excuse me," he said. "Twenty what?"

"Come the first of January, you will be a whopping twenty years old. How does that sound?"

"Young," he said, not altogether sure he liked it. "Couldn't I be twenty-one now, and twenty-two in January?"

"Too naive," she said. "Now, tell me how you ended up in Charleston? I didn't think whalers ever docked here."

"We docked first in Massachusetts, I think. Somewhere in New England. I walked off the ship to see a free black man being publicly whipped for not leaving the state two weeks after he entered. Many northern states have laws like that, I discovered: black people are only allowed in if they leave again. Then I went to New York City and saw the biggest, worst slums you can imagine."

"That's odd," Emma said. "I know many people who summer up in New York to get away from the heat and bugs here."

"On the seacoast, maybe, but not in that section of New York City, I'm sure. Thousands of immigrants brought in to provide cheap labor for the factories, none of them paid enough to survive on. So, I found a ship that would hire me for temporary crew and sailed south. I liked what I saw in Charleston – except the slave markets, of course. I don't think that will last though."

"Why not?"

"For one, slaves have been freed almost everywhere else in the world. Also, you have more emancipation societies here in the South than they do in the North, and many more free black people. It'll end, soon enough."

II

He suspected it was Emma, or possibly the Dragon, who started the rumor that he was the son of an earl. When asked, he did admit to growing up in the manor house, but he did not expound on the fact. Although some assumed he was a dispossessed younger son, others guessed he was born "on the wrong side of the blanket." Either way, people assumed he was high-born, and he found people treating him with a bit more respect. The Dragon actually smiled when he called to pick up Emma for church every Sunday, and never complained about how late he brought her back. Men and ladies at the services gave him a nod and tipped their hats which, of course, he reciprocated. Messengers running back and forth in the bank gave him a nod instead of ignoring him completely, and eventually Frost moved him into a tiny office connected to his through an open doorway, instead of leaving him sitting in the middle of the hallway.

December came, and both Devlin and Emma were forced to spend some of their "pennies". He bought a warm, caped greatcoat, she some leather boots instead of the too-fragile slippers women generally wore. For Christmas she gave him a watch chain.

"I know you don't actually have a watch, but this will look very distinguished stretching across your vest."

"It is beautiful," he said. "Thank you. I just hope no one asks me for the time!"

His gift to her was a scarf made of wool so soft and smooth and finely woven that it felt almost like cotton, but it was long and warm and she could wrap it around her bare neck and tuck it into her dress top to keep the winter chill off her neck and shoulders. Brown and green fibers were woven together in it. When he saw it, he thought instantly of her eyes: brown and green and gold all swirled together.

"I've never given a Christmas gift before," he said.

"Not even to your Young Lady?" she teased.

"I didn't really understand the custom," he shrugged. "She gave me little toys and candy. It was in the winter, so probably it was Christmas. You have to understand, though, that she gave the cat presents, too."

The winter was wet and dreary. The weather was not conducive to long walks around town or open-air cafés. They often walked to the public library on a Saturday instead of going on a promenade on Sunday. Sometimes, they checked out books to discuss with each other. More often, her tastes ran towards the life of Michelangelo, while he studied politics, philosophy and economics. On Sunday, after services, he merely took her back home and went back to his own boarding house. In their own environments, they each sat in the public parlor by the fire and read away the long, quiet afternoons. When Devlin's land lady discovered that not only was he an avid reader, but was good at reading aloud, she urged him to entertain her and the other guests at the house. He put his own books aside for evenings in his room and read the newspapers and romances that the others wished to hear, unknowingly setting a pattern that would be a major part of the rest of his life.

Charleston, South Carolina, March 1840

Spring came, eventually, and as it began to dry up and warm up, Devlin proposed a picnic by the sea.

Tired of the long winter also, Emma said, "All right. But let's splurge."

He rented a buggy, borrowed some plate and flatware and a blanket from his landlady. Emma brought fresh, still warm bread from her neighborhood bakery, then they drove to the docks to do their shopping. Emma found exotic Arabian pastries that had honey and nuts between the translucently thin layers of dough. Devlin purchased a large fish and half a dozen oysters, fresh-caught that morning. They picked out winter apples and imported asparagus to complete their meal, and he drove them off the peninsula and along the coast to a place he had scouted earlier. Much of the seacoast in the area was muddy and marshy, but he had found a place where there was more sand than mud. Although it was warmer than it had been and the sun was shining, the sea breeze held a chill that kept most people off the beaches, so they had the whole stretch of sea front to themselves. He spread the blanket above the high-tide line where the ground was dry and less marshy than below, and Emma sat down on it, tipping her parasol where the wind would not snatch it away. Devlin took off his boots and rolled up his pant legs to roam up and down gathering driftwood to build a fire. After it burned down to a good bed of coals, he buried the oysters and roasted the fish and asparagus.

"That was delicious," Emma sighed as she sucked her fingers clean.

"I didn't think of this," Devlin said, as he also licked the juices and sticky honey off his fingers. They had napkins, but no fresh water. He had known needing something to drink would be a problem, and he had brought a container for quenching thirst, but he had filled it with lemonade, not water.

"Does saltwater work?" she asked.

"I suppose it's better than nothing," he said. He took their napkins and waded into the low waves to rinse them clean. Then he wrung them out and brought them back for washing sticky hands and faces.

"Gritty," Emma commented.

"Wet, though," he said, sprawling on the blanket beside her.

"Better?" she asked, turning her face towards him.

"You missed a spot," he said. He took the wet napkin from her and leaned closer to wipe a bit of fish grease from the corner of her mouth. And then he leaned closer still, fully intending to kiss her. He stopped when she leaned back, not much, just enough to make her intention as clear as he had made his.

"Dev," she said, smiling. "Let's not spoil a perfect friendship."

He gave a self-deprecating laugh and leaned back on his elbow again.

"Thank you," she said.

"What did you think? I would force unwanted attention on you?"

"Of course not!" Emma said. "And that is exactly why I like you so much."

"Because I'm so easily manipulated?"

"Not at all! Because even though you actually have much less claim to being a gentleman than many men I know, you act more like one. Now, run along and play while I work."

"Yes, Young Lady," he said, accepting her words as teasing, exactly as she had intended. She pulled out her sketch pad and pencils. After watching her awhile, he did get up and walk along the edge of the water, letting the cold surf splash over his feet and up his legs while he tormented miniature crabs and collected pretty shells. It was still early in the year, though. The days were short, and the drive back was not. When she saw him returning, she packed up her art supplies and reopened her parasol.

"Sure you don't want to dip your feet in the water?" he asked, as he sat down on the blanket to right his own clothing.

"How is the water?"

"Frigid."

"I'll pass, thank you."

"Someday I'll get you into it," he promised. He stood up and offered her a hand. He pulled her to her feet so easily that he almost lifted her off them.

"Maybe in the summer," she said. "You won't believe what a summer in the Deep South can be like."

31

"Probably not," he agreed. He carried their picnic basket, the blanket and her art supplies back up the long walk to the buggy, settled her and everything else in, and drove them back to town.

That night, lying alone in the narrow bed of his boarding house, he considered her words. Would it be so bad, he thought, to marry a friend? Wouldn't friendship be a strong base for a lasting relationship? He had imagined once being married to a Lady, an unknown ornamental woman doing lady-like things, like embroidery. Now he imagined life with Emma. She would not be easy to live with. She had too many strong opinions and disliked very much anyone who tried to dominate her. But a good husband didn't dominate, he merely led. And provided, and protected. A lady necessitated servants. He knew how much work a woman did in a house: he saw his landlady and her two black servants (he didn't even know if they were slaves or not) struggling with cooking and cleaning and laundry all the time. Emma deserved some household help. But, if they could not afford it, she would not demand it. And it would be good to have someone to talk to about important things, who could discuss politics and art, poetry and business with intelligence and interest. Someone like Emma, who had that wicked sense of humor, but who could laugh at herself as easily as at anything else, who had both a cynical and a romantic view of the world at the same time. Yes. Marrying Emma was something definitely to be considered.

But, the next day, he met Larissa Sebastien.

II

When he stopped by Emma's boarding house in the morning to walk her to church, the Dragon told him Emma had a cold from sitting out in the chill wind all afternoon yesterday. When he asked if he could see her, he was refused, and the door was closed smartly in his face. Monday he would learn that Emma had a scratchy throat from a songfest some of the other tenants had initiated in the parlor Saturday evening and was not sick at all. But Sunday morning, he felt guilty and at loose ends. What to do next? After a moment's consideration, he went to church alone, since it had been his habit every Sunday since November, and he could think of nothing better to do. He sat, as always, with the bachelors, paying even less attention than normal to what went on around him. When he stepped outside, he paused at the top of the steps and replaced his hat. But then he recalled he had no one to wait for, and he started down the steps. Peripheral vision made him vaguely aware of a female presence nearby, but as there were a number of people exiting the building at the same time, he paid little attention. Until a soft cry caught his ear. The steps were slippery from a light rain that had fallen while they were inside, and a soft-soled ladies' shoe skidded on the top step. With the reflexes of a sailor used to snatching things that tried to fall overboard, he caught the falling woman around the waist before she could tumble headlong down the stairs, and righted her on the step beside him, two steps lower than she had started out. She was barely shoulder-high on him, so all he saw were the flounces of her wide skirt and the wide brim of a pink and blue silk "Victoria" bonnet. She could have been a child, or an elderly woman for all he knew.

"Are you all right, ma'am?" he asked.

"I… Yes. Yes, thanks to you!"

Immediately, they were surrounded by concerned people, men, women, even children worried about her fall. A large, well-dressed man pushed through the crowd to the step below.

"Larissa! Are you all right?"

"Yes, Father. Yes, everyone! I am fine. I just slipped! This kind man caught me before I could get hurt. Please! I'm fine!"

The big man tried to climb another step to catch her by the elbow and help her down, but she slipped her hand into the crook of Devlin's arm and hung on to him, so he escorted her safely to ground level, where a large brougham was waiting for her.

There were more concerned questions, but the crowd began to disperse, and Devlin helped the young lady into the brougham. She was young, he could see that now, even though the big bonnet still covered her hair and most of her face. Her father paused to shake his hand before entering the vehicle himself.

"My thanks to you sir," he said.

"It was nothing, really," Devlin replied. At the sound of his voice, the older man looked at him more closely.

"I know you from somewhere, don't I?"

"Yes, sir. I work at the Merchants' Bank."

The older man shook a finger in Devlin's face. "I recognize you now! You used to sit at that desk outside Perkins' office! Haven't seen you around in a while, though."

"My own office was... finished finally," Devlin said.

"Excellent! I'm..."

"Josiah Sebastien," Devlin said. "Yes, sir. I recognize you also."

"Very good! Yes, I do a lot of business with Merchants'. I like to invest in this community." He looked around himself proudly as if he had built the entire town. And possibly, Devlin thought, he had built a good portion of it. He had done enough of Perkins Frost's paperwork to know at least a few of the pies Sebastien had his fingers in.

"It is a beautiful town, sir," Devlin said politely.

"Do you really think so?"

"Yes, sir. I do. I'm not exactly a world traveler, but it's the nicest one I have ever been to."

"Very kind of you to say so," Sebastien said, puffing his generous chest out proudly.

"Father," came a soft voice from the brougham. "Perhaps we could invite this young man to luncheon with us, since he probably saved my life."

"That is an excellent idea, my dear," Sebastien said. "If not her life, you did save her from a nasty fall, perhaps even broken bones! Please do come home with us for a Sunday meal. It's the very least we can do for you."

Devlin accepted, having nothing much else to do that afternoon. He climbed into the brougham and sat next to Sebastien, across from a roundish woman who was introduced as "Mrs. Sebastien." On the drive through town, Sebastien proudly pointed out several elegant buildings and businesses which were part of his investment empire.

"I am a lawyer, actually," he said confidentially. "Inheritance and real estate law mostly. But there is no point, is there, in letting money just pile up in a bank. Investing is much wiser, and it helps the community, also."

Devlin agreed. Eventually, they left the business district and moved into an area of largish homes with generous lawns around them. The brougham pulled into a wide curved driveway of white crushed seashells. The house at the apex of the drive was three stories and generously built with white columns holding up a second-floor balcony and many windows on the face. The ladies were helped down and preceded the men up the few shallow stairs to the front hall, parlor to the left and dining room to the right, broad sweeping staircase to the rear. Their wraps were left in the charge of a tall, thin black man, and Devlin was instructed to leave his stick and hat near the door. *Quality folk*, he thought, looking around at the high ceilings, polished floors and rich carpets. He was used to a butler, uniformed maidservants. The house, though, was much newer and airier than the manor house he had grown up in, which always seemed very dark to him in his memories. Perhaps it was. Perhaps here, where the winters were less harsh and the summers – so he had heard – were long and hot, people needed this openness more than farther north, where things tended to be closed against the elements.

Devlin followed his host into the dining room. Big windows and multiple candelabras illuminated the room, which was dominated by a huge table that could easily have accommodated twenty people. Only the end near the kitchen had a cloth over it, and even as they entered, a fourth place was being set there.

"You sit here, by my right," Sebastien told Devlin. "You ladies can sit across from him."

They were seated, Sebastien blessed the meal. And Devlin looked up to find himself face to face with the most beautiful woman he had ever seen in his life, now that the huge, sheltering bonnet was finally discarded. Larissa Sebastien had a fine-boned face and slender figure, pale blue eyes accented by the pale blue silk gown she wore. Her mouth was small, the lips rose-pink to match the glow in her cheeks. Her shining gold hair, piled high on her head, looked too heavy for her slender neck to support. Her skin was as white as Southern ladies preferred it, but it was also clear and smooth as the polished marble staircase out in the hall. When she smiled across the table at him her teeth were small and white and even.

Devlin was only vaguely aware of the fine meal that was served him, of the silent-footed servants who brought in course after course, even of Sebastien's economic discussions throughout. He heard the man's words, he made the proper responses, but he was so enthralled by the beauty across the table from him that later it was all he remembered. Her delicate mouth, pursed to sip at the soup, her sparkling eyes laughing at some remark of her father's. The dainty way she held the heavy silverware. Her gentle voice as she and her mother excused themselves from male company at the end of the meal.

"Nice to have a man in the house for a change," Sebastien commented, helping himself to the brandy bottle on the mantlepiece. He offered it to Devlin. "You don't imbibe, do you?" he asked, indicating the three glasses of wine, one served with each course of the meal, which still stood untouched by Devlin's plate.

"I never cared for wine, sir."

"Ah! Perhaps a bit of bourbon then," Sebastien said. "Or no, with that accent... scotch!"

Devlin accepted a small crystal glass of golden, smoky scotch, easily the best he had ever tasted. He sat across from Sebastien in the comfortable chair indicated and sipped and listened, and hoped that the ladies would return. They did not. After an hour or more of Sebastien's real estate discussions, Devlin gave up and asked to excuse himself from the company on the pretext of needing to get home. He was offered the brougham, or a smaller carriage, but he said it was not far and he preferred to walk.

"Once again, I must thank you," Sebastien said, shaking his hand. "I hope to see you at the bank again sometime. And of course, services every Sunday! If you ever need anything, call on me." And he passed over a business card reading "Sebastien, Tindale & Scott, Attorneys," with an address near the bank.

Devlin walked down the wide drive, his boots crunching on the seashells, and out onto the cobblestone sidewalk still in a daze. Larissa's smile, Larissa's eyes, Larissa's delicate hands covered his mind so completely it was a wonder he walked in the right direction to get home. About half-way between the elegant neighborhood of the Sebastien home and the business district where his boarding house was located, he was suddenly accosted by a man who stepped in front of him and invited him to lunch.

"I just ate," he said, feeling confused. He had never seen this man before in his life.

"Maybe dinner?"

"No, thank you," Devlin said, and he started to proceed again when he noticed the man accosting another passer-by. He paused and watched and realized finally that the man was trying to drum up business for a nearby restaurant. He looked around and found he was standing in front of a large brick building, flanked on either side by a narrow alley and even taller buildings. Four steps led up to a wide, arched double doorway, but the opening for the door had been shortened so that a rectangular wooden door could be inserted into the space. "BAYVIEW" was printed on the space between the flat top of the actual doors and the arch of the doorway. Curious, Devlin went up the stairs and into the building. There was no entryway. The door opened directly into the dining room, which was both impressive – and not. The room itself was two stories high, with dirty skylights in the ceiling to let in some light, and high arched windows running down the right side, fortunately too dirty to see much of the bare brick wall across the alley. To the rear, on the left, a rickety stairway ran up to a series of closed doors fronted by a narrow open balcony that ran the length of the left side of the room and left a gaping empty space below. And dead center of the whole place, a large, rust-stained pump stuck incongruously out of the flagstone floor. The floor of the main room seemed to be littered with small round tables with no cloths and only a small, single candle lighting each one. Only one table was occupied, and apparently the two people sitting there were waiters. As he stood looking about, a man hurried up to him.

"Welcome, sir, welcome! You can have your pick of tables, as you can see. We are having a special on fish today…"

"I'm really not interested in dining," Devlin said, still looking about. "I was just curious about this building. And you're being open on a Sunday. That's unusual isn't it?"

The man's effervescent good humor fizzed away suddenly. "We're open every day of the week, but it doesn't seem to help. We get a few workmen in for breakfasts, but the evening meal… well, you can see how that is working out for us."

"Are you the owner, or just the manager?" Devlin asked.

"Both, actually. Why, is there a problem?"

"No. I was just wondering if you would consider selling it."

"Selling this?" The man looked amazed. He stammered a bit and said, "Oh! If only I could at least get back my investment… Are you serious?"

"I think so. I'd like a few days to really think it over, but… What would you take for it?"

The man named a price. Devlin, well aware of real estate values in this area, countered immediately. A number was settled upon with little more dickering, but again, Devlin said he would have to think about it. He tipped his hat and walked out, already thinking as he walked. The possibilities. Larissa. Those windows! Larissa. Wine. Larissa.

"So, you rescued the richest new debutante in town, did you?" Emma said.

"Did you know that they come to the same church that we go to every Sunday?" Devlin asked.

"Of course. You hadn't noticed?"

"I don't spend much time looking over the men," Devlin said. "And honestly, when you woman are out in public, you all look the same."

"Really?" Emma sounded more amused than offended, though.

"Yes. Big, wide skirts. A shawl hanging over big, puffed sleeves so the upper body is as shapeless as the lower, and those ridiculous, huge face-hiding bonnets. Anything female out on the streets could be Cleopatra or Seaman Willoughby."

"Who exactly is Seaman Willoughby?"

"A man I worked with who was about four feet tall and five feet wide."

"You wouldn't make much of an impression with Larissa Sebastien if you told her that," Emma laughed. "You didn't, did you?"

"No, of course not."

"You are totally besotted, aren't you?"

"Well, I…"

"Don't apologize. I think it's adorable. What a pretty face can do to a grown man is amazing, sometimes. So, is this your plan, now?"

"Excuse me?"

"You don't have to climb the social ladder any more. You can just marry it."

"I do think about marrying her," Devlin admitted. "But not for that reason. In fact, in order to be worthy of her, I have to elevate myself first."

"That's not going to be easy. I don't see anyone lining up to hand you a big promotion to vice-president of the bank."

"No. I'm going to quit the bank," Devlin said. "I have another idea. Listen, I know it's late when we get out, and you may miss dinner, but if you would come with me after work… It's the opposite direction from your boarding house, but I can hire you a cab to get back. I want to show you something."

"Cryptic," Emma said. "All right. And if I am late for dinner, you can buy that too."

"Done!"

IV

"Are you out of your mind?" Emma demanded. The space was empty, lit only by the hand lantern Devlin lifted high so they could see around. "This is an abandoned warehouse! You're…"

"Don't say 'naive' again."

"I was going to say 'idiotic!'"

"Just wait. Listen. I've been around Charleston enough to know that this entire town thinks of itself as a place of leisure and respectability, a playground for the wealthy and well-to-do. I mean, look at it! All these imports and exports, and no railroad coming through town to the docks. They want the money, they just don't want to look like anyone here has to work."

"I know that. What's that got to do with this lunatic idea…"

"Just wait, would you? Look. To start, we take out those upstairs rooms. Then we have a broad balcony where tables can be spaced far apart for the very well-to-do to be able to sit up above and look down on the lowly rabble."

She considered a moment. "All right. You have my attention."

"Now, under there is wasted space. But we separate it into six or so individual alcoves, closed on the back and sides but open to the front so people who don't want to walk up the stairs can also sit in relative privacy and look out on the common people. It could also give businessmen enough privacy to feel they can discuss business, but… always open so no one can be accused of anything unseemly going on."

"What about the floors and walls? You'll never get anywhere with plain brick and stone. Whitewash…"

"Is tacky. No, the brick and flagstone stay. But it will be scrubbed, the floor sanded down and polished."

"Of course, this has to go," Emma said, walking up to the large, over-sized pump.

"No. Well, yes, but no. If there's a pump, there's water. This is going to be a fountain, not raised up, but at floor level. We'll cut the floor into a big, broad, shallow basin. The fountain goes up to a smaller basin, and above that a smaller one, and above that a very small one, with a small pipe – well, more ornate than just a pipe, but you see what I mean – sticking out the top." He raised his hands as he spoke, indicating a total height of nearly seven feet. "On the very top, the water won't spout, it will just bubble up out of that top pipe and flow into the first basin, overflow in a curtain all around into the next, and the next and the next…"

"And pour all over the floor."

"No! I admit I don't know exactly how fountains work. If I can't figure it out at the library, I'll find someone who does know. But you know that fountains never fill up, the water… circulates or something. Anyway, it will be like a little lake in the middle of the floor, with a cascading spring of water flowing into it. Brass if we have to, but I am hoping for ceramic tile and basins, preferably blue. Now, these windows…"

"Looking out onto an alley, didn't you say?" Emma asked, because in this light, they were just black.

"But they won't look out. We'll cover them on the back, remove the glass, install paintings of landscapes and re-install the glass, light them up so that instead of seeing a seedy alleyway and a blank wall, the customers will have what looks like a magnificent view. That's where you come in. I need you to paint the 'views.'"

"That would take weeks of solid work, it wouldn't be something I could do in my free time."

"I know that. You'd have to quit the bank and come to work for me."

"For free?"

"Of course not! I'm going to be working on borrowed money for a while, so I can't pay you more than the bank does – to start. Hopefully we can up that soon. Also, I want pictures – paintings, behind the balcony and all around the alcoves – with price tags on them. Unlike a gallery, I wouldn't charge you a commission on anything that sells out of the restaurant."

"What if nothing sells?"

"Then you're no worse off."

"Until your windows are done. Then what? The bank isn't likely to hire me back after I leave. I think they'd be too glad to be rid of me."

"You'll stay on with the restaurant. I haven't given you all the details, yet. I want potted plants all over the place, even small trees, so it looks like…"

"A forest?"

"I was going to say 'a sylvan glade'. I'll need help with the plants. Also, I know nothing about wines. I don't like them, and it seems to me the nastiest tasting ones are the ones people like the most. But the best restaurant in town has to have the best wine. You'd be in charge of that. Procurement, storage. Matching wines to the menus. And you'd be the hostess…"

"What would you do?"

"Books, money management, run the staff. Buy the food. Pay the bills. Cook. Wash dishes. Scrub floors: whatever needs doing. And running things, of course."

"You have thought this out, at least a little bit," she said. "You'll need better furnishings than this…"

"The best. Padded chairs, nice tables, fine linen tablecloths and napkins, good, elegant china and heavy silver. I know. And I want blue satin drapes around those scenic windows."

"It could be fun," she said thoughtfully, "to paint streets scenes of Charleston, maybe the harbor…"

"No, I want them to get out of Charleston. 'Sylvan glade', remember? I want something very pastoral: rolling green hills, low stone fences. Blue sky with fluffy clouds, maybe a lake in the background…"

"Lambs frolicking in the foreground?" she teased.

"Only if you think it fits," he said seriously.

Emma looked around at the dark, vast space. "There is no way," she said, "That you can borrow enough money to do everything you want to do here, and still hire a staff, buy food and furnishings… No one's going to loan you that much, even if you do work in a bank."

"I know. But that's the main part of the plan. No one who can afford to start their own business needs to work! A good business needs a good investor. And Josiah Sebastien spent most of Sunday telling me about all the businesses in this town he has invested in. How much, where they are, what they do. He doesn't own a restaurant, but I am sure he is a man of vision and I can convince him to invest in the business of the man, incidentally, who saved his daughter. And, once I'm his business partner, you see, I will be much more eligible to call on Miss Larissa."

"That's a lot of work for nothing," Emma said.

"What does that mean?"

"Think about it. You said women in public are hard to see. Well, the same is definitely not true of the men! I'm sure Larissa Sebastien noticed the tall, blonde, elegant stranger in her parish the moment you first set foot in the door. And the first time you were there without me on your arm, she conveniently slipped, right where you were standing. I am sure if your reflexes hadn't kicked in to save her, she'd have saved herself by falling into you. She'd have met you and have invited you someplace where she could show off her good looks without the bonnet and shawl and mittens she wears in public. I'll even make you a wager that you get invited to her coming out ball, being the big hero and all."

"You really think so?"

"Sweetheart," Emma said, reaching up to pat his cheek. "I know women."

"I'm still not going to marry social position," Devlin said. "I'll get up there on my own. I need you, though, Emma."

"And you knew exactly what would get me out of that dreary basement at the bank. A chance to paint and be admired by all of Charleston! I won't quit there until you're more set up here. I'll need a place to work free of dust, and that won't be immediately available. But, yes. I will assist you in your social-climbing and entrepreneurial endeavor."

V

The papers were all signed the following week, and Devlin found himself in possession of a large, still furnished building, and an even larger mortgage. He put in his notice at the bank and went home that night to tell his landlady he'd be moving at the end of the week. When she asked where he was going and why, he told her about his restaurant, the plans he had for it, the work to be done.

"How is a gentleman like you going to take care of all that carpentry work?" she asked him.

"I spent more than half a decade helping a ship's carpenter," he said. "I imagine there's a good deal of similarity between woodworking on the ocean and woodworking on land. Same tools, same principals…"

"But that is so much work for one person!" she cried.

"It will take time alone, but I'm sure I can get it done," he assured her.

That night, as he was undressing for bed, there was a tap at his door and he called "Come in," without asking who it was. When one of the young maidservants stepped into his bedroom, he quickly grabbed his shirt and put it back on.

"I'm so sorry," he said. "Chloe, isn't it? How can I help you?"

"I was thinking," she said shyly, "that I can help you."

"I don't really think…"

"I know a carpenter," she said, before he could continue with entirely the wrong idea.

"Oh?"

"Samuel. He's my husband. He was… he was not in town before, but he's here now. He has no work and no place to stay. I've been feeding him out the back door for a couple weeks, but… He really is a good carpenter, Mr. Lachlan. He grew up working with wood. He could make your work go much faster, and then you'd be able to open faster, wouldn't you? And start making money?"

"Well, yes, I… uh…"

"You could just meet him," she said.

"Yes. I could at least do that," he said.

Saturday, after breakfast, Devlin packed up what few belongings he had, said goodbye to Mrs. Chambers, and any of the other tenants who were down that early on a weekend, and left the boarding house. Skipping lunches would not save enough pennies any more: he would be living at the restaurant. Although the dining room was two stories high, the kitchen was only one, and there were three rooms above it, opening one off the other in a chain rather than having a balcony in front like the side doors. The first room had served as an office for the warehouse and for the previous restaurant owner, and it still had (now empty) filing drawers, chair, and a large roll-top desk. The next two rooms had been used as storage, and still had some junk piled in them. He planned to clear them out and use the end one for a bedroom and the middle for a sort of sitting/dressing room. It may have been the space above a restaurant kitchen, but it was the largest room he had ever had all to himself in his life. Whistling, he walked down the steps to the sidewalk with a large bundle in his arms and found a big black man waiting for him on the sidewalk.

"Mr. Lachlan?"

"Yes. Can I help you?"

The man was easily as tall as Devlin and even broader in build, but his clothes were dirty and disreputable, and he was, despite the cool morning air, barefoot.

"I'm Samuel," the man said.

"Oh. I see. Well, uh… Why don't you come along with me and see what I'll be trying to do. It might not be to your liking."

"Working in a rice paddy was not to my liking," he said. "Snake-filled swamps were not to my liking. I think about anything to do with woodwork would be, though."

Devlin began to have a sinking feeling about hiring this man. Married to a woman he did not live with, not in town, then in town, swamps and rice paddies…

"Are you a free man?" he asked.

"I am now," Samuel said.

"We'll discuss this off the street," Devlin said. They walked the rest of the distance to the big brick building in silence. Once they were inside, in the gloom of the unlighted main room, Devlin set his bundle down on one of the tables and turned to face the big man.

"Are you a runaway?" he asked flatly.

"Yes, sir, I am," Samuel said.

"Well, points for honesty, I suppose. Chloe is your wife?"

"Yes, sir. We was married about two years ago on a cotton plantation down in Georgia. I was never no field hand, I was the carpenter for the whole plantation, and my Chloe, she was a house servant. Master died. Missus couldn't keep the place up, and she sold off most of the slaves. I was sent to a Louisiana plantation as a field hand, and Chloe ended up here in Charleston. Took me over a year to find her again. If I can't find work here in the city, I'm taking her north with me."

"She's a… she's not really free either, is she?"

"Does it matter to you that other folks bought and sold us like we was race horses or hunting dogs? I'm still a carpenter. She's still my wife."

"I come from a place where slavery was outlawed, and I worked with

45

free black deck hands for years on a ship. But when we came to American ports, they weren't allowed to leave the ship. People here, and even in the North, are terrified of slave revolts. They see helping slaves get free as inciting revolt sometimes. I don't really want to go to jail, or be hung for starting an insurrection."

"I understand. I reckon we should move on…"

"I didn't say that." Devlin sighed, looked around, considering. "There's some storage rooms under the kitchen and part of the dining room. I think some of the ones on the side even have some small windows, high up. If you want to stay there, kind of out of sight, at least for a while, I think we can work something out. I can't pay you more than, say, what a foot soldier gets. But you'd have free room and we can share meals. I am a bit concerned about your wife, though…"

"If we can be in the same city for now, that's a start," Samuel said. "Someday I'll figure out a way to get her with me permanent again."

They spent the day moving into their respective quarters. The small upstairs rooms, for reasons Devlin did not want to consider, were outfitted like bedrooms. Each had a narrow bed across the back wall, and most had some other piece of furniture: a table, a chair, a chest of drawers. It was sparse, but it was enough to furnish two comfortable bedrooms. Samuel helped Devlin clear out the junk from the upstairs storage rooms, to be sorted through later. And then the two of them cleared out a small rear storage room in the basement.

"Can't use this for storing food or wine anyway," Samuel commented, pointing to the two small windows.

"You know about that sort of thing?" Devlin asked in surprise.

Samuel shrugged. "Common sense. And my Chloe worked in the kitchens."

Beds were placed in the two bedrooms. Devlin took two bedside tables, a small bookcase and a chest of drawers also, while Samuel preferred one of the dining tables and two chairs for his room.

"I need to hit the stores before they close up," Devlin said. "Is there a way to get a fire going in one of those kitchen stoves?"

"There's some wood and such left behind," Samuel said.

"Get it going, then. I'll be back soon."

He had taken some of the extra mortgage money out in cash, knowing he would have to outfit himself for staying in the restaurant. Husbanding it carefully, he was able to buy overalls, work boots and shirts for himself and Samuel, as well as some blankets. He bought flour and sugar, coffee, butter, fish and vegetables and a few other main staples, including small packets of spices, and two loaves of bread. Fortunately, the previous owner had been glad enough to be shed of the place that he had left behind quite a few handy items: lamps, pots and pans, even the mattresses and pillows on the beds. That evening, Devlin and Samuel sat by lamplight at one of the tables in the dining room, enjoying a meal of fish and bread and vegetables, with fresh fruit for dessert, and water from the kitchen pump.

"You're a pretty good cook," Samuel commented.

"I went through a number of positions on that whaling ship," Devlin said. "Someday, I may even try baking our own bread. Tomorrow, though, I will be out. Church. What about yourself?"

"There's an AME church in town," Samuel said. "It was through them I found Chloe. I'll be back sometime in the afternoon."

"You be careful."

"Nobody's gonna be looking for such a well-dressed man as I am now," Samuel grinned back.

That night, Devlin found himself lying in a narrow bed, in a small room, much like when he lived in the boarding house. But this room felt entirely different. This room was his. This room was in a building that belonged to him. It was a new feeling, and he liked it very much.

Charleston, South Carolina: April 1840

It sounded easy enough: tear out the flimsily built rooms upstairs. But it was harder than it sounded. Using a claw hammer and a catspaw, starting on opposite sides of the balcony, they pried boards off the walls and hammered the nails out, carried and stacked the wood downstairs. It took the entire week, and when they were done, the place looked worse than ever. Sawdust, scraps of wood, stacked wood, and all the things they had piled when they cleaned out the bedrooms filled the big downstairs room. Before they started sanding, they tore out the staircase, also. Devlin didn't know yet how he would replace it, but he knew it was too narrow and too steep for any ladies who might want to accompany their husbands upstairs. It would have to be extended, which would be difficult, since it already reached as far as the kitchen door. Go over the door? No, that was odd-looking. He'd work on it. Meantime, they built a ladder for their access, and the bricks, ceiling and floors upstairs were sanded and buffed and all the wood varnished. Again, it sounded easy, but it took up more than two weeks with both of them working six full days a week. In the evenings, while Devlin prepared dinner, Samuel tended to disappear into the basement rooms. When he was asked what he was doing down there, he said, "Just fixing things. In case someone other than me has to stay here overnight sometime.'

"Just be sure to leave the cool rooms for the food and wine," Devlin said, not liking much the sound of "other people" staying in the basement.

"I will. I'll even build some shelves and wine racks down there once we know how much wood we'll be using upstairs."

"Go ahead and start," Devlin said. "We shouldn't need everything we've saved so far."

But he was thinking: *wine racks?*

Emma explained it to him. "Wine bottles are sealed with corks, but if the corks get dried out, they can shrink, let air into the bottles, and spoil the wine. Racks keep the bottles lying not-quite-flat so the wine always touches the corks and keeps them from drying out. And by the way, how do you like your new job?"

"Very much," Devlin said. "The work is hard, but it beats sitting at a desk in an office all day long, wondering if I can look busy enough to keep the job. The only real hard part is after work every day heading into the kitchen to make dinner. Cooking's a tough job after a long day. What we really need around here is a woman."

"Don't look at me," Emma said. "You just said it's a tough job. Anyway, I'd be about as useful in the kitchen as your precious Miss Sebastien."

He recalled that she had called herself "Southern Aristocracy," when they first met, and he knew now how true that was. One Sunday when the Sebastiens stopped outside the church to greet him and he introduced Emma to them, they recognized her name. Sebastien knew her grandfather, had done business with him, and had actually handled the transfers of property when her father lost everything. Mrs. Sebastien had heard of the plantation, recalled fondly how it had looked decorated for a ball she had once attended there. Emma was, Devlin realized then, of that pampered upper class, used to being waited on, used to having slaves to do the hard work. She had told him that when they first met, but she seemed so capable and independent that he had never really thought of her that way before.

The upstairs was organized, if not finished. They began building the partitions for the downstairs alcoves. A trip to a lumber yard, and Devlin brought back several four-by-four beams of heavy, dark wood. They were set under the edge of the balcony, and the walls built back from there, four inches wide, dead space between the panels. The problem was, the question of the staircase had to be addressed before they could finish all the partitions. In the evenings, by lamplight, Devlin and Samuel sketched and figured and finally decided the bottom stairs would point towards the front door, then make a sweeping curve to follow the kitchen wall up and to the balcony.

"How do we get the wood to go into that shape?" Devlin pondered when they had their final sketch completed. It was one thing to do the math. It was another to get the wood to curve.

"It ain't easy, but we can do it," Samuel assured him. It involved huge tubs filled with steaming hot water. They soaked the wood thoroughly then carefully bent it into a mold Samuel had built and left it in the kitchen to bake dry. Fortunately, the kitchen was huge. Otherwise, they would have had to heat the entire dining room to get that wood dried out properly. Summer was coming on, and sleeping above the kitchen, Devlin found it stifling after they had been drying wood, but the end product would be worth it. Of course, the new design left a dead space under the stairs that could not be used for dining, or much of anything else. Although the staircase itself was not yet completed, they boarded up the space, punched a hole in the wall back into the kitchen, and hung two of the discarded bedroom doors over the front and rear openings of the space. It would be a closet for storing buckets, brushes and brooms for cleaning, to be camouflaged, eventually, with potted and hanging plants.

Every Friday morning, Devlin washed up, put on his business suit, and walked down to the bank to draw out wages for Samuel, cash for their personal needs, and enough money to purchase the materials needed for the next week's work. He also stopped by the basement of the bank to collect any new sketches Emma had for him. The second Friday of the month, what she had for him was a sketch of the fountain and some designs for the windows. He was studying them when he came back upstairs, and he almost literally ran into Larissa Sebastien, who was loitering around the first floor.

"I am so sorry, Miss Sebastien! Do excuse me!"

"No excuse necessary, I was not watching where I was going either. And it is good to see you again, Mr. Lachlan. I must say, I was sad you did not take up our invitation to come to lunch again."

"Open invitations are rather difficult to schedule," he said.

"We'll have to decide on a specific date then. What is it you have there? Do you mind if I look?"

She held out a slender, lace-mittened hand, and he let her take the pages from him.

"This is lovely!" she said. "Pictures of some place you've been?"

"Pictures of some place I am building," he said, unable not to feel pride in what he had already accomplished, and what he still hoped to accomplish. It must have shown in his voice, because she was immediately intrigued.

"Really? You are building this? You must let me see it!"

"You can come by any time…" he started.

"How about right now?" she asked.

He was caught completely off guard. "I don't know… that is…"

"I'm waiting here for Father. He's supposed to take me to a dress fitting after his meeting here, but he has a tendency to get long winded and have his meetings go way over time. I have the brougham waiting outside, and a chaperone, too. I'll just tell father you will escort me to the dressmaker, and he can pick me up later."

She smiled up at him, so that the bonnet framed her face instead of hiding it, and he could not help but admire her warm, generous smile.

"If your father agrees…"

Sebastien agreed readily, glad not to have to cut his business short, and Devlin rode in the brougham once again, this time sitting opposite Larissa and a pretty, young black woman who was not introduced to him at all. He gave the directions and the address, and the driver took them to the front door, which was still, unfortunately, a blocky looking little entrance inside the partially boarded up big, arched doorway.

"It doesn't look very promising from the outside," Larissa commented as he helped her down from the carriage.

"Wait until you see the inside," he said. He led her in and gave her the spiel, what would be where, how it would look. Unfortunately, at the moment, that was hard to visualize. They had cleaned the skylights so there was a good deal of natural light in the big room. But the stairway was gone, just the rough ladder led up to the balcony, and under the balcony, plain boards separated the individual alcoves. Sawdust and construction materials were scattered everywhere, the big pump still dominated the center of the room, and the windows were still dirty and still looked out onto the alley. He explained, he tried to show her how things would be eventually, but she didn't seem to be greatly impressed.

"Well, I'm sure it's a lovely idea," she said." Good luck with your decorating."

Her bright smile didn't salve the sting of her words. He escorted her and her chaperone to the dressmaker, which fortunately was on the south side of town, not too far from the lumber yard he needed to visit anyway.

As he was handing the ladies out of the brougham, the chaperone smiled up at him and said, "it will be wonderful!"

Her words were kind, but they, also, did not relieve the sting of

Larissa's response.

Decorating, he thought bitterly, as he paid an exorbitant price for the walnut boards that Samuel would make into the big arched doors that would, soon, hopefully, grace the front entrance. *Decorating!*

Saturday, Emma paid her usual visit to see how things were going, and she couldn't help but notice that Devlin's mood had soured considerably. When she pried out of him the events of Friday morning, she was angry. Not with Larissa, but with Devlin.

"Don't you ever stop to think before you act?" she demanded.

"She was impressed with your pictures. She wanted to see it. I thought…"

"You thought everyone has your grand vision or my artist's eye. Most people don't, Devlin. They can't see what will be, only what is, and right now, what is isn't too impressive. This could spoil everything!"

"How? She'll see it done later and she'll see how she was wrong…"

"If you can get it done without her father's money! You go to him now asking for an investment, and she'll be there to tell him just how hopeless this place is!"

"Is it that bad to try to share a dream with a girl you care for?" Devlin asked.

"When money is involved, yes. Okay, look. It's not completely hopeless yet. What we can do is fix up this front corner to fit your vision. It'll have to do. Meantime, I know you don't have a fountain yet, but put something up in that big hole in the floor, something to show the scale, if not the elegance."

"But, what…"

"We'll invite them to dinner. After dark, so they can't see all of it, just the part we want them to see. I'll get that one painting done. While I work on that, sand and refinish this window frame. Have Samuel get those doors up, even if they are not finished. That big, curved piece of wood you will use to support the rounded part of the stairs, can you get that in place?"

"I think so. We can put in a rough frame, but not the stairs themselves very fast."

"We'll need tablecloths, napkins, at least one set of drapes, preferably two. I wish I were two people so I could paint and sew at the same time."

Samuel, who had been listening in, said, "I can help with the sewing."

"You sew?" Emma asked him in surprise.

"Not me, no. But I know someone who can help. And Chloe has Sunday afternoons off. She can help too."

"We still need food," Emma said. "Something impressive."

"I can cook... Devlin said.

"Invite them on a Sunday, and Chloe can help," Samuel said again.

"We need wine if we're going to impress Sebastien," Devlin said.

"Get me a menu and I'll get the wine," Emma said. "And by the way, this had better work, since we're going to be using up the last of your mortgage money, I'm sure."

The next day, Sunday, they met the Sebastiens on the steps of the church once again and were invited to lunch again.

"Larissa said we should give a specific date," Sebastien said. "How about... two weeks from today?"

"I accept," Devlin said. "Only if you will come to dinner that night at my place."

"A boarding house?" Sebastien asked uncertainly.

"No, it's a business I am starting. It will be the best restaurant in Charleston when it's done, maybe in all of the South. It's a bit rough yet, but I think we can impress you sufficiently."

"Well, let's just see if you can!" Sebastien said, accepting the challenge.

"Two weeks is more than enough," Devlin told a worried Emma as he walked her home.

"You dream big," she said.

"I have more help," he said.

After their discussion Saturday afternoon, he had told Samuel, "If you are bringing people in to spend a night or two here that is fine. But never do it behind my back, is that clear? You have a seamstress hidden downstairs, I take it?"

"It's a whole family," Samuel admitted. "The seamstress is the daughter."

"I'm not running a hotel or the Underground Railroad," Devlin said. "I will allow people passing through to spend some time here. It's better than on the streets. But, if we're feeding them, they will have to earn their keep."

"A day's labor for a day's meals?" Samuel asked.

"That seems a little steep. You get that plus wages. But whatever you think is fair."

In two weeks, Devlin saw numerous new faces, some came and left again in one night, a few stayed longer. Skilled labor helped Samuel. Unskilled cleaned or helped him scrub the floors with buckets of sand and stiff brushes. The curved stair rails were placed, even though the stairs themselves were not built yet. The first window was removed and cleaned thoroughly, and while it was set aside, Emma worked painting the stretched canvas that filled the window well. She quit the bank, somewhat sooner than she had planned, so that she could work full time on this ambitious project. Chloe and three other women hemmed and stitched the cloths. Another man scrubbed and organized the kitchen. He said his name was Pierre, and it might have been. There was a trace of Louisiana Creole in his speech. Pierre wasn't a great chef, but he was inventive and interested in staying on. He took Devlin's suggestions and recipes and added to them where needed, feeding the group that now shared the building with his experiments.

"I want three separate meals for Sunday," Devlin told him. "But just one serving of each. For the guests, anyway. I'm thinking something with chicken, something with beef, and maybe something plain south, like ham and sweet potatoes. And three kinds of desert, too. Maybe, Emma can find that Arabian baker again and get some of those honey-nut things…"

"Baklava," Pierre said. "I can make that."

"Where did you learn to make that?" Devlin asked in surprise.

"You brought some home once, remember?" Pierre said. "I tasted it and figured it out."

"And you can make it now?"

"Sure! It's work, but it can be done. Also, something with a custard, maybe? And a rich pastry with chocolate and cream. And, if you will buy the ice, I can make a nice sherbet for between the courses. That is what elegant restaurants do."

"I'll take your word for it," Devlin agreed.

The second Sunday came, finally, and Devlin and Emma traveled in the brougham to the Sebastien house for a lunch of baked white fish and early spring vegetables. Sebastien had obviously told his chef to try to impress also, and it was good. After lunch, he invited Devlin and the ladies to enjoy the lovely spring weather by having a game of croquette on the lawn. It was a pleasant way to spend the afternoon, and it helped Devlin with the growing sense of worry and panic he was having trouble holding down. After two rousing games, they all retired inside for sherry and conversation.

"About this restaurant of yours," Sebastien said.

"It's really quite funny, Father..." Larissa tried to interject, but Devlin held up a hand.

"I'd rather not discuss it at all until you can see it for yourself," he said.

So, they talked about the high cost of living since the tariffs had gone up again. Eventually, the clock chimed the half-hour past seven, and they all rose to gather their wraps as Sebastien ordered the brougham to bring them to the restaurant.

"Do you have a name for it?" Sebastien asked as they all climbed in.

"The Lakes," Devlin said.

They pulled up at the front door as the gas lamps were being lit on the street. The glow cast a shine over the polished walnut arched double front doors. They were not carved or varnished yet, but they still looked much more impressive than the inset doors that used to grace the front of the building. Devlin helped Mrs. and Miss Sebastien out of the brougham, and escorted Miss Sebastien and Emma up the steps, while Mrs. Sebastien walked up on her husband's arm. As they approached, the door opened, and Devlin had a moment of panic. But there in the doorway, bowing low to welcome them all in, was Samuel, dressed in one of Devlin's good white shirts, with a white apron tied over Devlin's second-best suit trousers.

"Welcome to The Lakes," he said, bowing low. "Your table is ready for you, sir."

Devlin swore to himself he'd find out later whose idea this was. Meantime, Samuel accepted the ladies' capes and bonnets, the gentlemen's hats and canes, and hung them respectfully by the door. He bowed again, indicating the table, and he seated Emma, while Devlin seated Miss Sebastien and Sebastien seated his wife.

Most of the room was darkened, but overhead lamps and table candles lit up the front corner where they were seated. The flagstone floor was sanded and shining. The brick walls looked rosy in the lamplight. A few potted plants graced the room and hid the worst of the construction. Several tables were scattered about, with long cloths to cover them, but only the front one had chairs: petit point cushioned dining chairs Emma had bought for this occasion at an estate sale. Having had most of her own estate disposed of this way, she knew where they were held and what bargains could be bought there. The table where the chairs waited was covered with a fine white linen cloth, edged at the bottom in lace, with pale blue linen, lace-trimmed napkins. The table was set for five with the fine, blue-patterned china and heavy silver Emma had also acquired at an estate sale. In front of the Sebastiens, at Emma and Devlin's backs, blue satin drapes were pulled back from the tall, arched window with thick, pale green ropes, and discreet lighting glowed on the realistically painted pastoral scene.

First came a fish course: small fillets of fresh-caught fish, seasoned and cooked perfectly and served with a dry white wine that Sebastien spun around in his mouth judiciously before swallowing.

"Acceptable?" Devlin asked.

"Perfect!" Sebastien declared.

Next Samuel brought out a tray of bowls and placed three different soups on the table. Sebastien (and Devlin) received the French onion soup, complete with a crusty piece of French bread and melted cheese floating on top. Larissa was served a light vegetable consume, and Mrs. Sebastien and Emma were served a creamy soup with chicken and mushrooms. Crusty fresh bread, still warm from the oven, soft, fresh butter and raspberry preserves were served with the soup.

When that was whisked away, three main courses came out. Ham, spiced with cloves, served with sweet potatoes swimming in butter, prime rib with asparagus and tiny new potatoes, and white meat of chicken cooked in mushrooms and white wine with French beans and slivered carrots. As Devlin had hoped, each member of the Sebastien family offered tastes of their meal to the others, so all three dishes were appreciated by all. White wine was served with the chicken, and red wines with the other meats. Following the main meal, there was a scoop of lime sherbet to cleanse the palate and then, not three but five, different deserts were brought to be shared around and savored. There was an egg custard with caramel sauce, a French eclair, baklava, three-layer chocolate cake, and hot apple pie served with a slice of cheese and a dollop of whipped cream.

As the last of the plates were taken away, and a rich, dark coffee served in delicate china cups, Sebastien leaned back in his chair and looked around.

"The food is definitely impressive," he said. "How much will you have on the menu at any one time?"

"I am thinking of the menu just being chicken, beef and pork, or lamb, and the actual meals being a sort of chef's choice, depending on what's fresh at the market on any given day, with some kind of fish or seafood course, soups, and a choice of probably no more than three deserts at a time."

"But what if I want the baklava, and it's not available the night I come?" Mrs. Sebastien asked.

"Then, hopefully, you will come again and again until you can have it!" Devlin said, giving her a mischievous grin.

Sebastien roared with appreciative laughter. "I like you're thinking! And I think I like your decorating. I saw there was a building next door when we drove up. I approve of your windows. Quite ingenious. Will you have paintings in those upstairs windows across the hall also?"

"I'm thinking just framed paintings, covering the windows. Let me show you around a bit."

Sebastien, primed with the beauty of this front corner and the delicious meal, was much more receptive to Devlin's explanations and promises than Larissa had been.

"I underestimated him," Larissa said as the men moved off, talking, with Mrs. Sebastien trotting curiously behind.

"It's easy enough to do," Emma said. "He's a bit naive still. But not at all stupid."

Larissa looked across the room to where her father and Devlin stood in front of the thinly disguised pump. Devlin was obviously talking about his proposed fountain, his arms raised, his hands coming down again and again, broadening out, to describe the cascading waters.

"And he's your... cousin?"

Emma laughed. "He's all yours, my dear. Trust me. He has been since the first time he clearly saw your face."

"I would like him to be interested in more than just my face."

"Now, don't you be naive," Emma said.

"Of course, I would want a piece of this!" Sebastien was saying as he and Devlin returned to the table. "I think you are right in saying it could be the greatest restaurant in the whole of the South. And the name! Perfect! You come by my office first thing tomorrow morning, and we'll dicker out how much you think, say, thirty percent of this business would be, and we'll get the paperwork done at once. Impressive. Very impressive."

"There is one more thing that I think would get it off to a better start than just throwing open the doors," Devlin said as he escorted the family to the front door again, where Samuel was waiting to hand them their wraps.

"Yes?"

"A grand opening. A special night that only select individuals are invited to. It would be a good way to get initial interest in your investment. And anyone who approves of what they see – and taste – can make a dinner reservation while they are here."

"Excellent idea!" Sebastien agreed at once. Then he paused, setting his hat on his head. "Now, here's a question, though. If we invite them, do they get to eat for free? It seems wrong to invite someone, then charge them for dinner. On the other hand, considering the type of meals you serve, free dinner for a roomful of people could set us back quite a bit."

"Tickets," Emma murmured.

"I beg your pardon, Miss?"

"You invite them, the way people are invited to a political dinner. If they want to come, they have to buy a ticket. One ticket entitles them to one dinner of their choice. We charge a regular meal price for each ticket, and perhaps a little extra…"

"Extra?" Sebastien sounded outraged.

"For the three glasses of wine and the free champagne."

Sebastien laughed again. "I like the way you think, too, Missy."

"Father," Larissa said as they were stepping outside, "Since Mr. Lachlan is your business partner now, shouldn't we invite him to my coming-out ball next Friday?"

"Oh!" Sebastien said. "Why, yes! Of course, we should. Eight pm, Lachlan. You know the address. We'll be looking forward to seeing you."

"Told you," Emma whispered to him as Sebastien was helping his women folk into their seats.

"Told *you*," Devlin said. "I was the business partner before the invitation."

"You are getting less and less naive every day," she said, giving his cheek a pat. "Soon you won't be fun any more."

He gave her a hand into the carriage. He felt like laughing. He felt like dancing. What he did was click his heels and bow in his best European fashion as the brougham pulled away from the curb.

The Lakes, Charleston, South Carolina, October 1840

Dozens of couples, a few families, and a number of single men milled about or sat at tables in the newest restaurant in Charleston: The Lakes. The place was, in fact, packed, thanks mainly to Sebastien who invited friends, relatives, political cronies and business associates to the grand opening. Wandering through the crowd, Devlin was gratified to hear the murmurs of appreciation for the decor, the window scenes, the bubbling fountain, the quality of the china and silver. It had all come together as he had envisioned. With, he had to admit, Emma's help. He was a bit worried at first about all the black faces in the room, more than a dozen men to serve the meal, a wine steward and his two assistants. But Pierre had been right. He had said these "quality folk," as Devlin still labeled them in his mind, were so used to being waited on by black people that they wouldn't even notice that all the waiters and kitchen workers were black. They, in fact, would expect it. All they saw was the blue-and-green livery Emma had designed for all the workers who would be visible to the public, and never looked at any faces. Which was fortunate, as many of them should have been in hiding, not so prominently displayed.

"Your Mrs. Chambers could be here," Pierre had said, "And Samuel's Chloe could wait on her, and she'd never realize it was her own parlor maid."

Devlin had made sure that no escaped slaves from the immediate area were waiting tables tonight anyway.

Besides the half dozen busboys to clear the tables and scrape the leftovers, Pierre had three kitchen cleaners and dishwashers and two men and two women helping him with the actual cooking: one made only sauces and gravies, one who baked the bread, one whose job was rolling out the fine layers for the pastries and baking them to perfection, one who helped him with the main courses. Also added to the permanent staff was an older man named Abel, who was in charge of the wines, a job Emma gladly gave up after testing his expertise. Emma herself was manning a stand-up desk at the front of the room. Devlin, recalling the shop where he had once dropped Larissa Sebastien for a dress fitting, had taken Emma to the same place and ordered work clothes for her. Blue was to be the color of The Lakes, with soft greens to match the pastoral landscapes, but he didn't want her blending into the background like a piece of drapery. He had found a rich, deep, slightly greenish blue that reminded him of the waters he had once seen off a Caribbean Island for one gown, a soft spring green, trimmed in yards of off-white lace with brown velvet ribbon trim to set off her eyes, for another. He had more plans for future dresses. He wanted her to be arrayed differently every night of the week.

"Just not pink," was Emma's response to that. She was wearing the Caribbean blue tonight, with something that caught the light and sparkled in her hair. She had said she was not beautiful enough to catch a husband on her abbreviated debutante season. He thought the men in this town must be blind.

"How's it going?" he asked her.

"We're booked for months already. I think you'll be able to pay off your loans sooner than expected."

"Even if I pay things off *as* expected, that's good enough for me," he replied, and went in search of Sebastien.

"Well, we've done it!" Sebastien said, clapping him heartily on the back.

I've done it, Devlin thought, but he smiled and nodded in agreement. He had done the work, he had come up with the vision. But, in fairness, Sebastien had supplied the lion's share of the cost. They were looking about the room, both pleased with what they saw, when a small, rotund man can up demanding attention.

"Josiah! You've got to do something! You own this place don't you?"

"What's the problem?" Sebastien asked.

"It's that… that *girl* over there! I said I wanted to reserve the entire building for Christmas Eve, and she said it was already booked. You tell her that if I want Christmas Eve, I can have Christmas Eve! The nerve of that girl! She has no idea who she is dealing with!"

"I'm terribly sorry, Arthur," Sebastien said. "It was my idea that we take bookings on a first come, first served basis so as to avoid any favoritism. I got caught in that myself! I wanted to book for New Year's Eve, and that's already taken as well."

"Well! I never! There are places in town where my name means something. I'll just take my business someplace else!" He turned to stalk off and added, "Snobbery!" as he passed the splashing fountain in the middle of the floor.

"Don't worry," Sebastien said. "He's not as important as he thinks he is. And the fact that even I can't get the dates I want shows you we are doing splendidly already! Is it everything you envisioned it could be?"

"Exactly as I envisioned it."

"Well, you must have that famous Scottish 'Sight'. I couldn't have foreseen this ugly warehouse turning into this. The food is excellent as well. Where did you say you got your chef?"

"Savannah," Devlin said at once, although Pierre had escaped from a restaurant in New Orleans.

"Good choice! They have wonderful cuisine down there. By the by, who exactly is Roger E."

"Who?"

"The artist who signed all your windows. I noticed you have a couple of his paintings for sale upstairs also."

"A local artist," Devlin said, careful not to use a pronoun. Emma had reversed her name and initial as he had once suggested, but though it was like masquerading as a man, he could not bring himself to refer to her as "he."

"His work is different from the usual in these parts. I like his use of color, though. I don't suppose he would do portraits?"

"I can ask," Devlin said uncertainly. How would Emma feel about being brought out, by having Sebastien pose for a portrait?

"I had a portrait done of Larissa before her coming out, but, honestly, the fool made her look like a man in woman's clothing."

"I don't see how that could be possible."

"Well, he managed it. Maybe, we can arrange some sittings here, during the mornings when the place is closed. She can bring Maisie for a chaperone. I'm sure you can talk your man into it," Sebastien said, unconsciously assuming, as his friend had, that his importance was enough to change people's minds.

"I'm sure something can be arranged," Devlin said.

"Excellent. Oh, excuse me, I see someone whose good will we simply must have!"

Devlin gave him a bow as he left, then he himself turned and looked for a specific person in the crowd. He found her finally, up on the balcony, the farthest table towards the front where she could watch all the comings and goings. He signaled one of the waiters and ordered two glasses of champagne to be taken up, then he went up himself and sat down with her at the small table, built only for two.

"I fear I must apologize," Miss Sebastien said.

"For what?"

"I scoffed at your vision. I could only see the grime and the pointless windows, and the ridiculous pump standing in the middle of the floor. You saw all this, didn't you?"

"Yes," he said simply.

Abel himself brought their glasses and hovered for a moment while Devlin tasted it. He hadn't known much about wine before. Emma had schooled him carefully, taking him on buying missions to various seaports north and south, including New Orleans. Devlin nodded, though in fact, he still didn't care much for wine of any kind, even with bubbles.

"Was this part of your vision?" Miss Sebastien asked, sipping her own glass.

"Sort of. I didn't know enough about wine to begin with, but I knew I wanted the best of everything."

"You certainly have accomplished your mission. I feel I should do something to make up for my lack of belief in you."

"There is one thing I have been meaning to ask you to do for me."

"Yes?"

"Marry me."

She didn't quite choke on her champagne. "Excuse me?"

"You heard the first time."

"I think, sir, that you get a little ahead of yourself."

"No. I know exactly what I am doing. You see, Miss Rogers explained to me this whole 'coming out' business to me."

"Did she now? And what exactly did she explain to you?"

"How it all is meant to work. So, I look at you and I see a young woman who can never be considered less than beautiful by any standards."

"Thank you, kind sir."

"And I'm sure your father has put up a generous dowry for you, and as his only child you stand to eventually come into considerable wealth."

"Well, eventually…"

"I know how that works, too. Anything you own belongs to your husband. You belong to your husband."

"And that's what you want?" Her voice was suddenly much cooler. "My father's fortune and a blonde slave?"

Devlin grinned. "Not at all. I mention these things only, because with all those attributes it makes no sense that after a season on the – shall, we call it the 'marriage market…'?"

"Please don't!"

"After a full season, someone as beautiful and wealthy as Miss Larissa Sebastien comes home with no offers of marriage."

"There were many offers," she said. "And as many refusals."

"That was my guess. I further guess that you are waiting for a man who is wealthy in his own right, to be sure that he has not chosen your father's money, but yourself."

"You guess well."

"I come from more humble beginnings than your father knows."

"Your father was an earl or something, wasn't he?"

"I never claimed him as a Father. I said, honestly, that I grew up on his estate. I don't even know who my real parents were. My intention has always been to make something of myself, by myself."

"I see…"

"No. You don't. You are too used to seeing yourself as a commodity to see what I saw the first moment I laid eyes on you: a beautiful, intelligent, caring woman with whom I would like to spend my life."

"Not so intelligent if I couldn't see your dream of this place!"

"Everyone has their faults," Devlin smiled. "Larissa… if I may be so bold as to call you that…"

"It is my name."

"A beautiful one. It suits you. Larissa. My goal in life has always been to make something of myself. But I never wished to do so by marrying money or a title or social standing. What I am and what I will be in the future is what I can do for myself."

"With father's help."

"As I once told someone else about business, if you can afford to start one on your own, you don't need to. If you want to fish for a living, you need a boat, and nets and buoys, lifeboats and laborers and food and freshwater tanks, and buyers! The list goes on. To start a restaurant you need a building, and food, but also all this…" He indicated the place settings, the tablecloth, the wine. "As I said, if you can afford all that, you probably can afford not to work for a living at all. Investors is how business works, here and everywhere. And quite honestly, yes, I was hoping for your father as an investor for a specific reason. I needed him to see me as a business partner – even if a junior one – not as a clerk because that was the only way I could ask him for your hand. Not the hand of a rich young woman. The hand of the most beautiful woman I have ever seen in my life. A woman I can respect, and who I can hope will respect me. A woman who will not expect to spend all her time visiting exotic places, but who will understand that her husband is the working half of a business relationship, will be busy most days and often on holidays, but who will always love and care for her and keep for her a special place and time in his heart and in his life."

"Whew," she said. "That has to be the best proposal I have ever heard."

"Will you consider it?" He reached in his pocket and pulled out the ring. It was not a large one, but he felt the thin gold band and small, well-cut diamond suited her better than anything big or gaudy would have done.

"Oh, I don't have to consider it," she said, looking at his offering. She smiled up at him. "You had me worried there for a moment, but you convinced me you are not a fortune hunter. Which is good because I have liked and admired you from our first meeting also."

"Was that a yes?" Devlin asked after a moment of silence.

"Most emphatically," she said, and she allowed him to slip the ring on her finger.

"I must warn you," she said. "We do believe in long engagements around here."

"I can wait a long time, as long as it means eventually you and I will be together."

"Shall we tell father, then, that he will get the most famous restaurant in South Carolina and a future son-in-law on the same night?"

"I was thinking of waiting a bit. On the other hand, he is in a very good mood right now."

He stood, offered her a hand to rise also. Downstairs, Emma caught his eye, and closed one of hers slowly.

New Orleans, Louisiana, June 1842

Considering she had claimed seasickness the entire voyage and stayed locked in her private stateroom with her maid, Larissa looked lovely and healthy when she came out on deck to meet Devlin so they could go to their hotel. He had already engaged a cab and had their luggage loaded. He accepted the small valise Maisie handed him and helped both women down the gangplank and into the cab.

It had not been his idea to bring Maisie along on the honeymoon. He had tried to fight it, arguing that now that they were married, they hardly needed a chaperone. Larissa had won however, on the grounds that Maisie would not be their chaperone, but her personal maid.

"Why do you need a maid?" he had asked.

But, she laughed and patted his arm and said something vague about how hard it was to dress oneself alone.

"You won't be alone, you know," he said.

When Larissa just laughed again, it was Maisie who whispered to him, "You'll never convince her. I'll stay out of your way, don't you worry, sir."

He did worry. He wondered, in fact, if perhaps Emma had been right all along. He hadn't meant to marry social position, but it seemed, like it or not, he had married into it.

The wedding itself had been an impressive show, far beyond his grandest imaginings. He had had a bit of a problem picking someone to be his best man. All his closest friends in town were escaped slaves. He even considered asking Emma to stand with him, which was vetoed immediately. He needn't have worried. Mrs. Sebastien loved throwing lavish parties and had been thrilled to be able to organize the wedding of her only daughter. She pulled up cousins, nieces, nephews, relatives and friends of relatives and not only supplied him with a best man but with fourteen groomsmen as well. A tiny pair of distance cousins had marched down the aisle first, the little girl strewing flower petals all over the floor, the little boy balancing the wedding bands on a silk pillow. Then fourteen couples, the women in pale blue silk gowns, the men in tuxedos (which apparently was formal enough for them, although Devlin, his best man and Sebastien had had to dress in something more elegant, called a "morning suit"), had marched down the aisle before Larissa's cousin, Jasmine Sebastien, walked down in a dark blue satin gown with a huge bouquet in her hands to stand opposite… Devlin didn't even know his best man's name. John, he thought. Not a Sebastien, though, he was from the other side of the family. Larissa had made an entrance worthy of a queen, which he supposed she was in Charleston society. Yards of satin and silk in her gown, acres of something filmy for the veil, a bouquet that trailed flowers and ribbons to below her knees, a train several feet long following her down the aisle. None of that was as important to him, though, as seeing her face when her father lifted her veil, kissed her cheek, and put her hand in Devlin's. It rested there, warm and smooth as if it belonged, and she smiled at him. He had smiled back. Overwhelmed. The service was long and formal, but it ended the way all such services end, with the groom given permission, finally, to kiss his bride. He had panicked a bit when they were taken back to the Sebastien home where even more guests than the hundreds (literally) that attended the wedding itself were already gathering. He had thought that every flower in the south must have gone into decorating the church as well as pinning flowers on the men, passing out bouquets to the women, but there were even more flowers in the big house, bouquets and vases in all the big rooms downstairs and decorating the lawn and the extra tables set up out there. But flowers were the least of it. Gallons of wine and champagne were sitting on (very expensive) ice, and there were tables and tables of food, including the sweets Mrs. Sebastien had ordered from The Lakes, so many that it had been hard to even keep the restaurant open the past couple days.

"We do have to be on board the ship before it leaves dock at six," he reminded Larissa. Again, she patted his arm and smiled.

"We will be love, don't worry," she said, and she swam into the crowd, accepting compliments and congratulations like royalty. Devlin had followed, less and less certain as the afternoon wore on. Eventually, he had climbed upstairs, away from the mobs, just for a moment alone.

"You look like someone who's wondering what he got himself into."

He turned, and Maisie stepped into the room, taking a liberty with him that she probably would not have with any other white man. She felt

68

comfortable with him because of the intimate time they had been forced to spend together – her tagging along behind the girl he was courting. She had always been Larissa's official chaperone and so had had to be present while Devlin took Larissa for buggy rides or walks along the bay. He knew that she had been Larissa's personal servant since childhood, but he also knew that like himself, she had learned reading and writing, arithmetic and grammar, sitting next to a more privileged person and silently sharing the lessons. If the world were fair, she should have been Larissa's maid-of-honor, not her maid. *She would have looked much better than that vapid Jasmine in that blue dress*, Devlin thought.

"You know, Maisie," he said hesitantly. "If you were interested in working at the restaurant…"

"I know what goes on in your restaurant," Maisie said, surprising him.

"You do?"

"I'm not exactly blind or deaf, you know. And I appreciate the offer, Mr. Devlin. But I think I'll stay here a bit longer. Miss Larissa needs me." She smiled at him and added, "Does that surprise you?"

"That you are loyal to your sister? No."

Her eyebrow quirked up in a gesture that was hauntingly familiar. "Now, how did you know that?"

"I think it would be obvious to anyone who isn't blind. I always wondered, though, what a little thing like you was supposed to do to protect Larissa if I… er… wasn't trustworthy."

Maisie shrugged. "Scream for help, maybe. I think the presence of another person is just to make you feel less comfortable – or to let the world know if the wedding had to be sooner."

Devlin had thrown back his head and laughed, and that was when Maisie assured him that the bride and groom were allowed to leave before the party broke up.

"Good thing," she had added. "This could go on all night!"

So, they had made it to the boat in time. Devlin had booked two cabins because his memories of bunks on a boat where not auspicious and he wished for something a little more comfortable for his wedding night. A luxury cabin on a cruise ship was somewhat different from a shared bunk in a whaler, however, and he somewhat regretted his decision – until Larissa got seasick. They were still at dock when she said the motion made her light-headed and queasy. She went below and he didn't see her again until they reached New Orleans. He tried to talk her out of the cabin several times, telling her the sea was not rough and that the fresh air would make her feel better, but she stayed in bed.

"I think she's a bit afraid of you," Maisie confided to him when she answered his knock at the cabin door.

"Am I scary?" he asked.

Maisie grinned. "Terrifying," she said.

The suite at the hotel had one bedroom, but it also had a sitting room and a dressing room. He stayed in the dressing room while Maisie prepared Larissa for bed and only came out when Maisie tapped on the door in passing. *At least*, he thought, *Larissa had arranged that Maisie would be staying in separate quarters downstairs, not in the same suite.* But, as he heard the suite door close behind her and started to turn the knob on the dressing room door, it occurred to him that he was probably as scared – if not more so – than Larissa was. His desire and passion were so powerful, and she was so dainty and fragile. And he had no more been with a woman before in his life than she had been with a man. Oh, he understood the basic mechanics of a conjugal relationship. He was unprepared, however for the joy of discovering the secret glories of a woman's body.

II

The sea voyage back and forth took up half of their brief honeymoon. He had wanted to be gone only a week or so from the restaurant, but his in-laws had insisted they have some time to themselves, even if he refused to spend a year visiting relatives with his bride, as was local custom. In the time they had, they explored New Orleans. Devlin had been there before, but only around the docks and warehouses. He and Larissa enjoyed walking along the tree-shaded boulevards, taking carriage rides to explore farther, sipping dark coffee while sitting on wrought iron chairs at patio cafés. Apparently, every blossom in the south had not gone into their wedding, since all the streets and lawns seemed to be graced with flowers. He discovered as they dealt with waiters and cab drivers that Larissa spoke fluent French. She discovered that he had a little French, but it was rusty.

"It's been years since I even knew anyone who could speak it at all," he said.

"I will speak from now on only in French, then, so you relearn it," Larissa laughed.

He thought it was silly, but knowing more than one language wasn't a bad thing. And apparently French class was one of the lessons Maisie had sat in on as well.

After the first night, Devlin did not allow Maisie to get Larissa ready for bed any more. He helped her out of her petticoats, crinolines and corsets himself. She did insist, however, on Maisie bringing up a breakfast tray and helping her re-attire herself in the morning.

The Lakes, Charleston, South Carolina, October 1842

Devlin was sitting at the desk with the accounts leger in front of him and invoices spread out all around when there was a tap at his door.

He never took his work home with him. The books, the day-to-day business of the restaurant stayed in the restaurant, as did the bedroom he had originally set up for himself to sleep in, even though he now lived with his wife in her parents' home.

He didn't like the fact that they lived in the Sebastiens' house, even though it was big enough that he and Larissa had a large bedroom and sitting room all to themselves. He would have preferred they have a place of their own but living with her parents had a double advantage. For one thing, honestly, it saved him money, and he was able to both pay his mortgage down faster and invest more in the restaurant than would have been possible had he also been paying rent. Also, if they were on their own, he would have had to hire servants. He was not fond of the fact that the servants in the Sebastien home were all slaves, but he had long known that a lady of quality did not soil her hands with common housework, and Larissa did not have to do that while they were living with her parents, any more than she had as a child. She was still tended by Maisie, something that also gave him a pang of discomfort. He would not buy slaves, but he allowed himself and his wife to be waited on by them? It was wrong. But, the arrangement benefitted Larissa in another way as well. He was gone working at the restaurant six days a week. They were only open for dinner, but he was often gone the entire day. There were bank deposits to be made, bills to be paid, menus to be planned, purchasing to be done. Besides which, he did a great deal of the physical work also. He hauled beef carcasses and helped cut meals out of them. He hefted fifty-pound bags of flour and cases of wine down to the storage rooms. He helped every morning with washing and ironing all the linens used the night before. He scrubbed floors and dusted and replaced candles in the chandeliers, even cooked and washed dishes when needed. Living with Larissa's parents meant she was not all alone every day while he was away. Her mother was always there, and her mother's and father's many relatives came by, often visiting, Southern style, for weeks and even months at a time. When they were alone, Larissa chatted with him about who had come to visit and what was happening in the family. She didn't ask much about the restaurant. Didn't, for example, ask him why the wait staff changed over so frequently, new black faces replacing ones that stayed only a short time and vanished again, or why they bought a great deal more food than they ever served, or why no one was allowed to go downstairs except Pierre and Abel. Or why Samuel disappeared so suddenly about the same time Mrs. Chamber's maid ran away. He was not even certain that Larissa knew what he had gotten involved in. Was she wise enough to know that discussing it, even just between themselves, was a good way for him to get caught? Or was she just oblivious? He wasn't sure. But he felt much more comfortable discussing family, the plays they could see at Sunday afternoon matinees, and books they had shared – even when they were alone.

"Come in," he called out, and was a little surprised that Emma walked in. Usually, she left after greeting the last incoming customer, long before the rest of them finished with serving and cleaning up. They had a standing order for a cab to take her back to her boarding house, as well as special permission from her landlady to stay out later than the usual nine o'clock curfew.

"Everything all right?" he asked.

"Never better," she said.

"No problems?" he asked, turning his swivel chair to look at her.

"None."

"Um. In that case, why are you here?"

She sat down on the edge of a low bookcase in the corner and said, "I wanted to tell you, in private, that I'm getting married."

The announcement staggered him somewhat. He hadn't been expecting it. Emma had never really shared her private life with him, or anyone else that he knew of, so he had no idea she had been seeing someone seriously enough to consider marriage. Or when she found the time. Although, since he started courting Larissa, long before their marriage, he had stopped spending Sunday afternoons with Emma. The restaurant was always closed on Sunday. It was the day of rest and family, and apparently flirtations, for all of them.

"Is it anyone I know?" he asked, trying to hide his surprise.

"Everett Dawson," she said. "He's an independent fisherman. We get most of our fresh seafood from him."

"Oh, yes. I think I've met him," Devlin said, trying to picture the man's face. "Well. Congratulations."

"Thank you."

"So, I suppose you'll be leaving us, then, is that what you are coming to tell me?"

"Yes. Everett has a cottage on a small island barely in sight of the coast. I'll be spending my days painting and gardening and raising a family there."

"It sounds romantic," he said, still feeling off-balance by the whole thing.

"It is. Very romantic. That's why we're getting married Sunday."

That took several seconds to sink in completely. "In two days…? Oh. Oh!"

"I thought you'd figure it out eventually," she said.

"It's just that you always seemed so… er… so…"

"Let's just say 'not a romantic,' all right? But I am a woman, Dev. We all have that streak in us somewhere."

"Is it going to be private or can I… can we…"

"It's very small and private, at the minister's request. But Everett doesn't have any close friends here in town, and neither do I. We were hoping you and Larissa would stand and witness for us."

"We'd be delighted!"

"You are speaking for another person, without consulting her first," Emma said.

"This is one time I feel confident she would not be angry with me for doing do. I'm also sure she's going to offer to loan you…"

"Her gown? I don't think white is entirely appropriate at this time. Anyway, Sunday. Two o'clock. You know the church."

Sunday at two, Devlin and Larissa were there, dressed in their best. Larissa had brought a big bouquet of flowers she insisted on giving to Emma, who was wearing the blue-green gown that always reminded Devlin of the Caribbean. It seemed to have a similar effect on Everett, as he looked

74

as pleased and dazed as Devlin knew he had felt when he first saw Larissa heading towards him down the isle of this same church. There was no procession this time. The four of them sat in the front pews until they were called, and the service was short and to the point. There was no music. No flower petals or guests. But when it was over, Devlin insisted the newlyweds come back to The Lakes for a late lunch, where he surprised them with a pre-planned combination wedding supper and baby shower. Pierre and Abel outdid themselves with a wedding dinner and fine wines. There was a bride's cake in tiers of fluffy white, and a grooms' cake of dark sugar, fruit and nuts. Samuel and Chloe were long gone, but one of the women who was at the moment helping out had taken the unstained parts of a discarded, wine-stained tablecloth and made a lacy baby dress and bonnet. Larissa gave them the wedding band quilt she had been making for their own bed ("I have years to make a new one for us, but only this one opportunity to give this to you!" she had said at Emma's protest). And Devlin presented them with the six-place setting of china and silver that they had used to entice Sebastien into investing in The Lakes. It was a small gathering, but a sincere one. Pierre insisted they take away with them enough leftovers that Emma would not have to cook, perhaps for days: "So you can have something of a honeymoon!"

"Too late!" Emma laughed. "But appreciated."

There were hugs and kisses, and Devlin walked them down to the Sebastien brougham that would take them in style to the dock where Everett's *Brown-Eyed Girl* was waiting to take them home to their island.

"I'm going to miss you," he said to Emma before helping her up. "You were the first friend I ever had in this country. In fact, you're the first and best friend I ever had."

"I'll miss you, too," she said, patting his cheek as she always did to put him in his place.

"I should have asked you to marry me," he said.

"Are you unhappy with what you have?"

He did consider it before shaking his head. "No. No, I'm very happy."

"So am I. Friend."

"Friend," he agreed, and he kissed her cheek then helped her up to sit by her husband. Only he and Larissa stood on the step to wave goodbye. Most of the others never came out of the building in the daylight.

Charleston, South Carolina, March 17, 1844

Devlin ran lightly up the front stairs of the Sebastien house, tossed his hat in the general direction of a nearby table, ran up another flight, and pushed open the door.

"Larissa!" he called.

"In here!" she called back, and he strode through the sitting room into the bedroom. There she was indeed, propped up on a mound of pillows, looking altogether too beautiful. He sat down on the edge of the bed and took her hand in his.

"How are you doing?"

"Fine," she smiled back. "Altogether too fine, it seems. Mother is very upset that I'm not languishing or moaning in agony."

"Why would she want you to be in agony?"

"Apparently, it's bad form for ladies not to be in unbearable agony when they are in labor. How's the restaurant? I thought you never liked to leave it alone."

"I told Abel and Pierre to take care of the people who were already seated, and we put up a sign saying 'Closed due to illness.' The doors are locked, with a man standing by to let people out, but not in."

Larissa laughed. "I think," she said, "when Mother had the message sent to The Lakes, the idea was that you would spend the night there and not come rushing home and get in the way."

"I'm not in the way. This is where I belong. Are you all right? What's happening?"

He still had one of her hands clutched in his, but she took his other hand and rested it on her belly. He felt the muscles there tense, harden even, and then slowly begin to relax again.

"Are you doing that?" he asked.

"Not intentionally. It just happens. Kind of like a muscle cramp that goes away quickly on its own."

"Does it hurt?"

She shrugged, that careless tossing of one shoulder that had always lifted his heart. "It's not comfortable, but if this is all I have to deal with, you should just go back to work."

"Oh, I think it'll get worse. Anyway, as I said, I belong here."

"Well, apparently you'll be here for a very long time, then. That only happens about every twenty or thirty minutes. The doctor was mad at Mama for sending for him. He said it won't be until sometime tomorrow."

"Then think of it as a good excuse for me to miss work."

She smiled at him, touched his face gently and said, " If it's a girl, will you be very disappointed?"

"If it's a rabbit I might be disappointed. Girl or boy doesn't matter a bit."

"Rabbit!" She burst into laughter, which caused her mother to poke her head in the door and frown disapprovingly.

"You should leave, sir! You are disturbing her!"

"He's not disturbing me, Mother!" Larissa promised.

"I'll call if we need you for anything," Devlin said. He grinned at Larissa. She smiled back, and they both laughed quietly as her mother slammed the door.

"Who are all those people downstairs?" Devlin asked. "Bad timing on their part or are they here to witness the event."

"They had better not be witnesses! No, three cousins are in so Mama can give them a grand coming out in the city here. Jaqueline, Willhelmina and Rose Doherty. You might remember them."

"I don't remember them being so masculine," he said, feigning puzzlement, and she laughed again.

"You must have seen Frank and Donavan. They're second cousins, vising for a week from school."

"Ah! That would explain the moustache. I knew Wilhelmina had a bit of one, but I didn't remember it being so luxurious…"

She laughed again, but a contraction cut it off. "No more jokes for a while. That was a bit more than uncomfortable."

"I could read to you, maybe."

"That would be nice."

He picked up the book she had lying by the bedside, opened it to the page marked, and began reading to her. He read aloud to her often. Before they were married, he had often come to visit on Sunday afternoons. If the weather was nice, they'd take a buggy and ride out into the country to have a picnic, sit on a blanket in the sun to admire the scenery. If it was cold or blustery, they'd sit by the fire in her parent's big living room. Sometimes they talked, but more often, he read because there was always a chaperone: Maisie, or Mrs. Sebastien herself, and sometimes even Mr. Sebastien if they were inside on a damp, cold day. Reading was intimate and enjoyable, but less personal than any conversation they could have – and he didn't care to share personal things in front of others.

Two hours passed, during which there were only eight more contractions. In another two hours, eight more.

"She's just too comfortable to want to come out," Larissa said.

"And you?" Devlin asked.

Again, that elegant one-shouldered shrug. "I'm fine. Really."

The doctor came after dinner, examined her, then called Devlin and Mr. Sebastien together in the drawing room.

"This is taking altogether too long," he said. "I don't like it."

"But there's nothing we can do about it, surely," Devlin said. One of the women he had met who stayed for a few days in his restaurant basement, had discussed childbirth with him when he mentioned his wife was pregnant. She had been a midwife, had told him early-stage labor could last more than a day, especially on a first born, and that the only downside to that kind of labor was that it made it hard to get any sleep. Later, labor would get more intense, but the early stage, light and far apart, was where Larissa so evidently was now. He didn't mention this aloud, though. He doubted Mr. Sebastien would appreciate hearing he had been discussing Larissa's condition with a runaway slave.

"There is a procedure," the doctor said. "It's not uncommon. I've done it before. It's called 'Cesarean' because Cesar's child with Cleopatra was born that way."

"Do it," Mr. Sebastien said.

"Now, wait a minute," Devlin said. "Just what is this 'procedure'? What exactly are you talking about?"

"It's a minor sort of surgery…" the doctor said.

"No," Devlin said. "Absolutely not. Don't even think about it!"

But they did think about it. In fact, they did it. Frank and Donavan,

Sebastien's personal valet and a large slave who worked in the gardens were recruited to hold Devlin down while Larissa's screams echoed through the house. Surgery had been invented at this time. Anesthesia had not.

He fought. He screamed her name. He felt hot tears running down his face, but he couldn't get free of all of them.

Then it was over. Maisie came out of the room with an armload of bloody sheets, towels and blankets, and Devlin was released. He took the stairs three at a time, and burst into the bedroom to find her, lying back flat now, drenched in sweat, looking worse than just exhausted. He knelt by the bed, grabbed her hand, and brushed the sweat-soaked hair back from her face.

"I tried to stop them," he said.

"I know. I could hear you," she smiled, a weak, pained smile, and reached up to touch the tears that still stained his face. "It's a boy. Would you like to see him?"

"I only want to see you," he said. He pulled back the bedclothes and lifted her nightgown to see the great stitched-shut wound on her belly, and his anger was so intense he was shaking.

"It's all right," she said. She stroked his arm until he knelt down by her again, holding her hand in both of his. "It's all right. It's over."

"I'm the one who should be comforting you," he said.

"I had the easy part."

"Easy...!"

"Pain," a little shrug, about half as much as her shoulder normally moved. He noticed that, and it tore at his heart. "You had to endure for me."

"I wish I could take it all away."

"It's over," she said again.

Talking seemed to exhaust her, and he couldn't read, not with his throat so tight still. So he just sat there, holding on to her, and the faint smile that touched her lips even when she closed her eyes told him that that was all she wanted of him at the moment.

The infant had been taken downstairs, washed and dressed and wrapped in a blanket. It was brought up again for her to nurse.

"You best leave the room, sir," the woman who brought the baby said.

"I've seen her breasts before," Devlin said.

If she was shocked by his words, he didn't care. Neither did Larissa, who smiled at his comment and reached both arms to accept the squalling bundle that was handed to her. Devlin was not favorably impressed with the red, wrinkled, screaming infant. He was still too angry about how it had been brought into the world. Larissa loosened the front of her gown and held the baby to one breast. It latched on, squalling stopped instantly. Sucking and gulping could be heard despite the small size. Then Larissa screamed, and fainted.

"It's not to be unexpected," the doctor said, after things had calmed down again. "Nursing often causes some latent contractions, and with the surgery…"

Devlin leaped at him. Only the two cousins prevented him from killing the doctor with his bare hands, then and there. One young man dragged at him while the other pried his hands off the doctor's throat. He fought loose this time, lunged after the man again. A house maid had already screamed out the backdoor for reinforcements, though. As the doctor squirmed away from Devlin again, several men grabbed him and pulled him back. Neither the cousins, Sebastien, nor the doctor could calm his rage now, but the voice that whispered in his ear, caught his attention.

"Calm down, sir, or they'll arrest you!" Maisie whispered to him. "They need you here! Miss Larissa and the baby. She needs you. You can't do her any good if they hang you!"

So, he went back to their bedroom. Larissa passed into a more normal sleep, and he pulled a chair up next to the bed and sat holding her hand while she slept. He didn't think to ask where the baby was. Larissa did that in the morning when Maisie came upstairs with a tray of food, the kind of heavy meal that a woman in her condition could not begin to eat.

"This is what the doctor said," Maisie said apologetically.

"Broth," Devlin said. "And tea. Take this away."

"You eat it," Larissa said, and before he could say he didn't want it, she asked about the baby.

"There's a woman down in the quarters that has a baby still suckling," Maisie said. "She'll be feeding your child on until you feel better. I've been caring for him"

"Can I see him at least?"

"You get stronger. Then you can see him."

At first, it seemed things might be all right after all. But the next day, she was flushed and uncomfortable. Devlin called for water and clean cloths and bathed her face and neck, and that helped. But it didn't take the fever away completely.

"You go on now and get some rest, we'll take care of Larissa," Mrs. Sebastien told him.

"I think you people have done enough," Devlin said, harshly. He escorted her out of the suite and locked the door. Of course, it didn't stay locked. Sebastien had a key to every door in his own house. But Devlin had made his intentions clear enough. He stayed with her. He bathed her face and neck and, when that wasn't enough, all of her body with cool water. But the fever not only stayed, it increased. The wound on her belly turned dark, angry red, then an ugly yellow with red streaks radiating out from it. She seldom knew who he was or where she was. Her slender body wasted away to thin, parchment-like skin stretched over her bones. Her face became drawn. Her hair started to fall out. The smell in the room was the smell of something already dead.

Two weeks passed. He left her bedside only for moments at a time when it was necessary and when Maisie could take his place. He didn't trust anyone else. He slept in the chair. He ate the food that came up on trays only when hunger gnawed at him strongly enough to catch his attention. It was late evening when she sighed softly and opened her eyes.

"Bring him to me," she said, in a voice so faint he had to lean over to hear her. In his worry over her he had completely forgotten what caused this illness.

He went to the door, hollered for someone to come up, and passed on the request. Then he went back to her bedside and picked up her hand again while they waited. She could no longer hold his hand. He clutched hers in both of his, and her hand was weak and limp and hot.

"I want to see him," she murmured.

"He's coming," Devlin said, but she didn't hear him. The breath rattled out of her and her chest didn't rise again. When the nurse came in with the baby he just said, "Never mind. Go away!" At the tone of his voice, the nurse scurried out of the room, glad to be away from him.

He sat there for over an hour, just holding her hand in his. It was when a servant came upstairs with another tray of food that he stood finally. He looked down at her face. It didn't even look like her any more, he thought.

The pale, stretched skin, the thinning hair. He bent down and kissed her cheek, feeling the warmth that the fever had left behind still there. Then he pulled up the blanket. Up to her chin. Up over her head. He heard a gasp behind him, but he didn't respond. After a long moment, with nothing else to do, he turned and went downstairs. He should wash, he supposed. He'd been in the same clothes, unbathed, for her entire illness. No doubt he stank. He didn't much care. He walked into the parlor and looked down at the selection of decanters and crystal glasses displayed for the man of the house and his guests on a round, marble-topped table. But he didn't want a drink. He wanted to swipe a hand across all that useless finery and smash it to the ground.

"There he is!"

He turned at the sound of his father-in-law's voice and found Sebastien and two uniformed men coming into the room. The uniformed men grabbed him roughly, shoved his hands behind his back and fastened steel manacles to his wrists.

"At least, you left my daughter's room so she would not have to witness this... this disgrace." Sebastien sneered. "She talked, you know! She told us everything!"

There had been a few moments in the past few weeks when he had to be away from her bedside, or when he had slept. She had talked in her fevers. Apparently, she did know what was going on at the restaurant, and apparently someone other than himself had overheard. He had not thought about Pierre and Abel and all the others in the restaurant for two weeks. He had been too consumed with Larissa's illness. Now he realized that in his own grief, he had deserted them, left them to a fate they could not have guessed was coming. When he left on his honeymoon, they had had weeks to prepare, to limit the number of reservations, to stock certain supplies, to make things easier to run in his absence. He had a white face, Emma, to run things. This time... he hadn't prepared anyone, hadn't given them warning, never even sent word where he was. He had abandoned them all.

"How does it feel, you insolent dog?" Sebastien demanded. "How does it feel to know that all those ignorant darkies you thought you were helping are even now being beaten or jailed and taken back to their masters where they belong?"

"How does it feel to murder your only child?" Devlin said back.

Sebastien blanched. "Women die in childbirth all the time!"

"Especially when a butcher and an ignoramus hack into her body with knives and saws for no reason! Get me out of here," he said to the men who had come to arrest him.

"You're filth!" Sebastien screamed at his back. "You lied to us! You're less than those darkies yourself!"

Devlin stopped in the doorway, causing the men who were dragging him to stop also. There must have been some sentiment in them, knowing he had just come down from his wife's deathbed, because they didn't jerk him on through the door, but let him turn to have a last word.

"All my life I wanted to be like you. Like her. 'Quality,' that's what I thought of you. But if this is how 'quality folk' treat their wives and daughters, I want nothing to do with any of you. Ever again."

Northern Georgia, April 1844

The men arresting him didn't have to drag him through the door. They had to hurry to catch up, to unlock the back of the prison wagon for him as he stood there waiting. He climbed inside, held his hands in the proper position so they could slide his chains through a bolt on the wall and fasten them with a padlock.

The trial was swift and somewhat pointless. They had already decided. Their fear of their own slaves dictated that he and anyone like him must be punished severely. He had expected to be hung, honestly. He tried to work up some feeling for that, but he was still numb. He was left in a small, dank prison cell, no other prisoners nearby, no exercise time outside. Food was pushed in, slops were changed. There was a small, high window in the cell, so he had some concept of passing time, and after about a week he began counting off the days. Another week passed, and another, and finally they opened the door, manacles in hand. He allowed himself to be chained up again and led outside into daylight too bright for him to even open his eyes after all the darkness. But they didn't take him to the gallows. He was shoved into a wagon with a dozen other men, all of them manacled as he was. He was chained to another man, their manacles padlocked to the floor of the wagon, along with those of the other men, and the wagon drove off. They didn't go far, though, before they were unloaded and herded up a horse ramp into an empty freight car to be locked in with a single armed guard.

"We could rush him," one of them men suggested. Devlin shrugged. They could. And one of them would die quicker.

The trip took a couple of days. It was evening when the train stopped, and the big door opened for more than just cleaning out soiled straw or sending in dinner. They were unloaded and put in another wagon and driven out of town to a small camp made up of several canvas tents, lots of men and horses. They were taken to the tent that served as a mess hall first, given food. Then they were billeted in a long tent that had rows of bunks along both sides of a narrow central isle. The beds were arranged in groups of two because the men would remain chained in pairs day and night.

"Get some sleep," a guard told them. "You got a long day tomorrow."

They were in north-western Georgia, although they did not know that for several days. They had been taken to help build a rail line from the infant town of Atlanta up to Chattanooga, Tennessee. Their job was mostly breaking up the rock that was blasted out of the mountains so the roadbed could be made smoother. The manacles tore at their legs, and they had to learn to walk and work in careful rhythms to avoid jerking their mates. The work was brutal. The muscles in Devlin's body, unaccustomed to this sort of labor, stiffened unmercifully. When he rolled out of his bunk in the morning, he could barely stand, let alone walk. His hands blistered. The blisters tore open, and new blisters formed on the raw skin. His face and neck burned in the sun. The rough, ill-fitting shoes they had been issued blistered his feet. But slowly, he grew stronger, as they all did. His muscles became used to the work. His feet and hands and ankles developed tough callouses. His skin darkened instead of burning. And the railroad moved north.

"You don't talk like a Southern boy," Josh Tyler, the man to whom he was chained, commented.

"I was born in Scotland," Devlin said.

"What are you in here for?"

"Life," Devlin said.

"That's funny," Josh said. "Cause I'm in here for death!" He laughed, but it wasn't really that funny, and no one laughed with him.

It was a man named Colbert who first suggested escape. Some of the men ignored him. Others chewed it around, considering. But the last men who had tried to escape had been tracked by the dogs and shot like animals, their still-connected bodies drug back to the camp and left to rot in the sun for days before they were taken away for burial as a warning to anyone else who considered escape, convicts or slaves. Devlin turned the idea over and over in his mind. To escape required getting free of the chains, which not only made running hard but alerted anyone who came across them of who and what they were. It also required fooling the dogs, which was not so easy, but he had heard talk from men who had managed it.

"Some dogs follow a trail on the ground," he'd been told. "But a good dog can lift his nose and smell you in the air half a mile away. Crossing rivers and walking through the swamps doesn't fool that kind for long."

Chains first, was his thought. Then dogs. It was not so much the idea of freedom that caused him to spend so much time on the problem, as it was a problem to spend time on. The work may have been long and hard, but it did not need a great deal of thought. Thinking, planning, had gotten him far in life. It was what would save him, not just from the drudgery of forced labor, but from the pit of blackness his mind had sunk into for so long. He picked up a variety of sticks and splinters of log wherever they were working, carefully palming the bits and stuffing them in his shoe while bending down, pretending to rub his chafed ankles. But none of the bits he found were thin enough and strong enough to slide into the hole and tease open the tumblers on the lock. The sticks broke or splintered. All of them.

"Shoot, if it were that easy, we'd all be free!" Josh teased, watching him work by moonlight. "Anyhow, you ever pick a lock on a manacle before?"

"Yes," Devlin said. He'd become quite adept at it, actually, removing restraints from men and women and even children who were hiding in the basement of his restaurant. What he needed was a piece of metal, but that was something they kept away from the prisoners. The flatware they ate meals with was carefully counted. Their wash buckets were wood with rope handles. Then one day he found something that might work: a piece of bone was wedged in the rocks they were working on. He had seen bits of bone before: rabbit, deer, and bird. But those were too brittle, broke too easily. This was bigger. Part of a cow he guessed. Leg bones, even from large animals, tended to be hollow and split lengthwise easily, but this was something thicker: a ball joint. He hit it with his sledge as he was hitting rocks. Kicked it surreptitiously towards where he had to swing his sledge and hit it again. He called a pause so Josh wouldn't hit him with the sledge, and bent down to massage his ankle, slipping a bit of bone into his shoe.

"You need to rub your ankles more than any other man here," the guard noticed.

"Something bit me," Devlin said, straightening up again.

"Yeah, sure. Buck up!" the guard said, and he wandered down the line. Josh swung his sledge. Devlin did. Work continued. Going home that evening, Devlin stumbled and fell onto the ground. Josh and another man hauled him back up.

"Idiot," the other man said.

Josh knew, however, that he had fallen on purpose.

"Whadja get?" he whispered that night as they lay on their bunks in the darkness, listening to men snore almost as loud as the insects in the woods around them.

Devlin displayed a single, small piece of rock.

"What good is that?" Josh asked, disappointed.

"I needed a tool," Devlin said. He fished his bit of bone out of his shoe and used the rock to shape and smooth it. For weeks he worked in the night, scraping and shaping the piece of bone, probing the lock works, shaping some more. He had to get another piece of rock, and another. Josh gave up watching him after only a few nights and used their precious down time to sleep. Then one night as he probed, he felt the shape, he pushed the right way, and heard the click. With more work than opening it, he managed to re-lock the lock. He hid his piece of bone, and went to sleep, wondering about the dogs.

As the planning woke up his mind, he noticed something else, also. Every Sunday evening a wagon load of preachers came to the camp and held meetings for the prisoners. There were Lutheran, Episcopalian and Methodist ministers who came in rotation, and one Catholic priest who came out week after week and sat alone in a small area reserved for Catholics but attended by no one. Devlin asked to be allowed to attend Catholic services. He suspected that he would be unchained from Josh, and he was, since Josh had no interest in papists. He was escorted to the place of meeting and locked inside a prison wagon that had a barred back door, so he was able to see and hear the priest without being an escape threat.

"Do you need Confession?" the priest asked him.

"I don't know what that means," Devlin said.

"Are you Catholic?"

"No."

"Then why are you here?"

Devlin indicated the bars, but the lack of a leg chain.

"I see. Well, instead of holding Mass for you, then, I think some instruction is in order."

"Does religion take much instruction?" Devlin asked. "I thought it was just a matter of belief."

"God is infinite," the priest told him. "Theology, or the study of God, is also infinite. Do you have belief?"

Devlin admitted that churchgoing for him had been a matter of social concern rather than belief. He had gone to help Emma, he had gone to conform to the Sebastiens' demands. He had never considered what it all meant.

"But you have been baptized?"

"It was required for us to get married, but it wasn't a Catholic church."

"We recognize 'one baptism for the forgiveness of sins,'" the priest said. "And by that, we recognize that all legitimate baptisms, done in the name of the Father, the Son and the Holy Spirit are one baptism. Other churches may demand you get re-baptized if you join their faith. We demand that you only get baptized once."

And that day, his instruction began with the meaning of baptism.

He immediately began to look forward to these weekly meetings. For the first time since he could remember, he had no books, no pamphlets, no newspapers: nothing to read and study and learn. But the priest, Father Ignatius, rekindled his love of learning. Father Ignatius did not lecture. He sat on a stump outside the prison wagon, while Devlin sat cross-legged on the floor as close as he could get to the bars, and they discussed. Devlin had a whole week between their meetings to consider what he had learned and to devise new questions. He was always intrigued by the responses, and each answer brought to life new questions. Once or twice, Father Ignatius admitted he was not sure of the answer, but came back the following week prepared to give a proper response.

"I don't know everything," he apologized. "But we have two thousand years of writings in which we can look things up."

That in itself was a question. "Not just the Bible?" Devlin asked.

"The Bible is the Word of God, and nothing in the Church ever goes against it. But the best minds in the western world have been pondering and learning and discovering since Christ walked the Earth. We have the Gospels, of course, the writings of St. Paul and the other letters of the New Testament. We also have the writings of the early Church Fathers, some of whom were trained by the men who walked with Jesus himself. Then there are the saints and Doctors of the Church, the Councils. Anything you can ask has probably been researched by someone in that long history."

"Can you explain the Trinity?" Devlin asked.

Father Ignatius smiled. "No. I can't tell you the exact number of stars in the Heavens either. Some things you will have to wait and ask God himself."

"That's the best reason to try to get to Heaven I have ever heard," Devlin grinned.

He was given permission to have a Bible to keep on his bunk and read in his free time. A few other men had Bibles, it was the one book they were allowed to have. But the guard who brought Devlin his Bible thought it was a good joke to bring him one written in Spanish rather than English.

"You can't read that!" Josh protested, as he sat doing nothing, watching Devlin read.

"I'm getting it, actually," Devlin said. "It's not that different from Latin."

"You speak Latin?"

"No. But, I can read it. Anyway, I am learning Spanish, which might come in very handy someday."

II

"How long have we been here?" Colbert asked. He was a big man, chained to another big man named Weeks. In fact, Devlin had early noticed that they were all big men. Not one man on the chain gang was under six feet tall. It saddened him somewhat that no matter what he did, learned, or envisioned, it was his size that people noticed. On the other hand, people noticing his size had opened doors for him. It had gotten him a regular job on the whaling ship instead of being used as a cabin boy. It had gotten him a job upstairs at the bank. And it had gotten him here. Hard labor, maybe, but labor was better than just being hung – or even locked up forever. Locked up there was no hope. Here, hope was blossoming.

"A year?" Weeks guessed.

"More like eight months," Devlin said.

They had moved the camp numerous times in those months, which is why the cook shack and the barracks were tents.

"No," Josh said. Can't be.

"It was early May when we came. It's almost February now. You haven't noticed the change in the weather?"

"Only maybe that we sweat less when we're working," Colbert said.

"And shiver more at night?" Devlin suggested.

"Is it true," Weeks asked, leaning close across the plank dining table and dropping his voice, "That you can pick the locks on these leg irons?"

"Yes," Devlin said.

"So, we could take off any time we want?" Weeks asked.

"I wouldn't say any time," Devlin said. "We do need to be a bit circumspect..."

"Say what?" Colbert demanded loudly. "You ain't cutting anything private off me!"

Devlin was confused. Josh grinned.

"Circumspect, not circumcise," he said. "He just means you got to be careful who's watching."

"Right," Devlin said. "But let's not forget the dogs. Do you know how to confuse a hound dog?"

"Can't be done," Weeks said.

"It can. It's just not easy." Devlin sighed and scooped a spoonful of food and let it slide back into his bowl. "Boiled goober peas again! It wouldn't be so bad if they could put some spice in it. Salt, at least!"

"I suppose you are a connoisseur of great cooking!" Josh laughed at him.

"Actually," Devlin said, opening up a little for the first time in all the time they had been, literally, chained together, "I used to own the finest restaurant in Charleston, South Carolina."

Weeks laughed loudly and raised his unchained leg off the floor. "Here! Pull the other one."

"I'm serious," Devlin said. "It was called The Lakes. It was..." He hesitated, and decided finally to just say, "it was worth it."

"Worth what?" Josh asked.

"Getting sent here," Devlin said.

"Why were you sent here?" Josh asked.

Devlin looked carefully at his three companions, knowing that if he told them everything, and if they felt like Sebastien did, he would be dead before morning. On the other hand...

"I hired runaway slaves to work for me," he said. "Sometimes let them sleep in the basement on their way north."

"Hired?" Weeks asked.

"'A man is worthy of his hire,' according to the Bible. I would never expect anyone to work for free. I always wondered what happened to them, though, Pierre and the others. My father-in-law was sending men to pick them all up the night he had me arrested."

"Your father-in-law!" Josh was shocked.

Devlin just shrugged.

"So, you know something about escaping?" Colbert said.

"Yes. But I don't know how to get hold of what we need to get past the dogs. They can run faster than we can, you know."

Two days later, as he was leaning over to pour slightly muddy creek water into their tin drinking cups, the black man who helped in the kitchen dropped something in Devlin's lap. Although he had no idea what it was, Devlin had been incarcerated long enough to know what to do. He stuffed the item into the waistband of his pants and waited until lights out that night to see what it was. Josh leaned over the space between their bunks to watch as Devlin pulled out the bundle and untied it.

"What is it?"

"Exactly what we need to escape. We'll take Weeks and Colbert. We'll leave Saturday night."

"Before you get your weekly dose of religion?" Josh teased.

"Can't be helped. Sunday isn't a workday. The guards drink more than usual on Saturday night and are sluggish rousting us out on Sunday. Surely you've noticed that, at least."

"I lost track of what day it was long time back," Josh said.

They waited to move until heavy snores filled the tent. Devlin had told Josh ahead of time to remove his shoes and tie the laces together. After months of practice, Devlin slipped his chain in seconds. It took only a few seconds more the unlock Josh. Then in the pitch black, with their shoes draped around their necks, and blankets tucked under their arms, they tiptoed across the tent to where Weeks and Colbert were waiting anxiously. The front of the tent opened into a communal area where the guards were gathered, drinking, around a big fire, so they pried up a tent stake near the rear and slid themselves under the canvas. Devlin took direction from the moon, and they headed out. It was a thin moon, very little light, and the underbrush in the area was heavy. It was slow going until they got to the creek, which was rimmed with ice this time of year. Still, it was the clearest path through the heavy brush and trees. They put their shoes back on for what protection that provided and waded into the creek.

"This won't fool them dogs!" Weeks whispered.

Devlin didn't answer. He kept them moving until well after sunup, then shifted away from the creek, looking for someplace to trap the dogs. He found it finally, early that evening: a rocky ledge that led down into a ravine choked with underbrush and with a tiny creek flowing at the bottom. The far side was higher and steeper and was topped with heavy timber.

"Here," he said.

"But water won't…"

"I know. Get across, go downstream and find a place where you can get out and up the other side."

They could hear the dogs, had been able to hear them for some worrisome time. But Devlin waited until the others were all across and working their way up the far side. He opened the packet he had been given and sprinkled its contents on the flat limestone at the edge of the ravine, then he climbed carefully down, trying to leave as little trail as possible, and walked upstream in the small creek to find a good place to climb out. At the top, they reunited and Devlin had them lie down in the brush, hidden but able to see out as the dogs swarmed the bank of the ravine, sniffing anxiously at their trail.

"We're dead," Colbert whispered.

"Shshsh!" Devlin said.

Suddenly, the dogs began yelping and rubbing their noses with their paws, rubbing them in the dirt also.

Devlin grinned. "Come on! Before the men catch up to them!"

They crept away through the brush, then began to run. Exhausted from a night and a day of running, foot sore from their ill-made shoes, hungry and wet and cold, they kept moving.

"I have to stop!" Josh said, sometime after dark.

"We stop, we'll die from the cold," Devlin said, leaning forward himself, hands on knees, to catch his breath. When he caught it, he reached inside his shirt and pulled out a piece of stale bread.

"We'll take a short break," he said.

"Where did you get that?" Weeks asked.

Devlin just looked at him a long moment. "You've been planning this how long? Didn't anybody think to hoard a few bits of food for the trip?"

No one had. He sighed and took out his second piece and split each of the pieces in half. It was not nearly enough to feed them, even had they each had a full piece of bread. But it was better than nothing at all. They walked through the night, blankets wrapped around themselves and moving to keep from freezing. In the morning, they found a spot above a river where the sun would warm the rocks, eventually, and they huddled together for a bit of rest.

"What was it you had in that little packet?" Josh asked as they all shivered and tried to sleep.

"Pepper," Devlin said.

"Pepper? You mean plain table spice?"

"Ground black pepper, yes. It might irritate your nose, make you sneeze if you inhaled a load of it. Dogs have very sensitive noses. It burns them. Not permanent, but they won't be able to follow a trail for about a day. The guards have a choice of waiting – until about now! – to continue or going back for more dogs. Either way, we still need to make more distance."

"Boy that is something!" Colbert said. "You complain about the lack of spice in your food, and that black boy gives you pepper! We all complain about the food! How come only you get flavoring for it?"

"I don't think it was meant for my dinner," Devlin said. "It was meant to help us escape. That man didn't eavesdrop on my culinary complaints: he heard me talking about The Lakes. He must have heard of it, maybe knew someone who went through there."

"He helped you because you helped some of his kind?" Josh asked.

"You know what they say about casting your bread on the water," Devlin said.

"It gets soggy?" Josh asked.

Colbert slapped him on the back of the head.

"Well, it would get soggy! You wouldn't be able to eat it at all!"

"He's talking about if you do something nice for someone, they do nice things for you," Colbert said. "It's, you know, in the Bible. I think."

"Speaking of bread," Weeks said. "You got any more?"

"One piece," Devlin said. They split it four ways as the sun began to heat them up and savored it slowly. When he pulled it out, a piece of cloth also fell out of his clothing, and he picked it up. It was the bit of rag the pepper had been wrapped in. He had not wished to leave it behind because it might incriminate whatever unknown benefactor had given them the pepper. But seeing it now, in full daylight, he realized something had been written on the inside of the cloth. He brushed away the remnants of the pepper dust and looked at it carefully.

"P + 18 FREE. M Warnd," it said.

"What does that mean?" Josh asked.

"P plus 18…" Devlin said. "P plus eighteen. Pierre plus eighteen!" He laughed aloud for the first time in months. He had left the restaurant in the charge of Pierre and Abel the night he went home because Larissa was in labor. Besides the two of them, there were seventeen other people in the restaurant that night, some of them working as busboys, kitchen help or waiters, some of them just waiting in the basement for a chance to move on. With all that had happened, he had not thought to send a message to them all until it was too late, until he was in jail and unable to warn them. But someone had "warnd" them. P plus Eighteen Free meant that all of them had gotten out, and Devlin felt an enormous weight lifted from his heart.

"Forgiving others is difficult," Father Ignatius had told him. "But forgiving yourself, that is much harder."

How true those words were! Part of the darkness that had clouded his mind and heart all this time, never lifting even when learning and planning had helped to make him think again, was the guilt that he had abandoned and let down all those people who had depended on him. Sebastien had said they were all being beaten, jailed, returned to slavery. But he knew now that they were free. They had escaped. They had been warned… by "M". "P" was undoubtedly Pierre, but who was "M"?

He repeated the letter aloud, trying to think. "M…M…"

Suddenly he realized "M" was not an initial: it was an abbreviation. Not "M", "EM". Emma had warned them! He had still seen her fairly often after her marriage. She came into the restaurant to drop off paintings and collect her earnings for the ones that sold. And she and the baby often accompanied Everett when he came to deliver fresh fish, oysters and crabs.

He doubted there was any way Emma could have known to take the message to them the night he was arrested. But she probably had visited sometime during his two-week absence. She would have known, through the high society she still had contact with, about Larissa's lingering illness. And she would have known that if Devlin stayed away for an extended period of time, sooner or later, Sebastien would come to check on his investment. Or maybe, to find out why food was still being delivered and cook fires lit even though the doors were closed and locked. Emma had told Pierre and the others to get out. Maybe Pierre himself and a few others stayed nearby, at least until Devlin's arrest, just in case they could come back. But either way, they were out of the way when Sebastien's police came.

Devlin lifted the cloth to his face and kissed it, ignoring the peppery smell and taste of it.

"God bless you, Emma!" he whispered. "And God bless you, whoever sent this to me!"

That night, they found an abandoned wood-cutting camp.

It was, mainly, a large, cleared area where trees had been cut, littered with sawdust and the small branches that had been removed from the logs. A tiny creek ran nearby, but otherwise there was nothing much that would be of use to them. Certainly, no food or clothing had been left behind. But in the midden heap they located some tin cans they could use to boil water in, and one of the cut trees had uncovered a squirrel's cache of nuts. Using rocks, they smashed all the acorns and put them to boil. The result was bitter tasting and weak, but it was more nourishment than they had had since Saturday evening.

"What are these?" Devlin asked, picking up round, green balls that were also in the cache.

"Walnuts," Josh told him.

Walnuts, Devlin knew, had hard brown shells. He had never seen any with this greenish stuff around them.

"Does this soft coating harden into shells?"

"No, the shells you usually see are inside that green stuff. And by the way, your hands will be brown and purple for a week just from touching that thing."

Brown and purple was better than hungry. They boiled the walnuts first and soaked their clothing in the juice. Devlin was certain the dye in the shells would not completely erase the black and white horizontal stripes on their clothing, but it would at least dim the bright contrast. It did, although they had to wait until morning to see the difference. After boiling the nuts, they roasted them in their campfire and peeled off the outer coating using ragged tin can lids as makeshift knives when they needed to tear more than their fingers could. Then they used rocks to break open the harder inner shells. There weren't enough nuts to assuage their hunger, but again, it was an improvement.

"Complain about a lack of salt," Weeks joked. "Maybe someone will hear and bring us some!"

Devlin didn't laugh. But he did ask them that night as they laid down to sleep in the piles of thin branches they had made into beds what their plans were for the future.

"What do you mean?" Colbert asked.

"Personally," Devlin said, "I plan to go to Mexico."

"I was thinking to go north," Weeks said. "It'll be easier to get lost in some of those big industrial cities, and you don't need a lot of skill to work in the factories."

"Yeah. That sounds good to me," Colbert nodded.

Devlin looked to Josh. Josh shrugged.

"If you don't mind, I'll head to Mexico with you. At least we'll be warm, finally."

"We would be if we were going south. I plan to go west."

Josh shrugged again. "Fine. Just somewhere where we can eat."

In the morning, in their still-damp but now somewhat less noticeable clothing, they split company. Weeks and Colbert went north, Devlin and Josh continued west, and by noon they had reached the river.

This was not the most navigable of rivers in the east, but there was still some traffic on it and, before the day was out, they found a steamboat captain who was badly enough in need of labor that he would trade them meals and a place to sleep (on the deck) for work. The river continued southwest for a way, then twisted back north for a longer way, but eventually it met up with the Ohio. There was a great deal more traffic on this river, but there were also numerous men looking for work. Still, the size Devlin had once found a hindrance served them both well and they were hired, again for meals and a place to sleep, but it was, for the moment, all they needed. When they got down to the Mississippi, they again found good luck, or so it seemed at first. A flotilla of rafts moving down river had lost several men and were more than willing to hire them on. It turned out, however, that the men had died of typhus, which Devlin and Josh both caught, after staying free of it all those months in the prison work camp. They were off-loaded by their raft-mates at a shack above the river, just below the Confluence with the Missouri, where a man lived who cut and sold wood to the passing river boats for their steam boilers. The man was not happy to have the two sick men in his barn, and he begrudged them every sip of soup and drink of clear water his wife fed them. But, despite the hardships they had endured since leaving the prison camp, both Josh and Devlin were young and strong, and they beat the fever that gripped them. As soon as he could stagger around, Devlin helped the man stack and load wood. He was very weak for a long time and could only do a few moments of labor with long rests in between, but he helped all he could to pay back their benefactors. Josh recovered more slowly and was still weak and shaky when a boat carrying, among other passengers, several squads of soldiers stopped for wood.

"I've had enough of this," Josh said. "I'm joining up."

"You can't join the army!" Devlin told him. "You're a fugitive. They'll throw you back in prison if you try that."

"What are they going to do? Send riders out to question every prison in America to see if they're missing a fella who looks like me? If I tell them my name is John Smith, who's to say different? Come with me. They'll feed us, give us new clothes, and take care of us when we're sick."

"I'm not signing away five years of my life for a little comfort," Devlin said.

"Well, I think it's worth it," Josh said. "I'm going."

"I feel like I'm saying goodbye to my left foot," Devlin said.

Josh chuckled and looked at the raw marks still on their ankles. The wounds were starting to heal, but the scars would be there forever.

"Kind of are, aren't we?"

"Write to me in a couple months," Devlin said. "General Delivery in Santa Fe. If I get it, I'll write you back."

They shook on that deal, and Josh went down to the boat to talk to the sergeant.

"You leaving too?" the wood cutter asked.

"I feel like I still owe you," Devlin said. "I'd like to work for you awhile to pay you back for your kindness."

The wood cutter was happy to take him up on the offer. As the days faded into weeks, Devlin grew stronger. He learned how to handle the big two-man saw that was much more efficient than an axe for felling trees – the only drawback with it was that it required, as the name implied, two men to handle it. With Devlin on the other side, the wood cutter was able to fell many trees which he could trim and block later on his own. The wood cutter's wife traded Devlin his poorly dyed prison suit for a pair of overalls that left his ankles bare and a shirt which was only a size or two too small.

"This is the most interesting shade of green-purple I have ever seen," she said, pretending not to notice the black stripes. "I'd like to cut it up and use it for quilt patches. I wish I had something bigger to give you in return."

"This is more than enough," Devlin said. "Thanks for everything you have done for my friend and I."

It was only a few days later that he managed to get a job on a small stern-wheeler that was heading up the Missouri. Devlin's plan was to get to the Santa Fe trail, and the steamboat left him in Independence, where the trail started and ended.

Independence Missouri, August, 1845

When he stepped off the boat in Charleston, South Carolina, Devlin had enough money in his pockets to outfit himself nicely, buy a bath and a haircut, and pay a week's rent on a boarding house while he looked for work. Six years later, when he stepped off the steamboat onto the crowded docks in Independence, Missouri, he had in his possession a torn blanket, a Spanish Bible, and one penny. The penny was a tip handed to him by a lady whose luggage he had carried off the boat as they were both disembarking.

Independence was not Charleston, but it was a thriving frontier town, a trading stop for goods coming up the trail from Mexico, up the river from New Orleans, and down from all points east. There were a dozen steamboats at the docks, and on the shore were rows of warehouses and business offices for the goods that were coming and going. Beyond the docks were the shops: bakeries and tanneries, dry goods stores, fresh produce and feed stores, milliners and drapers, lumber yards, furniture stores. Spreading out to the sides were the corrals for the mules that were trade goods themselves as well as the locomotion for the wagon trains that came and went. The place was alive with activity. And it was alive with people, too. Missouri traders, slaves and free blacks, American boatmen, mountain men, Indians and Mexicans crowded the streets. In such a mix, Devlin still stood out. Of the elegant and dapper owner of the finest restaurant in South Carolina, there was almost nothing left. His clothing was mostly rags that had not fit to begin with. His bare feet showed through the open seams of shoes that were literally falling apart. Seared by illness, strengthened by labor, his hair bleached almost white by the sun that had burned his face and arms dark, he was leaner and harder than he had ever been in his life, and he looked it. If his bright, blue eyes had not still held that quality of gentleness that had always been part of him, people would have been crossing the street to avoid him. As it was, many people looked twice, and tried not to antagonize him. But Devlin was unaware of that. All he was thinking about was what he would do next. Work, he supposed.

Work had gotten him this far. Work would keep him surviving. Dreams of living the life of "quality folk" were long past. All he wanted now was to find out how to keep eating regularly, and maybe be able to afford real clothing before winter came on. And he still wanted to continue down the Trail into Mexico.

For the moment, he stepped inside a general store that held everything from ladies' dainties to harnesses for oxen teams, and looked around, wondering if there was anything he needed that he could get for a penny. A comb was too much, as was a razor. He was considering a small amount of lye soap when a little girl came into the store and walked up to the counter. She as a Mexican girl, small, but already rounding out into promised womanhood. She wore a loose-fitting green blouse, gathered at the neck and sleeves over a skirt that was gathered at the waist, but also flared out in two more gathered flounces, ending about halfway between her knees and her bare feet. Each flounce was of different material: pink with red flowers, red with pink polka dots, white with red and pink roses. She also wore a thin shawl, mostly hanging down her back and caught in the crook of both elbows. Her hair was braided into two thick plaits which hung far down her back, even though they were both doubled up into loops that were tied with green ribbons at the back of her neck. He remembered once thinking that Larissa Sebastien's neck looked too frail to hold up her mass of heavy hair. This little girl had a sturdy little neck, as everything about her was sturdy. But what hair! It had to have been past her knees if it was let loose. He had never seen a woman of any age with so much hair.

The little girl stepped up to the counter and laid a dime on top of it. She smiled up at the clerk and said, "*Por `favor, señor. Diez de esos.*" She pointed to a jar of bright colored candy sticks, clearly labeled "One Cent". The clerk looked at her, looked at the dime, looked at her again. Then he scooped up the dime, laid it in his cash box, and opened the jar to hand her a single candy stick. The little girl looked disconsolately at the stick.

"*Por favor. La mujer dice que este es diez centavos. Este dulce cuesta un centavo. Por favor, quiero tener diez dulces. Son por los niños en el campo.*" She pointed to the jar of candy and held up both hands to show the number ten. Ten candies. For the children at the camp. The man just grinned at her and said,

"I don't speak Mex."

"I do," Devlin said, moving closer. "The young lady gave you ten cents for ten pieces of candy. You gave her one. You owe her nine candy sticks, or nine cents change."

"She gave me a penny," the man said. "You can't prove otherwise. It's in the box."

He smirked, obviously feeling superior to both the child and this ragged man. The little girl, not sure what the exchange was about, did see the ugly smile on the clerk's face, and started sadly to take her one candy stick.

"*Deja un momento*," Devlin told her. He turned back to the clerk. "I saw the money she put down on the counter. I was standing right here. It was ten cents."

"You calling me a liar?"

"Obviously, you are calling me one. I don't appreciate that."

"You gonna pick a fight with me cause some fat little Mex kid wants more candy?" the man asked.

"No," Devlin said, and the man's smirk grew larger, until Devlin leaned forward, his face inches from the man's. Both his fists were balled on the counter, causing the muscles in his arms and chest, visible through his ragged shirt, to bulge. "I was thinking of calling for the law. But, now I think I might just bypass the marshal and do a little vigilante-ing right here, right now, and take that nine cents change out of your hide. Personally, I've seen better hides on two-week old carrion. I don't think yours is worth much, so it will take a lot of tearing off of flesh and snapping of bones to get nine cents worth out of you. Or. You can give her the candy."

The gentle blue eyes were no longer gentle, but hard as gunmetal. The clerk swallowed once, seeing a seriousness, and an ability, he had not realized was there. He picked up the jar of candy sticks and counted out nine more.

"I made an honest mistake! There's no call for you to get so aggressive about it!"

"Add one more," Devlin said, laying his one penny on the counter also. The clerk did so, and the girl picked up the eleven candy sticks, wrapping them in a corner of her shawl so they wouldn't get sticky from the warmth of her hands. She bobbed a curtsey to the clerk and thanked him. She thanked Devlin also and left the store. Devlin turned to the clerk.

"Mistakes happen," Devlin said, much more mildly now.

"Yes," the clerk agreed.

"Did you really need nine cents that badly?"

"I…"

"Don't answer. Just let me say that I don't know you and I don't have any reason to come back here. Unless I hear round about that you've been stealing candy from babies again. Then we'll have to see just how much money that thin hide of yours is worth."

He walked out before the man could answer. He sighed as he stepped out onto the sidewalk. Nine cents. That man was cheating a child over nine cents! What was the world coming to anyway?

"Señor?"

He looked down to see the little girl had waited for him.

"You speak Spanish, no?"

"Yes."

"I just wanted to thank you. I didn't know if the lady was wrong about how much the coin was worth, or if I misunderstood, or if the man lied…"

"He lied," Devlin said.

"Oh! Well, thank you then! My name is Esperanza Catalina Ordoñez y Valencia."

She made a little curtsey, and Devlin gave her a small bow.

"Hope. What a beautiful name. My name is Devlin."

She looked confused. "My English is not so good, but… you are named *el Diablo?*"

Devlin laughed. "No! No, not 'de*vil*,' Dev*lin*. You can call me Dev." He looked around and said, "You're not here in town on your own, are you?"

"Oh, no! I came with my father and my brother. There they are now!"

Two men were in fact running towards them, one about forty-five or so, the other a few years younger than Devlin. The older man was shouting, in English and Spanish, "You! Get away from her! Leave her alone!" At his shouts, other men seemed to materialize. Out of saloons, stores, alleyways, Mexican men appeared, all of them pounding towards Devlin. Instinctively, he took a step back and found his back against the wall of the store. No retreat, then. He raised his hands, spreading them wide to show he was unarmed, his thread-bare blanket dropping to the ground as he did. Esperanza also saw instantly how things were, and she stepped in front of him, holding her own hands up as a sign for them to stop.

"Papá! No! He's good! He helped me! Jaime, no!" she added, insinuating herself between Devlin and her brother. Although he was several years younger, and barely shoulder high on Devlin, his fist was cocked, ready to fight.

"What are you doing with my daughter?" the older man asked. "Do not touch her! Where are you taking her?"

"I am not taking her anywhere!" Devlin said.

"Papá!"

"You keep quiet! You, sir, what are you doing with my daughter?"

"Papá, please!" Esperanza begged. "He helped me, I told you. I came here to…"

The man turned his attention to the girl, although her brother and the other men were keeping close watch on Devlin.

"You came here? After I told you not to go anywhere, to wait right by the door…"

"I know! I know, Papá. But listen, please? Remember, the door where you told me to wait, the lady was playing the music. Remember?" She moved her hands back and forth, together and apart.

"The accordion?" her father said.

"Yes! Remember, the music was so pretty, and I was so happy! We got here safe, and you and Jaime got a good price for our things. And the music was so pretty, my feet just started to move…"

"All the way down here, all by themselves," her father said drily.

"Yes! No! I mean, they seemed to move by themselves. They were dancing. The music was so pretty, my feet just had to dance. And then a man came by…"

"This one!"

"No! No! A dark-haired man. In a suit. He came by, and he gave me a coin. Oh! Papá! I was so embarrassed! He thought I was begging on the street! I wasn't! I was just dancing because I was happy, and the music was so pretty! The lady was playing so well…"

"Yes, yes, daughter. And a man gave you a coin."

"Yes! I wanted to give it back. I was so embarrassed! But he was gone in the crowd, and I didn't know who he was. I tried to give the coin to the lady, but she said he had given it to me, so it was mine. I didn't know what to do! She said it was worth ten cents! Then, I remembered the store with the pretty candy sticks in the jar that said one cent each, and I thought, I can buy a candy stick for each of the children at the camp. That way, I wouldn't be taking the man's money for myself. Since I couldn't give it back, I would give it away!"

She smiled prettily up at her father, but he wasn't impressed.

"So, you left. After we told you not to."

"I thought I could run down here and be right back, really, I didn't mean to disobey, but I didn't want to take the coin for myself, so..."

"Yes, yes. So, you came here."

"Yes, and I gave the man inside my coin and asked him for the ten candy sticks. I showed him the jar, and counted," she held up one hand, showing five fingers, and the other hand, still clutching the shawl corner and the candy. "He took my coin, but he only gave me one candy. I didn't know what to do! I didn't know if the lady lied to me, or if he knew it wasn't my money, or what. Then this man, *el Diablo*..."

"My name is not *el Diablo*!"

"He spoke to the man," Esperanza said, talking over Devlin. "And the man was not nice to him, and then he got mad." She hunched her shoulders and spread her arms out from her sides, clutching her fists, making a fierce face. The men around were starting to look more amused than alarmed.

"Like this! And the man gave me nine more of the candies!" Esperanza said with a grand finish.

"Ten candies?" her father said.

"Yes!"

"Then why are you holding eleven?"

"Oh, because *el Diablo*..."

"My name is not..."

"...gave him another coin, a different one, a brown one, and he gave me the extra piece!"

The older man looked up at Devlin thoughtfully.

"Why," he asked in a deceptively mild voice, "did you give my daughter a piece of candy?"

"She said she was buying candy for some children in a camp," Devlin said. He got a hard stare in return. "Well. I also was given a coin as a tip this morning. I was in the store trying to see if it would be of any use to me, when the young lady came in. I saw and heard the shopkeeper try to cheat her, and it made me angry. So, yes, I told him he had better… be more honest. And it seemed to me that the best use for the coin would be to buy one more candy for the children in the camp."

Several of the men were trying to hide grins. Esperanza's father sighed heavily.

"Are you feeble minded?" he asked Devlin.

The question surprised him, until he realized it was not so different from Emma's accusation of naiveté.

"No," he said.

"New in town?"

"I came in this morning on a steamboat," he admitted.

"This morning?"

"About… half an hour ago."

Esperanza's father turned to the other men and thanked them.

"I think everything is all right. Thank you. Thank you."

Hands were shaken. Men went back to their business. Devlin was left with Esperanza and her father and her brother.

"Excuse me," Devlin said. "Your daughter misunderstood. My name is Devlin. Devlin Lachlan."

"That is a terrible name," her father said. But he took the hand Devlin offered and introduced himself. "Francisco Maria José Ordoñez y Barela. My son, Jaime. I take it you have met Esperanza."

"Yes, we've met Mr. Barela."

"Ordoñez. You said you just came in. Are you heading somewhere, or stopping here?"

"I suppose I'll have to stop here to get a stake. I was planning to go to Mexico eventually."

"I see." Ordonez did not look pleased. "And why is another American going to Mexico? You didn't steal a big enough piece of it when your compatriots immigrated to the province of Texas and proceeded to attack the federal government for the right to break all of our laws?"

"I'm not an American," Devlin said, and he found himself standing straighter as he did. "I haven't been in this country long enough to become an American, and I'm not so sure now that I would like to be a citizen anyway. I don't think I can pledge my allegiance to a nation that spends so much time idealizing freedom and independence and buys and sells people like cattle."

Ordoñez considered him thoughtfully. "Good argument. Is it the truth?"

"It is true," Devlin said. "But it is not the whole truth. I escaped from a prison work camp a few months ago. Leaving the country seems to be my best option at the moment."

"What were you in prison for?"

"Helping escaped slaves," Devlin said.

"I apologize for thinking you were feeble-minded," Ordoñez said. "I think your problem is that your heart is too big. Makes you do foolish things. How do you plan to get to Mexico?"

"Work," Devlin said. "Get together a stake to pay for the trip, I suppose."

"It is costly. What sort of work have you done in the past, besides harboring fugitive slaves?"

"I learned bookkeeping and carpentry on a whaling ship. I worked as an assistant to a loan officer at a major bank. I owned and operated a very nice restaurant, where I was not only the business manager, but also had to learn cooking, laundry and dishwashing. Since my fall from grace, I learned how to use a sledgehammer so well that my partner and I were promoted from breaking rocks to drilling with a double jack. And more recently, I've learned to use a two-man saw and an axe. I have loaded and off-loaded boats and wagons, poled a raft down the river, stoked and maintained a steam boiler."

"Can you ride? Shoot? Drive a six mule team?"

"No, and no. I have driven a one-horse buggy before, but never a team of any kind."

Father and son looked at each other. Jaime shook his head.

"Esperanza would be more help," he said.

"Labor is always needed on the trains," Ordoñez said. "A man willing to change and learn can be an advantage."

"What trains?" Devlin asked.

"The mule trains along the Santa Fe Trail. We will be heading back that way in about a week. If you are willing to work, we can always use another hand."

"I would be very much obliged," Devlin said sincerely. "All I have to offer is my labor, but I will willingly do whatever you need."

Ordoñez nodded. "That is what I had hoped to hear. Jaime, take him to the camp and turn him over to Tia Dolores. You, Espe," he added, looking at the girl, "you come with me. We'll buy you some shoes so you are not running around town barefoot like a street urchin. But not at this store. Somewhere where they won't cheat you for a few cents."

Esperanza passed her fistful of candy to her brother before going off with her father. While he walked, she pranced along at his side, not quite skipping, not quite dancing. It was easy to believe her story of being given money for her street performance. Every move she made was full of both grace and exuberance. Devlin bent and retrieved his blanket. The leather-bound Bible fell out of it, and Jaime picked it up and looked at it before handing it back to him.

"Did you know Spanish before, or is this how you learned?"

"This is how I learned," Devlin said.

"That explains it."

"Explains what?"

"Why your accent is strange and your grammar too formal."

"I have been accused of having an accent when I speak English as well."

"Yes, but you know how to pronounce it. We'll work on that. Come along, *el diablo*, I'll take you to the camp."

"My name is not…"

"I know," the boy just grinned.

II

Most of the wagons that had come up with this group of Mexicans from Santa Fe were parked at warehouses and freight depots, unloading what they brought, waiting to load what would be taken back. A handful of the men had brought families with them, however, so half a dozen of the wagons were gathered in a camp outside of town. The wagons made a half circle around two large cook fires. Two of the wagons, parked about six feet apart, back-to-back, had ropes strung from the two rear corners of each with blankets hanging over the ropes, creating a small area of privacy in between. In that area, a large wooden tub had been placed. The tailgates of the wagons had been removed to lay on the ground and make a wooden path through the mud that surrounded the tub so that a person could get in or out of it without sinking up to their ankles, because the ground all around was soggy from the water having been dumped out of the tub and replaced multiple times.

Presiding over the fires and the bathing space was a handsome woman whose strong, aristocratic features were lined from sun and wind. Her dark hair had streaks of white in it, and a corner of her skirt was tucked up into her belt to keep it from dragging in the mud. She looked over Devlin as he approached and asked Jaime, "He's a big one. Where did you get him? From under a rock?"

"He speaks perfect Spanish, Tia," Jaime grinned.

"Do you?" she asked Devlin.

He shrugged. "I wouldn't say it was perfect, but I seem to get along with it."

"I see. And what are we doing for you today?"

"He's going to come with us," Jaime said. "But he needs some clothing, and some cleaning up."

"Understatement." She blew upwards to get a strand of hair out of her eyes and asked, "What are you called?"

"He is *el diablo!*" Jaime laughed.

"A slight problem translating from English to Spanish," Devlin said. "My name is 'Dev*lin*.' His sister heard it as 'devil.'"

The woman swatted at Jaime, not meant to actually strike him, just to shoo him away as one would shoo livestock away from a cooking area. Laughing, he left.

"Devlin what?"

"Devlin Matthew Lachlan."

She considered, blowing at her hair again. "Mateo," she decided. "And you will call me Tia. Everyone else does. What's in the blanket?"

He showed her. She set the Bible on a wagon seat and said, "This you keep. Everything else goes. Undress in there and start washing."

Devlin obeyed. Entering the blanketed area, he undressed, sat himself down in what was obviously used bath water, and began cleaning himself with the soft lye soap that sat on a stump nearby. He was there only a few moments when Tia called from the other side of the blanket.

"That was part one. Dump out that water now, and some boys will bring you fresh."

He dumped the tub over and snatched his trousers to hold in front of him while several boys staggered into the privacy area, carrying buckets. When the tub was half full, two more buckets were brought and set next to it, and he was instructed to continue washing.

"Do a good job," Tia threatened from the other side of the blankets, "Or I shall come in there with my scrub brush."

"I promise to do a good job," Devlin called back. "But I might want to borrow that brush!"

It flew over the blanket and splashed into the water right in his lap.

"I hope you weren't aiming," he murmured to himself. "That came too close!"

He scrubbed himself more thoroughly than he had been able to do in a long time, using the scrub brush on his hair and beard and on his feet, which were stained so badly from mud seeping through the cracks in his shoes that he despaired of ever seeing their normal color again.

The prisoners had been allowed to bathe in the prison camp. Once a week on Saturday nights, still chained in pairs, they were lined up in front of a plank bench on which were laid out a single bucket of icy creek water for each man, a piece of torn and dirty toweling, and a small wad of soft soap. Stripping was impossible, chained as they were, but they cleaned themselves as best they could, and he and Josh had washed their shirts in the buckets, and had at least soaked their trousers as well, when the weather was warm enough. Traveling, he had washed himself in creeks now and then, but he had a fear of water moccasins, so would not immerse himself in the great green and brown rivers he had traveled. This bath, with water that was clear from a nearby creek and at least partly heated on the big cook fires, was luxury. Finally, he stood and poured the buckets of clean water over himself.

"Are you finished yet?"

"Yes."

A clean piece of toweling was draped over the top of the blanket, along with a pair of trousers. He dried himself, standing on the tailgates, and held up the trousers. A strip of matching cloth had been sewn onto the bottom of each pant leg, making them long enough for his legs. A year and a half ago, they might not have fit around him, but they did now. He pulled them on and tied them at the waist, and asked, "I don't suppose you have a shirt?"

"Hair cut first, then shirt," Tia said. "Come on out, now."

He came out then, feeling cleaner than he had in longer than he could remember, and Tia had him sit on an upright piece of log. She wrapped an apron around his neck and laid out several instruments on another piece of log nearby. The scissors she had were sharp and the tips pointed as swords. There was also a razor, water and soap, and brushes and combs. She started by working the tangles out if his hair, which was now almost down to his shoulders.

"The bath felt very good, thank you," he said. "But I think I can comb my own hair."

"You just sit there, I'll be your barber today. How long since you had a real bath?"

"Oh... I don't know. It must have been in March."

"Four months ago? That's not too bad."

"A year and four months ago," Devlin said.

"Tell me about it," she said.

So, he talked, while she worked on his hair. He did not tell her everything about himself. His early childhood, his marriage and Larissa's death were never mentioned. But he did tell her he had worked on the ocean and in a bank, and about his time in the prison work camp, and the months since his escape.

"I guess I was very lucky," he said. "I met many kind people, so although I was hungry now and then, they let me work for food. I never starved."

"It is not luck, *'jito*. You were blessed. Jaime told me about the incident in the store. You have a good heart. People see that, they respond to it."

"Good things happen to good people?" Devlin shook his head. "I don't believe that. Because if it is true, then the opposite is true and I can't believe that people who suffer are all bad. Some of them are very good, but they suffer terribly anyway. And people who are bad, nothing bad ever seems to happen to them."

"I understand what you say. But you must remember that obtaining goods of this world is not the same as good things happening to a person.

We were not made for this world, you know. God created men to live in unity with him in Heaven. Our first parents lost Paradise for us, by choosing sin over God. But we can't just lay the blame at their door. No human being is perfect." She paused to make the sign of the cross. "Except the Blessed Mother, of course. But every time a person chooses to do that which he knows is not God's will, he commits Original Sin again. And again, and again. Heaven can be ours again, thanks to the great sacrifice of God, who came as a human being to walk this Earth, to suffer and die for the sin of Adam and Eve and for all of us who choose poorly. But how can we enter Paradise if we are not perfect?"

"I thought no one is perfect."

"Not here on Earth, no. You know about Purgatory?"

"A second chance for sinners to make it to Heaven?"

"No, no! It is only for people who die in a state of Grace, who are headed for Heaven anyway. In Purgatory, their desire for the fleshly things of this world, for sin, too, is burned out of them. If we yearn for these things, how can we be happy with God, even though His Heavenly Paradise is perfection itself? We don't desire perfection. We desire a warm fire, good food, nice clothing, respect, ease and prosperity. But those are things you don't need in Heaven. And sometimes, God gives a bit of Purgatory to special people, to help cleanse them of the desire for this world so they can be perfectly happy with him in the next."

"So... God's punishment is for your own good?" Devlin asked skeptically.

"Not punishment, exactly," Tia said, working on a particularly knotted bit of hair. "Do you know your Bible?"

"Not by heart."

"Many people in the Bible suffered trials that were not punishments, to strengthen them, to... well, purify them. It's like metal. We heat and work iron to make it stronger, we heat gold to purify it. By sending us trials, God purifies us, makes us stronger in our faiths, closer to perfect."

"So, anyone who suffers, gets into Heaven faster?"

"No. It's not that easy! First of all, God gives trials to many people. But some people spit them back, they curse God for not making them more comfortable or wealthy or happy here on Earth. They throw the gift in His face and curse Him for it. Only if you accept the suffering, know that you are not so great yourself that you deserve better, know that your suffering here on Earth can not only help yourself, but can be offered for the souls of others, does the suffering begin to cleanse and purify you…"

"How do you suffer for others? A priest told me about that. How does that help you?"

"I can't explain all of it to you now. Some of it you will have to eventually learn for yourself. But the simple part is offering up your suffering for others, even as our Lord suffered for us. You can suffer gladly pain or illness or hardship if you ask the Lord to let that suffering be for someone who needs it more than you do: someone who is locked in sin, or who is in dire need. Our Lord suffered not only a painful death, and the tearing away of the spirit from the body, but also terrible ignominy in His death. But he did it willingly, even happily, because he did it for His beloved: us."

"Why did God put us in this world if He didn't want us to be happy here?"

"First, remember, He put us in a better world, we chose this one instead. But mainly, I never said He didn't want you to be happy. Suffering, in fact, can also make you happy in this world. By losing things you thought were important, you realize what is truly important."

"I don't know," Devlin said.

"When you first arrived in this country, what did you want? What was important to you?"

Devlin felt his mouth curve upwards. "Those things you said. Comfort, respect, prosperity."

"And what is important to you now?"

"I couldn't answer that easily. Surviving and getting free have been foremost in my mind for too long."

"Well, it will come to you. Eventually. Now that God has purged those other things from your heart. And anyway, you misunderstood before. I never said you were a good person, I said you have a good heart. That is not the same thing. I don't know if you are good yourself or not, but I know there is a generosity in you that makes you help other people. Besides, when you were hungry, did you ever go up to people and beg for food? Did you ever say, 'Gimme,' or 'what can I do for you to get this food?' Or did you say, 'What can I do for you?'"

"I asked people if they had work I could do," Devlin said.

"Not bargaining, just asking?"

"I won't take anything from anyone unless I have earned it," Devlin said. "I only accept your help now because Mr. Ordoñez made it clear there would be plenty for me to do to pay you all back in the coming weeks."

"Months, actually, if you come back with us. Is that still acceptable to you?"

"More than acceptable."

"Good. Hold very still now, I don't want to poke you."

She had left his hair long, just evened it out on the edges and bottom. Now she took those very sharp scissors and started trimming his beard, which was too long at the moment for shaving.

"I can shave myself," Devlin said.

"And I will poke your eye out if you move again. You sit still, and you will be safe enough. Don't worry. I shave Jaime every week."

"And this is significant… why?"

"Ah! You would not know, would you? Some of the men in that family, Jaime is one of them, have a disease of the blood. It doesn't ever thicken. The smallest cut never stops bleeding. It is hard to understand because for most of us, a little cut doesn't even need care, it just stops bleeding on its own. Not Jaime. You saw that scar on his chin?

"It looked like a burn."

"Yes. He nicked himself shaving, and it had to be cauterized. Even the smallest break of his skin has to be stitched or burned or he will die. On this trip at least, I have taken over his shaving. Much safer, I think. Fortunately, he doesn't need the service very often. About once a week."

"I'm more of a daily person."

"You will come to my wagon every morning to borrow the razor. You will strop it after use so it stays sharp. This is for shaving, but it is also part of my medical kit. I am a *curandera*."

"I don't think I know that word."

"It doesn't translate well. It means that I have been taught by my mother and my grandmother about healing and medicinal herbs and plants and I can treat illnesses and wounds. Someday, when she is a little less flighty, I will teach Esperanza as well."

"She's just a child, though," Devlin said.

"She is just over half a year from her *quinceañera*. Don't ask, your chin will move. It is a coming-of-age ceremony for girls. She should have started her training already, but she is not very mature for her age. She does not take to sitting and learning very well. She barely learned to read in all those years of school. But in eight months, she will not be a child any more, she will be a young lady, with suitors. Marriageable age."

"Too young," Devlin murmured.

"Like I said. Flighty. How do you want this beard now? Some bits here and there are fashionable," she said, touching his chin, his cheeks, to indicate the type of goatee or sideburns many men wore.

"Take it all off. It's too hot."

She stropped the razor, and began soaping up his face, a little at a time so that the soap would not dry in the hot sun while she worked on other areas. When she finished, she untied the apron from around his neck and folded it so the hair, the tufts of beard and the shavings were all locked inside, and she called to one of the children to fetch it and shake it out away from camp.

"Thank you," Devlin said, standing up. "For your care, and for the speech. I will keep it in mind."

"Good. But you are not done yet. You're not even half dressed."

Someone donated a newly knitted pair of socks. Someone else had worked while he was bathed and shaved remaking a shirt so that it was large enough for him. Tia Dolores gave him a wide leather belt to wear over the shirt, and a knife in a sheath to hang on the belt.

"This is too much!" Devlin protested.

"Necessary tools out here. A man without a knife is like a man with one hand. Or less."

He did not know if the straw hat he was given had been woven this morning, or if it happened to be sitting around, waiting for a new owner. Either way, Tia insisted he needed a hat to keep the sun off his face and neck.

"It's not too bad here, but when we get to New Spain[1], we have thinner air. The sun can fry your brains, even on a cool day. Heads must be

---

[1] Now called New Mexico.

114

covered."

"Yes, ma'am."

"And if you can wait here a few more minutes, your shoes are almost done."

Someone had traced his footprints in the damp earth just outside of the bathing area while he was inside and cut thick pieces of rawhide to match. More leather was cut, all of it punched with an awl, and while Tia was cutting his hair and beard, moccasins were stitched together by two of the women. It did not take long. He was outfitted then with the best-fitting pair of shoes he had had in a long time. Scrubbed, shaved, dressed in clean clothes that actually fit his tall, lean frame, his feet cradled in the moccasins, padded by socks, and his head shaded by the hat, he felt for a moment tears burning in the corners of his eyes.

"You people are too kind!" he said, fearing his voice would break.

"No one can put in a good day's work when they are cold and dirty and tired," Tia said pragmatically. Then she touched his hand and looked up into his eyes. "I told you you have a good heart. But that is not enough. A good heart must be tried, as gold is tried in the crucible. I don't think God is done with you yet. You be strong, though, and he won't give you anything you can't handle. Yes?"

"All right. Yes."

"*Ve'te entonces*, Mateo. Go help those boys bring the firewood for dinner. And Breakfast!"

He helped children gather wood that afternoon. He attended Mass with the Ordoñez family the next morning and watched afterwards as Esperanza broke her eleven candy sticks and passed them out to the fourteen children on the train, as well as some of the men and women. She offered one to Devlin, but he declined. The next day was a regular workday, and instead of helping children gather a day's worth of wood, Devlin went into the woods upriver with the men and equipment to start cutting, blocking and splitting the firewood they would carry in the slings under the freight wagons.

"We'll take as much as we can," Jaime told him. "We won't find many trees once we get out on the plains. When this runs low, we'll start gathering chips."

"What are chips?" Devlin asked.

Jaime grinned, as usual. "You'll find out!"

Devlin only worked with the wood cutters one day, though, before Ordoñez tapped him to come into town with him and some of the other men. This was Francisco Ordoñez's fourth trip up the trail. All the other men who were merchants, not just teamsters, had experience also and most of them were at least partially bilingual.

"Just listen," Ordoñez told Devlin. He did. After a few hours, he asked if he could read also. He only found about eleven discrepancies between what had been bargained for and what was written on the contracts, and for the next few days, as the loading began and continued, he moved back and forth between the warehouses with various men, checking the manifests as well as helping with the physical labor."

"I don't think I did anything that Señor Ordoñez couldn't have done himself," Devlin commented to Tia Dolores later.

"It may have been a test," Tia told him. If it was, he passed.

Soon the loading of the freight wagons was done, then the so-called "family wagons" were loaded with the food and supplies for the whole train for the trip.

"Dance tonight!" Jaime told Devlin, clapping him on the back.

There was neither time nor room for all the people of the freight train to wash in the big tubs, so the men went to a nearby creek and spread out up and down its length to make themselves presentable for the dance. A pig had been slaughtered the day before, and all day while the loading finished, pork roasts were slow cooked, and great kettles hung over the fires for the small pieces of fat to be boiled down. The lard this made would be a large part of their supplies for the trip, but the real prize was the bits of cooked meat and fat that were left when the lard was boiled out. They were called *chicharones*. They were crisp and sweet and rich, and sprinkled into a bean burrito with *chile colorado*, Devlin agreed that they were very, very good.

The fires blazed high, the food was excellent, there was beer and wine, and then the music began. Guitars, violins and other instruments were brought out and tuned up, and the women came out from their wagons, arrayed in skirts that had row after row of gathers so that if they clutched opposite corners and lifted their hands high over their heads, they could not begin to stretch out all the material in their voluminous skirts. Each row of flounces was decorated with rows of ribbon or lace, and more ribbons swung from braided and upswept hair. Tall combs made of tortoise shell, silver, ebony and even polished bone stood up from the piles of hair they held in place. Fans of oriental paper, silk and feathers fluttered in the ladies' hands as they stepped out to dance, skirts swishing and flaring in great wide circles around their bodies as they flung the corners back and forth to make the skirts dance as well as their feet. The men were not to be outdone. All those who had fandango trousers with them unbuttoned the silver buttons on the sides of the legs and released swathes of gold and red silk that spun and fluttered as they also danced. The men far outnumbered the women, but no one seemed to care.

They were leaving in the morning, so the party broke up well before midnight. Finery was packed away, kettles of beans carried to the creek to cool so they would not spoil before morning. Carrying one side of the kettle handle while Devlin carried the other, Jaime asked him: "Where have you been? You didn't join in!"

"I couldn't have possibly kept up!" Devlin laughed. "But that was... wonderful! I've never seen anything like it."

"You'll see more! And you'd better learn how to dance! The ladies are all disappointed that you did not participate." He wagged a finger in Devlin's face, and laughed, slightly drunk on wine and music and excitement. Growing more serious, he asked, "are you sorry to have joined up with us? There are trains of Americans coming and going all the time, you could still get passage with them."

"Never!" Devlin declared. "I would not trade this for anything!"

Jaime grinned again. "Good! I was starting to get used to you, Diablo."

Santa Fe Trail, Summer 1845

The entire train was up and working before the sun the next morning and, as all of them had been at least on the trip east, they fell immediately into a pattern. Fires were lit, coffee boiled. Burrito-sandwiches were built of the leftover beans, *chile* and *chicharones* to be passed out even as the big coffee pots were carried throughout the camp to fill the men's cups as they laid out the harnesses. A few men on horseback rode out to gather the stock, which was sorted and separated and harnessed to the wagons.

"How do you tell which animals go to which wagons in the dark?" Devlin asked. The dozens of mules all looked alike to him.

"Does it really matter?" Jaime grinned back. Then, "Teasing you," he admitted. "The animals know their owners, and the owners know them. You'll get to where you can tell them apart after you've been around them long enough."

Devlin moved through the camp, helping wherever he was needed. He held harnesses and moved animals into place for the men doing the harnessing. He gathered dirty dishes which would be washed in the evening, collected grills, packed bedrolls and food and shoveled dirt onto the fires until they were dead and out, and helped count the children so no one was left behind.

They started about the time the sun was halfway over the horizon. There was an order to the wagons, and each one pulled into the line in their assigned place, freight wagons front and rear, family wagons in the middle. There were forty wagons in all, fifty-seven men, six women and, counting Esperanza, fourteen children.

The first day was pleasant. Devlin had been assigned to help the women and children and as he walked along beside the train, he moved up and down the line of family wagons, checking to see if anyone needed anything. He lifted children who were tired of walking up onto the high wagon seats and lifted down the ones who were tired of the bouncing and jolting of steel-rimmed wheels traversing a road that was no more than wagon ruts on the open prairie. He quickly learned what chips were (round patties of dried buffalo dung) and helped the younger children, who seemed to have boundless energy to run out after them and run back to the train, gather them into baskets while they walked. At least six of the men, sometimes more, rode alongside of the train at all times. They spread out along both sides, rode in front and behind, watching for danger. Jaime preferred riding ahead on his flashy black-and-white pinto, scouting for the train and hunting for fresh game at the same time. But as the days progressed, he took his turn driving one of the four wagons his family had brought, insisting that Devlin sit with him while he drove and learn how to handle a team.

They stopped, daily, well before dark, made the wagons into two concentric circles, released the mules and horses to find graze, hobbling the ones who were likely to run off, leaving the others free, knowing they would stick with the group. Fires were lit. Mountains of tortillas were rolled and baked while stew or beans and coffee boiled. Devlin helped haul water, helped heat it and wash dishes, entertained some of the rowdier little boys, learned how to roll tortillas and how long to leave them on the hot flat rocks where they were cooking. When dinner was done and packed away, guitars were brought out, not for the wild dancing of the night before they left, but for the kind of simple entertainment that for Devlin had always before been reading aloud. He still sometimes read to anyone who wanted to hear and told stories about the great whales of the oceans, while the plains rang with music and singing. Women sat close to the fires, sewing now that they were not being bounced. Small children fell asleep on the laps of mothers and fathers and uncles. Bedrolls were brought out, guards were set on the wagons and on the animals. Devlin's place to sleep was under one of the family wagons, and he, like all the men, was rousted out in the middle of the night to take his turn at watch. In the morning, it all started again.

Devlin had always been able to get along with people, but he found it especially easy to get along with these trail-wise frontiersmen. True, the men laughed at his accent. They laughed at his inability to handle firearms or harness mules. They laughed at his long legs, and the fair skin that burned red even if he was careful about his hat. But Devlin was not offended, because it was very good-natured laughing. They weren't teasing, so much as enjoying. They laughed at themselves and each other easily as much as they laughed at him, maybe even more. Their laughter was an acceptance, not a division. They seemed to enjoy life and have a very easy-going attitude towards things. They were friendly, open and honest, and even as they laughed, they helped him learn the things he needed to learn: how to drive the teams and load the long rifles, how to use a bow and arrow when ammunition was scarce. He learned about edible roots and plants, how to find water, how to conserve water when there was none to be found, how to make the tortilla dough, how to build fires with buffalo chips as they left the trees behind and moved out onto the open prairie, how to field dress game animals, and butcher them into steaks and stew meat. He quickly became a favorite among the women and children. He was more than willing to do any work assigned to him, including cooking and babysitting. He even proved that he could handle a needle, a skill he had learned helping Chloe and Emma hem the napkins and tablecloths for The Lakes, although that seemed several lifetimes ago to him now. The children especially liked him. The small ones begged always for rides on his shoulders. The girls smiled up at his tall handsomeness. All of them begged for stories about the big city and the ocean, and the ladies discovered he had an eye for color and design and could describe what the well-dressed Charlestonian woman wore — even if his descriptions were more than a year old. The travel was long and exhausting, the labor hard. But, at the same time, the company was good.

Some days, the weather was good and the travel was pleasant, if exhausting — sometimes covering as much as twenty miles. Other days, the weather was against them. It poured rain, hailed and thundered, and the children rode inside the leaky canvas covers of the wagons, while Devlin and the men had to stand the weather to push the wheels out of the mud that sucked at them, and haul the mules out of the bogs that threatened to swallow them. There were creek and river crossings that took sometimes more than a day to make as they had to haul the wagons down to the water and up the other side using long ropes and extra mules tied on behind to prevent the wagons from rolling down out of control, and double teams to haul them back up the other side. Sometimes they could ford the creeks. Once they had to try to swim the wagons across, which proved not only dangerous, but difficult. Once they were able to cross a particularly wide river by loading the wagons one at a time on the three rafts someone had left on the river for just that purpose.

They were a month into the trip when suddenly, the prairie ahead of them was burned and black. If fire wiped out all the graze, they could not go forward with this many animals. Benito Alvarez, who was the husband of Tia Dolores and the leader of this group, called a halt. The wagons were unhitched, and the animals turned out to graze while Jaime and another man rode ahead to scout the burn. It was near midnight when they returned, but they agreed that the burn was a swath across their path, and they should be able to cross it in two days, if they pushed the stock hard. The animals were given another full day of grazing before they were harnessed up again and the train pushed forward. By late afternoon of the second day, Devlin and other men were pulling at the teams while the drivers lashed their whips to try to keep them moving.

"We won't make it," one of the women said.

"We will make it," Tia said. "Because we have to."

They made it. Not only did they reach tall grass again, but a creek had stopped the blaze on that side, so they stopped for another two days while the animals had all the food and water they wanted after their deprivation. Jaime took Devlin out on a hunting expedition while they were camped, and Devlin's shot brought down a fat young buffalo calf. There was fresh meat for everyone on the train that night, while Devlin was both teased and congratulated for his feat.

Teased: "Finally, you are almost as good with a rifle as my young daughter!"

Congratulated as if he were a boy on his first hunt. He enjoyed both.

They were attacked twice by Indians. On the first attack, Devlin helped the women and older children load rifles and pass them to the men. The men, Devlin learned, full of fun and laughter as they all were, were fierce fighters, and the Indians were fought off with no serious injuries to the people of the train. The second attack, coming weeks later, was more serious. The Indians were determined to get the goods in the wagons as well as the livestock, and before they were fought back, several of them breached the wall of wagons.

The only fight Devlin had ever had before was a fistfight on the docks with another sailor. He was unprepared for the hand-to-hand combat inside the wagon circle, but he was spurred on by the sounds of screams, screams pitched so high they could only come from the throats of very young children. He fought desperately against a warrior who, armed with a hand axe, tried hard to kill him. He snatched the knife at his waist which he had used before only for cooking and other chores, and by the benefit of his longer reach was able to hold off the tomahawk and slash at the man's throat. Blood gushed, but the man was still determined to make a kill before he died himself. Devlin hit him hard, grabbed the tomahawk and used the butt end of it to smash the man's head, bringing him down into the dirt where he would, in a few minutes, finish bleeding out. There were more. Now armed with the small axe, he waded into the fight, swinging fists and weapon until suddenly, there was no one left to fight. The Indians were retreating, and several men jumped onto horses to chase them. Devlin looked around and saw that while there were many bodies on the ground, few of them were Mexicans. The cover of one of the wagons was burning, but men were slashing it free, dropping it to the ground to be put out. Suddenly, he thought of Jaime. Jaime had been at his side when the Indians came over the wagon bows into the encampment. He looked around and found his friend leaning against a wagon wheel, clutching at his arm, from which blood was flowing freely. Devlin bent down and picked him up bodily, holding his own hand over the gushing wound, and shouted at one of the older boys, who had dropped down out of the wagon to help now that the danger was less:

"Run! Get Tia! Tell her it's Jaime!"

The boy dashed off, and Devlin staggered after him, carrying Jaime.

Tia, with the help of the other women, was already tending to other wounded, but on hearing Jaime was hurt, she laid out a bed for him in the wagon, and scrambled up herself, laying out her sewing kit. Except for the burning canvas, which had been put out, there were no fires already burning, just the smoldering remains of the fires from dinner, now hours past, so there was no time to heat up an iron. She pulled out her kit and threaded the needle as Devlin hauled Jaime into the wagon and stretched him out on the bed.

"Get a lamp," she instructed Esperanza, and the girl scrambled to obey.

Jaime had received a deep gash on the upper arm, from a knife or a tomahawk. It was about six inches long. Devlin held the ends of the flesh together while Tia started stitching. She made several stitches, far apart to hold the flesh shut, then, with the lamp Devlin held close over her head, she made smaller stitches, closer together. The blood slowly stopped leaking out. Jaime was pale and unconscious, though.

"Will he be all right?" Esperanza asked.

"We'll know by morning," Tia said. She ordered fires lit and water boiled, and Devlin jumped down out of the wagon to help the men. Two men were dead. Four more, not counting Jaime, were hurt: one had an arrow through his shoulder that required Tia's immediate attention, the three others had lesser wounds. Coffee and herbal teas were made and passed out, weapons were gathered and picked up, the dead dragged outside of the circle, children were counted, and graves were dug: two of them.

"What about them?" Devlin asked, pointing to the eleven Indians who had been laid out in a row outside the camp.

"We'll leave them here…"

"To rot, like animals?" Devlin demanded.

"To be picked up by their own people tomorrow and buried in their own fashion," Ordoñez said, smiling sadly.

They lost several of the mules but gained five of the horses of the dead Indians. Four were ponies, saddled with ropes and blankets. But one was a tall horse with a US brand on his hip and an army saddle on his back. They kept the Indian ponies, but turned the big horse loose, not wanting to be caught in American territory with an American military mount in their possession. They kept the saddle though.

"Now, we can teach you to ride properly!" one of the men said. They had made trousers long enough for Devlin by sewing those strips of cloth to the bottom, but they had not been able to find a saddle among them that would accommodate his legs. He laughed with the man, then walked over to the campfire. He sat down on one of the logs that had been placed around the fire for that purpose the night before, and suddenly found himself shaking so violently it was as if he were outdoors in the winter. He wasn't cold, but he couldn't seem to stop.

"Get some warm tea into him!" Tia shouted. "Get a blanket!"

The tea had a bitter, medicinal taste, but the heat of it seemed to help. Esperanza not only draped a blanket over his shoulders but wrapped an arm around him to help warm him. That was when she noticed that the blanket had soaked through that quickly with fresh blood. All the blood on him was not Jaime's.

"Tia! He's hurt too!"

He had a gash on his left shoulder and extending down his back from the tomahawk, which hadn't been a stone implement, but a small steel hand axe, decorated with rawhide and feathers. Tia came back and washed it out and stitched it up for him.

"That is one of the least pleasant things I have ever felt," he said as the needle bit over and over into his already damaged flesh.

"Necessary, though," Tia said, biting off her thread.

"I can't seem to stop shaking," he said apologetically. "I don't know what's wrong with me."

"Shock," Tia said, pushing another cup of hot liquid into his hands. She rubbed his arms through the blanket to help warm him. "From the wound, of course, but also... have you ever been in a fight like this before?"

"No." He sipped at the tea. Between that, the blanket, and Tia's vigorous rubbing, his shaking was starting to subside. "I killed a man tonight. Maybe two. I have never killed a man before."

"The first time is difficult," Tia said. "If you are lucky, it will never get easier. And thank you."

"For what?"

"For saying you killed 'a man.' Most people would use some other word. You gave him his dignity."

"Why is no one else affected?" Devlin asked, looking around. The men who were not wounded were still busy, checking the livestock, dealing with the aftermath, passing out hot beverages.

"They are. But most of them have done this before, so it is not so obvious. They hide the shakes, treat them. Young Jaime in there killed a man when he was fourteen. It is a way of life out here."

"I don't know if I can get used to that," Devlin said.

"You will learn to deal with it. That's not the same as getting used to it. I told you before that you have a good heart. I can say the same about most of these other men. But a good heart is not enough. There has to be an inner core of hardness to go with it, or you bleed for your loved ones, but you don't protect them."

"They have that," Devlin said looking around, remembering the fierceness of the fight. "I don't."

"Let me ask you. Would you have hurt that man for trying to cheat Esperanza out of her nine pieces of candy?"

He had to consider. "If it was me, I definitely would not have. It wasn't worth it. I'd have probably done just what Señor Ordoñez did and merely tell others not to trade in that store. But when he pulled that trick on an innocent, helpless little girl, it made me so mad! I threatened to hurt him, but... I don't know. I honestly don't know."

"You felt the anger, the ability to fight. But, only when it's needed. This is why you fit in so well here. You are like us. You have a good heart, but you have the hardness in you also. I have seen it. I have heard your stories: you have been hungry and cold, you have been hurt and cheated by people. You were jailed and badly punished for trying to help people. I think you lost someone very close to you, too, although you never talk about it. A good heart, without that inner core of strength, would have just broken. You can fight when you have to. And when people you care about are threatened, you will do it again."

"I think you have more faith in me than I deserve."

"You give people faith in you," Tia said. "That is how I know you have that strength."

He patted the hand that was still on his uninjured shoulder, and he leaned closer to the fire to heat his shakes while she went to check on her other patients. The children of the train were also shaken by the events, although all of them had been safely tucked into the bottom of the largest wagon and had come through without a scratch. While their mothers and fathers and the older children were busy getting an only slightly earlier than usual breakfast and getting ready to leave, the youngest children congregated around Devlin. Two sat on his lap. One sat by his feet. Two more sat next to him on the log and leaned up against him, and three others curled on the ground near his feet or stood behind him, touching his shoulder for reassurance. Fernando, who was only a year and a half old and who didn't like anyone but his mother or Esperanza to ever even touch him, leaned against Devlin's leg and allowed himself to be picked up and added to the pile on Devlin's lap. When Tia came around later with plates of food for everyone, a good hot breakfast instead of the usual cold leftovers, she found him dozing, looking like a big dog covered in puppies.

No bones had been broken, but Devlin's wound was deep. He had lost a good deal of blood before he ever realized he was hurt, so he was weak and shaky for the rest of the day. He was loaded into a wagon, on top of the bedrolls and blankets, with Jaime and the man with the arrow wound, and the three of them slept most of the day. Jaime had lost a great deal of blood also, and when he wasn't sleeping himself, Devlin was told to feed Jaime salt water and broth to help him regain his strength. By the next day, Devlin was still not up to walking, but he had been promoted to driving the wagon instead of trying to sleep in it. The man with the arrow wound was in the far back, fading in and out of consciousness, with Tia Dolores staying close to him with compresses and cool water for his fever. Jaime was still very weak, but he could sit up, propped among the bedrolls in the front of the wagon, right behind the driver's seat. Although Fernando had gone back to his mother, several of the other youngsters took turns sitting up on the wagon seat with Devlin. The smallest, Joaquim, sat with his legs dangling and the two first fingers of his left hand stuffed in his mouth. Apparently, it was a habit like thumb-sucking, just using different digits, because although he was almost four, Joachim would not remove the fingers, except to eat or if he had something to say, which was seldom, and fairly garbled anyway.

"Thanks for coming to look for me so quickly," Jaime said.

"You're welcome. Have you ever considered that maybe, with your special problem, that you shouldn't engage in things like hand-to-hand combat?"

"You mean I should hide in the wagon with the women and children?" Jaime gave a short bark of laughter. "Not my style. And what good would that do anyway? The two men who died did not have my 'special problem'. Having blood that coagulates didn't help them any. You live out here, you take risks, every day. Everybody. It's worth it though."

"We'll see," Devlin said.

"Wait until you see the mountains!"

On the wagon seat, Joaquim leaned against Devlin, eyes starting to sag shut. It was a miracle, Devlin thought that kids could sleep in these bouncing wagons. He had only managed to sleep a little yesterday because he had been so weak.

The wheel hit a large rock and the wagon gave a hard jolt.

"Think you can aim for more rocks?" Jaime said. "I haven't been in pain for almost three seconds."

"Sorry."

Joaquim tucked a hand under Devlin's arm and sucked harder on his fingers.

"These kids are going to run you ragged," Jaime commented.

"I don't mind them," Devlin said, giving a big smile to the boy next to him. Joachim clutched his fingers with his teeth so he could smile back without them falling out of his mouth.

"You're a natural-born family man," Jaime said, settling back into his padding. "It's a wonder you never married."

After a moment of silence, Devlin admitted, "I was married."

"Was? What happened to her? Or did you just have to abandon her when you were put in prison?"

"She died," Devlin said.

"Oh. I'm sorry to hear that. Our mother died. Cholera. Terrible disease. It took two younger children too. Espe and I had a brother and sister, but this was at least five years ago. Was your wife sick?"

"She was pregnant."

"Childbirth? Yes, that happens. It's very hard on the man, usually. Makes him feel kind of guilty I think."

"I don't feel the least bit guilty," Devlin said. "I blame my father-in-law."

"That's a new one on me. How is her father to blame for her dying in childbirth?"

Devlin looked down at the little boy sitting next to him. He was once again leaning against Devlin, dozing off. He glanced back and saw that Tia was occupied with the wounded man and several feet away. He sighed, then, and told Jaime the entire series of events surrounding Larissa's death, the first time since it happened that he had described it to anyone. When he stopped, and there was silence, he glanced over his shoulder to see Jaime making the sign of the cross on his chest.

"That is the worst thing I have ever heard," Jaime said. "Weren't there any women around to help her?"

"Black women. Apparently, no one wanted to ask them."

"And they arrested you as you came from her deathbed?"

"For inciting slave riots," Devlin said. "That's what they called helping families stay together."

"Whatever happened to the child?"

"What child?" Devlin asked, thinking of the woman and two children who had been at The Lakes the night he walked out of there for the last time.

"Your child. Or didn't it live?"

Devlin was silent so long that Jaime reached out and touched his back. "Dev?"

Devlin gave a ragged half-laugh. "Child! I guess I… forgot there ever was one! It lived. They had a wet nurse for it, I think."

"Was it a boy or a girl?"

"A girl. No, wait. We talked about having a girl, but I think someone said it was a boy. I guess… I don't really remember."

"You don't remember if you have a son or a daughter?"

"I was a little preoccupied. And all I ever saw was a blanket with a red face sticking out. Larissa called it 'him,' just before she died. She asked to see 'him.' But at that stage, she might have been asking to see her father. Or me. She didn't always know when I was in the room."

"Will you try to get in touch with him? Or her?" Jaime asked.

Devlin considered. "Sebastien was pretty angry. I don't know why he was so angry with me, it was all his decision. But he seemed to put a lot of blame on me. That's the main reason he had me arrested: punishment. No, I doubt he would ever let me see the kid, much less bring it out here with me. Not to mention the fact that if I go back there, I go back to prison."

"What will happen to it?"

"It will be raised in a big house, with nice clothes and good food, private tutors or good schools, slaves and servants, doting grandparents and lots of cousins and aunts and uncles. If it is a girl, there will be a coming-out ball, eventually, and a good husband will be chosen for her. Or maybe she'll have her mother's personality and choose for herself. If it's a boy, he'll probably go to Harvard or some other big school back east and become a lawyer like his grandfather. I guess he'll be better off without me anyway."

"No child is ever better off without their real parent," Jaime said with conviction.

"Well, there's nothing I can do about it."

"You'll marry again," Jaime predicted. "And be covered in kids, just like you are half the time on this train."

Devlin smiled to himself and wrapped his arm around the boy who was now fast asleep, leaning against him.

"What are you planning to do once we get to Santa Fe?" Jaime asked.

"You know, I never thought about that. I've spent so many months just planning to get to Mexico, that was as far as things got. Anyway, I've found work before, I suppose I will again."

"Ever do any prospecting?"

"For gold? No, why?"

"I've been thinking about it. We have gold in our mountains. It will be winter in the high country when we get back, but maybe we could take off in the spring, look for a stake. Maybe buy some land if we get enough gold."

"You're not coming up the trail again?"

"Four times in three years is more than enough, believe me. Father is ready to retire also. We have a little place west of town on the Santa Fe River, but I wouldn't mind getting together a stake for a place of my own."

"Not a bad idea," Devlin said.

III

They smelled it two days before they reached it. Dead buffalo, stretched across the plain as far as they could see. No meat was taken, not even the hides that were so valuable in the east: just a slaughter of hundreds of animals.

"Why?" Devlin demanded, staring at the carnage.

Jaime's jaw was hard. His eyes glinted with fury.

"The Americans murder the buffalo. Remember those Indians the other day? With no buffalo, they are forced to raid instead of hunt. The Americans are hoping to wipe us both out, the Mexicans and the Indians, so they inherit what is left."

"A dead land," Devlin said.

"Land," Jaime said. "That is all they care."

It was almost a week later that they met up with the squad of Mexican soldiers, sent out to guard them on the last leg of their journey.

"What do they want?" Devlin asked.

"Not you, don't worry," Jaime grinned at him. "They're for protection."

"Yeah? Where were they last week?"

"Ah, yes. You see, the Mexican military is not allowed in American territory to escort Mexican trains, even though the American Army often escorts American traders all the way into the village of Santa Fe. The American Army won't escort Mexican trains though, just American ones. So, we get protection, but not before we reach this point."

"Politics certainly complicates simple things," Devlin said.

IV.

"I see you are only carrying one bucket of water," Tia said as Devlin came into the center of the wagon circle after helping water and bed down the stock.

He glanced down at the bucket in his right hand and shrugged. "I'm not riding children on my shoulders this week either."

"Let's have a look, see how the stitches are doing."

She passed the bucket off to a boy of about eleven, who held it two-handed and struggled with the weight, and led Devlin over to the log-chair she had set near a wagon, under a lamp. He pulled his shirt off and let her open the bandages to examine the wound.

"Where are the soldiers?"

"They are camped out there."

"Outside the circle? Seems like taking a bit of a chance."

"I think they are between the two circles, some protection, but not with us. That is a good thing. All of us have been together for months, having them move into camp with us might be uncomfortable. I'm going to leave the center stitches for another two or three days. It is deepest there. But the edges will start to grow into your skin, so I will be taking them out now. Don't worry. It doesn't hurt as much as putting them in."

She had a small, curved pair of scissors for sliding under the stitches and cutting them, and a pair of tweezers to slide them out of the wounds.

"Almost painless," she said.

130

"Almost," Devlin said.

"I have been wanting to speak to you," Tia said. "You said before that you studied for a while with a priest. Did you intend to become Catholic?"

"I don't think I ever thought about it that much," Devlin said.

"Then why did you ask for a priest?"

"A bit of rebellion. You'd be amazed how much people hate Catholics. Partly because, I think, if they admit there is nothing wrong with the Catholic faith, then they have to admit that breaking away from it was wrong. But I found it interesting, too, that Catholics are considered weaklings."

"Weaklings?"

"In America, real men don't take orders from anyone. That's what freedom and independence means to them. They see Catholic men drinking and fighting and doing what they do during the week, but on Sunday, they go meekly to church where they are under the direction and rules of the pope. Taking orders."

"That is ridiculous!" Tia snorted. "How does their military work then?"

"Not that well. I have seen schoolboys taunting soldiers for being cowards and being like slaves. So, I asked to see a priest. Well, I did get unchained from Josh for an hour every week. Not that he is a bad person, but it is not entertaining to drag someone else around with you everywhere. And it was a bit of a dare: call *me* weak. Foolishness."

"But you found much of what he said interesting?"

"Yes, it was, actually."

"You do know, don't you, that if you wish to live in Mexico, you have to agree to live by our laws, including becoming a Catholic."

"I didn't."

"Do you have a problem with it?"

He thought about it seriously, wincing at the odd feeling of the thread sliding out through his skin.

"There is one thing I have a little trouble with. Forgiveness. 'Forgive us our trespasses *as* we forgive those who trespass against us.' There is one man I am not sure I could ever forgive."

"Your father-in-law."

When he turned to look at her she said, "I have ears. I heard. I heard what Jaime said too, about men feeling guilt when their wives die in

131

childbirth. That is very true, I have seen it often."

"But I don't feel guilt," Devlin said.

"Don't you? It was your child wasn't it?"

The words sliced into some deep part of his heart that he had not even realized was there. For a moment, he could not even breathe.

"All men, all *decent* men, will have some twinge of guilt for their wife dying giving birth, whatever specifically causes the death. It is natural. But you had a very real scapegoat to pass that guilt onto, and good reason to do so. All his fault, no one else's. What he did was not smart, but the fact that he did it gave you what you thought was a clear conscience. Consider this, Mateo. Consider that he also felt guilt, probably a great deal more than you ever felt. His anger against you, his violent action, having you arrested and put in jail, was the only thing he could do to assuage his own guilt. And I'm sure it was not enough. You twisted the knife into his heart when you accused him of murdering his own daughter. Maybe it was true, but you hurt him, he hurt you, and you both suffer for it. Maybe not today, maybe not now, but someday you will see how much he hurt, and you can forgive him his horrible mistake, knowing it is a guilt he will have to live with as long as he lives."

"I don't know…"

"Not now. Like our other talk, let it soak in. By the way, have you seen Esperanza? We have already started dinner, but I haven't seen her in a while."

"She's not with the children? Or Jaime?"

Tia waved a hand in front of them. As usual, there were four cook fires in the middle of the wagons. While there were a number of men and the usual few women working, sitting, eating around the fires, Devlin counted the children. Twelve, not counting Fernando, who was probably asleep in the wagon already, and not who they were looking for anyway. In case he had confused Esperanza with one of the women, he counted again. Five. Six with Tia standing behind him. And Jaime was sitting near the fire with a plate of food.

"She was off that way when I came in," Devlin said, indicating the western end of the camp.

"That is the direction of the soldier camp," Tia said.

Devlin replaced his shirt and went to find Ordoñez and Jaime. Several other men stood up or came near as Devlin was asking if anyone had seen the girl. No one had.

"She took several tortillas," one of the women said. "I thought for the children, but maybe she wanted to share with the soldiers."

Ordoñez turned and walked towards the west end of camp. Jaime and Devlin followed, and after a moment more than a dozen other men as well. As the rumor went through the camp, more men joined the group. Some had their long rifles laid casually across their arms. Devlin found he was resting his hand on the tomahawk that he now carried in his belt, spoils of war as well as a useful tool. The music and eating in the camp went still and silent as the group crossed between the circled wagons into the space where the soldiers were camped. They also had a fire, larger than was needed for cooking. While the teamsters' camp had gone silent, there was still music and laughter here. Someone was playing a harmonica, several men were laughing and clapping and Esperanza was dancing in front of the fire. At the arrival of the group of men, the music faded. There was no sound but the crackling of the fire.

"Papá!" Esperanza said in surprise, stopping her dance.

"Go back to the wagon," Ordoñez said.

"Oh, Papá, you don't understand! I was just…"

"You have happy feet, I know. Go."

"But these men were…"

Ordoñez had been watching the men, now he turned his eyes on his daughter. His eyes were cold and hard and unyielding. His look brooked no argument.

"Now!"

She sought her brother's eyes, and Devlin's, looking for support, but found instead looks as hard as her father's. Defeated, she broke into tears and ran back towards the teamsters' camp, pushing through the mob of men who now outnumbered the soldiers almost three to one, and were armed besides.

The officer of the group stood up and moved forward, insinuating himself between the teamsters and his men.

"We meant no harm. The young lady came in and brought us some tortillas. We appreciate the gift very much. There was music, and…"

"You are welcome to the tortillas," Ordoñez said. "We should have come earlier to offer them, or anything else you might need. I know you travel light. But my daughter is too young to understand some things. From now on, please keep your men away from our women. And our children."

"Of course," the officer said. There was no point in arguing. He bent his head to show compliance, and the men faded back through the wagons into the main camp, Ordoñez, Jaime and Devlin leaving last of all.

"Papá!" Esperanza cried when they were all back around the family fire. "That was too humiliating! There was nothing wrong there…"

"Never," Ordoñez said, lifting a finger towards her face, "never go off alone with one man, much less with ten of them!"

"But no one…"

"Listen to me!" he said, so loud and so sharp that everyone in the camp listened. He lowered his voice again. "You have no idea how lucky you were to fall into the hands of this man," he indicated Devlin, "when you took off wandering around Independence alone! It was not what you told me, but what he told me that made me trust him, and I knew how very fortunate you were. You have no idea what could have happened…"

"But nothing…!"

"No idea! I know some of those men! You were not as safe as you thought you were!"

"Papá, I…"

"No. You listen, you don't talk! If I cannot trust you, I will lock you up. Not with chains, but you will be watched much more closely from now on! I only hope," he added softly, " that someday you will learn."

He turned his back on her then. Esperanza spun on the ball of her foot and ran back to the wagon, sobs of humiliation breaking from her chest. Around the fires, all the other members of the train were silent for a moment, respecting the interchange. Then someone began softly picking at a guitar. Dinner recommenced.

"Was I too hard on her?" Ordoñez softly asked Tia Dolores, as he sat again near the fire.

"Knowing her, probably not hard enough," Tia said, gripping his shoulder. "She is…"

"Foolish," Jaime said.

"I was going to say *inocente*," Tia said.

"Of course, she wasn't guilty!" Devlin said.

Jaime grinned at him. "It doesn't translate well. What she was saying isn't innocent or guilty, she meant it as… well, innocent of the way things are. A child's heart, that kind of innocence. Pure and simple and trusting."

"Ah! Naive!" Devlin said.

"When I said I hope she learns someday," Ordoñez said, "I meant, I hope she does not have to learn the hard way."

"We'll keep a closer eye on her, father," Jaime promised.

"Yes," Ordoñez looked around the camp. "There are a lot of good men here. But not all of them. I should never have brought her on this trip!"

"It hasn't been so bad," Tia said, patting his shoulder. "You lost her for a few moments twice. Both times it was her exuberance and generosity that made her wander off. She is not one of these silly girls who can't stay away from the men. The only trouble you will have with her now, I think is that her feelings will be hurt for a while. But she'll get over that too."

"*Gracias, mi tia,*" Ordoñez said. Because while everyone called Dolores "Tia," she was in fact his father's sister: his actual aunt.

Santa Fe, New Spain (Mexico), October 1845

It was snowing when the train finally reached Santa Fe. The thick, heavy flakes turned rooftops and tree branches white, but churned into a muddy mess in the streets. The tired mules dragged the wagons more than rolled them through the muck around the ancient village square and along San Francisco Street to the shops that were waiting for the goods.

Devlin had two part time jobs before they had completely off-loaded the cargo. As he was introduced around and gave the list of his experience, he was immediately hired by the loan department of the bank, and by one of the larger merchants in town as an inventory clerk and bookkeeper. He spent the night with the Ordoñez family, but by the next day he had already found himself a place to live: a small single-room building outside a larger house about two city blocks from the house where the Ordoñezes lived, plenty close enough to help Jaime and his father with the fall hunting and butchering. Because of Devlin's job, they went hunting on weekends only, but still brought back several fat deer and an elk, more than enough for their own family, but they were also supplying Tia Dolores and her husband. The meat was hung where it would stay frozen all winter, and the hides were turned over to Tia Dolores and came back in the form of fringed leather coats for Devlin, Jaime and Ordoñez: dark brown buckskin for Ordoñez and Jaime and soft blonde elk hide for Devlin.

Winter passed quickly. As the snow set in too heavily to do more hunting, Devlin took another bookkeeping job and was working now six days a week. Sundays he attended catechism classes with the young people who would receive their First Holy Communion and Confirmation at Easter services. Father Anthony was not as relaxed and interesting as Father Ignatius had been. He tended to be a bit pedantic, but if he took too long to explain some minor points, at least he was full of information that he was more than willing to pass on.

Christmas came, and Devlin was invited to celebrate with Ordoñez, Tia and Benito, and the other relatives who all squeezed into Ordoñez's home.

He brought chocolates and lace for the ladies, and surprised everyone by baking French puff pastries, filled with heavy whipped cream.

"You really did own a restaurant," Jaime said in surprise, licking cream off his fingers.

Spring was wet and early, but Devlin and Jaime had agreed to postpone their trip until the completion of two important events. At the Easter Vigil Mass, Devlin and a dozen youngsters were formally initiated into the Catholic Church. Two weeks later was Esperanza's fifteenth birthday.

Santa Fe, New Spain (Mexico), April 1846

Esperanza Catalina Ordoñez y Valencia turned fifteen on April 20, 1846. The occasion was marked by the family with a celebration called a *quinceañera*. There was a church service in which the girl, now a young woman, dedicated her life to being a good Christian woman and was blessed by the priest. Her gown for the occasion was made of white satin, modeled after pictures in Godey's Ladies' Book and a description they had gotten earlier from Devlin. Instead of a fiesta style skirt, it was a full skirted gown with a snugly fitting bodice, the neck and waist cut in a V shape. The neckline covered her shoulders, though, unlike the pictures in the book, and the V was not too deep and had a satin rose at the center to make it even more demure. Four inches of imported lace hung from the neckline and over her otherwise bare upper arms, and the skirt was gathered and flounced with white silk cord and soft pink satin roses. The dress was designed to fit her round figure, rather than having been made three sizes too small so that a corset was needed to fit her into it.

"The ladies in the book looked much thinner," Esperanza fretted.

"The ladies in the book looked downright abnormal," Devlin told her.

There followed a banquet for all the friends and family. Plank-and-sawhorse tables were set up outside in the greening spring grass to make enough room for everyone, and a large dance floor was made of fitted boards, hung about with paper lanterns for lighting for the dancing that would take place after dinner. The dance started with Esperanza tossing her doll into a crowd of young girls, much like a bride tosses her bouquet over her shoulder into a crowd of single women. Then her little lace-up boots were traded for a pair of satin dancing slippers. Her older brother, Jaime, had escorted her to the Mass and at dinner, but it was Francisco Ordoñez who had the privilege of the first dance before turning her over to be squired about by other young men. The dancing and feasting and drinking continued until dawn.

"That was some party," Devlin commented as he and Jaime watched the sun peek over Santa Fe Baldy.

"Maybe we should wait until tomorrow to start into the mountains," Jaime said.

Devlin grinned. "Yeah. We said 'the next day' right? That will be tomorrow." After a moment, he added, "I didn't mean to step on any toes when I danced with Espe."

"She didn't complain."

"I didn't step on her!" Devlin laughed. "I meant figuratively. I think I was supposed to wait for all the family men to have a dance first."

"You are family. Besides, she's had a crush on you since you rescued her from the big, mean shopkeeper."

"I wish people would quit bringing that up! It was embarrassing. Besides, I'm way older than her."

"She's officially an adult today. Anyway, you're not that old are you? Or are you? Sometimes you seem as young as Espe is."

"I have been accused of being naive," Devlin said. "That's like *'inocente.'* It has been a few years though."

"So, how old are you?"

"I never did know. Something between twenty-four and twenty-seven, I suppose. A friend of mine made up a birthday for me once: January first. By her reckoning, I guess, I am twenty-six." Devlin sighed. "I feel old though. The last two years alone seem like a lifetime. I've had at least three different lives already and I'm starting on a fourth now. That's old, even for a young man."

"Maybe you're part cat, and you still have six lives to go."

Devlin laughed. "I don't know if that is a good thing or a bad thing!"

Jaime slapped him on the shoulder and stood up, and they started clearing away the party mess. Other hands helped also, but it still took half a day to gather up and dispose of the torn paper lanterns, dying flowers and now-dirty ribbons, stack the boards, gather and wash the dishes and redistribute them to the people who had loaned them for the party. They spent the afternoon preparing their pack saddles and checking their supplies, and though they intended to go to bed early and get an early start in the morning, they ended up sitting up with Jaime's father, Tia Dolores and Benito and Esperanza, talking long into the night.

Sangre de Cristo Mountains, New Spain (Mexico), April to October, 1846

April 22, they finally left around mid-morning. Jaime rode his pinto. Devlin now had a big dun gelding he had bought over the winter but was still using the Army saddle they had captured from the Indians.

The snow was still deep in the high country, but they traveled upwards following the snowmelt as the summer progressed, panning their way up creeks and streams.

"There's not much here," Jaime said. "But you need the practice!"

Jaime guided them around one peak, down into a deep valley, and up another line of peaks, and they began to get more color as they panned, working their way upstream and up a mountain side.

As summer came on, Devlin understood why Jaime had said before that this country was worth the hardships of living in it. He had seen Scottish moors, the ocean, southern cotton fields and rice paddies, the thick timberland of the upper southern states, huge rivers, and broad plains. But he had never seen anything like these mountains. The climate of the mountains, once the snow began to fade, was cooler than the lowlands, but it was lush and green as well. The grass was belly-deep on their horses, the springs plentiful, and the aspen trees sang with the softest breeze that blew through their leaves. The evergreen forests were dark and cool and, when the summer heated up, rich with the scent of pine. They came upon deer and elk, bear and bobcats, and once discovered a sated and lazy mountain lion looking down on their work with sleepy interest. Beaver dammed the streams and made pools full of trout, and eagles soared high above the valleys, but below from where they watched from the heights. Beautiful, but wild and untamed as well. The storms were violent, with thunder that echoed deafeningly through the mountains and lightning striking so often and so close it caused their hair to stand on end and exploded trees near them more than once. It would not be an easy place to live. The growing season was short, the winters long, but Devlin had already decided he would like to set down roots right here, somewhere in these high mountain valleys. He could buy some land, he was sure of that already with just the dust they had panned out of the creeks. Around mid-July they were standing near the crest of a long ridge of mountains where they discovered what looked like more mounds of snow. It was, in fact, deposits of quartz rock, laid bare of dirt by the violent weather of the high country, and Jaime was certain there would be veins of gold running through some of it. They had brought with them, among other things, a small amount of dynamite. Because of his experience in the prison work camp, Devlin knew how to drill holes to place the dynamite, and how to break up the shattered rock it produced. Between the placer gold they had panned, and the veins in the quartz, they weren't rich, but once they took it down to assay offices or banks, they would definitely be very well off. Despite Indian raids, prairie fire and other hardships, Devlin had thought his trip down the Santa Fe Trail was the best time of his life. This summer topped it by a mile.

Santa Fe, New Mexico Territory, October 1846

Summer was short. By late August, the leaves of the aspens were starting to turn gold, and their trunks faded from dark green-brown to silver. Then one morning they awoke to find a light snow had fallen during the night. They shook it off their bedrolls and started packing up their camp. They were in no hurry to get back, however. Doing more gold panning on the way, they followed a different gold, the gold leaves of the aspens, down the mountain, as autumn came earlier in the high country than down below. By the time they followed the Santa Fe watershed down to the village, the cottonwoods in the river valley echoed the gold colors of the aspens up high. They laughed together often as they were coming back successful from a restful, soul-healing summer.

It was late in the afternoon when they reached the outskirts of Santa Fe and headed west towards Jaime's home. Their high spirits faded as they noticed something seemed to be wrong in the village. People hurried from place to place instead of lingering and talking with friends, and there were American soldiers everywhere.

"They come in with the wagon trains," Jaime reminded Devlin.

Devlin nodded. "But why is there an American flag flying over the Palace of the Governor?"

"Come on," Jaime said, and they increased their pace through town. When they reached the back lane where the Ordoñez house was, it was nearly dark, but they smelled no smoke and saw no welcoming light in the windows. Jaime jumped off his horse at once and ran to the door, while Devlin followed more slowly, tying the animals to the posts out in front of the house before ducking through the front door himself. He could hear Jaime calling, his voice echoing through the empty rooms.

"Papá! Espe! FATHER!"

The house was built in a typical southwestern style, a square of rooms surrounding a center courtyard. In the summer, the courtyard was a pleasant place to sit in the hot afternoons, but with winter coming on, it was empty of furniture and full of leaves. But as his eyes adjusted to the gloom, Devlin saw it was not the only thing that was empty. Much of the fine furniture, imported from New Orleans and Mexico, was gone. The only rugs on the floors were the rough, locally woven ones meant to clean mud off shoes, not the more expensive, decorative ones. Candelabras were missing. The pantry in the kitchen was empty. And Jaime was still running from room to room, calling his father's and his sister's names.

"Jaime!" Devlin said sharply, grabbing his arm.

"Where are they? Dev, where can they be?"

Devlin knew what was in his mind: cholera, which had taken his mother and younger siblings. Typhoid and smallpox and other diseases that were always rampant here.

"Let's go to Tia Dolores. She'll know," Devlin said as calmly as he could. They went back out, closing and latching the door firmly behind them, and rode through the warren of streets to another house, this one built without the center courtyard, and with the thorny vines of summer roses around the front door. There were lights here, smoke from the chimneys. They tied their horses and knocked on the door. But it was opened by a stranger, a white man wearing military boots and trousers, but with his jacket discarded for comfort.

"What do you want?" he demanded.

"Where are they?" Jaime shouted. "What did you do with them?"

"I don't speak Mex," the man said, and he started to close the door.

Devlin forced Jaime behind him and removed his hat.

"Excuse me, sir," he said in his best aristocratic English. "We were looking for the *curandera*, the woman who lived here. Where can we find her?"

"She was a witch, huh?" the man said, scratching at his beard. He shrugged. "I got no idea where she is."

"May I inquire as to how you came into possession of this house?"

"It was deserted, so by law, we're allowed to move in," the man said. "You got a problem with that?"

"No," Devlin said. He gave a half bow and backed Jaime away from the door.

"Shut up!" he hissed as Jaime started to protest. The man was armed. Devlin had noticed how he kept one hand out of sight behind the door while he talked. Devlin half dragged Jaime away and shoved him up onto his horse. He climbed onto his own horse, and they rode off, still leading the pack mule.

"Think!" Devlin said. "What other relatives do you have in town?"

"Um," Jaime said, his mind obviously not clear enough to think. "Um, Florencio. Pancho…"

"Where would Tia Dolores most likely go?"

Jaime managed to pull a name out of the muddle of his thoughts finally. "Doña Isabel. Yes! Isabel Gallegos."

"Lead," Devlin said, and they crossed town again, winding along Canyon Road to a house with a large yard, enclosed by a tall adobe fence. They left the horses in the street and went in through the front gate to knock on the door of the house.

Isabel Gallegos was a half-sister of Tia Dolores, not related to Jaime directly, but like family. Her husband Eduardo answered their knock.

"Where have you been?" he demanded.

"Up in the mountains. What is happening here? Where are Father and Espe and Tia Dolores?"

Eduardo didn't answer immediately. Instead, he said, "Do you have horses?"

"Yes. Out on the road."

"Bring them in. We can put them in the tool shed to get them out of sight. Hurry!"

They went back for the horses to bring them through the narrow walk gate. The packs had to be taken off the mule for it to get through the opening, but they got everything inside and threw the packs back on to lead the three animals around to the back of the house. The Santa Fe River was just outside the walls of the yard, so there were big cottonwood trees inside and outside the fence. They provided protection from prying eyes while the horses were unloaded, brushed down and watered. Hay was tossed onto the floor of a tool shed, and all three animals were crowded in there.

"What are you carrying?" Eduardo asked, trying to heft one of the paniers from the pack saddle.

"Gold," Jaime said.

"Ask a silly question," Eduardo murmured.

Devlin took one of the paniers, Jaime dragged the other into the

144

kitchen. The room was lighted and hot, but the shutters were all latched against the cool night air, and Eduardo closed the door quickly. There were two women in the room, Tia Dolores Devlin recognized. The other was introduced to him as Doña Isabel. Tia hugged them both. Isabel hugged Jaime and gave Devlin a smile.

"Give them some dinner," Eduardo said.

"Give us some answers," Jaime said.

"Eat," Eduardo said. "And we'll talk."

Plates of hot food were served up, and although they had evidently already had dinner, Eduardo and the two women sat at the table also with cups of coffee and buttered fried bread.

"I'm sure you heard the rumors even before you left," Eduardo said. "There was some fighting down near Matamoros on April twenty-fifth…"

"We left the twenty-second," Jaime said.

"Oh. Well, from what I understand, some Americans marched into Mexico, down near Matamoros, claiming it was 'disputed territory,' and actually belonged to Texas. They were captured. A few of them were killed, and the American president called for troops to fight a war that we had started! A general named Kearney left Missouri around June something, came down the trail to Santa Fe. Governor Armijo called for troops to fortify Apache Canyon…"

"You could hold off a whole army from there!" Jaime said. "What happened?"

"Armijo sent about five thousand men out, and waited for another two hundred trained soldiers, and when he got there with them, it was all over. No one was defending the pass!"

"Why not?"

"Confusion. Lies. I don't know. The captain in charge said most of the men just went home. Some of the men said they were ordered to leave, I heard others say that Armijo turned the canon around to point at our own men and said he would open fire if they tried to fight."

"I thought, he wasn't there," Devlin interrupted.

"Orders sent ahead? I don't know. Anyway, this Kearney acted like he was liberating us from something. He sent out letters saying how friendly his troops were. He even marched in a procession the church was having for the Blessed Virgin."

145

"If only he knew we were praying to get rid of him!" Isabel said.

Eduardo patted her hand on the table. "Anyway. It was about the eighteenth of August he came marching into town. But he had all these civilians with him. Mormon settlers getting out of Missouri, hundreds of them. They came in first, and the army followed. We didn't really know what was going on. You know the American Army sometimes escorts settlers coming through on the Trail to California."

Devlin and Jaime nodded.

"But then he put up the American flag, said he was in charge of all of New Mexico. And he wrote out these new laws, a hundred pages of rules we had to follow! And the punishments for anyone who didn't obey. Lashings, hangings! Who can follow a hundred pages of new laws?"

"Was one of them that women can't own property?" Devlin asked.

"Yes. How did you know?"

"My father-in-law worked in real estate law. That's a big rule back east but it's one of the things I always admired about Mexico. You treat women as if they were real people. They tend to treat them like property."

"What can you expect from people who won't outlaw owning slaves?" Eduardo said.

"Where is Tio Benito?" Jaime asked suddenly.

"He died, *'jito*," Tia said. "Remember, he was sick even before Easter last spring. That is why I was thrown out of my house. I was not allowed to own it for myself. Fortunately, Isabel lets me stay here…"

"This house is yours forever," Isabel said.

"At least until I die," Eduardo said glumly. "How do we provide for our families with laws like that? I have two daughters. How do I provide for them if I can't leave them this property?"

"And no one has murdered this Kearney yet?" Jaime asked angrily.

"Oh, I think he knew which way the wind was blowing early on. He took off before anyone got organized enough to kill him, with most of his Mormons, I think. But he left George Bent in charge as governor."

"Bent? From that fort on the Santa Fe Trail?" Jaime asked.

"That's the one. He and his pal DeVries have been cheating people for years, now they have the law on their side to help them. He's staying away from most of the anger, up in Taos. I'll bet," Eduardo added, " he's got some nice Mexican and French furniture in his new house – thanks to your father! Your house was pretty well stripped last time I saw it."

"Where are they?" Jaime asked, quietly. It was not lost on either him or Devlin that that was one set of answers that had not been volunteered. The three older people around the table looked at each other.

"Tia," Jaime demanded. "Where are they? What happened?"

"Esperanza was raped," Tia said finally. "They came out to the house and found her alone…"

"They," Jaime noted, grimacing in pain.

"Five American soldiers," Tia said as gently as she could.

"According to Kearney's laws, rape is punishable by castration," Eduardo said. "But apparently, that's only if a Mexican gets caught raping one of their women — which they didn't bring with them anyway! There doesn't seem to be any punishment for Americans raping Mexican women. It has happened too many times since they got here."

"And Father?"

"He couldn't get them all," Eduardo said. "But he killed two of them. He scalped them while he was at it — one of them before he was dead."

"Good for him," Jaime murmured.

"He got caught, though."

"I don't suppose he's in jail?" Devlin asked softly.

"They hung him immediately…"

"But left his body to rot in the gallows as a warning to others?" Devlin guessed.

"Not very civilized, are they, for people who want to come out here and 'civilize' us!"

"Is Espe here, with you?" Jaime asked.

"No," Eduardo said. He glanced at the women. "We have to tell him."

"Tell me what?"

"Some of the soldiers did get in some trouble for raping women, I think," Tia said. "Not much. They were just told to use prostitutes instead. So, they gathered up a bunch of women and opened a whorehouse. Apparently forcing oneself upon a woman is legal if you give a dollar to some strange man at the door for her trouble."

The dinner had gone cold on Jaime's and Devlin's plates anyway. Now Jaime put his elbows on the table and his head in his hands.

"We were having such a good time," he murmured. "And while we were enjoying ourselves..."

Tia came around the table to wrap her arms around him. "If you had been here, you would be dead too," she said.

"I think I would prefer that."

"No. God kept you away for a reason. So you can save her."

"It's too late..."

"No! No, you can get her out of there! The two of you," she added, looking at Devlin.

Eduardo reached across the table and grabbed Devlin's hand as he started to stand up.

"Not right now! You need to rest your horses. We need another horse for Esperanza. And a plan. You won't be able to stay here once you get her free. They'll just track her down and take her back, probably kill you in the process."

"Where would we go?" Devlin asked.

"Missouri?" Jaime guessed, thinking of the Santa Fe Trail.

"No," Eduardo said. "And I wouldn't go south right now. I think there's a lot of fighting down there."

"Alta California!" Tia said suddenly. "Our family is here, 'jito, but your mother's family comes from up... northeast, I think, of Yerba Buena! On the San Francisco Bay."

"I thought they all died."

"Your uncles. But your grandfather is still alive, I'm sure. Your father got a letter from him in April. He sent a gift for Esperanza's *quinceañera*."

"That's right," Eduardo said. "A silver hair comb, with *la vigen* carved on it."

"Alta California," Jaime sighed. "*Northern* Alta California. That's only about twice as far as Missouri."

"If anyone asks," Devlin said suddenly, "tell them we are going to Missouri. In fact, spread the word. Tell them Jaime knows the trail well, speaks English well. That is where he would go!"

"But that doesn't even make...Oh," Jaime said. "You think they'll fall for it?"

"We can only hope. How soon can we get Esperanza and go? Midnight?"

"Tomorrow evening," Eduardo said.

"That's too long!" Jaime objected.

"You need supplies. You need another horse for Espe. Your horses need rest if you are going to go fast tomorrow. Nighttime makes good cover, especially now when the moon is almost gone. But, if you wait until night, there will be... um... customers. Early evening should be the best time to go in there, and you will have the cover of darkness after you leave."

"What are we supposed to do in the meantime?" Jaime demanded.

"Try not to go crazy," Devlin said. "And that won't be easy. For either of us."

Santa Fe New Mexico Territory, October 29, 1946

They emptied and repacked their paniers. They no longer needed the picks and sledgehammers, but they kept one small shovel. That lightened the load somewhat, although they kept the rocks they had collected, with the veins of gold in them.

"Not bad," Eduardo said, examining them. "I would buy them from you, save you the weight, but I would probably be murdered in my home if I tried to cash it in somewhere."

"Trade one for the horse you are getting," Devlin said, but Eduardo shook his head.

"Done deal. Don't worry about it. I'm sending her Isabel's saddle. Isabel is much taller, but you can shorten the stirrups."

"She rode my horse once on the trail," Devlin said, "by tucking her feet into the stirrup straps."

Eduardo chuckled softly. "Barefoot, no doubt! That girl…" His voice trailed off, though.

Isabel and Tia made stacks of tortillas. The flat bread traveled well and wrapped in damp cloths would stay fresh for days. They packed flour and coffee, lard, salt, butter and beans, and anything else they could think of. Tia had rescued some of Esperanza's clothing from their abandoned house before it had been completely stripped by looters, and she packed that, and made a good warm bedroll for the girl. Devlin and Jaime tried to rest as much of the day as they could, but they only fell asleep after lunch from sheer exhaustion. As the sun lowered towards the Jemez mountains in the west, Eduardo shook them awake.

"You be careful," he told them. "You have a plan?"

"Part of one," Devlin said.

"I suppose that is better than nothing. She may not be my actual niece, but she is a special child. You two take care of her."

"We will," Devlin promised. Tia touched his arm and held him back a moment while Eduardo and Jaime got all four animals out of the yard through a back gate.

"Take this," she said, handing him a small paper-wrapped packet.

"What is it?"

"It's an herbal tea. It will help her. Boil water, steep it for five minutes." She handed him another bundle also and showed him it had a sewing kit – nicer and cleaner than the one they had carried in the mountains all summer – and a few medicinal herbs. He thanked her, took the liberty of giving her a warm hug, and left, tucking the packets into his saddlebag as he caught up with Jaime outside the fence. They were right on the bank of the river, which compared to the Mississippi and the Missouri was barely more than a narrow creek. Jaime leading the extra saddle horse, Devlin leading the pack mule, they dropped down into the shallow water and followed it towards the business area of town. Devlin had gone out that morning with Eduardo so he knew which building it was. While most of the town was single-story adobe, this building was two-stories tall and built of wood, practically in the yard of the largest saloon in town, a place that had always catered more to the *gringos* who came down the Trail than to the local people. The building was about a block from the river. They tied their animals in the shadows of the cottonwood trees on the riverbank and walked the rest of the way. Dusk was settling, and except for a few squares of lamplight from open windows, the streets were dark: no streetlamps here, like the ones Devlin had known in Charleston. He reached into the pocket of his leather jacket and pulled out the small partial stick of dynamite they had left over from their prospecting.

"You know what to do," he said to Jaime.

"Tell me again why I am the distraction, and you get to go inside."

"Because I look more like a customer. And I am slightly," he held his thumb and forefinger apart, but so close they were almost touching, "less likely to kill someone than you."

Jaime gave him a ghost of a grin, and took the dynamite, a bit of fuse and two thin narrow strips of wood.

With a nod to each other, they parted company.

It was too easy, Devlin thought, for him to get inside the front door. The man sitting there in a chair only cared that he had the right amount of money, in American dollars, and let him go upstairs on his own. But what next? He opened the first door and found a young lady, probably no older than Esperanza herself, sitting in a chair, half-dressed. She stood and started to take off her chemise.

"I'm looking for Esperanza Ordoñez," he said.

"She's busy," the girl said.

"Where?" Devlin asked in a low, but hard voice.

"Two doors," the girl said.

He started to close the door, then he looked at her and said, "there may be a bit of confusion in a few minutes. If anyone wanted to walk out of here, that would be the time."

She stared at him without speaking, her dark eyes wide. But he noticed as he closed the door, that she was reaching for a dress.

Devlin skipped the next door, and softly turned the handle and pushed open the second one. There was a man standing there, his back to the door. His shirt was on, but his backside was bare, and he was reaching to unlace his belt from the trousers that were on the chair beside him.

"Stop that racket! You'll enjoy this if you know what's good for you!"

Devlin grabbed him by the shoulder and spun him into a fist. The man went down as if he were dead, and Devlin found himself fingering the tomahawk he still wore on his belt. But he remembered why he was here, not Jaime: a runaway prostitute would upset them, maybe, but a murdered man would have the whole American Army down on them. He gave the man a couple good kicks while he was down though. One in the ribs that would make breathing hurt for days, and another one that would guarantee he would not be bothering young ladies for maybe a whole week. Then he looked at the bed and looked away again quickly. She also had a thin, white garment on, but it was shoved up to her neck. He folded the blankets around her and called her name softly.

"Espe? Esperanza, it's me. Dev. I've got you!"

There was no response. She was breathing, he could feel her chest rise and fall through the blankets, but her eyes were squeezed shut. Tears leaked out of them, and her breath was ragged, like sobs.

"I got you," he said again, and he scooped her up, blankets and all. The man on the floor was starting to move. Devlin kicked him again and stepped on his hand on the way out. When he stepped into the hallway, he heard the bang. It was bigger than he had expected, probably because the blast was not buried in rocks, but was wide open. In his arms, Esperanza whimpered at the sound. He clutched her tighter and ran down the stairs, relieved to find the man at the front door was gone, out in the street with all the other men on this part of town, looking to see what was happening. Jaime had done well. The dynamite had gone off near a group of tethered horses, and they were all kicking and fighting to escape. Several did, and at the same time, a fire sparked in some rubbish left on the village square. Devlin turned the opposite way and ran with Esperanza in his arms back to the river. Jaime was there waiting.

"Espe!"

"She can't ride," Devlin said. He handed the bundle to Jaime and swung up on his horse, then leaned down to take her from Jaime's arms.

"It's us," Jaime whispered to her. "You'll be all right!" And he passed her up to Devlin, who had the bigger horse and the stronger arms. Jaime swung onto his own horse, grabbed the two lead ropes, and they headed off downstream, the horses splashing through the rocky bed of the river rather than threading their way through the underbrush on its banks. In the town, the shouting and noise began to die away. Eventually, they hit the Camino Real, little more than a wagon road, despite its fancy name. They galloped for about ten minutes, rested the horses by walking them for twenty, and galloped again. Around midnight, they stopped for a longer rest. Esperanza lay on the ground, wrapped in her blanket, silent, while Jaime and Devlin lengthened the stirrups on the spare horse. They were still short for Devlin, but he climbed up and took Esperanza in his arms again.

"Is she sleeping?" Jaime asked.

Her eyes were closed, but they were closed too tightly. Devlin shook his head. With a fresher horse, they were able to gallop for a few minutes every hour or so. Twice more Devlin traded mounts. Shortly after dawn, they left the road and went down to the banks of the Rio Bravo[2], traveling along it until they found a place shaded by cottonwoods, with a shallow, sandy bank leading into the water. Devlin gently set Esperanza on the ground, sitting her up, leaning against the bole of a big tree. She let the blanket slip, and he pulled it up again, as the thin material over her breasts

---

[2] Americans call it the Rio Grande.

153

did nothing to hide them. She did not speak to him, or even acknowledge that he was there. After trying to get her to talk, he walked back to where Jaime was tending the horses.

"How is she?" Jaime asked.

Devlin shook his head. "Not good. I don't know. Some form of shock, I guess." He sighed, stripping his own saddle off his horse, letting it loose to drink and roll in the grass. "She's... been beaten, I think. She's lost a lot of weight."

"I noticed when I lifted her," Jaime said. He glanced over to the tree, but Esperanza just sat there, staring at the water. "When we get to Albuquerque, maybe we can find a doctor or something."

"Why are we going south?" Devlin asked. "I thought this place we're heading is northwest."

"Yeah. But we'll never get across the mountains this time of year. Eduardo suggested we go down to the Mojave. We'll still have to cross mountains, but he thought it might be easier. Then we can follow the coast north. There's a whole string of Spanish missions there. Better than spending all our time in the wilderness. What are you doing?"

"Getting the blankets Tia packed for her. That one she has on stinks of... Well, I don't think it's helping her any."

"Good thought."

She didn't seem to care when he tried to trade her blankets. At first she just sat there, immobile. But then she stood and stripped off the filthy one and let him wrap her in the clean one. She sat down again. Closed her eyes.

"Tia packed some clothes for you, too," Devlin said. "But, well, you just rest for now. We'll worry about that later."

He went back to where Jaime was setting up camp, finished dealing with the stock while Jaime kindled a small fire that would not put out much smoke.

"Coffee?"

"I'm done in," Devlin said. "I just want to sleep."

He untied their bedding from behind their saddles and laid it out in the soft grass under the trees. He had a slicker and another blanket that was part of Esperanza's bedroll, and he glanced over towards her again, wondering if he should put her to sleep closer to them. She wasn't there. Something in his movement alerted Jaime. He stood also and stared. The blanket was there, but Esperanza was not. At the same moment, they noticed the bubbles in the river. Without pause, they both ran into the water. It was not deep, maybe waist-high on Devlin. He bent and felt in the water, while Jaime dove in. They found her almost at once, and both of them hauling on her arms got her up out of the water and onto the land. Devlin did not know if she was breathing, but Jaime grabbed her around the chest and squeezed. Muddy water and air shot out of her mouth, and he realized she had been holding her breath. She gasped, choked, and started sobbing. Devlin ran for the blanket, and they covered her nakedness again, laid her down on the bedroll Devlin had put out for himself, and each of them, still wet and cold themselves, laid down on either side of her. Ideally, to warm a person one stripped out of their wet clothes and huddled together under a blanket. But they both knew that would not be a good idea considering Esperanza's state of health and mind at the moment. The breeze was chilly, though. Devlin got up, put a thick blanket over both Jaime and Esperanza. He pulled a small cook pot out of their gear and got some water from the river to heat over the little fire. He pulled off his soggy boots and clothes, laid them out to dry in the sun and dressed in his spare clothes. The water boiled. He steeped Tia's special herbs in it and sat Esperanza up enough to get her to drink it down. She choked at first, sobbing making it hard to swallow. But with his gentle talk and insistence, she finally drank down the entire cup. While Devlin force fed her, Jaime got up and changed also. Then, grabbing the blankets of his own bedroll, he snuggled down by Esperanza again, spreading out the blankets to catch all three of them. Devlin crawled under on Esperanza's other side, feeling her shivers slowly begin to subside. It wasn't long before all three of them were asleep.

II

No one felt much like eating, but Devlin boiled some jerky, added salt and torn bits of tortilla to it, and they all three drank down the broth it made. That whetted Devlin's appetite, and he ate the softened jerky and a tortilla, sharing them out. Jaime had some and added butter to his tortilla. Esperanza refused all offers of food other than the broth, but Jaime did convince her to have a few bites of his tortilla. She did not seem to be feeling well. She clutched at her stomach and almost threw up the broth. But then she calmed down a bit. She still wasn't interested in moving much, and as neither of the men felt comfortable stripping her down and dressing her again, they just wrapped her in her blanket. When they were ready to leave, shortly after sundown, Devlin carried her in his arms again. She was not as still and silent as the night before, however. She moaned often, shifted uncomfortably so it was hard to hold onto her. Moving his hands to get a better grip, Devlin realized the one that had been under her was wet. It was dark, but wetness was thick and had a strong, vaguely familiar odor.

"Jaime, there's something wrong," he said. When Jaime rode closer, he held out his hand to show him.

Jaime looked away, embarrassed. "That happens with girls," he said. "It's normal."

"No. This is not normal," Devlin said.

"How would you know?" Jaime snapped. "How many sisters do you have?"

"How many *wives* do you have?" Devlin snapped back. "I'm telling you, I have lived much more intimately with a woman than you have, and this is not normal. In fact, it smells…"

"What?"

"More like… afterbirth. But that's not possible."

Jaime jumped down from his horse and tore open Devlin's saddle bags. "What did you give her?" he demanded.

"That herbal tea Tia sent. She said it would help…" Calm her nerves, he had assumed. That's why he had given it to her after she tried to drown herself. But Jaime found the packet and smelled it.

"What is it?" Devlin asked.

Jaime sighed heavily. "When grass is scarce," he said, "the cows will eat the needles off the pine trees, just to get something green. But it makes them lose their calves. I've heard that some women know which pine needles can do that for them as well." He looked up at Devlin, agony in every line of his face. "She's pregnant. Tia gave her something to make her miscarry."

"Holy Jesus," Devlin breathed. "What do we do?"

"We get her to a woman as fast as we can. Preferably a *curandera*."

"Tia?"

"No. We're more than halfway to Albuquerque." Jaime considered.

156

"You take both the big horses. Push them as hard as you and they can stand it. If I can't keep up dragging this pack mule, don't worry about it. I'll find you eventually. You stop at the first house you come to and ask for help. Someone will know what to do, or who to reach."

"How far?"

"It's sixty miles from Santa Fe, so I'm guessing... twenty-five, maybe less from here. We did good last night."

"That's still more than a whole day!"

"With a mule train," Jaime agreed. "You can do way better than that on horseback. Trade horses now. Then go."

He may have missed a ranch house or two, tucked away from the road in the dark. The sky was getting lighter, though sunrise was still some time off, when he found a large adobe house near the road. There were already lights on inside. It was awkward, getting down without dropping Esperanza, but he managed it, carried her to the front door and kicked it, since both his hands were full.

"Closed for the night," someone called from inside. In English.

Devlin answered in kind. "Please, we need help! There's a girl. She's..." He wasn't sure how to describe her condition quickly. "She needs help. A healer! Please!"

The door opened, and a woman of about thirty-five stood there. She had pale brown hair, pinned up untidily and wore a simple skirt and blouse. She looked over Devlin and his bundle, and Devlin showed her his hand.

"I think it's... a miscarriage?"

"Bring her in," the woman said, opening the door wider. He entered into a large, comfortable room with many couches and chairs. He had the brief impression that there had been a party last night that no one had cleaned up after yet as there were empty and half-empty glasses scattered about the room, and a few plates with crumbs on them. He followed the woman through to a hallway and down that into a small bedroom. She lit a lamp while he laid Esperanza down on the bed.

"You go on now," the woman said.

He'd heard that before, or similar things. "I should stay."

"You should not! Go take care of your horses, they look sweated. There's a stable around back where you can take them. She's in good hands," the woman added more softly when he hesitated. "You couldn't have found a better place to bring her. We know what to do."

When he stepped back into the hallway, he saw other bedroom doors were open, heads peeking out. All female. Another woman was cleaning up in the main room when he went back through, and a third was heading through an open doorway into a large kitchen to start stoking the fires. He went out to where he had left the horses, reins dragging on the ground, but both of them were too tired to run off. Esperanza's mare hesitated when he tugged on the reins, but then they both followed him around the big house to the yard behind. There was a chicken pen, and a milk cow in a small enclosure, and the promised stable. It was a large building with many stalls, a full hay loft, and all the usual equipment for horses. But there were no horses, though some of the stalls had fresh droppings in them. He didn't want to think about what that meant right now. He led each horse into a different stall and unsaddled them, hanging the saddles and tack on the doors of stalls across the way. He gave each of them a quick brushing, then rubbed them down more thoroughly, working blood back into their tired muscles. He climbed into the hayloft and forked down straw for their bedding and hay into their mangers, then went outside to bring buckets of water from the well. The sun was over the mountains then, and since direct light was coming into the stable, he was able to give the horses a quick check, making sure they had no sores or bruises, checking their feet. Then he went outside again. After a moment's hesitation, he went to the back door of the big house and knocked. When the door opened this time, it opened only far enough to accommodate the barrel of a rifle that was shoved into his belly.

"What did you do to this little girl?"

Devlin automatically raised his hands. He knew there was no use asking for them to listen, so he just started talking, from the beginning.

"Her brother – he's coming behind me – he and I were prospecting up in the Sangre de Cristos all summer. We just came down a few days ago, and when we got to his house…" He talked fast, covering everything from finding the house deserted and ransacked to the herbal tea Tia Dolores had given him for her, and his hard ride last night. The gun barrel lowered. The door opened wider.

"That story seems to match up to her injuries. Come on in. Have some breakfast."

He stepped inside.

"Your name?" It was the same woman who had let him in earlier.

"Devlin," he said.

"Angela," she said. "This is Pilar." She indicated the younger woman who was working over the stove.

"Maybe we can ask the gentleman to haul some water," Pilar suggested. "We're going to have a lot of washing up to do."

"Good idea," Angela said. "Why don't you do that while we fix you something to eat."

"You don't have to…"

"You'll have earned it. You can fill that big tub there. We use it as a sort of reservoir."

There was a large copper tub in the corner of the room.

Devlin nodded but hesitated before leaving again. "How is Esperanza?"

"Is that her name? How pretty. She's fine. You men worry too much. She was uncomfortable for a while tonight, I'm sure. That tea gave her something like labor pains. But she's sleeping now. Don't worry about her."

He did worry. But he went out to the well and started hauling buckets of water. It took a lot of two-gallon buckets to fill what must have been at least a forty-gallon tub. He was almost done when Jaime found him. He introduced Jaime to Angela, and Angela sent Jaime out to care for his horse and the pack mule. Once he finished hauling the water, Devlin helped him in the stable, then they both went inside to find fried eggs, ham and potatoes waiting for them, with, of course, red chile on the side.

Angela sat down with them at the table with a cup of coffee.

"This is, shall we say, a place of business, isn't it?" Jaime asked. "I'm not so sure this is the best place for Espe to wake up in right now."

"The business has nothing to do with her," Angela said. "She'll be fine. And this isn't like the place you took her from. No one was raped and kidnapped into this house."

"Do you mind if I ask…" Jaime said, but he didn't actually ask.

"Three of us are widows," Angela said. "One girl lost her family to an Indian raid, the other was an orphan. We run this farm, but a little extra income on the side is very helpful. This is more of a private club than what you are thinking. We have our steady customers, whom we entertain. Strangers are not welcome. You still do not approve," she added, looking

159

at Devlin.

"He's a bit of a prude," Jaime grinned. "It's that aristocratic upbringing."

"Aristocrats are our best customers," Angela said, grinning herself as Devlin's face grew red. "Anyway," she looked at both of them. "Some of the women here have used something like that tea before. As I was telling your friend, it isn't quite as bad as you thought. She could use a day or two of rest, though. Where are you headed?"

"California," Jaime told her.

"Will she be able to ride?" Devlin asked.

"She did not give birth," Angela said. "True, she lost a child, but it was so small at this stage it was just part of the expelled tissue. What happened was more like a heavy monthly cycle than childbirth. So, there is no damage and no problem with going on almost as if nothing has happened. Now, she does have some bruising from other use. And there are bruises from being hit, with fists, I'd say. And she was lashed at least once by what looks like a leather belt. That is bad, but it is not serious damage. No tears, no broken bones, no internal damage. She may be uncomfortable for a week or so, but it will not stop you from continuing your journey."

The two men looked at each other across the table, both of them repulsed by the thoughts her words brought up. Devlin shuddered and looked down at his plate with a sudden loss of appetite.

"Has she spoken to you?" Jaime asked.

"No. Why?"

"She hasn't said a word since we found her."

"That wasn't so long ago. Give her time. Give her lots of time."

They did finish their breakfasts, and at Angela's suggestion, laid down on their bedrolls in the hayloft for a rest since they had been up all night. When he awoke in mid-afternoon, Devlin saw Esperanza's shift and blanket flapping on the clothesline, along with a number of sheets and towels. He knocked on the door to see if he could help with anything, and a young woman who identified herself just as Jane suggested that they might want to move their horses down to the river to graze, as a few visitors were expected for the evening. The next day, they left Esperanza with the women and took the pack mule into town. Neither of them had ever dealt with gold before, but they found an assay office, where they were told their rocks were indeed valuable, and a banker who was willing to buy them and take them to be processed later, along with a small shipment of other gold. They kept the bags of gold dust they each had but getting rid of the rocks lightened their packs considerably, and they used the extra space to purchase a few more supplies and a pretty cloak and boots for Esperanza.

"But now we have all this to deal with," Devlin said, indicating the bag of silver and gold coins, they now carried.

"Trick I learned on the Trail," Jaime said. He had gotten hold of some rawhide while they were in town. Now he cut it into four squares. He punched holes in the edges using an awl they found in the stable and laced two of the squares together on three sides, then the other two, making the four squares into two pillows. He divided the coins into two equal piles and stuffed one pile into each of the pillows, then stitched them shut. Once they were sealed, he dropped them into a bucket of water to soak through. When the uncured leather was completely soaked, he set the bags in the sun to dry. When they did leave, two days later, the rawhide had shrunk down tight around the money so there was no jingling at all to alert anyone of what they carried. They each stuffed one of the pillows in a saddlebag.

"If anything happens to me," Jaime said. "You take it all. I know you'll take care of Esperanza."

"Same with me," Devlin said, and they shook on it.

III

"Here she is, all ready to travel," Angela said.

Jaime and Devlin both stepped down off their horses and went to the front door where Angela, Esperanza, and four other women were waiting for them. Esperanza was washed and dressed in one of her own calico skirts and a comfortable blouse. But, due to the oncoming winter, she was wearing shoes and stockings, a warm bonnet, and the thick cloak of blue wool they had bought for her in town. She still seemed to have nothing to say, didn't look anyone in the eye. When Jaime led her over to her horse, she just stood there, and Devlin lifted her bodily into the saddle.

"Thank you," Jaime said sincerely. "Please, what do we owe you?"

The women exchanged looks. "Fifteen cents," Angela said firmly.

"Fifteen cents!" Jaime repeated.

"For hair pins," Angela said. "It took most of our hair pains to get her braids pinned up. What lovely hair she has! I think all of us helped comb and braid it. I have never seen such hair!"

Devlin was reminded that her thick braids were one of the first things he had noticed about her. On the Trail, whenever the weather was warm and they were camped near sufficient water, Tia had insisted on all the women and children having baths, and he remembered Esperanza walking around camp with her hair loose afterwards, drying in the sun. It was thick, and so black it gleamed blue when the sun hit it, and it hung down past her knees.

"Are you sure that's all…?"

"Fifteen cents," Angela repeated, and after Jaime counted the coins into her hands, she added, "Take care of her. And of yourselves."

"*Muchas gracias*," Jaime said. "*Dios te pague*."

"*Tú tambien*."

Leaving Albuquerque, they traveled west and south, threading the needle between Navajo and Apache country, traveling more quickly than a wagon train, but still pausing to make sure the horses and themselves were rested and fed. For weeks, Esperanza moved like a ghost in the camp: silent, unresponsive. She ate when they handed her food, she slept when they laid out her bedroll and told her to lie down. Eventually, she started lifting herself into the saddle in the morning, but still that was about all, until they hit the Mojave.

The Indians there were friendly enough, though none of them spoke either English or Spanish. The women helped Esperanza wash her hair with yucca root to make it shine, and they tried to temp Devlin and Jaime with things they must have considered delicacies, though neither of the men cared to try bugs or lizards. They stayed with them for a few days, resting the horses, but Devlin was never comfortable. None of the Indians had seen hair the color of his before, and it was still long, hanging past his shoulders now. Every time he sat down to eat or to compare maps with the men, someone would come up behind him and run their fingers through it. Once, he awakened in the middle of the night because someone was playing with his hair. He quickly grew tired of it. As they were preparing to leave, several women came to touch his hair one last time. He took off his hat, pulled his hunting knife out of his belt, grabbed a handful of hair and, to gasps of dismay from the women, chopped it off. But the gasps of dismay turned to squeals of delight when he handed the lock to one of the women. He grabbed another bunch of hair and cut it, and another, and another, until all that was left on his head was a ragged, uneven crown of gold that looked more like a dying dandelion than hair. Jaime laughed delightedly. Devlin clapped his hat over the mess and turned to mount his horse, when he saw that Esperanza had a small smile curving her mouth upwards.

Two weeks later, when they had crossed the last of the mountains, Jaime managed to slash his arm while he was struggling to cut through the gristle on a piece of meat he intended to cook. Esperanza quickly took out the sewing kit and stitched up the gash. Jaime went back to cooking the meat that Devlin had finished cutting for him. Meantime, Esperanza looked at the tiny scissors in the sewing kit. She signaled to Devlin to come and sit on the log Jaime had just vacated, and when he did, she used the scissors to even out the ragged clumps of hair on his head. When she was finished, he stood up, brushing the hair off his shirt, and said, "Thank you."

"You are welcome," she said in return.

Jaime spun from where he had been sitting at the fire. He stared at her in open-mouthed amazement, then jumped up to grab her in a hug so tight, it was almost as if he were trying to get water out of her lungs again.

"You're going to be all right!" he whispered into her hair. "*Gracias, Madre de Dios*! You're going to be all right!"

Dos Lagos Ranch, Near Aguas Amargas, Alta California. February 15, 1847

The old man was suspicious when they first knocked on his door. He answered with a long rifle in his hand, squinting at them in the faint light of dusk. "Who did you say you are?" he demanded.

"Jaime Francisco Ordoñez y Valencia. This is my sister Esperanza Catalina. Our Father is Francisco Maria José Ordoñez y Barela. Our mother was Catalina Rosario…"

"Valencia y Gutierez," the old man finished for them, setting the rifle aside and reaching for Esperanza. "*Mi 'jita! Mi bonita hijita!* You look just like her! So pretty. And you! Such a man! Come in, come in! Bring your friend!"

They had been told when they asked in town to bypass the big house and look for Señor Valencia in a smaller house on a hill to the south. Coming in at dusk, they had seen the hulk of a big building, but nothing of the details.

"Mother said the family had lived here for almost a hundred years," Jaime told Devlin. "She said the house had rooms for grown children to live with their families, lots of space. I imagine it is too much, since *mi abuelo* is alone now."

The small house looked as if it had been built originally as a bunk house for hired hands. It was long and narrow, with a cook stove at one end, and a bedroom divided off the far end. But it was clean and comfortable, and after he hugged and fussed over the grandchildren he had never seen before, Señor Valencia let Devlin and Jaime care for their stock and unload their packs while he and Esperanza made a simple meal for them all. She had never spoken more than a few words on the trip. She had not started washing herself until Jaime threatened to do it for her, and she had never helped with the camp chores, cooking and cleaning up. But here, with this old man who was her closest living relative now, except for Jaime, she seemed to relax a small bit more. She made dough and fried *sopaipillas* while he found honey and coffee to go with them. When the young men came back, they sat on the floor while Esperanza sat on the footstool, and the old man sat in his single rocking chair, and he told them what had been happening while they were on the road. Kearney, now promoted to Brigadier General for his successful conquest of Santa Fe, had arrived several months before them. Even more interesting to Devlin was the fact that clear back in July, American warships had sailed into the major ports of California and declared the ports to be the property of the United States.

"We came here for nothing!" Esperanza wailed. "He got here before us! He will make the same laws here! He will destroy everything!"

"No, he won't," Jaime said, holding her hand to calm her.

"He's a monster!"

"You've never met him," Jaime said reasonably. "Espe! Calm down! He snuck into Santa Fe behind a train of immigrants. He came here openly, and the people have been fighting him! We have strong fighting men. He is thousands of miles from support." He patted her hand. "Okay?"

"I should have guessed this was happening," Devlin said.

"Why should *you* have guessed?"

"Because I know something about economics. Yes, America wanted more land, but the seaports would bring in a very lucrative trade from the Far East! Silks and tea and spice, bypassing the European traders! It makes much more sense than just grabbing New Mexico."

"The Texicans have been trying to grab all of New Mexico ever since they rebelled against the government a decade ago. They've invaded more than once, wiped out villages east of the mountains. Their big contingent got lost on the Staked Plains, though. Our military should have shot them for spies and traitors instead of sending them home to attack us again!"

"Kearney isn't from Texas," Devlin said. "Neither are those ships out on the coast. That's the United States government, not a few rebel slave holders. What I don't get is how they got here so fast."

"They had boats," Jaime said.

"Yes, boats off the coast of Mexico, perhaps, that could get up here in a few weeks. But, Eduardo said the Americans went into what they called 'disputed territory' on April 25th. How long would it take for a message to get all the way to the president of the United States that there had been blood spilled, for him to ask congress for troops, and for a message to get back to these ships, here on the western side of the continent, to tell them to go claim the ports?"

"Three, four months?" Jaime asked.

"It took us two and a half to get from the western part of the United States to Santa Fe…"

"With mule trains!"

"An army that doesn't travel with mule trains starves to death – like your Texicans out on the plains. Some time to get to Missouri, then two and a half months from there, three and a half to get to here – I know we didn't push it, but we didn't have mule trains either. That's six months at least, and that doesn't count getting a message from Mexico to Washington in the first place."

Jaime and his grandfather considered the timelines carefully.

"A messenger, with a fast horse…" Jaime said.

"Or a fast ship…" Señor Valencia said.

"I worked with commerce, remember? It takes seven months for a ship to get around the tip of South America and back up this side of the continent. The fast horse, maybe, but still… I think it's too tight. I think the orders were set up ahead of time that those soldiers were to be sacrificed by their officers so President Polk would have an excuse to start a war he had already prepared for." He sighed. "Another reason I am glad I never applied for American citizenship!"

"So, do you consider yourself enough of a Mexican to fight these Americans?" Señor Valencia asked.

"Absolutely," Devlin said, without hesitation.

"We'll go in the morning," Jaime said.

"Not we. Me," Devlin said. "You're not going to join this fight."

"Because of my 'peculiar condition?'" Jaime demanded. "I thought we discussed that before."

"No. Because you have a grandfather and a sister who need you."

Jaime started to protest. Devlin interrupted. "Excuse me, Señor Valencia. I know you are a capable man who has worked this land for a lifetime. But you need help now, don't you? I can see how hard it is for you to keep things up. Jaime coming here now has been a godsend for you, hasn't it?"

"I admit," Señor Valencia said. "It is true. I do need help, *mi 'jito*."

166

"And Esperanza needs her brother here with her, not off somewhere where she may never see him again. She needs your strength. She needs your constancy. I know you have cousins and uncles in New Mexico, but here, you only have each other. You need each other. I'll take your place in this fight, Jaime. If our positions were reversed, I know you would do this for me."

There was more discussion, but in the end, Devlin won. He would leave early the next morning.

As he was stepping out the door, Esperanza caught his hand in hers.

"Thank you for coming for me," she whispered.

"Dear heart," he said, lifting her face so he could look into her eyes, "I will always come for you!" He kissed her forehead, shook hands with Señor Valencia, and went out to his horse. Jaime helped him get his saddle and gear in order.

"That rawhide pack," Devlin said as they worked, "and my bag of dust, I plan to leave here. That's not something to carry into a war anyway. If I don't come back…"

"I know," Jaime said.

Devlin hesitated before climbing into the saddle, not sure how to say just what he wanted to say. "I met a lot of nice people since getting off the ship in Charleston. I've had some good friends. But you aren't just a friend, Jaime. You and your father and Esperanza, you made me part of your family. I never had any family of my own. You'll never know how much this has meant to me."

"You had a wife," Jaime pointed out.

"Yes. But we lived with her parents, we never got to be our own family, we were part of hers, and I was never really fully welcome there. You made me welcome. I'll always think of you as my brother."

"You are a brother to me also," Jaime said. He grinned, and clapped Devlin in a hug instead of just shaking his hand. Devlin gripped him back, then swung up into the saddle.

"You come back," Jaime said.

"I will. You be here," Devlin said.

"I will be here," Jaime agreed.

And he was.

Dos Lagos Ranch, Near Aguas Amargas, California, August, 1848

The Treaty of Guadalupe Hidalgo was written and signed in Mexico by American and Mexican ambassadors in February of 1848. But by that time, the fighting in California had already tapered to almost nothing. The less than ten thousand Mexican residents – men, women and children – were outnumbered and outgunned by the Americans. Although the Navy left to blockade Mexican ports farther south soon after declaring California an American territory, they were back before the end of 1847 with trained sailors and marines. The bloodiest battle took place in December of that year, against Kearney's men. The Mexicans, mostly cattlemen, were all expert horsemen, but the American military had more men and more weapons. If fighting this influx wasn't difficult enough, in January of 1848 gold was discovered in the San Francisco Bay area. Long before word could travel east and hundreds of thousands of prospectors could come west, hundreds of sailors, whaling men and merchants jumped ship to look for gold. Towns that had been peopled primarily by Mexicans and Mexicanized Americans quickly became home base for a population of men who considered themselves racially superior to the Mexicans. And there were too many to fight. Before the treaty was ever signed, most of the *Californios* returned home to care for their families. Devlin was delayed by a bullet hole through the thigh. Once he fought off the fever and infection, he took a slow course back north and east to the tiny settlement and broad cattle ranches where the Valencia holding was located.

He rode in as he had the first time, late in the evening, past the great hulk of the ruined main house and around back to the old bunk house. It had changed a little since he last saw it. Jaime had partitioned off another section of what was being used as a living room/kitchen to make a second private bedroom and had added a couch and a rocking chair in the now smaller main room so there were more places to sit. Devlin was served a dinner that consisted of nothing more than a thin gruel made of roughly ground corn and water, with well water to drink. In the morning, after a breakfast that was a single egg, split three ways, Esperanza walked him up the hill to visit Jaime.

"Our uncle Diego died when he was just five," she said, kneeling in the grass. "He fell out of a tree and cut his head. He bled out before anyone found him. Uncle Juan got hooked in the leg by a cow's horn when he was herding cattle. He was alone, so he bled to death. Uncle Pablo got in a knife fight at a dance in town and bled too much for the doctor to save him. Uncle Hernán was fixing a wagon. The box dropped and cut his hand, and…"

"And he bled to death," Devlin finished for her, sitting down next to her in front of a carved wooden marker. "Please tell me Jaime did not cut himself shaving."

"Scarlet fever," she said. "Grandfather and I had it. It was very bad. Half the town was sick, so there was no one to come out and help us. Jaime took care of us both. He must have worked for days, weeks maybe, suffering from fever himself. Eventually, his heart just gave out."

"He always had a big one," Devlin said, touching the marker.

Jaime Francisco Ordoñez y Valencia. August 11, 1824 – February 18, 1848.

"Grandmother died seven years ago," Esperanza went on with her litany, indicating another marker. "Grandfather said she was just too old and tired. These others are…"

"Not important," Devlin said. "Espe?"

"Yes?"

He sighed. "Nothing." He stood, helped her back to her feet, and they walked back down the hill together. He had hoped, he and Jaime had both hoped, when Esperanza smiled for the first time, spoke for the first time, and thanked him before he left, that she would be normal again. Oh, he knew that the effervescent fourteen-year-old with happy feet was gone forever. But Esperanza had been much like Jaime: full of the joy of living. She had laughed and made plans. She had chattered, been full of life. What he saw now was a shell, almost lifeless inside. She went through all the right motions, said all the right things, but there was no real spark left inside at all. He had noticed it last night, as he and Señor Valencia had sat talking. When it was late, Esperanza stood and went to kiss her grandfather goodnight. She had given Devlin a kiss on the cheek as well, even

169

commenting on his scruffy beard. But… it was automatic, with no emotion. He had hoped it was because she hadn't seen him in over a year and was feeling uncomfortable in the presence of a virtual stranger. But no. It was more than that. She cooked and cleaned and kept house for her grandfather. But it was more as if she did what was expected than that she did what she wanted.

After walking her back to the bunkhouse, where she sat down in her rocking chair again as he suspected she did most days, he went out to look over the area. The firewood which Jaime had stacked last fall was down to a few sticks, and most of those looked to have been gathered this summer, dry deadfall from the forests above. The garden lay fallow: no one had plowed or planted it this spring. The cow had a calf, but the calf had been allowed to suckle with no one milking the cow, and there was no milk to spare now for the humans, even though the calf was well past weaning age. There were three chickens left, and they were starting to get too old to lay daily. Esperanza's horse and the mule had been turned loose to graze and fend for themselves. Jaime's flashy pinto as gone. He suspected they had sold it to buy food, but whatever they had bought or stored was almost gone. There were a few handfuls of cornmeal left, whatever the chickens laid. Nothing else. Of course, he knew Señor Valencia was old and Esperanza was just a girl, but they had done nothing to keep themselves alive after Jaime died, and Devlin felt himself a bit disgusted with them. They could have tossed a few seeds in the garden. Hell, they could have dug up the money he and Jaime had hidden in the fallen-down stable…

If they had known where it was.

"Jaime told us he buried some money in the stable," Señor Valencia admitted. "We looked, but we never found it."

They looked in the wrong stable, Devlin realized, seeing that the dirt floor of the lean-to that had been built for the horses up near the bunkhouse had been dug almost completely up. Devlin went to the ruins of the big stable near the old house, tossed aside some debris from the roof falling in, and dug up the cache. Most of it was still there. It looked as if Jaime had only used part of one of the bags of gold dust. Devlin re-buried it, after taking a fistful of coins out of one of the leather pillows. It was a lot of money, and all of it gold and silver, even if it was Mexican coins – no paper money at all.

He spent that afternoon hunting, and came back with a fat young buck, which he hung in the lean-to to skin. He cut some steaks off it for dinner, and more for the next day.

"I'm going into town tomorrow," he announced. "I may be gone overnight."

The only comment was, "Be careful," from the old man.

They had rich, dark deer meat for dinner that night, and in the morning, Devlin boiled the last bit of coffee from his saddle pack to go with the fried deer meat and one egg they shared for breakfast. It was, he thought, the most either of them had eaten in a long while.

He took the mule as well as his horse into town. The town may have been small, but he was able to get everything he came for: a wagon, another mule, flour, coffee, sugar, strings of dried onions and red chile, squash and pumpkins, sacks of beans and potatoes, cans of fruits and vegetables. He even managed to get some butter. But he had a bigger plan than just buying supplies. He knew the ranchers in the area routinely sold cattle at the seaports. He also knew that the Valencia cattle had not gone along on the cattle drives in many years. The herd would be big. If he could get the other men to help him round them up and let him join their drive, he would split the income with them.

"Not a bad idea," Señor Valencia said when he explained himself later. "But it may be more trouble than they are worth." Most cattle in those days were sold for tallow and hides, which were shipped east, all the way around South America, to make shoes in the northern factories, and candles to light those factories.

But, "They'll be worth more now," Devlin said. "They found gold down there. When I came through, there were already hundreds of men looking for gold. Winter's coming on. They all have to eat. That's why I bought all the goats and chickens, too."

"Can we keep some?" the old man asked.

"Of course," Devlin said. "That's why I bought so many."

For several days, he left the goats and chickens to forage for themselves, instructing Esperanza to lock them inside the tall coyote fence of the garden at night to keep them safe from predators. He gathered some tools from the ruins of the old stable and went to cut hay. Two men he had hired came up from town and pitched in to help immediately. Juanito Vega was a boy younger even than Esperanza who lived with his mother and younger siblings in town. The other, Miguel Vigil, was an older man with no family in the area except a married sister. With the help, Devlin was able to cut most of the hay in front of the big house. They left it to dry in the fields then and took a two-man saw, a hand saw and an axe up into the mountains to start cutting firewood. This Devlin had more experience with, so the work went quicker than the hay cutting, which he had had to learn as he went. He and Miguel felled the trees with the two-man saw and blocked the logs into lengths that would fit easily into the stove. Juanito started lopping off branches with a handsaw or the axe, a job Devlin and Miguel helped with when they were done sawing. The wood was loaded into the wagon and hauled down the mountain in multiple trips to be piled near the back of the bunkhouse. They took the wagon out then and gathered up the dry hay, piling it in the living room of the big house. Señor Valencia insisted the place was a ruin, but the roof was intact. It was the only building they had big enough to store the hay in.

Other men showed up by then: Antonio Gallegos, Lorenzo Ochoa, Manolo de Vargas and others, to round up the cattle that roamed free over all the open, unfenced public rangeland, Valencia cattle as well as their own. Devlin had become a good horseman over the past couple years, but he had no experience with cattle, especially the wild long-horns they had to deal with. He was willing to take instruction, even from men younger than he was, and that earned him their respect. The group was not quite as joyous as the men Devlin had traveled down the Santa Fe Trail with. These men, after all, had just been conquered. But they accepted Devlin more easily when Ochoa recognized him as someone who had fought with them, not against them, and when they learned that they could laugh with impunity at his inexperience with the livestock. They spent the better part of a month searching the hills and valleys for cattle and getting them together in the big meadows below the Valencia ranch which, being the westernmost property in the area, would be their starting point for the drive. Miguel and Devlin went back to the bunkhouse. They packed the chickens into crates, leaving behind a half a dozen good laying hens, and packed the supplies for the trip under and around the crates. The goats were a bit of a problem, but Devlin had convinced them to follow the wagon out from town by tossing handfuls of grain at them now and then, so they followed it again, baa-baa-ing

172

noisily. Devlin left behind a nanny goat, heavy with milk, that Señor Valencia had already begun milking.

"You can't make butter with goat milk," he said. "But Esperanza makes a good cheese from it!"

"I have to leave you here," Devlin told Juanito.

"Because I'm the youngest," the boy sighed.

"You'd probably be more use than I am on the drive, but I have a bit more stake in the sale than you do. I need someone to look after Señor Valencia and Esperanza while I'm gone." He gave the boy a handful of coins. "Three months' pay for you, and extra, in case you need to buy more supplies in town. Save the hay until the snow is too deep for the animals to find food on their own."

"Will you be gone long?" Señor Valencia asked.

"Probably," Devlin said.

"Why goats?" Ochoa asked, as they started moving their odd herd towards the mountains.

"Small meat, for people who can't use a whole cow," Devlin said. "Same with the chickens."

Ochoa shrugged. "We'll see," he said.

Taking the goats and chickens proved more difficult than Devlin had bargained for. The goats could fend for themselves, as the cattle did, but someone had to feed the chickens in their crates every day, clean the crates regularly and collect eggs.

"We'll eat well on this trip!" One of the men said. They all laughed.

The broad valley where their ranches were all located was between two sets of mountains, but they made it over the western ridges with their live cargo before the snows – which this year started by late September – were more than ankle deep. They stopped in Sacramento and sold twenty head of cattle to the American army, which most of them had just finished fighting, then continued on, south and west, until they reached the gold fields. The livestock sold well: the goats and chickens, and the dozens of eggs they gathered in the last few weeks of their trip, as well as the cattle. The cash was divided according to who put what animals in, and they headed back across the mountains. With the wagon, the goats and the chickens as well as the wild cattle, it took them much longer than it should have to get all the way to Yerba Buena. By the time they were headed back, the snow was heavy on the mountains and the going was rough. They would not have even tried it, had they not all had families waiting for them on the other side. Several times they had to sit out blizzards. Each time, they had to pack trails with snowshoes to move the wagon and the horses down again. Finally, they made it, much later than they had hoped.

"Next year, we sell the wagon, too," Ochoa said. "But… maybe we get even more chickens and goats."

"Agreed," Devlin said. They had sold well, and he had made a profit on them, but they had slowed the progress so much that it was only a few days before Christmas when they got back to where the road split, taking the rest of them towards town, and Devlin and Miguel towards Esperanza, Señor Valencia and Juanito. It was starting to snow again, heavily this time. He said a quick goodbye to the other men and drove the wagon past the big house up to the bunkhouse in the rear. There was a light inside, smoke coming from the chimney. When he knocked on the door, Esperanza flung it open and stepped back from the cold wind and blast of snow he brought with him.

"You came back!" she said.

"I told you I always would," he said. He and Miguel unloaded bags and packs, but then had to go out into the storm again. They drove the wagon into the ruined stable and parked it under the portion of roof that was still intact. Fixing this would have to be his first chore, Devlin thought, as he unhitched the mules and found them shelter inside from the coming storm. Each man rubbed down his horse. Juanito came out from the big house to help them haul out enough hay to keep all the animals for the night. There was a pump outside the stable, and they filled the water trough. The animals were not locked into stalls – there weren't any stalls left in the ruin anyway. They could come for water, and they could get outside if the weather let up, to forage more for grass. But for tonight, they had almost complete protection from the storm.

Devlin followed Miguel and Juanito into the big house. Devlin had told them it was the only place he had on the ranch for them to stay, but he was amazed when he went inside. Juanito had been living entirely in the kitchen, a big adobe room with a flagstone floor, a huge cook stove, and even an indoor pump. There were lanterns burning on several counters, and the stove was blazing so the room was bright and warm.

"Why does the old man keep saying this is such a ruin?" Devlin wondered aloud.

"The upstairs is fairly useless," Juanito said. "There's some nice rooms downstairs, though. But Boss? I'd kind of like to go back to town to spend Christmas with my family."

"Me, also," Miguel said.

"Of course! Anytime you want."

The two men glanced at each other. "In the morning?"

"If the weather permits. Stop by up at the bunkhouse before you go," Devlin said. "You both have some pay coming."

He had in fact paid Juanito almost entirely in advance, and he had paid off Miguel while they were still in the seaport so the man could purchase anything he wanted in a town much bigger than Agua Amargas. But they stopped as he requested and received anything left due to them, plus half a month pay for a Christmas bonus. Devlin had also purchased silk scarves for Juanito's mother and Miguel's sister, a box of candy for the children, tobacco for the brother-in-law, new spurs for Juanito and a good new hunting knife for Miguel.

"You must have gotten a good price for those cows," Señor Valencia commented, noting the generosity.

"Many times more than the two dollars for tallow and hides," Devlin said. "I think cattle will be a better paying business, at least while this gold rush lasts."

The snow let up for a day, making it easier for the two men to get back to town. But the next day, Christmas Eve, it started again. Devlin snowshoed out into the mountains and came back with a turkey he had shot, and a small evergreen tree. They had no way to stand it, no decorations for it, but he leaned it in a corner, the only festiveness or decoration in the house. He remembered the Christmas in New Mexico when Esperanza, Jaime and their father had wrapped pine boughs all over their house, decorated with big red ribbons and shiny bells. Well, with Francisco and Jaime both gone, things were different. Esperanza plucked and cleaned the turkey. Christmas day she put it in the oven to roast. Devlin baked sweet potatoes and corn and made soup from the canned oysters he had bought. And while the feast was in the oven, he laid out the gifts he had brought for them. For Señor Valencia, who used a stick to walk everywhere, he had brought an ebony cane with a gold-trimmed ivory top that would fit smoothly in his hand, and a pair of rabbit-fur lined slippers to keep his feet warm inside the cabin. Esperanza had already received hair pins and ribbons and lengths of bright colored cloth: those he considered necessities. For gifts, he had brought her a tall ivory comb for her hair, as well as a boar-bristle brush and three sizes of combs for combing out her long tresses. These combs were carved from fragrant red cedar to perfume her hair while she combed it. There was a box of white and dark Mexican chocolate for everyone to share, as well as walnuts, and half a dozen oranges that had survived the long trip carefully wrapped in straw. It was a week later that Esperanza presented Devlin with a pair of moccasins she made for him to keep his feet warm indoors.

"I forgot about Christmas," she admitted.

"That's all right," he said. "They're just in time for my birthday."

Dos Lagos Ranch, Near Aguas Amargas, California, March 1849

Miguel and Juanito were not able to get back to the ranch until the mid-February thaw. Meantime, the winter passed quickly. On good days, Devlin hunted for fresh meat and split more of the great pile of firewood. On days when the weather was bad, he trekked down to the old stable and worked on cleaning out the debris so it could be repaired. On all days he fed the chickens, goat, mules and horses, collected eggs, mucked out where they were living and piled the soiled straw where he could haul it away later. The wagon was not going anywhere in this snow, but the cattle learned quickly to come in front of the big house where fresh hay would be forked out for them daily. Esperanza stayed close to the house in this deep snow, going outside only when she needed water from the well or to stock up on firewood. She cooked and washed and kept house for the three of them, saying little, doing everything that was expected of a young woman. Señor Valencia tended to huddle close to the fire in his rocking chair, his old joints stiff and sore.

When he had the chance, Devlin also explored the big house, although Señor Valencia insisted it was a worthless ruin. It wasn't that bad, Devlin thought. The front door opened into a room he thought of as The Great Hall. It was broad and long with a ceiling that soared twenty-five feet above the floor – which was rotting away with weeds and even a small tree growing through the cracks in the wood. Right now, it was a great place to store the hay, but he could see it was a beautifully proportioned room. It had a huge fireplace on one side, and a dining room on the other – smaller than one would guess for a house like this, but he supposed that if the original builders had wanted a big party, they held it in the Hall. To the rear, a wooden staircase had rotted away, but it had once led up to six bedrooms that opened onto an indoor balcony that looked down into the hall. Each bedroom had a small, individual balcony that hung outside on the back of the house. To the right of the Hall was a smaller room, only one story high, set back from the Hall so that it was shorter as well, though still quite a large room. It also had rotting floors and a big fireplace, but the tall windows facing east and west were its chief beauty. The best part of the house was the hallway behind that rotten staircase. It had flagstone floors, like the kitchen, and it led to a row of bedroom-suites. There were two suites with two bedrooms and a sitting room, one with a single bedroom and a sitting room, and one with just a bedroom and a small dressing room. But all of them had flagstone floors, a fireplace and private, enclosed patios, also floored with flagstone. Each patio was surrounded by five-foot-high adobe walls which had flower boxes built around the insides.

A back staircase from the kitchen was rickety but intact, and when he explored up there, Devlin found the attic. Since the family had died out, not moved out, there was still furniture in some of the rooms, and more furniture and trunks of things like bedding were piled up in the attic. He also found trunks full of books, some of which were not completely destroyed by mice or worms. These he shared out with Miguel and Juanito, taking a pile himself back to the bunkhouse to read aloud to Esperanza and her grandfather to help pass the long winter evenings.

Juanito had originally slept in the kitchen, living in that one room while they were off on their fall cattle drive. But Devlin gave them permission to use any part of the house they liked, and when Miguel came back, the two of them hauled down comfortable furniture from the attic and fixed up one of the two-bedroom suites. They cooked in the kitchen, but they each had a private bedroom and shared a cozy common room, with a big fire cracking on the hearth, on chilly spring nights. The kitchen was comfortable enough, but this sitting room had plush chairs and foot stools. And although they had to travel the chilly gap between the kitchen and their suite of rooms, it was the nicest living space either of them had ever had.

The odd part of the big house, though, was a corridor that led south from smaller living room. It was built of stone with packed earthen floors and had small rooms, six of them, opening back off a narrow corridor.

"What are those rooms?" Devlin asked one morning while he rested from splitting firewood by the bunkhouse.

"Who knows?" Señor Valencia shrugged. The day was sunny and he was sitting on an upturned log, warming his aching joints in the sun. "They were already blocked off when I was a boy. Maybe that was the original house, or maybe it was a series of root cellars, or maybe there was some kind of Indian pueblo here."

"I don't think Indians in this area built pueblos," Devlin said.

"Whatever it is, it doesn't matter. You should not concern yourself with that house. It's a ruin. It needs to be torn down."

"It's not that bad," Devlin said. "Just needs some work. Anyway, the men need a place to stay."

Spring warmed up. The cattle had to be gathered, calves branded. Like last fall, many other ranchers came to help with this, to separate out their own stock and slap on the proper brands.

"I didn't think you would still be here," Ochoa said to Devlin as they sat around the evening campfire, sipping hot coffee.

"I feel I need to take care of Esperanza and Señor Valencia," Devlin said. "You know, when Jaime and I brought Esperanza out here, we didn't expect…" He let that trail off, and instead asked, "How did that old man survive up here by himself?"

"It doesn't take much for one person to live," Ochoa shrugged. "He slaughtered a beef every fall. Planted a small garden."

"He can barely move," Devlin said.

"He's gotten much worse in the past couple years," Ochoa agreed. "He really livened up when his grandchildren came out here, but after Jaime died, he went downhill fast. His sons all died without children, so did his brothers. He had real hope for the children of his daughter. She married well outside of the area, and that was a good thing. He never saw her again, of course, but the family had a disease that ran through it. He really hoped marrying so far outside, she wouldn't pass it on."

"I don't know about the ones who died young," Devlin said. "But Jaime had it.

"Ah! And the girl?"

"She doesn't seem to."

"Well, that's something. Maybe, she's the last hope for this family. Or maybe," he added with a leering grin, "you are!"

Devlin had wondered if taking Esperanza back to New Mexico would help her listlessness. She had more family there, cousins and aunts and uncles. She was part of a big family there. The letters they got from New Mexico were not that encouraging, though. And whether they left him here or tried to haul him over the mountains, their leaving would mean death for Señor Valencia.

"You like this place?" the old man asked Devlin as spring faded into summer.

"It is beautiful," Devlin said. "I had thought I would want to go back to New Mexico and buy me a place there. But California is nice, too. I doubt, I can afford anything as grand as what you have here, but I have enough for a good start. Someday."

"Buy this place," Señor Valencia said, surprising him into silence. He had been shocking the first cutting of hay, working near where Señor Valencia was sunning himself while Miguel and Juanito worked the opposite end of the meadow. He stopped what he was doing to look seriously at the old man.

"Like I said, I can't afford any place this nice."

"We can deal about the price."

"But this, this is Esperanza's heritage," Devlin objected, waving an arm around that encompassed the hills and valleys, the buildings and livestock.

"The first night you came here, Esperanza was terrified because the Americans were here. Now, they have conquered and taken this land as a prize of war, and you know what the first law they passed in New Mexico was: women cannot own land. They will do the same here. Esperanza is the last of my family. I cannot leave her my ranch. It will become the property of some American land-grabber, and when I die, she will be destitute and alone."

"You're not going to die soon," Devlin said.

"Sooner than I like to think," the old man said. He waved off Devlin's protests. "I know this body. It is old, and it is not getting any younger. I want to sell you this ranch."

"Why me?"

"Jaime told me how much you loved the mountains when you saw them. This is not New Mexico, but it is beautiful as well. You will take care of it. And more importantly, you will take care of Esperanza. If you own it, she can live here all her life. She will be taken care of and not be turned out to... to what women do when they have no one to support them."

"It would be an honor, sir, to take care of her heritage, and of her.

Besides, I owe her family. Jaime, Esperanza and their father treated me like family when they had no reason at all to even trust me."

"Good. I thought you would feel that way. Then there is one other thing I will ask you to do."

"What's that?"

"Marry her."

Again, Devlin was caught with nothing to say.

"You do love her, don't you?" the old man asked.

"Well, yes. She's like a sister to me! But I never considered her as a wife! I'm much older than she is! More than ten years!"

"Ten years is not so much for a married couple, not when the girl is as young and as in need of care as Esperanza. She does not show any interest in the young men in town when we go into Mass or to buy things, but she has always liked you very much."

"Does she get a say in this?"

"Of course. You ask her. I will bet you this ranch she says yes!" Señor Valencia grinned wickedly.

"If I take this ranch, I will pay you for it," Devlin countered. "And I think you are wrong. I'm her other brother, like I said. That's not romantic."

"But you are not her brother. Not really. No, I seriously think that if she would take any man, it would be you. If you two are married, and you own my ranch, her children will still inherit it, yes?"

"If she can have children," Devlin said.

The old man made a waving motion with his hand again. "Do not worry so about that business with the tea. The effects are temporary, I assure you."

"Am I the only person in the world who did not know about that foul brew?" Devlin demanded.

"You did not grow up in this country. How would you know? Anyway, how do you feel about this proposition?"

"If she'll have me," he said finally, after consideration. "If not, maybe I should not buy your ranch."

"You buy it anyway. Even if she chooses not to marry you, why let someone else snatch it away from her? Jaime considered you his brother. That makes you my last heir. But yes. Do ask her."

He didn't. Not right away, anyway. There was too much work to be done while the weather was good. After stacking the first cutting of hay in the Hall, this time properly shocked, he and Miguel and Juanito went into the forest to cut trees. They needed firewood for next year, yes, but also they needed logs: long ones for beams and poles, thinner ones for the cross bracing, tall logs to be peeled and saved for future woodworking needs. They made adobes and rebuilt the back wall of the stable with thick log ends sticking out into the walkway for draping saddles over. Devlin and Miguel rebuilt the rafters for the stable and made a strong pole corral to one side, while Juanito planted the garden. Devlin went to town to buy lumber to build a barn but came back instead with a water-powered sawmill, and they cut more logs and began to process lumber. The rains came, and the sun. The garden needed weeding, and the grass grew tall enough for a second cutting of hay. The neighbors arrived at a pre-arranged date for a day of barn building, the men working outside, the women gathered in the kitchen of the big house to prepare food for them all. There followed an evening of dancing and music. People camped out in the big house and in the meadows and left again after a breakfast of mostly leftovers to get back to their own chores. Even Esperanza seemed to enjoy herself, at least more than she had in a very long time.

Dos Lagos Ranch, Near Aguas Armagas, California, August 1849

Devlin had removed his shirt while he split wood, but he grabbed it and put it back on when Esperanza came outside with a handful of donuts and a cup of water for him.

"I thought Sundays were a day of rest," she said.

"We kept running out of wood last winter," Devlin said. "This year, we have more fires to feed. I want to be sure we have enough."

She sat down on his chopping block, and he sat cross-legged on the ground to eat his snack. "These are very good. Thank you."

"Your recipe," she said.

"Is it? Well, they're still good. Espe...?"

"Yes?"

He couldn't pretend to be too busy now. Not with her just sitting there, looking at him.

"Could you... That is... would you ever consider marrying me?"

"I thought you were never going to ask," she said.

"What? I mean... Is that a yes?"

"Of course. Do I get a ring?" she asked, waggling the fingers of her left hand at him.

He had never thought that far ahead, but now he said, "Of course! Although, I doubt I could get you a good one here in town. You'll have to wait until we go to Sacramento. Your grandfather and I have some business there..."

"Getting the deed to the ranch in your name," she said.

"He's talked to you about all this?"

"Oh, yes."

"How do you feel about that?"

She just shrugged. "I would rather you have it than some stranger. This isn't land I grew up on, you know. I don't know it any better than you do, or feel any ties to it. Anyway, I don't think I would want all the responsibility myself. You make ranching look like a lot of work!"

"It is," he said. "But it's good work."

"Can I go with you?" she asked.

"Go with me where?"

"To Sacramento. With you and Grandfather."

"Oh! Yes, of course. In fact, I hadn't thought about it, but it's much better that you do go, if we're both going. Not for a while yet, though. We'll stop by there when we take the cattle to market again."

"Can you see the ocean from Sacramento?"

"No. It's too far. But we'll be going down to Yerba Buena after... well, perhaps first, then stop in Sacramento on the way back. Yeah. Can't do business with a herd of cattle waiting. And yes, Yerba Buena is right on the water."

"Will we see sea monsters, like you used to talk about to the children?"

"No. Maybe the whales will be passing. But that giant squid I saw once... that was deep in the Atlantic. Way out there. And rare. No one on the ship had ever seen one like it before."

"Too bad. I'd like to see a real sea monster."

"Not if you were close to it," Devlin said. He stood up and brushed the wood chips off his seat.

"Back to work?" she asked, standing also.

"Yes. I'm afraid so. Thanks," he added, handing her back the cup.

"You're welcome," she said, and she went back to the house.

So, he had done it. And Señor Valencia had been right about her accepting him. He just wished either of them had been more enthusiastic about it.

San Francisco, California, September 1849

It was no longer Yerba Buena, a sleepy little Mexican coastal village. It was San Francisco. It had been booming last year, but now it was unrecognizable. There were thousands of people there, maybe tens of thousands. Boats were pulled up on the shore and beached, no men available to sail them back where they came from. The town was several times the size it had been, packed with honkytonks, assay offices, loan brokers, whore houses, theaters, restaurants, laundry and barber shops, every conceivable type of business, including stores selling mining equipment and stores catering to the upscale desires of the newly wealthy. It was easy to find a diamond ring in all that, and Devlin bought two gold wedding bands as well. He bought yards of silk for a wedding dress, pale rose, the color she asked for, and the first suit for himself he had owned since he left The Lakes. There were new shoes all around, new clothes, store-bought soap and other fancy items. They didn't stay long. It was too raucous and noisy. Too dangerous, with all the drunks and fighting. But Devlin did take Esperanza to the end of the peninsula to look out at the ocean, and they did see migrating whales pass by, though from the distance, all they saw were some backs and flukes.

"How big are they?" she asked. The flat expanse of ocean played tricks with her sense of distance and size.

"Longer than those boats pulled up on shore back there. Maybe not as tall."

"How do you catch them and put them into your boat, then?"

"You don't. You kill them, take the parts that are worth money, and leave the rest for the scavengers."

"There must be a lot of dead whales floating around the ocean," she said.

"They aren't there very long."

"Not like the herds of buffalo men have killed."

"Right. Not quite like that."

II

Señor Valencia insisted Devlin pay only a few hundred dollars for the entire ranch.

"I will barely live long enough to enjoy that much," he said. "Why should I be greedy and take more?"

"Esperanza," Devlin began.

"Will be your wife. And it is your money. Think about it."

"We're still not married," Devlin said. "She can change her mind. If you want to give her the money, that's fine. It will be hers, not ours, hers to do with what she wants. But I cannot in good conscience cheat you out of such a fine property."

"How will you pay for it? Selling my cows at two dollars a head?"

Devlin set the unopened leather pillow on the lawyer's desk. He was glad now he and Jaime had traded their gold for cash back in New Mexico. The price of gold had not been very high then, but the value had actually gone down here with the gold rush on. The lawyer used a pen knife from his drawer to open the bag and spilled out all the coins onto his desk. He looked up and said, "are you sure? All of it?"

"All of it," Devlin said.

Señor Valencia shrugged, and the papers were drawn up. Señor Valencia had brought with him all the ancient family paperwork that granted the land to his grandfather, the deeds that went through his grandfather, his father, and himself.

"You have a good paper trail," the lawyer said. "This will be strong and legal. But I suggest a survey as well. I can give you the name of a man who can do it for you. We'll get the deed registered with the state and county now, but get the plat registered when you get it from the surveyor."

They stayed in Sacramento several days while the paperwork was all taken care of. The money was counted twice, and then repackaged as it had been before at Señor Valencia's request. The brand was transferred and re-registered in Devlin's name. There were documents and seals, signatures. And when it was all put together, they took it back to Aguas Amargas and placed the paperwork in a safety deposit box in the vault of the new bank.

"You know, I never asked you," Devlin said, as he stood looking out the door of the bunkhouse at the valley spreading out to the east that was now his. "What does that brand mean? It's the symbol for infinity, isn't it? A sideways numeral 8?"

"Two Lakes," Señor Valencia said. "Dos Lagos. That's the name of the ranch."

He did not understand why Devlin laughed aloud. Devlin had only peripherally been aware of the name of the ranch. He thought of it as The Valencia Holding, which is what it was called on the maps. He had heard someone call it Dos Lagos, but he hadn't really thought about what that meant. Lakes. Two of them this time. For the man named for lakes.

Twin Lakes Ranch, Near Aguas Amargas, California, February 1850

Devlin had heard somewhere that June was the proper month for weddings, probably some romantic nonsense he had picked up in South Carolina. But Señor Valencia vetoed that. He wanted it to take place much sooner. Señor Valencia said December. Devlin got him to hold off until mid-February, mainly because there was usually a thaw around then and they would be able to get into town without snowshoes. Meantime, Devlin traded the bunkhouse for the big house. Most of it was still unusable, but he hoped to eventually fix that. Even as it was, it would give him and Esperanza more privacy than sharing the bunk house with her grandfather. He and Juanito spent considerable time scrubbing and sanding the flagstone floors in two of the bedroom-suites. They fixed up the suite with one bedroom and a sitting room for himself and Esperanza. Miguel helped them find, and when necessary, repair, furnishings, garnering items from the attic, and bedding from the metal, mouse-proof trunks up there. Miguel and Juanito, still being the only two hired hands, each got a private room in the bunkhouse, not quite as nice as the ones they had had all summer, but still better than usual accommodations. Devlin set up Señor Valencia in the smallest of the suites, the one with a bedroom and a small dressing room, almost a closet, which he could use for storage or whatever he wanted. For himself and Esperanza he fixed up the one-bedroom suite. In the bedroom he put a big wardrobe, a wide double bed with thick quilts and soft sheets, a dressing table with a tall mirror, a small table and chair. He moved a big chair and a reading table into the sitting room and moved Esperanza's rocking chair and a bookcase full of books in there. There were new rag rugs for the floors, and, though they wouldn't even begin to grow until spring, he planted some rose trees he had bought in San Francisco in the flower beds of the patio. He moved Esperanza and her grandfather into their new rooms, careful to get back down there early each morning to light fires and start coffee for them, but he slept in the bunkhouse on the couch until after the wedding.

"It's still a ruin," Señor Valencia complained. But he slept warm and comfortable in the big, soft bed in his room, with a lively fire crackling in the fireplace.

Although Aguas Amargas was nowhere near the size of Santa Fe, and there were few if any relatives in residence, Ochoa and some of the others felt that Devlin and Esperanza deserved a real wedding. Some of the women had gotten together over the winter and stitched up the gown for Esperanza. When the thaw hit, the fruit trees blossomed, and they gathered several branches of peach and apple blossoms for a bouquet. They cooked up pots of beans and tamales, enchiladas and sopaipillas. Thaw or no, it was cold, but the men laid out a board dance floor outside, piled up wood for bonfires, and laid out plank-and-sawhorse tables.

They held the ceremony early in the day so the feasting and dancing could take place in the warmest part of mid-day. Señor Valencia served the dual purpose of giving away the bride, and standing up for the groom, taking what should have been Francisco's, and Jaime's places. With no female relatives or even good acquaintances in town, Esperanza's matron of honor was Miguel's sister. Esperanza was beautiful, though, Devlin thought, as he watched her come down the aisle. She had matured since he had first met her, something he had never really paid attention to before. Her figure, always round, was soft and womanly, and the lines of her face were more beautiful than cute and sweet. The pale rose silk set off her golden complexion magnificently. Her veil was pink lace draped over the tall, carved ivory comb he had bought her for Christmas a year ago, and her dress was all flounces, silk roses and ribbons. The ceremony was similar to what Devlin remembered from his marriage to Larissa, High Anglican being not too much different from Catholic. Then came the feasting and the dancing that lasted until after sunset, when the chill settled in too deeply even for the bonfires to quench. Devlin and Esperanza left early, however, making the long drive back to the ranch alone. Señor Valencia and the hired men would come back the next afternoon.

It was late when they arrived at the big house. Devlin led the way through the kitchen, into the back hallway with a lantern held high. He kindled a fire in the sitting room fireplace, then went outside to tend to the mule while Esperanza prepared herself for her wedding night. Devlin himself was not sure what to expect. His wedding night with Larissa had been two inexperienced youths learning together. He had experience now. So did Esperanza, but hers was not of the good kind.

He washed his hands and face in the cold pump water in the kitchen when he came back in, so he would not smell of horse sweat. He toweled himself off, and went to the sitting room, where he took off his boots and jacket. There was no light through the open bedroom door, but the crackling fire lit both rooms with a cheerful glow. He stepped into the bedroom.

And froze. Appalled.

Esperanza was lying flat on her back on the bed, arms stiff at her sides, hands clenched into fists, eyes squeezed tight shut, and her chemise wadded up around her neck − exactly the position he had found her in when he rescued her from the forced prostitution in Santa Fe. He crossed to the bed in two long strides and whipped the blankets over to cover her body. Still dressed, he laid down beside her, wrapping his arms around her blanketed body, feeling her tremors.

"No, Espe!" he whispered in her ear, stroking her long, braided hair. "No, dear heart. Never like that. Never!"

He kissed the top of her head and felt her break into sobs. It was not the most auspicious of beginnings.

Señor Valencia died six weeks later.

"You almost waited too long," was the last thing he said to Devlin. Devlin now understood why the old man had not wanted them to postpone the wedding for nicer weather.

He also understood that if Esperanza was not terribly broken up by the death, it was most likely because she hardly knew the man in any real way. He was her grandfather, true, but she had never met him before they fled to California in '46, and as Ochoa had said, Señor Valencia's health had been declining. He had been more of a burden to her than a replacement for her other lost grandfather, or father or brother. She stood on the hill, looking at the newly carved wooden marker for several long moments after the burial was completed, but it was against Jaime's marker that she laid her small bouquet of flowers. Devlin threw the shovel over his shoulder, and wrapped his other arm around her shoulders, walking back down the hill with his arm around her. With a soft sigh, she allowed the embrace, as she would have allowed a similar embrace from Jaime, he realized, in a similar situation. He had thought once that marrying a best friend might not be a bad idea. Now, he was not as sure. He had been friends with this girl for several years, much closer than most friends, but how would he ever move from that into being her husband?

No, he realized. That was not fair. It was not their friendship that was the block to their relationship now. All he could do was be as slow and gentle as possible, and maybe someday she would accept him as a real husband.

For now, though the big house was still not a real home, and they lived only in their bedroom and the kitchen, those two rooms were clean and cozy. Esperanza took good care of her small domain, and of Devlin. She had come to enjoy the feel of him lying next to her in bed, liking his strength and warmth. It took several months of careful trial and error on his part, but before he left for his annual cattle drive, she had at least once acquiesced to his advances. It was, he hoped, a beginning. The marriage was, at least, comfortable.

Devlin threw himself into work. With the two hired hands, there was still much to do around the ranch, and he did want to eventually make this old house into the elegant home he knew it could be. He bought some dynamite and a single jack and spent part of the summer quarrying flagstone out in the public lands. He stockpiled iron bars he had bought in San Francisco and spent time with a blacksmith in town learning how to twist it into elegant shapes. With the help of the men and the mules, he milled more lumber and stacked it to dry. The ranch work took up too much of his time to spend much time on these beginning chores for fixing the house. But he knew how it would look with flagstone floors all through the downstairs, wrought iron balcony railings, and glass in the windows…

Someday.

Summer warmed and waned again. They harvested the vegetables, and a good crop of potatoes to sell in San Francisco. He and Miguel and Juanito cut firewood and hay. He left Esperanza in town with Miguel's sister while he went with the men on the yearly cattle drive, a process that was becoming more lucrative as more and more people moved into the area. The Gold Rush of '49 would increase the population of California by 300,000 people.

"And they all," he was fond of saying, "have to eat.

Twin Lakes Ranch, Near Aguas Amargas, California, April, 1851

"You are on private land," Devlin said.

The man who was camped by the creek looked up, and he looked, Devlin thought, rather smug.

"Looks deserted to me," he said.

"Well, it's not. You can spend a night here if you are passing through, but then you'd better move on."

"No, I think I'll stay here," the man said. "Looks like a nice place for a cabin."

Devlin looked around at the camp. The man had a covered wagon, which he had partially unloaded. There seemed to be a wife and two… no, three kids. And, he had started to cut trees.

"I don't think you understand what I'm saying here," Devlin said. "This is my property. It is not available for settlement. You are trespassing. You need to move on."

"No, you need to move on, Mister," the man said, pulling out a shotgun and leveling it at Devlin. "By law, I can settle any land I think is vacant. I think this is vacant. I'm settling here."

"And I'm telling you it doesn't matter what you 'think.' This is not vacant land."

"Prove it!" the man sneered.

"I can, you know," Devlin said.

"I bet you squatted it yourself, stole it from some Mex. Well, we're taking it from you!"

"No," Devlin said. "What I'm telling you is that I'll be back in the morning with the sheriff. Maybe, you don't mind going to jail, but you might want to think about your kids."

"Bluff!" the man said.

"Have it your way," Devlin said. He mounted his horse and left the camp. Behind him, he could hear the man laughing. He rode back to where he and Miguel had been cutting wood when they smelled the campfire and told Miguel to get back to the ranch.

"I can get to town a lot faster from here than if I go back," Devlin said. "You watch the place for me. Make sure that crazy man doesn't threaten Esperanza or any of the buildings or livestock."

"I hope the sheriff comes," Miguel said. "I've heard rumors about men like that one."

"Squatters?"

"Plague of them. Like locusts."

"Worst than locusts," Sheriff Morales said when Devlin found him in his office. "They passed a law. A man can claim any land he thinks is vacant, and if it isn't, it's up to the real owner to take him to court and prove otherwise."

"How do I get him to court?" Devlin asked.

Devlin was the one who had started making the cattle business lucrative in the area. He was always ready to help his neighbors. He had made a lot of friends, Morales included.

"I'll take him there for you," the sheriff said.

Devlin took his paperwork out of the bank. He rode back home, packed for a trip, kissed Esperanza, and left for Sacramento. A very angry squatter arrived there the day after he did. The man was furious at being dragged to court, but he was still smug. He came into the courtroom with a very well-dressed lawyer. The two of them found Devlin waiting there, without council, and they both grinned. The gavel banged, they all rose. The man's lawyer presented the case of a large tract of unfenced land. Devlin handed the judge a leather packet that contained his deed, with all the proper stamps and seals, including the inscription saying on which page of which book the deed was recorded legally. Besides his deed, he had the paper trail that led back to the original Spanish land grant to Valencia's grandfather. And he had the surveyed and recorded plat.

The judge looked at the squatter and said, "Didn't this man tell you he could prove his ownership?"

"Well... I..."

"Be more careful next time," the judge said. "The land belongs to Mr. Lachlan. Case dismissed." The gavel banged. Devlin gathered his paperwork. The lawyer handed the squatter a bill for five thousand dollars.

"What is this?"

"I told you ahead of time that my fee was thirty-three percent of the property, or its value, win or lose!"

"I can't pay this!"

"You should have thought of that!" the lawyer said. Devlin sealed the leather case and walked out, ignoring the insults shouted at him as he left. Outside, the covered wagon was parked, with the woman and children peering out of the canvas.

"I'm sorry," Devlin said. "The land does belong to me."

"What do you need with all that?" the woman screeched at him. "You're greedy! You could have shared a little corner...!" She shouted more, but he left, not wanting to hear it. He was very glad he was half-way out of town before the man got back to the woman and told her the rest of the story.

II

Unfortunately, the same thing happened a few months later to one of his neighbors.

"You take in your paperwork, and you fight it," Devlin said. "If everything is in order, there's nothing the squatters can do."

But there was a section of the new law of which he had been unaware. The law stated that anyone who thought – key word being *thought* – land was vacant could settle on it. Anyone could say they *thought* anything was vacant, even if there were fences, buildings, and survey marks. The law further stated that it was the responsibility of the owner to go to court and prove his claim to the land the squatter had settled on. But the law also stated that no Mexican could testify in a court of law against a white man. Pablo Cerrillos lost his land.

"I'm not considered a Mexican?" Devlin guessed. They were in the church building, about a dozen men, most of them with families. All of them were men he had convinced to go on that first cattle drive, and most of them had gone every year since, pooling their work and resources to make a better living for all of them.

"You're *juero*," a man named Gallegos said. A blondie.

"They don't care which side of the war you fought on," Valdez said. "You have blonde hair and blue eyes. You may speak Spanish, but you speak their language too."

"Suddenly, 'Mexican' isn't a nationality," said another man. "It's a race. All Mexicans are all at least a quarter Indian, that's what *they* say. And Indians don't count as people – to them," he added pointedly.

"So, anybody can come through here and take any land they want?" Devlin demanded. "That's not right! There's got to be something we can do."

"'We?'" Gallegos said.

"We," Devlin agreed. "I only bought that ranch because Señor Valencia wanted Esperanza to be provided for. We knew they would outlaw women holding land, but, this! This can't be legal!"

"Legal or not, they have a law that says it is," Sheriff Morales said.

"Maybe…" a man named Herrera started, hesitated again.

"Go ahead," Morales said.

"Maybe Mr. Lachlan can go to court for us if anyone tries to take our land. He's the right color. They'll listen to him."

"I'm sorry," Morales said. "Only the owner of the land himself can testify in court against the squatters…"

"And no Mexican is allowed to testify," Valdez added bitterly.

It was one of the wives who spoke up gently, hesitantly. "What if Mr. Lachlan was the owner?"

"What, give him all our land, instead of giving it to strangers?" Gallegos demanded. "Is that really better?"

"Could we… I don't know. Put it in his name. Like you put our ranch in your name only," she turned to her husband, "so they couldn't say a woman owned it and take it from us."

"If it is in his name, it's his property," Father Aurelio told her gently.

"You wouldn't steal it though, would you?" she asked Devlin. "Would he?" she asked Father. "He could hold it for us, until we can get rid of this terrible law…"

"They won't change it," Valdez said.

"They will have to, eventually," Morales said. "It does go against their constitution – and the treaty they signed with Mexico to end the war. It's not legal."

195

"Didn't Texas make a treaty with Mexico – then go back on it right away?" Devlin asked. "And doesn't America make treaties with the Indians all the time, then go back on them? I'm sorry to say I think we're stuck with this law, at least until they have all the land that used to belong to Mexican citizens, treaty or no treaty."

"*Dark-haired* Mexican citizens," Gallegos added.

"I am sorry, but you are right about that," Devlin said. "I lived in the American south, where they still hold slaves, some of them aren't even 'dark', like you say, but they belong to that group. Worse, though, I traveled through the American north, where they profess to hate slavery, but most of them seem to hate non-white people even more that Southerners do. All non-white people. And some white people," he added thoughtfully, knowing the hatred against Catholics and Jews.

"Perhaps, if you wish," Father Aurelio said, "For Mr. Lachlan to hold your land for you, we could make up some contracts."

"Like what?" Gallegos asked.

"Well… Suppose his heirs can't touch your land. If anything happens to him, it automatically goes back to you."

"That's more than fair," Devlin said. "I mean, fair *if* I were to do that, but it still feels wrong for you to trust me that much."

"It is because it feels wrong to you that I think we can trust you," Father Aurelio said. "It feels wrong to you, not because you are cheating an unfair law, but because you are unwilling to take, even if it is just in name, something that you know belongs to someone else, am I right?"

"I can't personally save the entire state," Devlin said. "Not even this one county."

"But you can help us," the woman insisted. "Most of us do not have as big a place as the Valencias had. A thousand acres was a small grant for the Spanish, but that was generations ago. They are the only ones who kept their's so intact – mainly because they died out."

"You can't just deed it over to me," Devlin said. "I'd have to give you some compensation for it, even if I never intended to really take it."

"Yes. There would have to be a bill of sale, with a price on it, for them to accept it all as legal in the courts," Morales agreed. "Can you come up with… a hundred dollars a ranch?"

"I may have gold hair, but I am not made of gold!" Devlin said.

Although… speaking of gold… he had never touched that second bag buried in the stable since he took out enough to outfit the first cattle drive to Yerba Buena. He had been making the ranch pay for itself. It could barely make expenses and payroll, but it was covered. "I don't know if I have twelve hundred," he said. "But I may be able to give a hundred a tract for at least some of it."

"But we'd give it back to you in rent, no?" the woman asked.

"I can't charge you a hundred dollars to live on your own land!" Devlin said.

"But you could pay us a hundred dollars, and still say it is our land?" Ochoa asked.

"There has to be an exchange of money for it to be legal," Morales said, again.

Devlin nodded. "Your land, all your lands, are worth much more than that. A hundred dollars wouldn't make me feel I had any claim to it at all."

Sheriff Morales and Father Aurelio hashed out some contracts. Devlin would buy properties for a hundred dollars, then rent them back to the original owners for a dollar a year, plus any property taxes owed on them. If such a time came that the owners wanted the land in their own name, and/or if the terrible law was repealed, the land would re-purchased by the owners for the same hundred dollars – minus rents paid. The land Devlin purchased would automatically revert to the original owners, or their heirs, if Devlin died. If and when he had heirs of his own, they would have no claims to the properties he was tying up. If the owners of the properties died, their heirs would own the contracts and have the same rights as the original owners. Ten of the men who had gathered in the church agreed to the terms. The other two decided to take their chances. Devlin and the ten landowners traveled the next week to Sacramento and met with the same lawyer who had handled the transfer for Señor Valencia.

"I know what you are doing," he said, privately, to Devlin.

"And?"

"Look, I don't like that new law. It's wrong. This whole deal with California becoming a state is wrong. America stole this place as surely as a thief robs a bank. So, yes. I'll get the paperwork as tied up and legal as I can, but I can't guarantee anything. You steal half a country, stealing a few thousand acres back is nothing."

"We appreciate anything you can do," Devlin said.

"I know. But listen, you were up in front of Judge Harris this spring. Well, he's gone. The new guy is a lot more... let's just say Anti-Mexican. This might not work. But more power to you. And don't forget those surveys!"

In the next two years, five cases from their county went before the judge in Sacramento, and Devlin won all of them. The deal even worked out for the men who decided not to trust their land to him, as word got out that squatters entered that county at their own risk.

Twin Lakes, Near Aguas Amargas, California, October 9, 1851

"You make beautiful babies," Señora Caldera, the midwife, said to Devlin.

"I don't think I can take credit for it," Devlin responded. "He looks just like his mother."

Devlin had sent Juanito on their fastest horse to town as soon as the labor started, knowing how great the distance in and out was. Still, the midwife barely made it in time. It was Devlin who sat by the bed, holding Esperanza's hand, letting her try to squash his big hand in hers as the contractions came on. He fed her sips of water and wiped the sweat off her forehead. When Señora Caldera finally came, it was already almost over.

"Time to push," she said, after a quick assessment of the situation. "You should sit up for that, it will be easier."

Esperanza was already tired, so Devlin had climbed into the bed behind her, his long legs extended down along her body, and held her shoulders and upper body in his arms while the birth was competed. He watched, he asked questions.

"Why did you spank him?"

"I hit him in the back. He's been living in a world of liquid. We need to dislodge anything that might be in his throat before he takes his first breath."

And his first breath had been followed by an angry cry that subsided again almost instantly, replaced by big eyes trying hard to focus on the new world around him. Devlin stayed where he was, arms around Esperanza, while the midwife washed the baby, diapered him and wrapped him up.

"Oh! Twins?" Esperanza said.

"Afterbirth," the midwife said. "Relax. That one will be easy."

It was. The baby was brought back and handed to Esperanza who stared down at the tiny face as if she wasn't sure what it was. Devlin stared down too. The baby was indeed good-looking. He was plump for a newborn, with the same soft gold skin tone that Esperanza had, instead of being wrinkled and red. He had a shock of dark hair on his head, and his eyes were dark, but filmed in blue.

"He has blue eyes," Devlin said.

"They'll most likely be brown," Señora Caldera said. "Most babies have bluish eyes at first. Up off the bed now, Papa. You have a job to do."

He reached down first, touching the tiny hand that was clenching and unclenching at the edge of the blanket.

"It's such a miracle, isn't it?" he said, looking up at the midwife. "Life. Out of... a person!"

"You are too romantic, sir. Now, the tradition is for the father to bury the afterbirth at the foot of a tree."

She handed him a blood-stained towel, heavy with something wrapped inside. He checked, just to be sure. It was what she said.

"On your way out, stoke up the fire and put some water on to heat."

"Why do people boil water when a baby is born?" he asked.

"Look around. We have lots of washing up to do."

He stoked up the fires as he was asked, put all the big metal containers he could find on top of the stove, and filled them all with water. He drug out the big wash tub, too, and added some soap to it before taking his burden outside to the barn to get a shovel. He dug a hole at the base of a big cottonwood tree that stood at the front corner of the house by the dining room. When he was finished with the chore, he stood for a moment and watched the moon rise behind the hills, up the valley from the back of the house. Beautiful night. Beautiful event. He felt full, and fulfilled, and happy. He took the shovel back to the barn and went inside to get himself recruited to wash laundry. There was indeed a great deal of washing up to do.

Señora Caldera spent the night, sleeping in Señor Valencia's old bedroom. In the morning, she checked on Esperanza, then came in the kitchen where Devlin was preparing breakfast.

"Good," she said. "I was going to suggest giving her a day or so off. She's not sick or incapacitated, but she's sore and tired."

"She can rest all she wants," Devlin said. "Um, Ma'am? She seemed a little off to me this morning."

"In what way?"

"Well, the baby was crying, and she didn't seem to notice or care. I had to take him to her for, um, breakfast. Does it hurt her?" He recalled what happened when Larissa tried to nurse after that horrible operation.

"Nursing? Well, her breasts may be a little sore and irritated at first, but nothing serious, and it clears up pretty quick. Probably she's just very tired. They call it 'labor' for a reason. Now, how much experience do you have at diapering?"

She showed him how to do it, showed him how to wash the baby and dress him. Showed him that the baby was not quite as fragile as he first thought, but still needed careful handling.

"How'd he get that bruise?" the midwife asked. "Something happen last night?"

Devlin examined the small, almost square blue mark on the back of the baby's right shoulder. "Well, I'll be. It's a birthmark," he said. "His uncle had the exact same mark."

His uncle also had a disease of the blood that had wiped out most of his family, Devlin recalled with a chill. After the midwife was gone, after Esperanza was asleep, Devlin collected the baby and a few things and took them out to the stable. He spread a clean blanket on the ground and laid the baby on it, kneeling next to him. He had a lantern, and a long, thick piece of wire. He put the end of the wire into the flame of the lantern, laid out a pile of rags and cloths, and picked up a sharp kitchen knife. He sterilized it in the lantern flame.

"I'm sorry," he said. "I have to know."

He lifted the baby's small right arm and cut a gash on the inside of his forearm. The baby screamed, of course. That was why he came out here, so the sound would not carry well through the thick adobe walls. He grabbed some of the folded cloth pads he had and stanched the blood, pressing down on the wound, while holding the baby to his chest to comfort it. The scream subsided slowly into soft sobs, then a wet snuffling sound, as the baby sucked on his own left fist. Devlin checked the wound. It was still seeped blood, but much less than it had been before. He put pressure for several more minutes. The bleeding stopped without the hot wire he had in case the wound needed to be cauterized. He bandaged the little arm and redressed the baby in his nightgown. Baby James did not have the same disease that his namesake had had. Devlin cleaned up, made sure he left nothing hot or dangerous in the stable, and went back inside.

Aguas Amargas, October 28, 1851

After the baptism ceremony, all the women in town seemed to want to cuddle and coo over the baby. Devlin left Esperanza in their care and sought out the midwife.

"There's something wrong," he said.

"Fever? Excessive bleeding? Red streaks and soreness?"

"No. No infections, nothing physical. I don't think. It's just… remember how she was the morning after the birth? Listless and uninterested in anything? Well, she's still like that. She doesn't do anything. She sleeps most of the day, she barely talks, except to agree to what I suggest cooking for her, or to ask for water or something. I have to make her get out of bed to change the sheets. I had to give her a sponge-bath to clean up before we came into town today. This is not normal."

"No, it's not, really. Yet it is. Mr. Lachlan, have you ever noticed, being a married man and all, that women have certain mood swings, usually on a monthly cycle. Some may get irritated easily, some may cry for no very good reason?"

"Yes…?"

"Well, giving birth is kind of like getting hit with nine months of that all in one big dose. All women feel some depression afterwards, but occasionally they get it very bad. I think your wife is one of the 'occasionally's."

"What does that mean?"

"It means just what you said. She seems tired all the time so she sleeps a lot, she doesn't have interest in anything or anybody, including you or the baby or even herself."

"Is this permanent?" Devlin asked.

"No, it should clear up on its own, but depending on how bad she has it, it could take a few days or a few months."

"What can I do?"

"To make it better? Nothing. To help her through it? Be there."

"I'm always there."

"I know. You're a good man. Just… take care of her. Don't try to jolly her out of it, or admonish her for not taking better care of you or the baby or the house. Don't throw it up in her face that she 'used to be better.' Just accept her as she is now. Be her strength until she gets hers back. I've seen you in a kitchen: you can cook and wash and you diaper a mean bottom. Do what she can't. Until she can."

When he looked thoughtful, she said, "Maybe we can find a woman to hire to come and take care of things…"

"Oh, no! That's not a problem. Winter is a slow time of year, and it's coming now. I can run the household by myself, and I have some men to run the ranch. It's just…" And he told her of Esperanza's past.

"Well, that certainly doesn't make things better," Señora Caldera said. "But I don't think that's the root cause here either. It's just a stronger than normal post-birth depression. I'm sure it will fade. But you will have to be very, very patient with her until it does."

That night as they drove home, Esperanza sat next to him on the wagon seat, holding the baby in her arms. Slowly, she leaned more up against him, until she was resting against his side. He put both sets of reins in one hand so he could put an arm around her, holding her against him so she wouldn't tip over as she fell asleep. He angled his grip on her so that his arm helped hold the baby she still held in her arms. This was what he needed to do now, he thought. Support them both. His arm ached with the tension after only a few minutes, but he held them all the way home.

Twin Lakes Ranch, Near Aguas Amargas, California, Winter 1851-52

He had planned on getting some work done in the big house during the slow time of the winter. Instead, he ran the household. Every morning he got up, lit a fire, changed the baby and handed it to Esperanza. He went out to the kitchen and lit that fire, put on the coffee and went out to feed the horses, cow and chickens and collect the eggs. He came back and washed the eggs, made breakfast, and took it in to Esperanza, moving the baby to its cradle near the bed while she had her breakfast. He learned not to make her much. She picked listlessly at whatever he served her, but she ate. He took his breakfast with her, sitting in the chair by the bed, sometimes holding the baby while he ate. He got very good at the one-handed fork maneuver. On various days he did the wash or the ironing – diapers had to be washed every day, he was amazed how fast the baby went through them. Other days he mucked out the stable or the henhouse, always coming back inside every half hour or so to make sure the fires didn't go out. He baked bread and simmered soups and scrubbed floors. He washed the baby and changed his nightgown daily, made sure the bedding in his little crib was always fresh. Every day he helped Esperanza get up and sit in the chair while he remade the bed. Once a week he changed the sheets. And every Saturday evening he filled the big washtub with warm water, got the fire blazing in the kitchen, and took her down the hall for a bath. He helped her out of her nightgown, helped her to step into the tub. He gave her soap, but if she didn't seem inclined to do much, he helped her with that also, and rinsed her with buckets of warm water. He soaped and rinsed her hair, which was so long, he had to set the small dish-washing tub on the floor behind her to keep it from hanging onto the floor while he rinsed the soap out of it with bucket after bucket of warm water. He helped her stand, toweled her dry, pulled a fresh nightgown over her head, and then sat her on a tall kitchen stool to comb out her hair for her. That hair he had noticed the first time he had met her, that the women always commented on, that hair was as long and thick as ever. It took over an hour to comb all the tangles out of it, sitting close to the fire so it would dry as he did. Long after the tangles were out, he would run the comb again and again down the length of her hair, enjoying the intimacy of it. Eventually, he would divide it into sections and with fingers used to working with leather and rope, braid it into long plaits that laid next to her in the bed when she returned to it.

Evenings, after dinner, he sat by her bed and read aloud, sometimes in English, sometimes in Spanish, from whatever books he could find. He drug Señor Valencia's rocking chair into the bedroom so he could hold the baby on his chest and rock while he read. The firelight flickered across the ceiling, the baby snuggled against the beat of his heart. Esperanza slowly slipped into restful sleep.

When he knew he would be in the kitchen for long periods of time, he unhooked the cradle from its stand and brought it in to sit on the worktable, so the baby was close if it needed anything. Eventually he brought Esperanza's rocking chair in there also, and she would sit and rock while he worked. It was a long, cold winter. But slowly, Devlin began to see changes. First, Esperanza picked up the baby and rocked it when she sat in the kitchen with him rather than just sitting by herself. She started responding to the child's cries, getting up and going to pick it up when it was hungry instead of waiting for Devlin to hand the child to her. She commented on the spices he was using in his soup. She asked him to help her change a diaper. Then one day, she walked into the kitchen in a skirt and blouse instead of her nightgown, and Devlin knew they had passed a crisis point. As the snow outside started to melt away, Esperanza became more and more her old self, taking care of the corner of the big house that was their home, taking care of the baby. She had been too lost in her depression to notice when the baby had a bandaged arm. She did ask about the scar one day, but accepted without comment when Devlin responded, "He got cut. Not serious." By the time it was time for Devlin to help with the spring round up and branding, he felt as if he could leave her at home alone with the baby all day and still find them both in good health when he came back.

"You did well," Señora Caldera told him when she saw the three of them in town for a few supplies.

He knew then that they really were a family.

Twin Lakes Ranch, Near Aguas Amargas, California, June 21, 1852

It was the longest day of the summer, but the back area, between the house and the outbuildings, was cool, shaded by the long shadow of the house. Because the dining room was not ready for use, and the kitchen could be like a big oven itself after a day of cooking, Devlin had set up table and chairs behind the house so they could have dinner and relax in the cool evening shadows. It was late, but neither of them was quite ready to jump up and start washing dishes. Instead, they both sat there, enjoying the cool breezes that slid down the valley, watching the baby play in the short grass near the table. He was nine months old, and amazingly fast for someone who needed hands and knees to get around. He had – many people had commented on it – a good personality. He wasn't prone to fits of angry crying, was more curious about things than upset by them most of the time.

"He'll be walking soon," Devlin commented, watching the baby use a chair to pull himself to an upright position.

"Boys don't walk," Esperanza commented. "They crawl, then they run."

Devlin laughed, remembering little baby Joaquim from the Santa Fe Trail trip. They hadn't let him on the ground much, but his short little legs had moved pretty fast when they did. Of course, with legs that short, even keeping up with older siblings required running.

"Maybe we can hobble him like we have to do that one mule," Devlin said.

He already had had to build a bed that the baby could not climb out of, after he landed twice on the hard flagstone floor of the bedroom. They watched him now, trying – unsuccessfully – to climb higher on the chair. He may not have been a fussy baby, but he was determined.

The sound of horse's hooves brought Devlin up out of his seat. He glanced towards the bunkhouse, but he knew that both Miguel and Juanito were back, even without seeing them sitting outside in the shade as he and

Esperanza were doing.

"Trouble?" Esperanza asked.

"Probably not," he said, and he moved to the corner of the house so he could watch the rider come in from the distant road. One man. Dark bay horse. He recognized neither the man nor the horse. Eventually the rider pulled up right in front of him. He leaned forward, resting his arms on his saddle horn, and looked down at Devlin.

"Boy, they were right in town. This place ain't so easy to find!"

"It's not that hard," Devlin said, wondering who the man was.

The man grinned. "You don't recognize me? Shoot, we were tied together for almost a year!"

"Josh!" Devlin realized at once.

Josh grinned even wider. "At your service! I suppose I'm late for supper?"

"There's more on the stove. We'll get your horse taken care of, then get you some."

Josh slid down off his horse then, and Devlin walked him over to where Esperanza had just stood and grabbed the baby up off the ground. James was not pleased at having his play interrupted, and he struggled in his mother's arms to get down again, but she held him while Devlin made the introductions.

"Espe, this is an old friend of mine, Josh Tyler. Josh, my wife, Esperanza, and our son, James."

"Pleased to meet you, ma'am," Josh said, removing his hat politely. He gave a little head-bow in her direction and reached to chuck the baby under the chin. James ducked his head away from the touch but looked at the stranger curiously.

"Good-looking family, Dev. But then, you always did attract the prettiest girls," he gave Esperanza a flirty wink, and then he and Devlin went to put up his horse while Esperanza went inside to bring out a bowl of stew, with several tortillas and a cup of coffee.

"Now, this is heaven," Josh said as he finished his dinner. "One thing I haven't had in a long time — shoot, ever! — is a good meal cooked by a pretty woman!"

While he had been eating, Devlin had told him at least some of his own adventures, mentioning the Santa Fe Trail, starting this ranch. Once Josh was done eating, he said,

"Boy, you always had a strange accent. It's worse now! You sound like some kind of Brit-Mex!"

"I guess I haven't spoken a lot of English in a long time," Devlin said.

"Yeah? I guess you got the last laugh on that guard who thought giving you a Spanish Bible was funny. Does the little lady here speak English?"

"Yes," Devlin said. Esperanza had not spoken much, if at all. After all these years with him, before and since their marriage, she did understand English perfectly, but she didn't like to speak it unless she had to, feeling always that her pronunciation and word order were wrong. Josh smiled her way, and she gave him a small smile back.

"Where have you been all this time?" Devlin asked.

"You know I joined up with the Army," Josh said. "The War came up shortly after I joined, and the volunteers, well, they were in for a month or a year or 'for the duration,' but me, they didn't let me back out until '50."

"Five years," Devlin said.

"It's still standard. And it wasn't so bad. They do feed and clothe you in the army. They tend to treat you bad, though. Slightest infraction and they would whip or torture fellas. I learned fast to keep my head down and do what I was told. Well, I had some experience on that score." He gave Devlin a wink, and Devlin just nodded.

"I was a corporal before the end of the year," he said. "And I made sergeant before the war started." He skipped over the war years, as Devlin himself always did if he was asked.

"By the time they let me out," Josh continued, "I figured the gold fields were probably all stripped bare, but I came west anyway. Did some prospecting. It was when I was filing my claim I found your name in the land office. I said, there can't be two men with a name that silly! So, when I had a chance, I rode on out here to see if it was really you. And here you are!"

"I made it to Mexico," Devlin said. "But then they changed the border!"

"Boy! Tell me about that! This place you got here, it ain't half bad. Ranching make much money?"

"It pays its own bills, that's about all for now. But the price of cattle is going up. How's prospecting?"

"I thought you'd never ask! I hit it, Dev! Oh, not the richest vein in California, not by a long shot, but enough to be more than just comfortable! I bought me a lot up on Nob Hill in San Francisco, gonna live up there with all the snobs. Here, let me show you the house. I've been working on it all winter. It's coming along real good!"

They had laid his saddle pack on the ground while he ate, planning to take it inside later. Now he rifled through it and came out with a rolled set of plans. When he laid them out on the table, even Esperanza leaned close for a look. It was getting dark now, the sun had set on the other side of the house and of the mountains, but Devlin lit a lamp and held it above the paper while Josh pointed things out.

"Real architect plans!" was Josh's first comment. Then he started pointing out details. The first was a drawing of what the house would look like finished. It was a monstrous Victorian affair, all turrets and bay windows, with a widow's walk, a wrap-around porch, ginger breading everywhere it could fit, and stained glass in the front door and in arches above the living room windows.

"Nice," Devlin said politely, though it was a style he had never cared for.

Josh flipped through some of the other pages. The downstairs had a parlor and a living room, besides the dining and kitchen.

"Gold wallpaper in the dining room," Josh said. "With red velvet fleur-de-lis and red carpeting. Here, in the parlor, off-white and blue striped silk wall coverings. And thick oriental rugs with pink and blue roses. Very elegant! And solid walnut wainscoting!"

There were four bedrooms upstairs, a large master bedroom, and smaller rooms for visitors or an expanding family, and on the third floor, a nursery and servant's quarters. Devlin admired the entire thing, then brought Josh inside to admire his big house.

"Got a bit of work left to do, don't you," Josh commented, looking at the big hall in the flickering lamplight. The flagstone was piled in one corner. Sand in another. There were stacks of lumber and iron bars and rocks for the fireplace repairs.

"Yes, but it's coming along," Devlin said.

Josh stayed for two days. Devlin took him for a ride around the ranch. They talked and Josh enjoyed Esperanza's cooking. But in truth, the two had nothing in common except for a stint on a prison work gang. When Josh said he had to leave again, Esperanza packed him a hearty lunch, coming outside to say good-bye while she brought it to him.

"It was nice to meet you," she said politely.

"It was a sincere pleasure to meet you, Mrs. Lachlan! I hope someday to have a nice family, like Dev here. But I despair of ever finding a wife as pretty and talented as you! I'll just have to make do with what I can find! Gold attracts them, though," he added, leaning closer to give her a wink. He kissed her hand, pinched the baby's cheek, shook hands with Devlin and rode away.

"He seems nice," Esperanza said. "Where did you meet him?"

"We built part of a railroad together," Devlin said.

Sacramento, California, September, 1852

They were preparing for the annual drive. It was never very far, not like the drives that would be so famous in Texas and Kansas in later decades, and now it was even closer. A railroad now connected San Francisco and Sacramento, so they only had a couple weeks travel to get to the railhead and the stock dealers there.

"Do you think we could go along?" Esperanza asked.

Devlin was surprised, but also pleased. For years, he had remarked on anything she showed interest in, and if she wanted to make a trip to the city, that was fine with him. Aguas Amargas only had one small general store, besides the feed store.

"That would be great," Devlin said.

James was walking already and climbing on anything he could get near. They had given up on cradles and cribs and let him sleep in a small trundle bed that he could climb out of by himself, without crashing to the floor. It was harder to keep track of him, but it cut down on bruises. When they made their infrequent trips to town, one of them had to hold him the whole way, which was not easy. Being restrained from his constant activity and exploration was the one thing that made him mad. This long drive would be a problem.

"You built him a cage?" Esperanza demanded.

"I don't want him falling out of the wagon and getting run over by one of those big wheels," Devlin said. "And he doesn't have to be in it all the time, just when one of us can't watch him."

He didn't like the cage at all, and Devlin didn't blame him. But a child too young to obey and as active as James was needed some kind of safety restraint for his own good. Mostly, they left him in it when he was sleeping, including overnight so he couldn't wander off and get eaten by something. When he could, when the cattle were moving along without too much trouble, Devlin would pick the boy up and set him in front of himself on the saddle. James liked that. His fat little hands patted the horse's neck and played in its mane, and he bounced happily along in front of his father. Devlin rode with one hand on the rein and the other arm wrapped securely around James at those times. He could feel the flutter of the baby's rapid heartbeat under his hand, smell the soft baby smell of him. It amazed him how fiercely he loved this little person, part of himself, part of Esperanza.

"It's his first birthday tomorrow," Devlin said, as they dropped their luggage on the bed of the hotel. "Think he would like to see a show?"

"I think he'd prefer to run amuck through town," Esperanza said. She looked tired. Bringing the baby all this way had probably worn on her more than it had on him, although he felt his heart had been in his throat the entire time, worrying about them both.

"Dinner out for sure, though," Devlin said. "I know a place that has good pastry. We'll get him a three-layer, custard-filled chocolate birthday cake, with cream and dark chocolate shavings on top. What?" he added as Esperanza smiled and shook her head.

"It's just odd, a man knowing so much about baking."

"I keep telling you…"

"You used to own the finest restaurant in South Carolina. I know. It still sounds odd."

"Listen," Devlin said. "I have to get some business done. I'll be back in two hours at the latest. You should get some rest. James has been a little fussy, I think you can get him to sleep too. Or I can take him with me…"

"No. We'll both get some rest."

"All right, then. I'll be back in a couple hours, and we can go do some shopping, go out to eat. Whatever you want."

"What heaven, eating something I didn't have to prepare myself over a campfire!" Esperanza said.

Smiling, he kissed her, then James, and he went to do the dealing at the stock offices. When he came back and asked at the desk for his room key, he was told he had already checked out.

"Of course, I didn't check out!" Devlin said. "I barely even checked in! I ordered hot baths, I paid for a week!"

"I gave her the money back, sir, when she checked out."

"What are you talking about?"

"Your wife. Mrs. Lachlan. I assumed you were not happy with the room, leaving so soon after your arrival. She was only up there a few minutes when she came back and asked about the train schedules. When I told her the train to San Francisco leaves today, she checked out. Oh, she left this behind though, for me to keep for you."

He held up the small bag that held Devlin's clothes.

"The other bags?" Devlin asked.

"She took them with her, sir. I helped her get a cab, carried the bags out myself, while she took the baby…"

She took the baby. Devlin could still not quite believe what he was hearing. "She asked about train schedules? And you got her a cab…?"

"To the train station, yes."

"Thank you," Devlin said, and he turned and rushed out. He did not know exactly where the train station was. The passenger stop was not anywhere near the stock-loading areas he usually dealt with, but he knew where the tracks went, knew where to look. He found it quick enough, pushing through crowds on the streets, running when he could. When he arrived, the small waiting room was deserted. But then, women alone were not allowed in public waiting rooms. There would be another room somewhere. He shoved aside a man who was at the ticket window, purchasing tickets, and demanded of the man behind the cage, "Did you see a young woman today? About so high? Very pretty, and carrying a small child?"

"Yes, sir," the man said.

"Well, where is she?"

"On the train, I imagine. After I sold her the ticket, we barely had time to get her and her luggage on the train before it left."

"What train? When did it leave?"

"The San Francisco train," the clerk said. "It left over an hour ago."

"And you're sure she was on it?"

"Yes, sir. I helped her on myself."

"When is the next one? Devlin demanded.

"In four days. Would you like a ticket?"

Without answering, Devlin left the train station and ran all the way to the livery stable. Miguel was still there, fortunately. Devlin paid him off, gave him the cash for the other men, and for the livery fee.

"When you're ready, go ahead and head back to the ranch," Devlin said.

"You and Mrs. Lachlan coming later?"

"Yeah, I hope so," Devlin said.

He got his horse, put together a quick kit from the cooking things in the wagon, and rode to the hotel to pick up his bundle of clothes. It took him two days to get to San Francisco. He almost killed the horse, pushing it too hard after the long drive. He had to stop and let it rest. But finally, he made it to San Francisco. He went straight to the train station to inquire about a young lady with a baby getting off alone.

"Yes, sir, I remember them," the station man said.

"Do you know where they went?"

"Yes, because she asked for directions to Number Eleven Cherry Hill."

Eleven Cherry Hill. He wasn't sure whether to be more alarmed or relieved. She had asked for directions to Josh Tyler's house. Josh was a friend. Or he had been. Devlin had to admit to himself, though, that he would never had had anything to do with the man if they hadn't been chained together for more than half a year. Josh was lazy and insincere. Josh had struck it rich in the gold fields. Josh had flirted with Esperanza the whole time he was visiting. On the other hand, Josh flirted with every woman, all the time, even the elderly cook's assistant at the prison work camp. All these thoughts and more raced through his mind as he rode through the winding and hilly streets, following the directions the station master gave him. He ended up in a neighborhood where tall trees and wrought iron fences hid the broad lawns and big houses inside. Sometimes he could see the tops of houses above the trees, or views of them between, but when he came to number eleven, he saw nothing. He opened the big gate and followed a dirt driveway around a curve. For a moment, he stopped in surprise. In the middle of the spot cleared for building was a foundation with a rough board floor laid over it, and two or three frames where walls would one day be. In front of the construction was a tent. Devlin spurred his horse forward and found Josh sitting in a low chair between the tent and a small campfire, sipping at a bottle of whiskey.

"Well, if this isn't old home week!" Josh grinned. "How come you didn't come to visit with your wife?"

Devlin leaped from his horse, grabbed Josh by his shirtfront, lifted him bodily from the chair and shook him so hard he dropped the bottle, which shattered on the ground.

"Where is she?" Devlin demanded.

"Whoa! What…? What are you talking about?"

"My wife! Where is she?" Devlin demanded, giving the man another hard shake.

"How should I know, Dev! Yeah, she was here a few days ago, but she left within minutes. I wondered why you didn't stop by yourself if y'all were in town, but…"

Devlin shoved Josh away from him, and Josh dropped heavily into his chair, almost missing it as he fell.

"Now that's uncalled for, Dev."

Devlin ignored him and looked around. There was no velvet flocked wallpaper. There weren't even walls to put it on. She couldn't have been inside the house, because there was no house to be inside of. He threw back the tent flap and looked inside, but there was nothing there but an unmade cot and a mess of dishes and clothes.

"When was she here?" he asked, coming back out.

"I don't know, a couple days ago. Why…?"

"Did she say anything? Where did she go when she left?"

"I don't know, Dev! I'm telling you! She and the kid showed up here about two, three days ago. She said something about men being all alike, and she left again."

"In a cab?"

"No. I think there was a cab, now that you mention it. But it left before we even spoke. She had a satchel of some kind and a smaller bag, and she just grabbed them up, tucked the kid under her arm and walked away."

"Walked away where? Which way did she go?"

"I can't see the road from here! Anyway, where would she go? Home, that's my guess. You must have missed her somewhere."

That was it, Devlin thought desperately. That was it, he missed her somewhere. She was here while he was there, she was there while he was here. Simple. He swung back up on his horse and rode off, with Josh still shouting behind him, "Hey! Aren't you even going to stay and visit? Hey! Boy! You broke a whole bottle…"

He checked everywhere in town he could think of. He asked at the train station and the stage station and checked every single hotel and boarding house in the huge, sprawling city, even the ones in an area he would never have let her enter alone, had he been there. She must have gone back to Sacramento, though how he wasn't sure. He was going to load his horse and take the train back, but then he thought, what if she was on the road somewhere, walking all by herself? So, he rode back. He checked the train and stagecoach stations there, checked hotels, especially the one they had almost stayed in before. He checked the livery stable. Miguel was gone, but no, no young lady had gone with him. No one had gone with him.

She probably went home, Josh had said. With no idea where else to look, Devlin headed for home.

He took every side trail he could find leading off the main road, following them for hours at a time before giving up and going back to the main trail. There were footprints and hoof prints, wagon tracks and the tracks of a hundred cows, but no sure sign of a woman and a baby. He finally caught up to Miguel just before they reached the ridge above the ranch road.

"I didn't see her, boss," Miguel said. "And if she was behind me, you'd have crossed her trail. She probably did go home. Where else would she be?"

Where else indeed? He rode in the deepening twilight alongside the wagon, all too aware of the empty cage tossed in the back among the returning cook pots and purchases.

Twin Lakes Ranch, Near Aguas Amargas, California, October 1852

"There, see," Miguel said. "I told you."

There was a faint glow from the windows of the big house, indicating lamps were lit deep inside somewhere. And smoke was coming from the kitchen stovepipe as well as the bedroom fireplace. Relieved, terrified, angry, he spurred his horse ahead of the wagon and drew up at the half-rotten front porch. He leaped down from the saddle and ran up the intact part of the stairs. His boots and spurs clattered loudly on the porch floor before he ever flung open the door calling, "Espe! James! I'm home! Espe!"

There was movement in the back of the big hall, where the door opened from the kitchen. Light spilled out from the kitchen as the door opened, but it didn't spill out on a pretty young woman. There was a man coming out of his kitchen. A grizzled-looking man of about fifty, holding a shotgun not-quite pointed at Devlin's gut.

He didn't pause, he didn't think. He grabbed the pistol out of his holster and shot.

The man fell, screaming in pain. The shotgun went off, blasting a hole near the ceiling above Devlin's head. Devlin strode across the room and pointed the pistol – which was a new six-shot Remmington, not one of the old single-shots – at the man's head.

"Where's my wife?" he demanded, cocking back the hammer.

The man was screaming in pain, screaming something else he couldn't understand. Two more people came out of the kitchen then, and for a moment, Devlin's heart leapt. The gun wavered and lost its aim as he recognized a gown of flounces and rosettes made of pale rose silk. But it was not Esperanza who had it on. It was some stringy-haired, pimply-faced teenager. The other person to come out of the kitchen was an older woman, wearing Esperanza's ivory comb in her grey hair.

Seeing the gun had wavered, the man on the floor reached for his shotgun again. Devlin kicked it out of his reach, and strode forward, shaking with rage, pointing his revolver directly into the girl's face.

"What did you do to my wife?" he said in a low, hard voice. "Where is she? Where is my son?"

There was no coherent answer. All three of them were sobbing and shouting and babbling. Devlin, gun still leveled, grabbed the front of the silk dress and said, "Take it off!"

The woman fell on the floor in a half-faint. The girl clutched at the material near her bosom and screamed. He might have stripped her there, he probably would have killed them all, if Miguel hadn't run in the front door just then, while at almost the same time, Juanito came running in from the back, both of them alerted from by the gunfire.

"Boss! No!" Miguel shouted. "Don't do it!"

Devlin let go of the girl, who sank sobbing into her mother's arms. Instead, he kicked the non-bloody leg of the man on the floor and said, "who are you? What are you doing in my house? And *where is my family?*"

"There was no one here!" the man said. "I swear to God there was no one here. It was abandoned property…"

"Where were you?" Devlin asked Juanito.

"I was checking the cows. I got in about half an hour ago, saw the smoke, and figured you were back. I was going to come down about now anyway to check on things… They couldn't have been here more than today! I checked the place before I rode out this morning!"

"What? What's he saying?" the man said.

"Boss?" Miguel said. "That man's going to bleed to death if we don't take care of that wound."

"Who cares?" Devlin said. "All I want to know is where Esperanza and James are!"

"I don't understand what you're saying!" the man wailed.

Devlin poked the barrel of his pistol against the man's nose. "Shut up!" he said. It was a confusing conversation as he spoke to the intruders in English, and to his men in Spanish.

"Boss?" Miguel said.

"Get some rags and things from the kitchen," Devlin said. He saw the women starting to get up and he swerved the gun their direction and said, "Don't move. Juanito, go get my rope."

Juanito ran out the front door and untied Devlin's lasso from his saddle.

It was a good, stiff working rope, but Devlin sliced it into sections with his belt knife and used it to bind the hands of the women, who shrieked and moaned until, disgusted, he said to them, "No one's going to rape you! No one in their right mind would want to!"

"Juanito, go get the sheriff," Devlin instructed. "And Señora Caldera."

Juanito started to leave, then paused again. "The midwife? Why do we need a midwife?"

Devlin explained it in English. Juanito knew enough of the language to get the drift, and Devlin wanted this family to hear all of it.

"Because these women are going to be stripped to the skin to see what else they have stolen, and if you can't find a woman to do it, I'll do it myself!"

This brought more screaming, but Devlin turned his back, disgusted, on the women.

He tied the man's hands tightly behind his back, stripped off his boots so he couldn't kick while Miguel washed and dressed the wound in his thigh.

"Don't let that dirty Mex touch me!" the man screamed when Miguel started to cut away his pant leg to see the wound. "Get him away from me!"

Devlin slapped the man across the face, hard enough to knock him over even in his sitting position.

"That man that you are insulting is the only reason you and your family are alive right now!" Devlin hissed at him. "You better treat him with respect or I might just ignore his desire to keep you alive."

"Oh, I don't care if they live or die, boss," Miguel said, in Spanish. "I just don't want you to have to live with murdering women and children."

In English, Devlin replied to him. "These aren't women and children. They're filthy, lying, murdering animals!"

"Yes, boss," Miguel said, and he finished bandaging the man's leg. Once he was done, Devlin tied his feet together too.

"Unload the wagon and take care of the mules," Devlin told Miguel then. "I'll watch them until Morales gets here."

"Boss?"

"Yes?"

"Don't kill them."

"I will if they give me any more reason to," Devlin said grimly. Miguel

219

left then, with one backwards glance to see that Devlin was still just squatting on the dirt floor of the hall, gun dangling between his legs.

"That Mexican could have poisoned the wound!" the woman wailed. "Ken is going to die because you let that dirty Mexican do that! You should have let me…!"

Devlin rose to his feet. "There are NO MEXICANS here!" he shouted. "The Treaty of Guadalupe-Hidalgo, signed on July 4, 1848 by President James K. Polk gave American citizenship to all persons living north of the new border. Everyone here is as American as you are!"

"He didn't know what he was signing," the man murmured.

"Are you saying the president of the United States was illiterate?" Devlin asked.

"I'll… ill…?" The man didn't even know the word.

"People like you disgust me! You call Miguel 'dirty Mexican,' but look at yourselves! You haven't bathed in a month! Maybe a year! You stink! All of you! And you walk into a man's house, steal his property…"

"By law, any land we think is abandoned we can take!" the man smirked. "You can't stop us! It's the law."

"I can certainly stop you if you're all dead," Devlin said, causing another round of shrieks from the women. "Abandoned property!" he added in disgust. "Are you out of your mind?"

"No one was here!" the man said. "And look at this place! It looks more like a lumber yard than a house!"

"Oh, yes? Hay in the barn, hens in the henhouse, horses in the corral, food in the larder, clothes in the closets! Abandoned! You didn't think it was abandoned. You thought someone who didn't speak English owned it, and you could swoop in and steal it all. People like you fight wars and pass laws to exterminate anyone different from you and steal what's theirs. It's you who should be exterminated! Maybe, I'll just do it myself, despite that 'dirty Mex' who said I shouldn't kill you!"

The women screamed. The man kicked at the floor as if he could get away. Devlin just stood and went into the kitchen, from where the smell of burning had been growing for some time. There was a pan of lard on the stove, smoking badly, burned and blackened chicken parts bubbling in the grease. He used a rag to slide it off the hot part of the stove, opened windows and the back door to get the smoke out. Then he walked past his captives to have a look at the bedrooms. It seemed that the couple had decided to move into his and Esperanza's bedroom. The bedroom and sitting room had been ransacked, other clothes as well as his and Esperanza's were scattered about. The girl must have decided to take over the smaller bedroom they used for guests since Señor Valencia died: some of Esperanza's things were tossed in there. Anger boiled in him again. He was shaking with it when he came back out. But just then, Juanito came back.

"Why are you back? I told you to get the Sheriff."

"I took the shortcut, through the Benevidez property, and the sheriff was there, having dinner with them. He'll be here in a few minutes. Mrs. Benevidez is coming with him, instead of the midwife."

II

It was near morning. Sheriff Morales came and squatted in front of Devlin, who was sitting on the cold flagstone floor of the hallway between the bedrooms and the big hall.

"I want them arrested," Devlin said. "They aren't just squatters. They're burglars, and thieves. And murderers."

"Dev," Morales said. "I've looked over everything very carefully. I know they made a mess, but there's nothing in this house to indicate Esperanza or little James has been here in over a month. They weren't here, Dev. Wherever they are, they weren't here when the Blunts showed up."

"Everyone said they probably went home. But they didn't..." Devlin stood up suddenly. "New Mexico! That's it! She probably went to New Mexico! I have to leave..."

"Dev!" Morales stood and caught Devlin's arm as he started to go into the bedroom to pack for another trip.

"They'll be there! I know they'll be there!"

"No, you don't know! You just hope. Devlin, listen to me! Winter's coming on. It'll take you months to get over those mountains, and months to get back. You'd be gone for half a year or more, and what if they come back here while you're gone? They'll think *you* abandoned *them*!"

Devlin started towards the bedroom again, turned again and started back to the hall. "What... I don't..."

"Write some letters. They'll get there as fast as you could, and you'll still be here waiting if they come back. If you take off, you won't be here for them."

Devlin sighed. "Okay. Okay, I'll write letters. But I want to press charges against those Blunt-headed people anyway. Abandoned property my... left foot!"

"I don't have much of a jail in Aguas Amargas. How about as soon as it gets light, we load them up and haul them off to Sacramento. It'll give you another chance to look there, too."

"Yes. Let's do that," Devlin agreed.

Mrs. Benevidez had earlier shown him some filthy women's underthings.

"Those are not Esperanza's," he'd said.

"What should I do with them?"

"Burn them," was his suggestion. Then he sighed and said, "let them get dressed again, but in their own clothing!"

He went into the bedrooms and searched and found a couple of faded old dresses that were probably what they'd worn into his house. The rose silk gown, and a plain brown dress Esperanza had worn for work were both folded up, along with the ivory comb, some jewelry, and Esperanza's best shoes to be taken by the Sheriff for evidence. The Blunts were loaded into their own wagon, their mis-matched, starved-looking mules hitched to it.

"Add this to the evidence," Devlin said, ripping a red silk kerchief from around the man's neck. It was a neck scarf Esperanza had made for him years ago on the Santa Fe Trail, when she was still a lively fourteen-year-old with happy feet.

Morales had to go into town first. Devlin packed, changed to a fresh horse, and left for Sacramento again. He met Morales there, and the judge was willing to get a trial started as soon as possible, so as not to keep white women in jail longer than necessary.

"You know, I'm getting tired of seeing you in my court," Judge Meyers said when Devlin came in with the sheriff.

"Maybe you should get rid of the Land Law of 1851," Devlin responded.

Meyers sighed, ignoring the comment, and said, "What is it this time? More squatters on Lachlan land?"

Sheriff Morales knew English, but not enough to speak in court. He had brought the town marshal with him, a man named Hughes, who was as bilingual as Devlin, and whose word carried weight.

"These people are being accused of breaking and entering, destruction of property, burglary, and attempt to do bodily harm with a firearm," Hughes said, speaking for the state.

"Really? You want to explain this, Mr. Lachlan?" Devlin described the incidents of the night he arrived at his house. Morales opened the bundle to show the gowns and jewelry the women had been wearing when he arrived.

"Those are our things!" Blunt shouted. "We brought them with us from Kansas! You can't prove otherwise! It's that man's word against ours!"

"You can identify these things positively?" Meyers asked.

"I can," Sheriff Morales said, with Hughes translating. "This is the wedding gown of Mrs. Esperanza Lachlan. I was at their wedding. So was most of the town, if you need more witnesses. My wife helped make this gown. Mrs. Lachlan also wore that comb in her hair that day, and these satin slippers. And I've seen her in town wearing this other dress as well. These items do not belong to the Blunt family. Besides, this dress didn't even fit Mrs. Blunt. I saw her in it, and it was obviously made for someone else. As I said, I can bring more witnesses, if we want to wait this trial."

"I think you've made your point. Anything else?"

"The Blunt family also slaughtered two chickens, stole food and drink from the larder, damaged beyond repair at least one cook pot. Rather than removing items from the premises, they moved their own things inside, and pulled a gun on Mr. Lachlan when he came home."

"He shot me!" Blunt said.

"In his own house, while you were pointing a cocked shotgun at him," Morales said.

Meyers sighed. "Mr. Blunt. The Land Law of 1851 was written so that land belonging to people who had died or moved on after the War could be claimed and used by someone else."

That was a blatant lie, Devlin thought. The law had been written to stuff into the pockets of white pioneers the land they thought they should have been entitled to after they fought a bloody and unethical war to steal it from peaceful and democratic neighbors, neighbors who had, incidentally, helped them win their war for independence against the British. But he kept his mouth shut. Meyers may have been lying, but he was obviously intending to chastise Blunt.

"The Law was never meant to allow people to move in on other people's property and help themselves to whatever they wanted. I'm afraid, sir, that entering a place that was so obviously not abandoned as the Lachlan ranch, you were indeed breaking and entering and burglarizing the property. I sentence you all to one year in jail and a fine of one hundred dollars. Sentence suspended." He banged his gavel. "Case dismissed."

"They're not going to jail?" Morales asked, not sure of the last thing the judge said.

"No," Hughes said.

"I'm sorry," Morales said to Devlin.

"It doesn't matter," Devlin said. "They were still convicted." He sighed. "I suppose I should start searching…"

"We did that for you," Morales said. "Hughes had four deputies checking every boarding house, every train, stage or livery stable in town. No one saw them, Dev."

"It's been awhile," Devlin said.

"Yes, and the man at the train station still remembers helping her onto the train to San Francisco. But he's dead certain she didn't come back. All you can do now is go home."

He did. There was smoke and lamplight again when he arrived, but he discovered it was Juanito, camped out in the kitchen.

"I wanted to make sure no one did that to you again!" he said. "I'm sorry I wasn't here before…"

"You were doing your job," Devlin said. "Exactly as you should. Are you going home for Christmas again this year? See the kids?"

"Yeah. They're getting big, but I still like to have Christmas with them. Christmas isn't Christmas without ki…" He stopped, embarrassed.

"Go see them," Devlin said.

Miguel had also waited for his return to make his usual winter trip into town. The three of them had dinner in the kitchen of the big house, and the other two men went back to the bunkhouse and left Devlin alone. He took a lamp and went to look at the bedroom he had shared with Esperanza. The Blunts things had been removed, but the room was still in disarray. Marge Blunt had evidently tried on all of Esperanza's dresses. Some of his own things were scattered around also, and the bed had been used, even if they hadn't spent a night there. Disgusted, he grabbed all the bedding off the bed and tossed it outside on the patio. Then he went and looked at Señor Valencia's bedroom. Some of Esperanza's clothing was in here, draped around like a dress shop. On the dressing table were some of her earrings, some gold and ivory bangles that Mrs. Benevidez had taken off the Blunt girl, her boar-bristle brush, and one of her beautiful cedar hair combs. He picked up the comb and smelled it, inhaling the fragrance of red cedar. But instead of the sweet smell of Esperanza's hair, there was something greasy and unclean-smelling in the teeth of the comb. Straggly, oily blonde hairs. He took it to the kitchen and threw it in the stove to burn. Coming back out, he stopped to look out over the big hall. A realization hit him then, and he dropped to his knees on the dirt floor, unable to stand on his own.

A lumber yard. Blunt had said his house looked more like a lumber yard than a home. And he was right. From the first time he examined the place, Devlin had seen the possibilities there. He had always seen it as it could be, not as it currently was. But Blunt was right: as it was, it looked like a lumber yard.

He had, all along, whenever he had the time, worked hard on this house. But the things that needed to be done first were things that took time and energy and hard labor, but didn't show visible results. He had hauled river rock and rebuilt the chimneys on both big fireplaces, up above the roof of the house. He had ripped out the rotting, half-collapsed stairway and the upstairs balcony that led to the upper bedrooms, so the floor of the big Hall lapped directly up against the flagstone of the back hallway where the useable bedroom-suites were, and the upstairs bedrooms were exposed and completely unusable. He had torn out all of the rotting wood floors downstairs and hauled wagon load after wagon load of clay and mud to fill in the gap between the ground below and where the floors had been, making the base solid for laying flagstone instead of having raised wooden floors. There were piles of sand he had collected from a streambed nearby for laying the flagstone, when he had time. He had pounded and tamped the dirt so the floors wouldn't settle and shift later. He had blasted and quarried flagstone for the job, piling it in the smaller front room. He had purchased and started twisting the wrought-iron for the railings he planned to build, iron that currently lay piled in a corner of the great hall. He had milled beams and lumber for reconstructing the stairs and balconies, and in another corner it was all air-stacked to dry so it wouldn't twist and warp when it was used. The bedroom and sitting room he had shared with Esperanza were complete, cozy, nicely decorated. The kitchen was big and warm and friendly. But in between was a construction zone, which he had simply never really seen. Suddenly, Esperanza's words to Josh made sense, "She said something about all men being alike," he had said. They were dreamers, she had meant. Or liars. And he could hear Emma Rogers' voice, as clearly as if she were again standing in front of an idealistic twenty-year-old, admonishing him: "You thought everyone has your grand vision or my artist's eye. Most people don't, Devlin. They can't see what will be, only what is, and right now, what is isn't too impressive."

This was definitely not impressive. It was almost as bad as Josh's foundation and two frame walls, rising up into nowhere. Devlin stood up then, looked around for a moment, and started in by faint lamplight to work on his house.

Christmas came. He laid out the lace shawl and brightly-painted toy train he had bought in Sacramento on the raised hearth of the fireplace in the hall. But there was no one to admire them, so he went back to work.

Daily, he did remember to feed the chickens and horses, fork down hay for the cattle when it was too snowy for them to forage. But he neglected the mucking out, barely remembered to light a fire and cook something to eat every now and then. Mostly he worked. He spread the sand, mixed the mortar. Starting in the side room, the room he was calling the study, he started laying the flagstone, a painstaking and laborious job for one man alone. The rocks had to be laid out and examined for size and shape and laid in a manner that left as few gaps as possible. Sometimes he had to use the hand-sledge and a chisel to chip the rock to the right size. All of it had to be hauled and laid and cemented in place. Floors first, he kept telling himself. Floors first, then he could start on the stairway and balcony. He never did go back to the room he had shared with Esperanza. For a while, he slept on the floor of the kitchen, living completely in that one room. But the hard stone floor was not restful for his tired muscles and sore back after a day of labor, and he built a ladder to reach one of the upstairs bedrooms, claimed that as his own.

He had never expected Esperanza to cook for the hired hands, but he had not liked to leave them alone to fend for themselves after a hard day's work, either. Over the years, whenever she made a big pot of beans or stew or a pile of tortillas, he had taken some to the bunkhouse and shared them with Miguel and Juanito. Now the role was reversed. It was Miguel who said they needed to leave him alone, but it was Juanito who said they needed to at least be sure he ate. They brought him beans and tortillas on occasion. They did the mucking out he had neglected, and eventually even started feeding the barnyard animals.

Twin Lakes Ranch, Near Aguas Amargas, California, April 1853

Devlin was on his knees, dragging a long board through the sand where he was going to lay the next pieces of stone, when Miguel came in to say, "Boss? The men will be here for the round up tomorrow."

"Oh? Already?"

"It's April," Miguel said.

"Oh. Well, I'll be down in the morning, soon as I finish this."

Miguel squatted next to him and took the board out of his hands. "Boss. You won't finish this tomorrow. You won't finish it next week or next month, maybe not next year. It's time to get back to running a ranch."

"You and Juanito…"

"Have been taking care of things. But it's not our place, Boss. It's yours. It won't do you any good to fix this house all up nice for her to come home to, if there's no ranch to support you both when she does."

Devlin seemed then to wake up as from a dream. For almost five months he had worked every day and long into the night trying to make the house into the nice home Esperanza deserved. He had neglected everything in his obsession.

"I'm sorry," he said now.

"It's Okay. We understand."

"I don't," Devlin said, with sigh. "Thank you, Miguel. And thank you for not saying 'if' she gets home."

Miguel just shrugged.

"I'll be up to the bunkhouse first thing in the morning," Devlin said.

"No, boss. You need to come now. Have dinner with us. You can sleep here tonight, or up there, but you need to have breakfast with us, too. You can't go on a cattle drive on an empty stomach."

"I have some things here," Devlin said. "Beans, I think, and some tortillas."

"The tortillas are gone, and the beans rotted. I gave them to the chickens two days ago. Come. Now."

He looked, at what he had accomplished and what he had not. But then he sighed and stood up and allowed Miguel to take him to the bunkhouse. There was stew for dinner, made of beef and last season's potatoes. He hadn't realized how hungry he was until he stepped inside and smelled it. He ate two bowls, but it was all right: Juanito had made plenty. There was fried bread and butter and honey as well, and eggs and bacon, potatoes and red chile, for breakfast in the morning.

"Thank you," he said again, as they prepared to head out for the round up.

"*De nada*," Miguel assured him.

They returned from the round up to find several of the families of the men camped out near the bunkhouse, preparing a barbeque for them all when they returned. No one had ever done this before, and although the food and music and dancing afterwards were very welcome, Devlin wondered why this time. Until he went inside the big house and found some of his personal belongings on the kitchen table. He looked then and found that the women had come to do what he had not been able to bring himself to do. They had washed and folded and stored away all of Esperanza's and James's things. They had stripped the beds in the downstairs bedrooms, washed and put away all the bedding, including what he had thrown outside last winter and left lying there. Both bedrooms were devoid of anything belonging to any member of the family, his own few personal items that had been left there were what was waiting on the table for him to put away. He could start over now. If he wanted to.

III.

Time passed. There was a garden to plant, hay and firewood to cut. Cattle to be drug out of situations they should not have gotten into, the annual cattle drive. As the first impetus of the gold rush waned, the price of cattle fell, and Twin Lakes made up the difference selling firewood, lumber, flagstone and potatoes. Miguel married and moved away. Devlin hired two more men, 'Berto Llamas and Sal – Salomon Rodriguez. Sal was an ex-miner who had been partially crippled in an explosion. He couldn't ride, but he had been hired to cook, take care of the bunkhouse and tend the vegetable garden. Devlin began taking his evening meal in the bunkhouse, since he had a cook. Juanito was promoted to foreman and received an extra three dollars a month in pay. The cabin on the Benevidez ranch burned and Oscar Benevidez and two of the children were killed. Mrs. Benevidez decided to move to San Diego where she had some relatives still, so Devlin borrowed enough from the bank to give her fair market value for her land and cattle, even though the law was still in effect that women could not own land, and the deed was in his name. He drove her and the two surviving children to Sacramento to catch a train, as he went in himself to change the deed for Twin Lakes. The lawyer he had dealt with in the past was now the senior partner of a law firm, Lancaster, Bailey and Gerrold.

"Do you want all of these smaller holdings incorporated into the big one?" Troy Lancaster asked him.

"No. Just the Benevidez one. The rest stay separate."

So, Twin Lakes and the Benevidez property were re-deeded as a single unit of seventeen hundred and fifty acres, and putting the Twin Lakes brand on the Circle B cattle took months of intermittent work to accomplish.

And Devlin continued to work on his house. The flagstone was finally laid throughout the first floor. He rebuilt the inside and outside balconies for the upstairs bedrooms, using strong beams and good flooring. He fixed the back staircase that went from the kitchen to the second floor and up to the attic, and he was able to take down the ladder he had been using to get to his bedroom every night. Instead of building a wooden staircase from the great hall up to the second-floor bedrooms, he designed a broad, curving staircase to be built from adobe. He drew it so that the steps would be shallow and the width plenty big enough for fashionable ladies' dresses.

"You're done this before, haven't you?" Juanito asked.

Devlin looked at his design and realized he had. Almost. It was easier to build it as a wall than to bend the wood.

Juanito helped him make adobes, showed him how to use string to line up each row so the wall was straight, how to use brick and mortar to tie the top so it was strong. They laid flagstone on the flat of each step, with brick on the risers. The heavy staircase and the balcony above made the hallway in front of the bedroom-suites downstairs private, and very safe. The only entrances were to the right of the big staircase, or through the door from the kitchen that also opened onto the back staircase. Then he started building the iron railings. One by one, he fixed or replaced windows. Step by step, it was starting to look like his vision.

Twin Lakes Ranch, Near Aguas Amargas, September, 1858

The fall round up would be starting soon. Devlin and Juanito rode out to locate where the cattle were so they would be easier to gather. Juanito went south and west. Devlin rode east, up into the timber along the side of the valley, then circled back to Hidden Lake, the easternmost of the two lakes that gave the ranch its name. It was in a large, deep bowl, surrounded on two sides by grassy hills, and on a third by rocky canyons. Water ran into and out of the lake year-round, so the water was fresh and clear, and the bowl it was in was filled with huge old cottonwood trees, making it a cool, shady glade on hot days. He had brought Esperanza and James up here often for picnics that one summer when there were three of them, enjoying the rustling of the leaves in the wind and watching little James splash in the shallows of the lake. It gave Devlin a pang to come here now, remembering. But there were memories all over the ranch. He couldn't avoid the memories or the places that reminded him of his wife and son, who had vanished so completely. He had received letters from New Mexico every year since he had first written to them, letters chronicling the deaths every year of more people he had known, but always ending with the note that no one had seen or heard from Esperanza.

He let the horse rest a few minutes in the cool shade, crop some of the green grass and take a drink from the stream entering the lake before he urged it up into the rocks. The trail through the badlands here was steep in places, narrow, winding up through dry, hard rock land. It was a rough ride. He paused for another brief break when they reached the top of the ridge before starting down through the canyons to the old Benevidez place on the other side. Here was another big, broad valley. It was not quite as well watered as Twin Lakes, but there was a stream through the middle than ran even in the driest times. There was also a spring where water ran out of one of the rock cliffs. Oscar Benevidez had put a pipe in the spring so that instead of just running down to make a marsh in the grass below, it trickled out of the pipe, which stuck out over a cistern he had dug and lined with rock. There was always water there.

All that was left of the Benevidez home was a pair of partial adobe walls that met at a corner. He had left them up because they provided a windbreak for the animals near the cistern. The barn was also still partially standing. It had three walls and most of the roof, and some of the interior stalls were still there. Outside of it was a big fire pit with iron bars over it for hanging coffee or cook pots on. It made a good stopover for men scouting for missing cattle, a place where they had fresh water and could get out of the rain if need be. The cattle also liked to shelter in the barn in foul weather or on hot days. But as Devlin rode down now, he noticed a few things out of place. The iron crossbar over the fire pit was missing. The bucket the men usually kept upside down on a fence post to prevent mice from nesting in it was sitting upright by the open side of the barn. And there was an unfamiliar horse grazing out behind the barn.

"Hello!" he called, sliding off his horse. "Hello! I have to tell you you're trespassing. Come on, I know you're in there!"

The voice that answered was high-pitched: female. And it spoke Spanish, which was unusual for a squatter. Unheard of, actually.

"Go away!" it said. From the shadows of the barn, a long, narrow iron tube poked out.

Devlin sighed. Switching to Spanish, he said, "I know you're not holding a rifle on me. That's the pipe from the fire pit! Now, come on out of there! I won't hurt you."

"I know you won't," the woman said in a threatening tone. She came out, but she had shifted her grip on the pipe so that instead of pretending it was a rifle barrel, she now held it like a club. She was not a large woman, a little taller perhaps than Esperanza, but woefully thin. Her hair had fallen from any pins that might have once held it in place and was tangled and dirty, but it was a dark red-brown, the color of an old penny, and it fairly glowed in the sun. She was dressed in a simple work dress and moccasins.

Devlin put his hands up at once. "Easy now. Careful! Where's your husband?"

"Dead," she said.

"I'm sorry," he said. "Just… let me have the pipe, all right?"

"I'm not leaving," she said, still threatening him with it. "We have

232

nowhere to go."

"No family?"

"No. This place has a roof. We'll stay here."

"It only has part of a roof," Devlin said. He took the last step towards her and jerked the pipe out of her hand. She staggered, and then to his surprise, fell in a dead faint. He dropped the pipe and caught her, laid her down gently on the ground, and went to look inside the barn. "We" she had said. But what he saw inside made him catch his breath. They had nothing, not even a blanket, but she had torn up grass to make a soft bed in the shadows where the hot sun didn't reach. Lying on the bed were two children, one maybe all of two years old. The other couldn't have been more than a month, if that. He stepped closer, squatted down, and saw that both children were thin, their cheeks pale and sunken. Both were awake, and both just lay there, listlessly, which was not, he knew, normal for children. He felt them, and the boy tried to move away from his probing hand. But he didn't try hard to move, and he didn't cry, even though his face looked as if he were crying. Both children were warm, but not hot. Not sick then. He left them and stepped back to the woman who was stirring, trying to lift herself up. He got his canteen off his saddle, and came back to squat by her, hold her head up and give her a sip of water. She also wasn't just thin, she was way too thin, her cheeks and eyes sunken. Defiant as she had been, she had used the last of her strength trying to chase him away. Resigned now, she let him feed her water. He propped her against the side of the barn and went back to his horse to pull his lunch out of his saddle bags. He had two tortillas, slathered with butter and folded over, wrapped in a bit of cheesecloth. He gave one to her. The other he took inside the barn and tore off a piece and handed it to the little boy. He helped the boy sit up and held out the piece of sandwich towards him. The boy grabbed it and gobbled it. Devlin started to tear off another piece when he heard retching behind him and saw that the woman was vomiting up the bit of food he had given her. Suddenly, the boy did also. He boy cried softly, and reached for more sandwich, but Devlin gave him only a drink of water instead. He went back to the woman.

"How long since you have eaten?" he asked.

"I fed the children this morning," she said. He considered that, and realized she was trying to nurse both of them to keep them alive. Most likely they had suckled, but there was nothing left for her to give them, and perhaps hadn't been for a while.

"How long since you have eaten," he asked again, making, in Spanish, the "you" singular and not plural.

She just shrugged without answering. He looked around. He had to get them back to the ranch. He had to get something softer than bread and butter into them, something their empty stomachs could handle. They'd be dead in a day if he didn't, all of them. But how to get four people back on one horse? They had a horse also, true, but the woman was in no shape to ride.

He had his slicker tied behind the saddle for emergencies. He took it off now and cut it with his knife to make it into a long, broad strip. He cut a few smaller strips also. Then he went to where the children were laying. The infant was sinking into sleep. The little boy was whimpering softly. He spread out the big piece of his slicker, laid the baby into it and wrapped it around the child's body, securing it in place so that when he picked it up, the child would not fall out. He tied the ends together, then he went back to the woman and squatted to feed her a bit more water.

"Señora? You'll have to help me here. I know you're at the end of your strength, but you'll have to dredge up a bit more. For them. I'm going to put you on my horse. You'll have to sit there just for a moment or two yourself before I can help you. Can you do that?"

She nodded. He scooped her up in his arms and set her astride his saddle. He went back for the boy, and set the child in front of the woman, draped her arms around him. He went back to the barn and picked up the infant and slung the tied slicker around himself, putting one side over his left shoulder, the other under his right so the baby hung suspended against his chest. He settled it into place as comfortably as possible, then used his stirrup to climb up and settle behind the saddle. The horse lifted his head and side-stepped at the unusual treatment, but Devlin got his boots in the stirrups and pulled the reins gently but firmly, showing he was still in control. He slipped both reins into his right hand, adjusted the infant in the sling so that its head rested on his arm as he reached around the woman and the boy with his left hand. It was awkward, not the same as riding with one small child in front of him on the saddle. But, fortunately, they were both fairly small, and he was big, so his arm reached around at least as far as the boy's chest. He snugged them both back against himself, careful to provide them support without squashing the infant, and he kicked the horse forward. Riding like this he knew he could not cross through the rock canyons again. There were places where the movement of the horse would toss them all to the ground if he tried it. It was longer through the road, but he had no choice. He headed across the meadow, climbed to the road, and turned left. His arm soon burned with the strain, but he dared not release the tension for a moment. The boy fell asleep, leaning into the arm that held him. The woman tried not to, but she seemed to drift in and out.

"Lydia," she murmured.

"Is that your name?" Devlin asked. Her head shook slowly, negative.

"The baby?"

She nodded.

"The baby's fine. I can feel her breathing."

"What... are you going to do with us?" she asked.

"Feed you," he said.

He had to walk the horse. It was evening by the time they came to the branch of the road that led off towards the ranch. So close to home, the horse wanted to move faster. He had to rein it in, force it to keep a slow, steady pace. Finally, they came to the house. The horse shook its head in disgust as Devlin rode past the stable, water and grain, up to the door of the bunkhouse.

"Juanito!" Devlin called. "Sal! Berto!"

All three men came to the door.

"Boss! What...?"

"I can't get down without help," Devlin said. "Juanito, follow me back to the house. Sal, do you have any kind of broth made, or can get some quickly?"

"I made chicken stew for dinner," the old man said.

"Wonderful! Perfect! We'll have chicken and vegetables for dinner. Send the broth to the house with Berto."

"What's wrong with them?" Sal asked.

"Starving," Devlin said.

Sal nodded, grabbed Berto's arm and disappeared through the door. Juanito took the horse's rein and led it back down to the big house. There he took the woman out of Devlin's arms.

"Put her in my room," Devlin said. "Then come back for the boy."

Juanito obeyed. He knew why Devlin had specified his own room: it was the only one with a mattress on the bed. With the big house empty, they had stored all the mattresses that had taken so long to clean and air out where, hopefully, they'd be safe from mice. Juanito was much smaller than Devlin. He could not manipulate his burden up the back stairs and had to carry the woman though the dark house and up the broad front staircase. He laid her on the bed and ran down the back stairs to take the child off the front of the saddle so that Devlin could slide down. They both went up to Devlin's room and laid their burdens next to the woman on the bed. Juanito struck a flint and lit the lamp, and Devlin dug some paper and a pencil out of his desk. He wrote something by lamplight and handed the note to Juanito.

"Grab dinner quick," Devlin said. "I need you to ride into town immediately. Get Mrs. Caldera. Ask her to come out right away. These people are in bad shape! Then you wait in town for the store to open, give this list to Gallegos. Tell him put it on the ranch bill."

"Our bill's a little thick right now, boss," Juanito said.

"I know. But he'll extend this much, what with the drive coming up. Tell him…"

"What?"

"Tell him if they die it'll all be returned unused," Devlin said. He went downstairs then to find Berto just coming in, juggling several containers. Devlin put him to care for his horse, then he lit the kitchen fire. He put the chicken broth in a pan on the stove and found that Sal had also sent a container of warm goat milk and a packet of white sugar. He blessed the man, and quickly began setting up a tray to take upstairs: cups, a pitcher of water, spoons, the sugar and milk, small bowls of broth. He carried everything upstairs and set it on his bedside table. Where to start?

He took a bowl, sat on the edge of the bed to lift the woman enough to spoon some broth into her. Two spoons, only. Then he lifted the boy and gave him some broth.

"*Tengo hambre, Papá*," the boy murmured.

"I know, son. I know. Just a sip though."

The infant could not have broth, he knew. She was far too young for anything that rich. He poured water into a clean cup and mixed several spoonfuls of sugar into it. He sat down in a chair then, picked up the infant, and tried to spoon a bit of the sugar water into her mouth. He was working on that when Berto came upstairs.

"What else, Boss?" he asked.

"I need you to haul a couple things around for me."

"Sure. What?"

"First, get some water heating downstairs. Then, go up to the attic and bring down a rocking chair, the cradle, and there's a small silver trunk, with roses stamped into the metal lid. If you're not sure, check. It has baby things in it. Bring that. Maybe a pillow or two if you can find them. They're also in a metal clad trunk."

Berto left.

"*Papá!*" the boy wailed, and Devlin felt tears pricking at his eyes: for the boy, for the family, for his own son: he didn't know. He had a pocket watch. He waited half an hour before allowing another sip of broth.

It was a long night.

II

Mrs. Caldera arrived just before dawn. She gave all of them a quick check and said, "What have you been doing?"

"One or two teaspoons of chicken broth every half hour, he said. "The boy seems stronger, so a little while ago, I gave him some of the goat milk."

"This baby is too little…"

"I know. I've been giving her drops of sugar water."

"Now, how did you know she'd be able to tolerate that?" the midwife asked.

"When James was real fussy once, Juanito said his mother gave it to babies for gas. It worked."

"It does. And the sugar probably kept her alive. Good thinking!"

"It was Sal who sent the sugar up here," Devlin said.

"Good for both of you then. Anyway, I have a little something here for her that I got from one of my patients."

She pulled a glass bottle and a rubber nipple out of her bag. The milk in the bottle looked kind of cheesy, but she shook it up, and he could see in the growing light it was thin, bluish milk. Mother's milk. He passed over the baby and stood so she could use the rocking chair. As he set the boy down on the bed and went downstairs to check the fire again, he heard the gratifying sound of a baby sucking and slurping. He was doing laundry when the midwife came downstairs, washing the diapers and baby dresses that had been in the trunk he had Berto bring him.

"I hope you have lots of hot water," Mrs. Caldera said, stretching her back. "We're going to have to do all the bedding as well."

"I know," he said.

"Maybe you should let me do that while you get some rest," she said.

"I got lots of rest, waiting between sips of broth all night. You were riding half the night."

"I don't suppose you have coffee boiling?"

He nodded towards the stove, and she helped herself to a cup from the cupboard and poured some.

"The little boy is doing all right," she said, sitting down at the table. "You were right in your guess that she was trying to nurse both of them, and I think he was getting more than his share. The baby might not have made it if you hadn't gotten them here when you did. The little girl's pretty weak, but I think she'll pull through if we can get the mother's milk up again."

She watched him rinse and wring out the things he was washing. "I don't suppose you have a clean nightgown lying around somewhere?" she asked.

"I sent to town for some women's things," he said.

Mrs. Caldera started to say something else, then she stopped. She understood what was happening. He could share the baby's things. His son had outgrown them before he had disappeared: they had probably already been packed away. But his wife's things were something else. They were too personal to share with a stranger, especially after what happened the night he had come back looking for his wife here. She knew the whole story: the whole county knew it. Devlin took the basket outside to hang the things on the clothesline. She helped herself to what was obviously fresh tortillas left by the bunkhouse cook and went back upstairs to check on the patients.

The warm late-summer sun dried the light cloth within a couple hours. The midwife bathed the baby and dressed her in fresh diapers, gown and bonnet. She hadn't been cleaned or changed in a long time, maybe more than a week. The little boy was just as bad, but she left him to Devlin while she took the infant back to its mother. Devlin soaked the boy in a warm tub in the sun outside, eventually scrubbing him up, and then letting him run naked while he washed up the boy's clothes in the bath water. The boy was old enough not to need diapers. He had only soiled himself in the last couple days when he was too weak to deal with such things properly. He explored the dooryard, Devlin watching carefully while he wandered as far as the stable and the chicken pens. He came back to stare thoughtfully at the tall, blonde man sitting in a chair in the shade.

"*Donde Papá?*" he asked. He had been calling Devlin "Papá," but now that he was better, thinking clearer, he recognized that this was a stranger.

"I don't know, son," Devlin said. "No *sé, 'jito*. The little lower lip started to stick farther and farther out.

"*Donde Mamá?*"

"She's upstairs. You want to go see her?"

The little brown head nodded, bouncing rapidly up and down. Devlin scooped up the sun-warmed little body and carried him upstairs.

"You need to knock!" the midwife admonished him as he entered his own bedroom. The woman was propped up on pillows on clean bedding, and as he entered the midwife quickly tucked the sheet up over her bare shoulders.

"Sorry!" he said. He passed the boy to the midwife, scooped up the pile of soiled bedding that had been left in the hall, and went back to the kitchen where, fortunately, he was still heating water.

It was past noon when Juanito returned with packages tied behind his saddle.

"Take the rest of the day off," Devlin told him. "Have a nap. And thanks."

"I got some of it from my mother," Juanito said. "She doesn't have any kids that small any more."

"That's great. Thanks."

As he turned to go back inside, Juanito called after him, "You get some rest too! If you need to stay in the bunkhouse…"

"I have nine empty bedrooms here," Devlin said. "I'll be fine. But thanks."

He took the things upstairs, gave them to the midwife, and went back to his laundry. He had just hung it all outside when the midwife came back downstairs.

"I'll have to go now," she said. "I have a woman due soon, I need to be close. Normally I wouldn't leave a sick woman and baby with a bunch of bachelors, but I know you can handle it. The question is, can you handle that boy as well?"

"I don't think he'll be any problem. Did she say anything yet? Do you know who they are?"

"Her name is Edwina Palacios. Her husband had a small place clear on the other side of the mountains east of here. About two or three weeks ago – she's not even sure – some men showed up…"

"Squatters," Devlin said. It wasn't a question.

"Maybe," Mrs. Caldera said though. "Apparently, the men had been around before. Horse thieves, I think more likely. She said her husband had a 'herd' of horses. Since those men had been around, her husband –I think she said his name was Jorge – brought her and the babies with him to go work so they wouldn't be alone in the cabin. The men came where he was fixing some kind of gate across a box canyon, a horse trap of some kind, or a corral. He threw her and the kids on the horse they had ridden out there and told them to hide out. I'm not sure if he tried to talk to the men, or just fought them, but he was killed. She had no choice but to just keep going. She got lost and turned around. She caught a fish once, and they had their lunch in the saddle bags when she left, but she might have been riding weeks before she landed here. What are you going to do with them?"

"Right now, get them healthy," Devlin said, "Like any decent person would. Then… well, it's up to her, isn't it? She said she had no family, but she wasn't in the best shape then."

"She's not in the best shape now," Mrs. Caldera said. "I want her on broth at least another day before you give her anything more solid, and then it had better be very light: no heavy meat, nothing fried. Probably want to avoid difficult things like cheese for a while, too. And I want her to stay in bed for at least a couple days, and then no work, nothing hard or difficult, just getting up and about on her own."

"That's no problem," Devlin said.

"Oh, it might be! This is not Esperanza. She's already trying to get up and do things she's not near strong enough to do. You may end up having to sit on her to keep her down."

240

"I'll try to avoid that," Devlin said, heat rising in his face at the thought. "How are the two children?"

"The boy – his name is Manuel by the way – seems to have come back completely. He can eat anything he wants. But he's an active kid, you're going to have to keep an eye on him."

"Yes, I saw that. The infant?"

"She needs to nurse on demand. That will keep the milk from drying up completely. Señora Palacios needs to be encouraged to keep herself healthy so she can feed the baby. If the baby is too hungry, you can give her a bit more of the sugar water."

"How will I know how hungry she is?"

"Check her diaper: nothing in, nothing out."

"Ah! Got it."

Sal had sent down more chicken broth and a small pot of stew. Devlin and Mrs. Caldera shared the stew, tortillas and coffee. Mrs. Caldera checked on her patients one more time, then left. Devlin put the broth and some water to warm up again and went to the attic to find himself some bedding. He drug a mattress down to the bedroom next door to his usual one, found some blankets and pillows and tossed them on top without getting sheets or making the bed. The broth was bubbling then, so he poured some in a cup. He poured boiling water in another cup and added some dried *yerba buena* – wild mint – and lots of sugar. He picked up a tortilla and a glass of milk also, for the boy, and took it all upstairs.

He set it down quickly when he found the woman out of bed and trying to walk around to the other side. He went to catch her, but she waved him off.

"I am all right!"

"What do you think you are doing?" he asked.

"I'm going to take care of my children!" she said, glaring at him.

"Are you? You can't even take care of yourself."

"I'm fine!" she snapped.

"No. You are not fine. Now, that little boy of yours is doing all right. If you kill yourself now, he'll survive. He'll be sad and alone, but he'll live. That little girl though, you don't even have to kill yourself to kill her. If you don't let yourself get healthy, she will die."

She stood there, shaking with the effort of standing, holding onto the foot of the brass bedstead. "I saw her diaper. She's fine,"

"What you saw was milk borrowed from another woman. You get back in that bed and get your health back, or I will take that child in to town where someone who is willing to help themselves can take care of her. I mean it," he added when she hesitated.

She tried to sit down, almost missed the bed to fall on the floor. He caught her, directed her back to the bed, lifted her in and tucked up the blankets around her. She let him pile up the pillows and help her to sit more upright. She sighed angrily but let him bring over the tray and arrange it.

"All of it," he directed. "But eat slowly."

"Yes, Papà," she said. She was being sarcastic when she said it, but she picked up the cup and sipped the broth.

"You are causing your mother worry," Devlin said, plucking the boy off the balcony.

He had been trying, unsuccessfully, to climb the bars of the railing, which is why the woman was getting out of bed. Devlin had dealt with a little boy who liked to climb before, however, and he had built all the railings in the house too close together for little heads to fit through, and completely upright so there were no crossbars for little feet to climb.

"Come on downstairs and get some dinner. I'm sorry," he added, looking at the woman. "I'll keep him closer until you are better."

"Good luck with that," she murmured.

He grinned at that, tucked the boy under his arm so he squealed with delight, and hauled him down to the kitchen for dinner. He let him romp around the dooryard for a while after that, but he was thinking, he would have to go on the drive, soon. He needed somewhere safer than a second-floor bedroom to keep him.

In the morning, Devlin took the boy with him to do the morning chores. He was obviously aware of how things worked on a farm or ranch, since he insisted on putting his own little hand in the bucket to grab handfuls of grain to scatter to the chickens, and he probed into the lower nests to find eggs. They walked the extra eggs up to the bunkhouse.

"Must be almost noon," Sal said when they arrived.

Devlin looked up at the sun, barely above the eastern hills, and looked back in confusion.

"Your shadow's only two feet long," Sal explained, looking down at the boy. Devlin laughed and gave out the orders for the day.

"Potatoes," Juanito guessed before he even started.

"Yes. We better get a wagon load at least to take with us to Sacramento, if you want to get paid. I think they're worth more than the cows right now."

"Will we be leaving on schedule?" Juanito asked.

"Yes. We'll manage that."

He heard giggling and saw that Manuel was sitting in a chair, swinging his feet, eating a fresh buttered biscuit.

"You have more of those, I hope!" Devlin said.

"Doubled the recipe," Sal said, handing him a basket full of fresh biscuits and another jar of goat milk. "Are you going to be needing more broth?"

"Yes. Please."

He walked back down to the house, going slow so the little one could keep up. Manuel sat in the kitchen and happily ate biscuits and peach preserves while Devlin fixed up a tray for his mother, and then he held Devlin's hand to climb the big staircase. He chattered all morning, but Devlin was not that well acquainted with toddler-speak. He had noticed the boy left parts out, like when he asked "*Donde mamà*," instead of "*Donde està mi mamà?*", and his pronunciation was sometimes hard to grasp. When they got upstairs, he clambered up onto his mother's bed and told her all about something to do with chickens and milk. She seemed to understand. Most of it, anyway.

"How are you this morning?" Devlin asked when the boy slowed down.

"Better, thank you."

Besides her breakfast, he left more broth and sweet tea for sipping at all morning.

"Rest and eat," he told her. "Don't worry about Manuel. He'll be with me all day. I'll be in and out, so if you need anything, give a shout."

"You don't have a little silver bell for me to ring?" she asked.

"I used to. But we put it on the goat," he said.

They both smiled at their joke, and he went to wash up dishes, then took Manuel on a short explore of the downstairs bedrooms. The very first room on the south end of the hall, close to the bottom of the staircase, seemed to be the best bet. It had a bedstead in the rear bedroom, a big wardrobe and chest of drawers. He carried soapy water from the kitchen to scrub out all the furniture, swept and mopped the rooms. Then he started carrying things to fill the other two rooms of the suite. Manuel must have worn out his little legs climbing up and down the stairs with him, but he trotted happily along, a little shadow, as Sal named him. At noon, they brought fresh broth, water and tea upstairs, along with some biscuits and butter.

"Real food!" Mrs. Palacios sighed.

"Just remember…"

"Eat slowly. I think someone mentioned that before."

After lunch, Devlin went to help dig the potatoes. Manuel ran back and forth, taking handfuls of tiny potatoes to the baskets the men had set out. He worked in the garden with Sal, also, digging randomly in the warm dirt while Sal gathered fresh vegetables. But, while he was an energetic, active and inquisitive boy, he wasn't naughty, and he loved being recruited to work with the men. At some point, Manuel started yawning widely, and Devlin lifted him to the wagon seat, where he curled up like a cat in the sun and gave himself a nap. When he woke up, Sal gave him an apple turnover sprinkled with cinnamon and sugar.

"We're not spoiling him much, are we?" Juanito grinned.

Mrs. Palacios got a whole stew for dinner, with bits of shredded chicken meat and lots of potatoes and fresh garden vegetables, and Manuel got another bath after working in the attic all morning and the dirt all afternoon. He waited in the kitchen, having a second desert, while Devlin finished washing the dishes, but fussed a bit when it was time to go to bed. Devlin sat with him in the rocking chair and started reciting a rosary. Mrs. Palacios joined in, and the soft murmuring sound of their voices quickly put the boy to sleep. Devlin tucked him into bed with his mother and picked up the baby to change her.

"You're getting better," he commented to Mrs. Palacios, wiping a bit of milk off the baby's chin.

"Where is your wife?" she asked, watching him handle the baby.

"I don't have one."

"You did," she said. When he glanced up she added, "No bachelor, in fact few husbands, handle infants as well as you do."

"I do have a wife," he admitted. "She left."

"Why?"

He shrugged. "If I knew that, she might still be here."

He handed back the baby, made sure there was drinking water, sweet tea and biscuits close at hand for nighttime snacking, and went, not to the room next door, but downstairs. He stayed for several hours working before peeking in on the Palacios family. All three were sleeping soundly. He went to the bedroom next door, kicked off his boots, and stretched out on the bare mattress, with an unsettled feeling in his heart.

They aren't yours, he told himself harshly. But found himself listening for the sounds of their breathing through the open door and windows.

IV

After breakfast and morning chores, Devlin found a wrapper for Mrs. Palacios to put on and asked her if she could walk, or if he should carry her, as he had something to show her.

"I can walk," she said.

He stayed close by, in case she could not, but holding onto the railing, she made it down the stairs. It was the first time she had seen any of the house except the one bedroom, and she paused on the stairs to stare at the great hall, peering into the open doors at the dining room and study.

"Why do you live alone is such a big house?" she asked.

"I never actually meant to live alone," he said.

He took her into the suite of rooms he had fixed up. The sitting room had a fireplace, with wood and chips stacked in a niche in the raised hearth. There was a soft chair and a rocking chair, a table with a lamp and another lamp on the mantlepiece. There was a case full of books, and a rag rug on the floor. To the left was a small bedroom. The little bed he had made to keep James from falling off a tall bed was set up in there, as was the hanging cradle, both made up and ready for use. There was a small cupboard, with all the children's clothes already stacked inside, and a shelf full of toys that made Manuel squeal with delight. There weren't many toys, just the few of James's he had found and washed up: blocks, a small wooden horse and a wagon with wheels that turned, a wooden top and a rubber ball, and the little train that was to have been James's Christmas present.

To the rear of the sitting room was the main bedroom. He had put a mattress on the bed and made it up with the sheets and blankets he had washed for himself, but not used. There was a lamp on a table on each side of the bed, a chair and the dressing table and wardrobe. He showed her that he had stacked clothing in the dressing table and hung dresses in the wardrobe. On the shelves of the wardrobe he had put the fabric he had bought for Esperanza, who never cared much for sewing so she had used little of it. There were also scissors, pins, needles and thread, and a basket of balls of wool.

"Are you adopting us?" Mrs. Palacios asked.

"I have to leave in a few days," he said. "You have more recovering to do, and I wanted to be sure you'd be safe – and Manuel would be safe." He showed her the completely closed patio beyond the bedroom. "If he happens to get up before you, he can't fall off the balcony."

She was shaky, so he sat her down in the soft chair in the sitting room and sat in front of her on the hearth while Manuel explored the suite.

"Sal and Berto stay here when we go," he said. "Berto keeps an eye on the ranch and the animals. Sal doesn't leave the bunkhouse much. His leg pains him, especially on hills. But he's going to keep supplying meals here until you feel up to taking care of yourself, and Berto will bring things down to you and wash up the dishes after. He'll be here three times a day, so if you need anything, you just tell him. And, both of those men are completely trustworthy, and they think Manuel is a gem. If you need to rest, just ask, and they'll keep him for an afternoon. You don't even have to ask: they'll probably just keep him."

"You don't have to do all this for us," Mrs. Palacios said.

Devlin shrugged. "I have a big house," he said. "Lots of potatoes and chickens. More than enough to share. Don't feel you have to get well and leave. Make yourselves completely at home. You can explore the other rooms, the attic, bring whatever you want wherever you want to make it all more homey. If it's something big, get Berto to help you. If you are not here when I get back from Sacramento, I hope it is because you have family to go to.'

"I don't really."

"You have Twin Lakes," he said. "And Señora?"

"Yes, Señor Lachlan?"

"Remember the children. You can't take care of them if you don't take care of yourself. You're not being lazy by resting. You're helping them."

Twin Lakes Ranch, Near Aguas Amargas, California, October, 1858

It was mid-afternoon when they got back to the ranch, but it took some time to get everything settled, packed away, put away, unharnessed and fed. When he stepped through the back door into the kitchen, he found Manuel trapped safely in a highchair he had forgotten was up in the attic, while Mrs. Palacios was frying chicken on the stove.

"Dinner will be at sunset," she said. "Do you need to wash up?"

He took that as a hint and took a bucket of warm water up to his room to sponge down and change into clean clothes. When he went back downstairs, the kitchen was dark and empty, but he could hear voices through the door. He stepped into the dining room to find them waiting for him at the near end of the long table, platters and bowls of food steaming. Fried chicken, mashed potatoes, red chile and white gravy, fresh bread and late squash. She waited, head bowed, and he realized she was waiting for him to bless the meal, something Esperanza had never done, so it was a habit he had gotten out of years ago. He made the sign of the cross, noting that although Manuel was not adept at it, he tried to imitate the action. Devlin recited the blessing, and the food was passed.

"This is excellent," he said appreciatively.

"It is a special welcome home dinner," Mrs. Palacios said. "Don't expect it every day."

"I won't. Thank you."

"How was the trip?"

"Everything went good. We're going to have to keep breeding chickens. One chicken is worth almost half a cow!"

"And the potatoes?"

"Sold them instantly, and they weren't even full grown."

"We harvested more here," she said.

"We?" he asked.

She shrugged. "I can dig potatoes."

After dinner, she said, "Shall we pray a rosary?"

"Yes," he said. He stood up and helped clear the table and wash the dishes. When they went into the study, she lit the lamps, while he kindled a fire in the fireplace. Smaller than the great hall, the room was cozy and pleasant as the cool autumn evening settled in. Somehow, both children ended up on Devlin's lap, and both were sound asleep before the twenty-minute-long prayer had ended.

"Babies like to fall asleep on a man's chest," Mrs. Palacios commented. "Their hearts are closer to the surface than a woman's. It makes their heartbeat louder. Babies like the sound of heartbeats."

"Here I thought they liked me because I was such a wonderful person," Devlin said.

"Well. There are men, and there are men. Not all men don't mind children drooling all over them and spitting up on them. I'll wash that shirt tomorrow if you leave it in the kitchen."

She picked up Lydia, and he carried Manuel, and they laid the children in their beds. It was late enough in the year that it wasn't that late, even though it had been dark for some time.

"If you want, we could read for a while," Devlin offered.

"That would be very nice."

He found a Spanish translation of *Paradise Lost* on the bookshelf and read it aloud while she rocked and sewed. After about an hour, his voice was tired, and she was wrapping up her work.

"Sunday," she said, "we should go to Mass. Is it very far?"

"We're twelve miles from town," he said. "It takes about six hours in the wagon to get there. Which is why I have seldom ever gone."

She nodded thoughtfully. "At dawn?"

"Dawn moves a few minutes right or left every week, depending on the season, so Father has it at eight o'clock."

"So, we would have to leave at… two in the morning. Perhaps, half an hour earlier than that."

"Why earlier?"

"If you have been intentionally missing Mass, you'll have to go to confession first, won't you? To be able to receive the Eucharist."

"You do realize you are making quite a strong demand on someone you hardly know," he said.

"I know," she said, "that you were the first to suggest we pray a rosary. And tonight when I suggested it, you did not come in here and sit and wait for me to deal with the leftovers, the dishes, the children and the fire. I think you would like to start attending Mass more regularly."

Señor Valencia had not ever gone to Mass, except for their wedding. He had the excuse of being old and sick, and that the drive would have been too hard for him. But even after he died, Esperanza had shown no interest in rising early enough to make it into town. Over the past several years, he had gone in himself now and then, usually in high summer and always on horseback, through the rock cliffs and the Benevidez place, a short cut that only took about four and a half hours.

"You are right," he said, "we should go."

"Do you have a suit to wear?"

"Seriously? Getting up at two in the morning is not enough for you?"

She grinned mischievously. "I saw one, actually. Stored away."

I haven't worn it in about a decade. I doubt it fits."

"We'll fit it for you before Sunday."

"What day is today, by the way?"

"Wednesday."

Sunday he was up at one-thirty. He washed and dressed and went out in the dark to harness the mules to the wagon by lamplight. He tossed hay into the wagon bed and spread a thick quilt over it so the children would have a place to lay down on the long trip. He filled two feed bags and three canteens and tucked them under the seat. By that time, he saw a light on in the kitchen. Mrs. Palacios was packing some things into baskets.

"The children are dressed," she said. "You can take them out."

He carried them to the wagon, laid them in the bed, wrapped in blankets against the pre-dawn chill. He picked up the baskets she brought out and set them in the wagon also. A clean outfit, more diapers and blankets. He helped her up onto the seat, and in the faint starlight, they started off, up the driveway, down the road. The children slept peacefully. The mules shook their heads in irritation at being up so early, but they soon settled and plodded towards town. The night was clear and chilly, but the wind was still, the stars a blanket of sparkling light overhead. It was, actually, not an unpleasant drive.

The night waned. The sky brightened slowly. They arrived in front of the little adobe church   just before the sun rose. Devlin helped Mrs. Palacios down from the wagon and handed her the baby. He took the wagon over to park it by the other wagons, leaving the mules harnessed, but munching in feed bags. Then he swung Manuel down and carried him into the church. He was wearing his suit. Mrs. Palacios had on a dress she had obviously made while he was gone. She had no hoop to wear under the full skirt, but there were flounces gathered above the hem and abalone buttons down the front of the basque. It was made of dark blue and dark green flowered calico, two kinds of material that had been in her cupboard, but that he would not have thought went as well together as they did.

After services, he paused to talk to some of the men. Mrs. Palacios introduced herself among the women, and they all admired each other's babies and gowns. Manuel met other children his age and they ran around between the adults' legs, shrieking gleefully after an hour of having to be still and quiet.

About halfway home, Manuel began complaining of hunger. Mrs. Palacios asked Devlin to pull up the wagon in a broad meadow, near a stream. When he did, she pulled out a blanket to spread on the ground and a picnic basket. He had been in a hurry to get home so they could have lunch. It had not occurred to him to bring it along, but it had occurred to her. She had packed fried salt pork, boiled eggs, pickles and bread and jam. They got out the canteens, stretched out in the sun, which was warm, despite the coolness of the breeze.

"This was a good idea," Devlin admitted.

"Every Sunday," she said.

"Well. I don't know about that."

"Until the snow is too deep."

"Deal," he agreed. "Anything else I can do for you, Mrs. Palacios?"

"There is one thing, Mr. Lachlan."

"Yes?"

More seriously, she said, "Can you please speak to the children in English? I think it will be important for them to know it."

"It will be," he agreed. "How about yourself?"

"Do you think I can learn it at my age?"

"Oh, I think so. We'll work on it."

II

They never slaughtered a cow until it was cold enough for the meat to stay frozen all winter, but Sal usually killed a pig or two earlier, salting the meat down in barrels. Mrs. Palacios, it turned out, knew how to smoke and cure hams and bacon, which none of the men had ever done before. She instructed Devlin in the construction of a smoke house. She helped Sal with the proper cutting and spicing of the meat. The day they slaughtered the animals, she spent the day in the kitchen, making beans and fried bread and chile to go with the *chicharones* Sal made as he rendered the lard.

Devlin stood as godfather to Lydia, and since Mrs. Palacios called him the girl's Papá, Manuel began calling him by that title also. As she was congratulated on the baptism after Mass, Mrs. Palacios began talking to the other women and discovered that many families traveled hours to get there and carried picnic lunches home. She organized a weekly potluck breakfast/early lunch on the church grounds after Mass. And, as everyone sat on the ground and on their wagons, the women further discussed tables. And a shelter. Plans were made – but for next year as winter was coming on fast.

Over dinner one night, Mrs. Palacios asked why it was they had piles of sawdust from the sawmill, and two lakes on the property, but no icehouse.

"That," Devlin said, "is a very good question."

"And do you have a very good answer?"

"How about… It just never occurred to me," Devlin said. Ice was something the restaurant had purchased in Charleston, but it was something he had considered to be available only in the winter elsewhere.

"How did you ever get along without me?" she asked.

Devlin made plans for an icehouse, but there was not enough time to build it all this year. He and Berto and Juanito threw together a quick frame structure, and when the water froze deep enough, they went to cut ice, hauling it back on the sled he used for hauling stone since snow was already beginning to make it difficult for the wagons. They did not have ice tongs, but the ones he used for logging worked fine for now to lift and move the heavy blocks and stack them in layers of sawdust to keep them from melting too quickly come summer. In the spring, while he was plowing the garden and potato garden, Mrs. Palacios asked why he did not plant more beans.

"Do we need more?" he asked.

"I noticed you bought some last fall. With all this good land around here, you really shouldn't have to."

"More planting means more work all summer," he said. "Some part of this all has to be weeded every day. It's not just about putting seeds in the ground."

"I will help," she said.

"All right then. One bean field coming up."

"Also, goat milk is fine," she said. "But you can't make butter out of it. Where are you getting your butter?"

"We buy it," Devlin said. "No?" he added, seeing her shake her head.

"One day a week for churning, and you have butter all winter," she said.

"Sal doesn't churn butter," Devlin said. "And you may have noticed a slight shortage of women around here."

"Not any more," she said.

"So, you intend to churn butter, milk the cow, weed the garden, the potato field and the bean field, and watch two kids?"

"Of course, not," she said. "You get to milk the cow."

Devlin laughed.

She discussed with the women where the picnic shelter should be, approved it with the men who would build it and with the priest. Some of the men in town were recruited by their wives to level the area for the shelter by the church. They dug and tamped, hauled gravel from the river to spread on it, and hauled rocks for a rear wall. Other men helped Devlin and Berto and Juanito harvest logs and haul them to the lumber mill for processing. They milled beams and boards, but the wood was green, and it had to be air stacked most of the summer before it could be used without later warping and twisting. Still, by the end of the summer, they had enough dry lumber for at least the tables and benches.

The icehouse Devlin designed was dug part-way into the north side of a steep hill and had walls and floors of rock. The digging and the laying of the rock took a great deal of time and much hard labor. The roof was laid and was then covered in a thick layer of dirt for more insulation so that next year's ice would last past July.

"This woman has us working double-time," Juanito said. "You know what my father would have called her?"

"No," Devlin said. "What?"

"A keeper," Juanito grinned, and Devlin laughed.

Mrs. Palacios did seem to come up with ideas that kept them all working hard. But the honest fact was, it was Devlin's ranch. He was not obligated to do anything he did not choose to do. He had to admit, though, that he had not done all he could have for the place. Part of the blame could, he had to admit, be laid on Esperanza. She had always cooked and kept house and done laundry, but that was all she ever did. She never tended the garden or fed the chickens he bred for sale in Sacramento. He got rid of the cow because even if he milked it, she would not skim off the cream or make butter. She never helped with anything outside of her small household domain. Devlin was not sure if it had something to do with her ordeal, or if – discounting her severe post-partum depression, which he knew did not count – she had always been a bit lazy. As a child, she had enjoyed parties and guests and dancing, but he did not recall ever seeing her work very hard. But then, she had been a child. Whichever way it went, though, he had taken up the slack when she lived with him, and after she left, he had thrown himself too seriously into fixing up the house for her. Miguel had said the house would mean nothing if he let the rest of the ranch fail, but it had still taken up all of the time that was not spent directly on the immediate needs of the ranch. And an icehouse was a luxury, not a need. As was a bean field, and a milk cow. Now that there was a woman who did not mind ranch work, things were becoming more like a real ranch, and less like four bachelors living in two houses, raising cows. And he was not alone in thinking that the idea Mrs. Palacios and the other women had come up with of making a gathering place outside the church building itself was a very good idea.

When fall came, not only did he not have to buy bacon, ham, butter and beans with his other winter supplies, he actually had beans to sell, all of which gave him a slightly larger than average profit. He used it to purchase a used buggy. The padded leather seats and suspension built for passengers, not for hauling freight, made the weekly trips into Mass much more comfortable, not to mention the fact that it only required one mule, not two, to haul. In fact, he began training a horse to pull it, one that would trot part of the distance and make the driving time somewhat less.

Although he was a little young yet, Devlin began teaching Manuel his letters and numbers. He not only made the boy speak English as much as Spanish but helped Mrs. Palacios with her English also. In the winter, dinner at sunset was much earlier than in the summer, and there was more time for sitting up in the study after evening prayers. There were lessons, there were stories, read and told, and there were games. Devlin even gave Manuel his first spanking when he threw a temper tantrum and hit his baby sister in anger. Once a week was bath night. Once a month, Mrs. Palacios set Manuel on a tall stool, then Devlin on a low chair, to give their hair a trimming.

Another spring came, and after the round up, branding and planting, all the men of the community put in some time on the building of the picnic pavilion. Carpenters built the supports and roof. Stone masons laid a rock wall across the back of the open-sided building, with a huge fireplace and niches cut into it for the placement of religious statues. Father Aurelio and some of the altar boys built three large *hornos* out behind the pavilion, outdoor ovens for baking bread and sweets.

During the round up, of course, Manuel stayed home, but when Devlin had simpler tasks to do around the ranch, such as searching for cattle or moving them to more friendly range, Manuel was allowed to go along, riding in front of him on the saddle, as James had just been starting to do when Esperanza took him away. Not only did both Manuel and Devlin greatly enjoy these day trips, but it gave Mrs. Palacios a chance to do something like churning or laundry without a rambunctious boy underfoot.

As it was barely over a decade after the War that forced them into America, the Fourth of July was not yet a popular holiday among *Californios*. But the church in town was *Nuestra Señora Reina de los Angeles*, Our Lady Queen of the Angels, and her feast day was August second. There was always a fiesta, though Devlin had seldom gone over the years. This year, however, the fiesta was combined with the official dedication and blessing of the new pavilion, even if it had been used part of the summer already. This was a party the entire town planned for weeks.

A fire pit was dug out and a bonfire kept burning all afternoon the day before. When the fire burned down to coals for the last time after midnight, the pit was filled with Dutch ovens of beans, sweet corn still in husks and soaked in saltwater, and the meat of a whole cow. Damp grasses were laid over it, then the whole thing was buried in dirt to be dug up for lunch. The *hornos* were fired up before dawn to heat them for the baking of fresh bread and pies. Everyone was bringing something special to the party, and Devlin surprised them all by preparing trays of sticky baklava, the recipe for which he had learned from Pierre all those years ago in South Carolina.

A solemn high Mass was held for the feast day around mid-morning, followed immediately by feasting, then a rodeo competition. There was wild horse riding, calf roping, and all the things that would later be known by rodeo fans, as the local ranchers and *vaqueros* competed with each other to see who was best at the skills needed for their jobs. Devlin lasted only seconds on the bucking horse, but he did not do too badly in the roping competition. And when some local miners added a double-jack competition, he got Juanito to hold the drill while he swung a two-handed sledgehammer, pounding the drill into a block of granite, to the cheers and screams of the crowd. When the holes were measured, they had come in second, outdistanced by less than a quarter of an inch by a team of professional miners. But there was one event peculiar to the great horsemen of the *Californios*, which involved burying chickens up to their necks in soft sand and having the men ride at a full gallop past them, sliding sideways out of the saddle to snatch the chickens live from the ground on the way by. All the men took a turn. Devlin tried it and laughed with the crowd when he rolled off the side of his horse. It was Juanito who took the prize in that competition and received more kisses from young ladies for his prowess than he had even for his bravery in the mining competition. Devlin grinned, watching, and recalled that when he once asked Juanito why he never married and settled down in a place of his own, Juanito had laughed and said, "But, Boss! If I chose to live with only one pretty girl, what will I tell all the other ones!"

The fiesta lasted for two days, and it was a good break, but summer was waning and there was work to be done all over the county. Hay, firewood, logging, harvest. The round up came too soon, it seemed, for the men to finish all they had to do. But the trip to Sacramento was more lucrative than ever. Rumors of war had upped the price of cattle, whose hides had to be shipped around South America to the factories in the east where heavy machines would stitch them into military boots. It was a successful enough year that besides being able to pay off his loan for the

Benevidez place, Devlin was actually able to bank a small amount for the first time.

The ranch was successful, and so was his home life. He loved Mrs. Palacios' two children, loved that they called him Papa. He loved playing with them, teaching them, guiding them. He loved Mrs. Palacios' sense of humor, her quick wit, her ability to laugh at him or at herself. He admired her strength and courage. The big house finally echoed with the laughter of children, and the relationship he had with Mrs. Palacios was stronger than most marriages.

In all ways but one.

He tried not to think about her as he lay in his bed at night, alone, but his thoughts all too often strayed the direction of that downstairs bedroom, with the strong, quick, funny, beautiful woman sleeping alone in it. Long after the ranch and house quieted into peacefulness, he often lied there awake, with no peace in his own thoughts. He considered many times getting up, going down the stairs… But he was certain that if he ever did make such advances, they would be rebuffed. She was Mrs. Palacios to him. He was Mr. Lachlan to her. This little bit of formality reminded him always of the distance that had to be maintained. He loved this entire family fiercely, but they could never be his. He had a wife. The fact that he had no idea where she was did not negate the fact that he was married, legally and morally bound to her, only her. No one else.

Esperanza, whose name was Hope, had left him none.

Nuestra Señora Reina De Los Angeles Church, Aguas Amargas, California, October 1860

"Father, can I speak to you a moment?" Devlin asked. The weekly potluck was wrapping up. People were beginning to pack away the things they had brought, round up their children from the groups playing in the meadow. But they lingered, talking, enjoying the crisp autumn day, one of the last, no doubt, before winter arrived in force.

"Privately?"

"Yes, please."

Father Aurelio nodded to the men among whom he had been standing and turned to lead the way into the church building. He glanced at the confessional, but Devlin shook his head. There were no pews in this church. The Protestant invention of pews had not yet reached this distant frontier. So, Father led him into the sacristy and they sat on a couple of chairs in there.

"What seems to be the problem, Mr. Lachlan?"

"I don't know quite how to say this, Father, but... I hope you can help me. I am going to have to find someplace else for Mrs. Palacios to live."

Father Aurelio blinked in surprise. "But why? I thought the two of you got along quite well together."

"That's the problem, Father. We get along wonderfully together. She would be the best wife any man could have. And her children...! But I can't have them! She deserves to have a husband, they deserve a Father. A real one, not some man who... lives upstairs."

"Oh, I see. Yes, I see," Father said slowly.

"I thought maybe you would know someone... I know there are several single men in the area..."

"Yes. Many of them are a bit afraid of her tongue, though."

"She's not like that, really. She's... well... joking when she talks sharply. She has a sense of humor that..."

"That you appreciate, but not everyone else does. I would hate to see it smothered out of her by a man who could not appreciate it, wouldn't you?"

"Yes, but…"

"Mr. Lachlan, if you were free to do so, would you want to marry her yourself?"

"If I were free, I'd have married her before I left on that first cattle drive after I found her two years ago," he said.

"I'm going to ask you something, Mr. Lachlan, and it may sound odd to you, but I want you to answer as truthfully as possible. Why did you marry Esperanza?"

"What?"

"You heard me. Please, just tell me."

"I… that is… I… What does that have to do with any of this?"

"Quite a bit, actually. I notice you did not immediately protest your undying love for her."

"Father, of course I…"

"Too late. I know her history, Devlin. I know her family and I know quite a bit about you – you have lived in this town for over a decade, after all. So, answer me honestly this time. Why did you marry her?"

"Her father took me in and treated me like family when I needed it most. He had no reason to trust me, in fact, he probably shouldn't have. But he showed me what family was. He let me be part of his. And Jaime was the best friend I ever had…"

"Yes, but you didn't marry Francisco or Jaime. You married Esperanza."

"I know. I was explaining. She was… hurt. You know about that. She needed taking care of, and she had no one left. Her father and brother were dead, her grandfather was sick. He actually asked me to marry her, to take care of her, keep his property for her…"

"I thought you purchased Twin Lakes from him outright."

"Yes, I did. But it is her heritage."

"But she abandoned it."

"She abandoned *me*, Father."

"Yes. She did. Why did she marry you, did you ever ask her that?"

"No."

"Do you think she was in love with you?"

"Well… uh… it's possible…"

"A woman does not leave a man she is in love with."

"That may be," Devlin said. "But the fact is, I did marry her. And she married me. It is, as you have often said in your homilies, an unbreakable bond. As long as we are alive, wherever she is, we are still married."

"This is true. But... Have you ever heard of an annulment?"

"I have heard of it, I am not quite sure how it works."

"We don't spend a lot of time talking about dissolving marriages. We want people to work on staying together. And actually, an annulment does not dissolve a marriage. An annulment says that there was some impediment, some reason that the sacrament was not a valid sacrament to begin with, and therefore, the bond doesn't exist."

"I'm not sure I understand."

"Sometimes people get married for the wrong reasons. Or perhaps, they are not capable of making the marriage vow sincerely for some reason: mental incompetence, perhaps, or being too young, not understanding the meaning of the sacrament. You know that the minister of the sacrament of Confession, for example, is a priest, and the minister of the sacrament of Holy Orders or Confirmation has to be a bishop. Do you remember who the minister of the sacrament of Marriage is?"

"Priest again, isn't it?"

"No. The priest witnesses and blesses the union. It is the couple themselves who bestow the sacrament on each other. This is the bond that cannot be broken. But if one or both of the people are not fit to bestow this sacrament, it isn't really a sacrament."

"You mean if they are in mortal sin?"

"No. I mean if one or both of them is lying, to themselves or to anyone else, about the reasons for making this commitment to each other."

"And you think that Esperanza or I were lying?"

"I put that badly. Let me put it this way. I did not know the two of you then. I know you very well now, and I know more about her, and if you came to me now with the request for marriage to her, I would deny it. Devlin, you did not marry a woman! You tried to make her your family to fulfill an obligation you felt towards her family − not even towards her herself! You, her grandfather, Jaime, you all decided she needed taking care of, and you ended up the one holding the short stick. You were the last one available to take care of her. Her grandfather asked you to marry her, you said. Did he speak to her also?"

"Yes," Devlin admitted.

"If you met her today," Father Aurelio said, "With no brother, no father, no grandfather to whom you felt obligated, if it were she whom you rescued from that barn, not Mrs. Palacios, would you ask her to marry you?"

"No," Devlin said. "That is, I mean…"

"Too late again. You are an honest person, and when I catch you off guard, the honesty comes out. Now, I cannot grant an annulment. That takes someone with much more authority than myself. Such matters may go all the way to the top. And it takes time. But I can tell you that I think you have a much stronger case than anyone I have ever counseled before. I can start the paperwork. I can send it off to my bishop. I may even take it to him in person. I do not believe your marriage to Esperanza is a valid one."

"What does that mean? That we were never married? That our son was born out of wedlock?"

"Not at all. You were married. We have church and county records to prove it. When I say it was not valid, I mean only that it was not a valid *sacrament*, and once the annulment is approved, in the eyes of Church and state, you are free to marry again."

Father Aurelio waited for several long moments in silence, watching the thoughts tumble past Devlin's clear blue eyes. Finally, Devlin nodded. "I suppose," he said, "it wouldn't hurt to at least begin the process."

"I will start the paperwork. I will need your signature on some papers… next Sunday all right? With winter coming, I hate to put it off longer."

"Barring a four-foot snowfall, we should be back by Sunday."

II

They were among the last to pull out of the church parking area. Lydia was fussy, exhausted after the long morning, which cut into her usual morning nap. Manuel was still bouncing with excitement after playing rowdy games with the other children, but the long ride home told on him, and eventually, he stretched out on the back seat of the buggy and fell asleep. Lydia dropped off sooner. Sitting between Devlin and her mother on the front seat, she leaned into his lap as she dozed off. Sunlight glittered gold off the autumn leaves, and waves of migrating ducks rose out of the fields to continue their flights. A buck and a doe stopped by a stream for a drink and watched the buggy pass with unworried interest.

"Mrs. Palacios," Devlin said eventually.

"Yes, Mr. Lachlan?"

"If I were free, would you marry me?"

"That's a very serious question, Mr. Lachlan. I'd have to think about it. Let me see." She looked down at the little girl curled half in Devlin's lap and half in her own.

"Of course, my children love you."

"I love them, too," Devlin said.

"I know. And that is a big consideration for a woman in my position. What else should we look at? *Hmm*. I clean your house, do your laundry, cook your meals, tend your garden, feed your chickens, darn your socks. In fact, we already live very much like a married couple. Except for the fact that every night I say good night to the best-looking man I have ever known and watch him walk away while I go alone into my bed. Of course, I would marry you!"

When he laughed, she added a little more seriously, "*If* you were free, as you said. But... Oh! Is that why you spoke so long with Father? Does he have some news of Esperanza?"

"Not exactly," Devlin said. And he explained to her the conversation he had had.

"Annulment," she said thoughtfully. "Is it possible?"

"Father Aurelio seems to think it is. But he said it could take a long time."

"How long?"

"That he did not specify."

"Well. If there was a chance, I think I would be willing to wait. I had been thinking myself that I should go. It's cruel, really, for me to stay here. For me, for you. For the children. But... I didn't want to go."

"I didn't want you to go," he said. "Don't want you to go."

"Then what's the problem?"

"What do you mean?"

"Ah, Dev! If you feel about this the way I do, you'd have come out of the church doing handsprings across the grass. Instead, you've been silent and moody since you spoke to Father. Something is on your mind. It's her, isn't it?"

"In a way. I just wonder if doing this would be fair to her. She's not here, she knows nothing about this, and I'm going to dissolve our marriage?"

"Have it declared invalid, not dissolve it."

"Right. Annul, not dissolve. It still feels like sneaking around behind her back."

"Did it ever occur to you that she already annulled you?"

"She knows where I live. I'd have gotten the paperwork."

"I don't mean legally. I mean walking out almost a decade ago. She left here, and she made sure you couldn't trace her. If she wanted to be married to you, she'd be here. Or is it because you feel the ranch is really hers?"

"No. I bought it. There was well over a thousand dollars in silver and gold coins in the bag I gave her grandfather for this place. I asked her if she wanted a claim to it, but she didn't. She never cared about the ranch."

"What happened to the money?"

"That old man kept it under his mattress until he died. When I cleaned out his room just a few days later, it was gone. It turned up under her side of our mattress. When I came back from looking for her, it was gone. I guess I knew then that I'd never see her again."

"Those people you told me about, the Blunt family, they might have taken it."

"No. If they'd found it, they'd have been sitting at the table, chortling and counting the coins. They weren't too bright, but they were very proud of themselves. Anyway, I had the sheriff and Mrs. Benevidez search their persons and every item that they claimed as their own that was packed into their wagon before they were allowed to leave. Esperanza didn't have any expensive jewelry, just a small diamond engagement ring, her wedding band, and a big gold locket I gave her when James was born. She took those with her. But that Blunt girl had all Espe's beads and bangles in her belongings, tried to claim them as her own. No. Esperanza took that money. She could have gone to Europe with that."

He sighed. Then he smiled. "Thank you, Ed," he said.

"Ed?" she said. "Oh, no! I don't think so."

"Eddie?" he suggested.

She considered. "All right. I guess 'Eddie' is acceptable. Barely."

"Eddie," he said. "You're right. I have nothing to feel guilty about on her account."

"That's true, but I have one more question before we consider this conversation finished."

"Yes?"

"What if she comes back? What if you get the annulment, and we get married, and out of the blue, she suddenly shows up on your doorstep, expecting to be your wife again. I know you, Dev. I think sometimes better than you know yourself. That sense of duty and obligation you have! You're still carrying legal responsibility for half the county! What would you do if she came back?"

"You like the hard questions, don't you?"

"I need to know."

"Yes. It's only fair. What would I do?" He considered. "I might build her a little cabin, one or two rooms, off on a corner of the ranch somewhere. I might even give her some chickens and some seeds to get her started. But I would never let her displace you! And I would never actually deed her any property. James, now," he added thoughtfully. "If he came back, I would feel an obligation to give him something, once he comes of age. He is my son. But even then, I wouldn't, say, will him the entire ranch. This is Lydia and Manuel's heritage now, as much as it ever was his."

"You're not just saying that?"

"You said you know me. James may be my son, but he would be a stranger to me. Manuel, Lydia... I've known both of them twice as long as I ever knew James. I have had twice as long to be their father. I'll never turn my back on them."

"Well, then, Mr. Lachlan. I guess we just have to wait."

"Father said it might have to go 'all the way to the top.' I hope it doesn't depend on the pope for an answer! That could take years!"

"Don't you think I'm worth it?" she asked.

"More than worth it," he said.

She slid her hand into the crook of his arm, and he held the reins in one hand to cover her hand with his. It was the closest thing to an intimate gesture either of them had ever made towards the other.

Nuestra Señora Reina De Los Angeles Church, Aguas Amargas, California, September 25, 1861

The day was chilly and blustery, even though summer was not yet over. Hail and rain came and went sporadically, and despite the blazing fire in the rock fireplace, the shelter was open to the wind and cold, and people were getting ready to pack up more quickly than they normally would. Devlin scooped up Lydia and stood her on one of the tables so he could more easily button her blue wool coat over her little pink dress and white linen pinafore, while Edwina Palacios started packing up their picnic things. Before either of them finished, Father Aurelio came out of the church and hurried towards them.

"Devlin! I'm glad I caught you before you left. It's done!"

"What's done?" Devlin asked, puzzled.

Several people nearby paused to listen as Father seemed so excited. When he held up a large envelope, covered in official looking seals, and said, "Your annulment!"

Nearer people elbowed further people, and everyone seemed to pause their packing up to listen.

"That was sooner than I expected!" Devlin said, although it had been nearly a year. "It's all legal?"

"It is all legal and official, my friend. You are free to marry again." He smiled happily, looking from Devlin, who held the little girl in one arm, to Edwina. "When would you like to schedule the wedding?"

"Right now," Devlin said at once.

There was laughter in the pavilion behind him, but he didn't notice. He didn't notice, either, that the people who were leaving were being stopped by others who were spreading the gossip quicker than wildfire. Oblivious of the crowd around him, Devlin looked questioningly at Edwina.

"Now? Sounds perfect to me," she said.

Father's grin evaporated. "Church custom has people wait at least six months…"

"I've been waiting three years," Devlin said. "We're here. You're here. Let's do it."

"Do you have rings?" Father asked.

That stumped Devlin. It was Edwina who looked down at her left hand and tugged off the gold band she was still wearing.

"We can get married with this," she said. "Then get some just for ourselves later."

"Right. That's will work, won't it Father?" Devlin asked, tugging the ring off his own finger.

"It is a little unorthodox, but technically, yes. I suppose it will work."

"Hey! Everybody! Don't leave!" one of the men shouted. "We're having a wedding!"

Laughing, chattering, people put their loads in their wagons and buggies and came back to the church. Devlin sought out Juanito, who did come in for services now and then.

"You want me to be your *padrino*, Boss? Really?"

"I've known you longer than any other man in this county. Seems right to me, if it does to you."

"I would be honored," Juanito said.

Several women vied for the chance to stand up with Edwina. She had become quite popular with the entire community. She picked one finally, by laughing and spinning in a circle with her eyes covered and one finger outstretched to point at the winner because, as she said, "You are all so wonderful and generous! How can I choose one of you!"

Despite the weather at the moment, there were still late summer flowers, and little girls ran through the fields, and even into backyards of houses in town to gather as many as they could. There were purple flowers for Juanito and Devlin to wear, small bouquets for Edwina and her chosen maid of honor, and a little basket was produced for flowers for Lydia to carry down the center of the church. She was too young to understand what was expected of her, but she saw her Papa standing at the front of the church, and she ran and jumped into his arms, to the applause and laughter of the community. It was, Father said later, the first time he officiated at a marriage during which the groom held his child throughout. Manuel, a manly five-year-old, was given instruction to take the rings to the front of the church and hold them, without playing with them, until he was asked for them. Proud and important, he was able to mostly comply, only losing one of the rings as he fiddled with them. But Juanito had been watching and saw where it had fallen.

"Boss, my mother will keep the children tonight," Juanito said afterwards, as they were accepting handshakes and congratulatory hugs. "I'll bring them home tomorrow."

"We all fit in the buggy," Devlin said.

"Round up tomorrow!" Juanito reminded him. "We can postpone one day, but this may be your only chance at a honeymoon!"

"Your mother won't mind?"

"My mother would kill me if I didn't bring them to her. They'll be fine. You two go on home now."

With much waving and shouting of congratulations and blessings, they climbed into the buggy and drove off.

About halfway home, Devlin had a sudden, unhappy thought.

"I guess that wasn't as romantic as you might have liked," he said. "We should have waited, had time for more flowers, a nicer dress…"

"Are you insulting my dress? This happens to be my best one, you know. And my new bonnet!"

"You look beautiful. I just meant… women usually want their wedding to be more formal…"

"I've been married before. You've been married before. Twice, in fact! This may not have been fancy, but it was the most romantic thing a woman could ever imagine. We all want to be swept off our feet. You really did it, didn't you?"

They both laughed, and Edwina laid her head on his shoulder, while he wrapped his arm around her and pulled her against him on the buggy seat.

Twin Lakes Ranch, Near Aguas Amargas, California, September 25, 1861

Mass, then the weekly picnic, then Mass again, it was after noon before they left the churchyard, and already dark by the time they made it home. Devlin went into the kitchen with Edwina to light a lamp, then went back outside to tend to the horse, and give the stock a quick feeding. When he came back in, she had lit the stove. Her bonnet was off and she had an apron on, but the stove wasn't even warm yet.

"Maybe, for dinner…"

He took her in his arms and kissed her, gently at first, then with growing intensity. When he paused for breath she said, "I think there are a few garments that should be removed…"

He scooped her up in his arms and went out into the great hall, but at the foot of the stairs, he paused.

"Your room, or mine?" he asked.

"The children aren't there, but my room is no place for a honeymoon. Yours, I think. And I can walk," she added, as he continued up the stairs with her in his arms.

"I don't intend to wait that long," he said.

Although he did wait. They both undressed carefully before climbing into his bed. Then, he reached for her.

This was no joining of inexperienced virgins, nor the careful treading around injuries and fears. In Edwina, Devlin had a mature woman, a woman who matched his desire and passion. Their first meeting was need and hunger and urgency. They both laughed afterwards at their own intensity, and so the second time was laughter and joy and playfulness.

"Do you want dinner?" she asked.

"No," was all he said, kissing her eyelid, her cheek, the corner of her mouth.

"Oh, good. Me neither."

The third time was gentleness and romance and loving care.

He didn't remember falling asleep, but he awoke in the pale, pre-dawn light to find her where he had always dreamed of finding her, wrapped in his arms. Her dark copper hair had fallen loose and was sprayed across the pillow behind her. She was snuggled up against his chest, breathing softly, but coming slowly awake with him.

"*Hmmm*," she sighed. "Now I know why Lydia likes so much falling asleep on your chest. It is a wonderful chest."

"I'm rather fond of yours also," he said.

"I think we should get up. The children will be here soon."

"If they got up before dawn and Juanito galloped them through the short cut, they'd still take hours to get here."

"Breakfast…"

"Can wait."

The fourth joining was exploration and learning, giving and more of accepting than taking.

"Those animals are getting angry out there," she said. "You'd better go feed them."

"I hate leaving you now that I finally have you," he said.

"Me, too. But it's just a few hours. We will have a lifetime."

"Make that a promise," he said.

"I don't suppose I have time for a bath?" she asked.

"Take your time getting up. I'll get one started for you."

He kissed her again, and got up himself, taking clothes downstairs with him. He lit the fire first, then gave himself a quick, icy washing up in the kitchen before getting dressed. As the stove warmed, he put as many pans of water to heat on the stove as would fit. Before going out to tend to the animals, he pulled the big tub down off the outside wall and set it up in front of the stove, added some cold water to it, and stoked the fire again. It took a while to feed all the chickens they would be taking for sale soon, feed and milk the cow. He fed their own chickens, the horse and mules that were in the corral, gathered the eggs and carried most of them up to the bunkhouse.

"Where is everybody?" Sal asked. He had biscuits baked already, and Devlin traded him most of the eggs for a handful of hot biscuits. He explained about the impromptu wedding.

Sal's response was, "About time!"

Laughing, Devlin went back to the house to find Edwina was already starting breakfast. She had washed quickly, apparently, and was boiling coffee and frying ham. Devlin set his basket down on the table and wrapped his arms around her from behind.

"That dress you had on yesterday may be your best," he said. "But this has always been my favorite."

She was wearing her workday clothes: a full skirt that hung in loose folds without extra petticoats or bracing to make it stand out. Because it had nothing to shape it, it held her shape, hugging her now-full hips before dropping to end several inches above the floor so as not to drag in mop water or dirt when she was cleaning or working outside. The blouse she wore with it was loose-fitting, gathered at the neck and the ends of the full, short sleeves with braided strings that ended in tiny tassels. Her hair was just braided and hung over one shoulder, and, as often when she was inside or working in the soft garden soil, her feet were bare.

"Men have no fashion sense," she said, but she leaned back into his embrace.

"As it happens, I have great fashion sense," he said. "It's just that this is pretty, and it looks comfortable and practical – and it looks like you with nothing to change your natural shape into something it isn't."

"You disapprove of corsets, do you?"

"Heartily! You don't own one, do you?"

"I do. But it makes it hard to do simple things like stooping to pick up a child…"

"Or breathing."

"Or breathing, yes, which is essential chasing those two around! I don't think I've worn it once since I bought it over a year ago."

"Which is what makes you so appealing."

"I'm burning the ham."

He released her arms so she could turn the meat, but still nuzzled at her neck, until suddenly he let her go, straightening and turning to the door.

"What?"

"Rider. Coming in hard," he said, and he flung open the back door and went outside, meeting, halfway to the stable, Juanito, who slid his galloping horse to a stop and jumped off.

"What happened?" Devlin demanded. "Are the children all right?"

"They're fine, Boss. My mother is bringing them. I just thought I should get here as quick as possible to give you a warning."

"Warning?" The word spread dread through him instantly, but Juanito grinned.

"Half the town is on its way out here to give you the wedding fiesta you missed by having it so sudden yesterday."

"People are coming here?" Edwina demanded. She pressed her arm to her chest as if she had been caught naked. "Now? I can't let anyone see me like this!"

"You got at least an hour, maybe all of two."

"Go ahead and go change," Devlin told Edwina, and she ran into the house. "Take care of your horse," he told Juanito. "Then see if Sal can make some more biscuits and come give me a hand in here. And thanks for coming to let us know."

"Sure. I wouldn't want a load of people showing up the morning after my wedding night without warning!"

Laughing, he led his horse towards the stable, but paused again when Devlin called "Get those eggs back from Sal!"

Quick and simple, Devlin thought, going back inside. He rescued the ham slices, then dug through the cupboards and found all the baking pans he could, four round pans and two oblong ones. He got out the biggest mixing bowl in the place, and he was measuring, multiplying mentally, when Juanito came back, bringing the eggs.

"What you got there, Boss?"

"Baking some cake."

"I don't suppose you can make that sweet stuff with the nuts in it?"

"Not today. It takes too long."

"If I ever get married, I'll give you plenty of warning so that can be my wedding cake! What do you want me to do?"

The day was still chilly and overcast. Devlin considered a moment, then said, "Light fires in the study and the hall first of all. Then go out to the barn and bring in all the sawhorses and planks you can. We'll set them up as tables in the big hall. I'll come and help you as soon as I get this in the oven. And then we'll raid every room in the house for chairs."

"What about that big table in the dining room?"

"You know, I think they built the house around that thing. Or built it inside that room. There is no way that can ever come out. But… let's get all the dining chairs into the hall, and we'll use that table for stacking food on."

"People are bringing more, you know."

"I figured. But we need to contribute also."

Juanito left. Devlin stoked and damped the fire again, finished his batter and got it into the oven. To his surprise, Sal came down from the bunkhouse.

"I figured it would be easier to work down here than to be hauling things up and down that hill," he said. "Say, this is a nice set up you have here."

"Now that you mention it," Devlin said. "Maybe it's time we build a bigger, better kitchen for the bunkhouse."

"The Missus suggest that?"

"I have ideas also," Devlin said. As Sal started laying out the things he had brought in his basket, Devlin said, "I have some cakes in the oven. If you could keep an eye on things…"

"Go do what you have to do. I've got this covered."

Devlin grabbed a biscuit, stuffed the partially burned ham into it, and ate it for breakfast while he went to help Juanito. They set up two long plank-and-sawhorse tables, then raided all the bedrooms for small side tables and all the chairs they could find. They brought out the dining room chairs, brought more chairs down from the attic, and also some wood and metal trunks that could be used as benches. Edwina came back, hair neatly pinned up, wearing her best dress, with shoes and stockings.

"Put on your suit," she instructed Devlin.

"Do you really think I need…?"

"Yes."

She covered her gown with an apron and helped Sal in the kitchen. The cakes were baked, turned out onto plates and baking sheets and sprinkled with white and brown sugar. They stoked the fire higher and made more biscuits. Edwina found bowls to set out butter and the raspberry preserves she had made just last month after Devlin took her and the children berry picking. He had insisted that they not go alone since bears like raspberries also, but they had gathered several small pails full without trouble, and she put out two jars of preserves now for the guests. She set out all the plates, cups, bowls and flatware in the house, and sent Juanito to the bunkhouse to raid that for eating utensils also. The bunkhouse had originally been set up for over a dozen men, so that helped. As he went up the hill, she fretted, "I wish we had something other than water to serve for drinking."

"I have that bottle of whisky I bought when Lydia was teething," Devlin said, "She only used a few drops."

"That's good for the men, but what about women and children? We have no milk, no buttermilk…"

"Those oranges and lemons I brought back last year, I saved all the peels and dried and ground them up. They're good for baking: I used some in the cakes today. But maybe we can make some kind of weak lemonade or fruit punch – with lots of sugar. And, we have coffee and good mint tea."

Sal and Edwina started on that right away. Devlin and Juanito were putting sheets for tablecloths on the plank tables when the first of the guests arrived. Lydia and Manuel ran to Devlin and Edwina for hugs and kisses, then there were adult hugs and handshakes. The food was laid out in the dining room. The big hall showed its worth as the rain came down hard outside, but all the guests were dry and warm inside. The guests brought pots of beans, baked squash and steamed vegetables, boiled meat and ham, trays of bread pudding called *sopa*, stacks of tortillas, pies and even doughnuts. The party did not last too late, since it was a long drive home for everyone. The rain let up about mid-afternoon, and the party started to break up. Many of the guests stayed to help with the clean up before they packed up: the men returned furniture to its proper location, women helped wash up and put away. Everyone took food home with them for the long trip back, and Sal, Juanito and Berto joined Devlin, Edwina and the children in the kitchen for a dinner of leftovers before they returned to the bunkhouse for the night. When everyone was gone and the house almost back to normal, they took the children in to the study for evening prayer. The children both fell asleep before it was over, and Devlin carried Manuel while Edwina carried Lydia back to their bedroom to dress them in their night clothes and put them to bed.

"We have a bit of a problem, don't we?" Edwina said, as they stood in the doorway, looking at the children.

"Do we?"

"Yes! In most houses, there would only be one or two bedrooms, and the children would be nearby even if the parents had a private room. But here, we're so spread out! We can't sleep way over in your room with the children clear across the house and downstairs."

"Even if I assure you that you can hear every sound they make from my room?"

"Oh, I'm sure you could in the past, when you were lying awake in bed pining for me. But you should sleep much more soundly tonight."

"You also."

"Exactly. I suppose we'll have to use my bedroom…"

"Is there anything wrong with that?"

"No. Although, I did rather enjoy the upstairs bedroom. You get so much more light and air, and the view. But that room is too small for us anyway, really."

"It is the smallest of the upstairs bedrooms. That's why I chose it originally. There are bigger ones, one even with a wardrobe already in it. And I don't need a desk in the bedroom, I do have an office in the study. Look. There are ten bedrooms in this house, not even counting that string of cells off to the side, or the fact that two of what I am calling bedrooms are two-bedroom suites. For now we will stay down here. But tomorrow, when we leave to round up and move the cattle, you can start exploring, planning how you want things arranged. Keep in mind that soon Manuel will be too big to be sharing a room with his sister – probably he is already. Lots of options. No hurry."

"This is a funny house," she said, leaning against his chest.

"Came in very handy today, didn't it?"

"I suppose that was the idea behind this design." She gave his chest a pat and said, "You go on up and get your nightshirt, and we'll get the rest of your things later."

"I don't have a nightshirt. And if I did, I wouldn't wear it anyway. Nor will you be wearing a nightgown."

"I won't?"

"No."

"You plan to keep me sleepless, I suppose?"

"I plan to feel my wife against me every night, all night."

"Put it that way, it sounds like an excellent plan."

She put her arm around his waist, and he wrapped his around her shoulder, and they went into the bedroom at the back of the suite.

Twin Lakes Ranch, Near Aguas Amargas, California, December 5, 1862

"I told you, you make beautiful babies," Mrs. Caldera said, handing the washed, wrapped child to Devlin.

"I will take some credit for this one," he said. He sat down on the edge of the bed, leaning into the pillows with Edwina so they could both admire the baby. It was a girl, small and delicate. The shock of hair on her head combined Devlin's bright gold with Edwina's dark copper to make a pale shade that was almost rose-gold. And her eyes had Edwina's gold flecks in Devlin's deep blue, making them, not green, but a clear turquoise. Manuel and Lydia, so long locked out of their parent's bedroom, were allowed to come in now, and they both jumped boisterously on the bed and leaned in to admire their new baby sister.

"What are you going to name her?" Mrs. Caldera asked.

"None of the names we thought of seem quite right now," Edwina said.

"It will be hard to pick," Mrs. Caldera commented. "She's got such pretty colors, she looks like a butterfly."

"Is she prettier than me?" Lydia demanded.

Devlin looked at her gently. "Is a deer pretty?" he asked.

"Very pretty!"

"And isn't a meadowlark a beautiful bird?"

"Well… yes…"

"But you wouldn't say that a deer is prettier than a meadowlark, or a meadowlark is prettier than a deer, would you?"

"No! Because they're not the same!" Manuel said.

"That's right," Devlin said. "You can compare two deer, or two apples or two rainbow trout. But people are all too different to compare like that. You are the most beautiful Lydia in the world. And your sister will be the prettiest…" He paused, then grinned. "Mariposa in the world."

"Oh, seriously!" Edwina said. "You would name your child 'Butterfly?'"

"It does sound better in Spanish," Devlin said. "Mariposa. What do you

274

think?" he asked the children and they bounced up and down on the bed shouting, "Yes! Yes!"

"She has to have a Christian name to be baptized," Edwina pointed out.

"Anne," Devlin said.

"Why Anne?"

"We were thinking of Mary or Maria anyway, for the Mother of God. But we'll probably call her Mari. She can't be Mari Mary, that's silly! Anne is the mother of the Mother of God. In fact, let's make it Spanish, like her first name. Mariposa Ana. Marianne, if she ever wants to shorten it."

"She'd better not!"

Mrs. Caldera took the children down to the kitchen for a snack, leaving Devlin and Edwina and the baby alone for a moment.

"Are you all right?" Devlin asked gently.

"I feel exhausted and stretched and flabby, but I think I will survive just fine."

"You know what I mean."

"If you mean will I lie around in bed for months, doing nothing… Well, it sounds rather appealing. I will take a few days, though, if you don't mind. Just for a rest."

"That's a given. Do you feel all right, though?"

"Oh, listen! There's always some depression. It comes with the territory. I'll probably cry over silly things, like hair ribbons that break or Christmas presents that I actually love. But I know you'll understand and not get upset with me, and that will make it all so much easier."

He bent to kiss the top of her head.

"I love you," he said.

"I know. I love you too."

"What do you think about a big family?" he asked, tickling the baby's chin so she pursed her mouth up tight. "I always thought a dozen children was a good even number."

"Sounds wonderful," Edwina said. "Provided you have the next nine."

He was still laughing when Mrs. Caldera came in with a tray of soup and tea.